TO LOVE A WOLF

A WOLF

PAIGE TYLER

Published by Sourcebooks Casablanca, an imprint of Sourcebooks, Inc.
P.O. Box 4410, Naperville, Illinois 60567-4410
(630) 961-3900
Fax: (630) 961-2168
www.sourcebooks.com

Printed and bound in Canada.
MBP 10 9 8 7 6 5 4 3 2 1

With special thanks to my extremely patient and under-standing husband. Without your help and support, I couldn't have pursued my dream job of becoming a writer. You're my sounding board, my idea man, my critique partner, and the absolute best research assistant any girl could ask for.

Love you!

Prologue

Outside Samarra City, Iraq, 2009

STAFF SERGEANT LANDRY COOPER MOVED CAREFULLY through the rubble covering the floor of the partially demolished building, inching his way closer to the target. The maze of shattered brick and broken pieces of wood weren't the biggest reason he was moving slowly, though. That had more to do with the hundred-degree temperature and the seventy-five-pound Kevlar bomb suit he was wearing. He despised the army's suit with a passion that few people outside the Explosive Ordnance Disposal community could understand. It wasn't simply that it was hot and heavy. No, what he hated most about the suit was the nearly complete sensory deprivation that came with wearing it. Inside the claustrophobic helmet surrounded by a neck gusset designed to keep your head from getting ripped off your body during an explosion, you couldn't hear much of anything, your line of sight was distorted by the thick, curved face piece, and your peripheral vision was non-existent. Having to make a manual approach—better known in EOD circles as the long walk—on a suspected improvised explosive device, or IED, was bad enough. Doing it when you had an armor-plated pillow wrapped around your head? That sucked.

But he didn't have a choice. Local construction

workers had come in this morning and found a suspected IED half buried in the dirt between two buildings. Cooper and his team had been able to use a robot
to drop a small demolition charge near the device, but
his disposal charge, combined with a bang from the IED,
had caused part of the surrounding buildings to collapse,
pissing off the locals and making it impossible to get the
robot back in to clear the area.

If there was one cardinal rule in EOD, it was that
you never released an incident location back to the good
guys without being one hundred percent sure all hazards
had been cleared. That meant doing a manual approach
in the bomb suit to make sure there weren't any explosive materials or secondary devices around.

Cooper wasn't too worried about walking up to the
package he'd just blown in place. While the relationship between the city's Sunni population and ruling
Shiite government forces would never be described as
anything other than tense, lately things had been better.
IED responses were way down, and they hadn't seen a
secondary explosive device, typically planted to target
police and other first responders, in months.

Still, he played everything by the book, keeping the
protected front of his suit facing the spot where the IED
had been, and using the building's structure for protection as much as possible. At the same time, he kept his
head on a swivel, looking for anything that seemed out
of place.

"I'm about twenty feet from where we blew the IED,"
he murmured over his suit's radio to his team members
waiting in the safe area three hundred yards away, and
then remembered he was wasting his breath. The damn

radio had stopped working about a month ago, and a replacement wasn't due for weeks. He was on his own.

Sweat trickled down his nose as he stepped over a low wall and moved toward the crater where the IED had been. He automatically lifted a hand to wipe the sweat from his face and thumped against the plastic face piece.

"Shit, I hate this suit," he muttered, forced to make due with wiggling his nose.

He reached the edge of the shallow crater and looked down. Two feet deep and six across, it looked like a big soup bowl. There were some rusty nails the bomb maker had added for fun, but the IED itself was long gone. Even better, his demo shot hadn't exposed another one buried underneath.

Cooper pulled a sharpened fiberglass rod out of his pocket, then jumped into the crater. If there was anything here, the blast from the disposal shot would have uncovered it, but it didn't hurt to check. Unfortunately, the heavy spine protector in the suit that helped keep an EOD tech's back from being crushed if blown backward against something hard meant he had to squat down like a sumo wrestler to stick the probe into the dirt. He ignored the sweat and aggravation and made it work.

He'd moved almost all the way around the shot hole and was about to climb out to walk around the rest of the area when his probe hit something hard. He tensed, but then relaxed. He was still here, so it couldn't be that bad. Dropping to one knee, he used his hand to slowly uncover what he'd found. When a horizontal, cylindrical pipe took shape, he assumed it was a water or sewer line. They weren't exactly common in structures as old as this one, but it could have been placed here to supply another building nearby. As he uncovered it, the pipe began to get smaller on one end. His gut clenched as realization dawned on him. He brushed off more dirt, revealing the nose of the 155-millimeter artillery round, as well as the metal electrical conduit extending out of it and running underground.

Fuck.

Cooper pushed himself to his feet and backpedaled toward the edge of the crater as fast as he could. An artillery round didn't usually have a conduit sticking out the end. This one had been booby-trapped so the bomber could set it off manually whenever he wanted. The conduit was there so the IED wouldn't cut the line if an EOD tech like him destroyed it. And with the conduit there, Cooper couldn't cut the line either.

This device was an EOD killer put there because somebody knew a bomb tech would come down and look around before turning the site over to the local police.

His mind raced. A projectile this size carried fifteen pounds of high explosive. When it went off, even a bomb suit as good as the one he had on was unlikely to stop all the frag that came off it.

He reached the top of the crater and backed away as fast as he could. He would have been able to run faster if he turned around, but the weakest part of a bomb suit was the rear. If this thing went off when his back was to it, he'd have no chance.

Time slowed as a thousand thoughts zipped through his head. How he seriously didn't want to die. How maybe the bomber on the other end of that firing line might have needed to go take a piss, and the 155 wouldn't go off. How his parents and brothers were going to be crushed when they found out. How he should have gone to the prom with that cute girl in his math class back in high school. How one of the junior members on his team was going to be forced to step up and take over his job. How the new unit lieutenant was going to have to write a condolence letter on his first fucking day on the job.

Cooper pushed those thoughts away, yanking his hands inside the arms of the suit to keep them from getting ripped off in the blast as he focused his attention on moving backward as fast as he could.

Just get twenty feet away. Then you might have a chance.

He didn't make it ten.

The blast threw him backward before his head even registered the flash of the projectile exploding. Luckily, he was so close that the wave took out the brick wall behind him before he could smash into it. But that luck ran out, and he slammed into the one behind it.

He felt a sharp stab in his back, then nothing from the middle of his chest down. The suit's spine support had broken—and so had his back.

He hit the ground hard, tumbling like a kid's toy until he came to a sudden stop against a pile of bricks. He felt pain—lots of it—at least from the chest up. He wasn't sure how he was able to, but he lifted his head enough to look down, and saw long, jagged fragments from the 155 sticking out of him like he was a damn pincushion.

Cooper let his head drop to the ground and swore long and hard. He was so fucked.

A detached part of his mind noticed that pieces of the building were burning around him. That was interesting, considering how little flammable material was in the area. The flames weren't too bad, but the smoke would probably choke him to death sooner or later. Not that he was likely to live long enough for that to happen. The frag had penetrated the bomb suit. He'd bleed out fast enough. He'd just be too numb to feel it.

Then someone was at his side, roughly prying up his face, telling him to hold on. That's when he realized his ears weren't working right. He could barely hear the person speaking. No shock there. The blast had blown out his eardrums.

He opened his eyes, expecting to see one of his junior teammates, and was shocked when he saw that it was Jim Wainwright, a fellow senior team leader and the best friend he'd ever had. Cooper hadn't even known another team had arrived.

"Get the hell out of here!" Cooper shouted. Or at least he tried to. The words came out as nothing but a gurgling whisper. "Jim, you know this is stupid. There could be another device down here."

Jim didn't answer, but simply shoved his arms under the bomb suit, as if he thought he could pick up Cooper and carry him out of here. He didn't bother to tell his friend how stupid that was. Besides all the frag sticking out of his body, making the task of picking him up akin to hugging a porcupine, Cooper and the bomb suit he wore weighed nearly three hundred pounds combined. There was no way in hell Jim could pick him up.

"Go!" he ordered again. "You know I'm done anyway."

Jim ignored him. Tears running down his face, he tried grabbing the heavy-duty rescue strap at the suit's shoulder and dragged him across the rubble.

"Shit!" Cooper wailed in agony, white-hot fire

shooting through his neck and shoulders. "Just fucking leave me alone and let me die!"

Jim disregarded that request too, grunting like a crazy man as he dragged Cooper over, around, and through the obstacles that separated them from the dilapidated building's exit. Cooper was stunned his friend could actually move him at all. He'd heard of soldiers doing some insane shit in battle to save a buddy, but this had to be the craziest. Too bad he was already a goner. Cooper only hoped Jim would get a medal out of it. Then, at least, one good thing would come out of this day.

Cooper didn't get much time to think about what the award write-up would sound like because the pain climbing up his neck like a wave of water drowned him until everything went black.

Chapter 1

Dallas, Present Day

IT MUST BE PAYDAY. EITHER THAT, OR GOD HATED him. As Cooper strode across the bank's lobby and got in line behind the twenty people already there, he wasn't sure which.

He'd been so exhausted after work he hadn't even bothered to shower and change into civvies at the SWAT compound like he usually did. Instead, he'd come straight to the bank in his combat boots, dark blue military cargo pants, and a matching T-shirt with the Dallas PD emblem and the word "SWAT" on the left side of the chest. He'd cleaned off the worst of the day's dirt, but he still felt grimy as hell. He couldn't wait to get home and throw everything in the wash so he could grab something to eat and fall into bed.

He bit back a growl as the man at the front of the line plunked down a cardboard box full of rolled coins on the counter and started lining the different denominations in front of the teller.

"You've got to be kidding me," Cooper muttered.

A tall, slender woman with long, golden-brown hair gave him a quick, understanding smile over her shoulder. He smiled back, but she'd already turned around. He waited, hoping she'd glance his way again, but she didn't.

Giving it up, Cooper glanced at the other line, wondering if he should jump over there. Definitely not. It was even longer.

He hated going to the bank, but his SWAT teammate Jayden Brooks had finally paid off the bet they'd made months ago about whether his squad leader and the newest member of the team would end up a couple. Instead of giving Cooper the hundred bucks in cash like a normal person, Brooks had given him a frigging check. At least he hadn't paid Cooper in pennies, or he would have been the one lining up rolls of change for the teller to count. But it wasn't Cooper's fault that he was more observant than most of the other werewolves in the Pack. Brooks had suggested the stupid bet. Cooper had simply agreed to it.

When Officer Khaki Blake had walked into the training room for the first time, every pair of eyes in the room immediately locked on her—except for Cooper's. Oh, he'd noticed she was attractive, make no mistake about that. But he'd been more interested in seeing how the rest of the SWAT team reacted to the first female alpha any of them had ever seen. While most of the guys had checked her out with open curiosity, none of their hearts had pounded as hard as his squad leader's—Corporal Xander Riggs. Cooper had immediately pegged Khaki as *The One* for Xander, and vice versa.

Other members of the SWAT team were still on the fence about whether they believed in *The One*, the mythical one-in-a-billion soul mate supposedly out there for every werewolf. But the way Cooper saw it, denying the truth was stupid. In the past ten months, three of the Pack's members had stumbled across their mates in the most bizarre and unbelievable ways. A werewolf would have to be an idiot not to see the women the guys had fallen in love with were their soul mates. It was obvious the moment you saw them together.

But just because Cooper accepted the concept of a werewolf soul mate didn't mean he automatically bought into the idea there were women in the world for him and the remaining thirteen single members of the Pack. Cooper wasn't jaded when it came to love, but he wasn't naive either. He'd been around the world enough times to know that not all stories had happy endings.

The jerk cashing in his lifetime supply of pocket change finally walked away from the counter, grumbling under his breath about the teller miscounting his nickels and dimes. Cooper leaned out and counted the number of people ahead of him and reconsidered whether it was worth his time to wait. Maybe he'd deposit the check on the way to work tomorrow. But that would mean getting up at least an hour earlier. He groaned at the thought. No way in hell was he getting up at four thirty, not after the day he'd had.

He and Brooks, along with their teammates, Carter Nelson, Remy Boudreaux, and Alex Trevino had been working with explosive investigative teams from the ATF and FBI since before the sun had come up. Some nut job had planted an IED in one of the parking garages of the Grand Prairie industrial area last night and killed a young Dallas PD officer moonlighting as a security guard. None of the investigators believed Officer Pete Swanson had been the target. He'd just been unlucky enough to be doing a security sweep of the garage when the bomb had gone off.

Instead, the feds thought the real target had been someone who worked for a company based out of the industrial complex. There were several defense firms that used the garage, as well as a biomedical research company and a consulting group that specialized in job outsourcing solutions. In other words, lots of people someone might want to blow up. Then again, it was also possible the bomber had picked that particular location purely by chance with no specific target in mind. Now that was a thought to keep any cop up at night.

But Cooper and the SWAT team hadn't been invited to the party to catch the guy. They'd been brought in to help with the long, painful process of combing the crime scene for every shred of evidence they could find to help the FBI track down the bomber.

They'd spent the entire day on their hands and knees searching the parking garage and surrounding area, as well as nearby rooftops, storm drains, and trees for pieces of the device. The FBI agent in charge was a friend of Cooper's and promised to call once they got all the pieces laid out so he could help put the IED back together. The SWAT team and the Dallas FBI field office weren't on the best of terms these days, and the feds would have a cow if they knew he was involved in the forensic part of the case. Between Xander and Khaki apprehending bank robbers the FBI had been chasing, and his teammate Eric Becker unofficially going undercover to save the woman he loved and taking down a group of Albanian mobsters, the feds weren't too happy with them. But what the FBI didn't know wouldn't hurt them.

The two people ahead of Cooper got fed up with

waiting and walked away. He quickly stepped forward
to fill in the gap and found himself behind the attractive
woman who'd flashed him a smile earlier. He couldn't
help noticing that she looked exceptionally good in a
pair of jeans. Or that her long, silky hair had the most
intriguing gold highlights when the sun coming through
the window caught them just right. She smelled so delicious he had to fight the urge to bend his neck and bury
his nose against her skin. Damn, he must be more tired
than he thought. If he wasn't careful, he'd be humping
her leg next.

He opened his mouth to say something charming, but
all that came out was a yawn big enough to make his
jaw crack. The woman in front of him must have heard
it too, because she turned around.

"And I thought I've been waiting in line a long time,"
she said, giving him a smile so breathtaking it damn near
made his heart stop. "You look like you're ready to fall
asleep on your feet."

Cooper knew he should reply, but he was so mesmerized by her perfect skin, clear green eyes, and soft
lips that he couldn't do anything but stare. He felt like a
teenager in high school again.

"Um, yeah. Long day," he finally managed.

What the hell was wrong with him? He'd never had
a problem talking to a beautiful woman before. But
in his defense, he'd never been in the presence of one
this gorgeous.

He gave himself a mental shake. *Get your head in
the game before she thinks you're a loser and turns
around again.*

"Catching bad guys, huh?" she asked.

"Something like that." He gave her his best charming smile. "Luckily, I'm off duty for the night."

She laughed, and the sound was so beautiful it almost brought him to his knees. Crap, he actually felt a little light-headed. He chalked it up to being out in the hot Texas sun all day. That could be hard on anyone, even a werewolf.

She tilted her head to the side, regarding him with an amused look. "Is that your way of saying you're free for dinner?"

Could she read his mind? "Depends. Would you say yes if I asked you out?"

Her lips curved. "I might. Although most guys tell me their names before asking me out on a date."

Cooper chuckled. He'd been attracted to her from the moment he saw her, but after talking to her, he was even more mesmerized. He'd always appreciated a woman who was confident enough to hold up her end of a verbal sparring match, and she seemed more than capable.

He held out his hand. "Landry Cooper at your service. Now that you know my name, how about dinner?"

He might have imagined it, but when she slipped her smaller hand into his much larger one, he could have sworn he felt a tingle pass between them—and it wasn't because of static electricity.

"I'm Everly Danu," she said. "And dinner sounds great."

Everly. Even her name was beautiful.

Cooper opened his mouth to ask Everly if she wanted to grab something that night—the hell with going home and falling into bed—when voices nearby caught his attention. Thanks to his keen werewolf hearing, he picked up every word.

"Are we still robbing the place with the cop here?" a male voice whispered.

"We're in too deep to back out now," another deep voice said softly. *"We were going to kill the guard anyway. Just make sure to take out the cop fast."*

Cooper snapped his head around, trying to figure out who'd said that. He scanned the crowded bank, looking for anyone who stood out, and immediately, zeroed in on a man over by the entrance. Average height with light brown hair, the guy was wearing mirrored sunglasses and a black windbreaker. On his own, the man wasn't that remarkable, but the small radio receiver in his ear sure as hell was. It wasn't hard to miss the telltale bulge under the man's left arm or the way he kept glancing at Cooper while keeping an eye on the door.

Cooper swept the bank lobby with his gaze, looking for the man's accomplice. He found him sitting by the manager's desk, pretending to wait for the woman to come back. Thanks to the identical sunglasses and the same black windbreaker the guy was wearing, he was easy to spot.

Cooper quickly ID'd two other men—one positioned a few feet away from the bank's security guard, the other near the big row of windows that looked out onto the main road. This one had a soft-sided computer bag big enough to hold several pistols—or a small submachine gun— hanging from his shoulder. Both were wearing sunglasses and windbreakers.

The guy by the door checked his watch, then nodded at his friend by the security guard. Cooper tensed. Shit, these assholes were really going to hit the bank with an armed cop standing right in the middle. Were they suicidal or just plain stupid?

Cooper's hand dropped to the Sig .40 on his belt.

"Landry?" Everly asked, her voice trembling a little. "Is something wrong?"

He didn't want to take his eyes off the four guys, but Everly's growing fear was so strong he could practically taste it on the air. Finding it impossible to ignore, he tore his gaze from the men and turned back to Everly.

"I don't want to alarm you, but the bank is about to be robbed," he said softly. "I need you to stay calm, okay?"

Everly had been ready to thank her lucky stars she picked today to come to the bank. It wasn't every day she met a man as attractive and intriguing as Landry Cooper, emphasis on the *attractive* part. Six-foot-four, broad-shouldered, heavily muscled, and gorgeous as hell, he looked like he should have been on the cover of a romance novel. His strong, scruff-roughened jaw and sexy lips were enough to almost make her start panting, but throw in that dazzling smile and sugary brown eyes, and she was nearly ready to jump him right there in the bank lobby.

Everly wasn't normally attracted to alpha males, especially not cops. She was an artist by trade and by nature, and she had never been into the overtly male types. Until now. When he'd asked her out, the thrill that rushed through her had been undeniable, and a little overwhelming. She'd never been the head-over-heels kind of girl.

But then everything had gone weird.

First, Landry's eyes had lost focus as he turned his head this way and that to look around the lobby in the middle of their conversation. When his gaze went sharp again, it was because he seemed to be sizing up the people around them. That was when she started getting a tingling sensation in her stomach that something was wrong. Then his hand slid down to the pistol on his belt, and Everly had really freaked.

When Landry told her the bank was about to be robbed, she prayed he was joking, but one look at his face told her he wasn't. She didn't have a clue how he knew what was about to happen, but she found herself believing him with a blind faith she couldn't explain.

Before she could ask what he was going to do, a man in a windbreaker by the door pulled out a handgun and fired shots into the air, shouting at everyone to get down on the floor. A split second later, men with guns barked orders and shoved people to the ground. Everly knew the smart thing would be to obey, but instead she stepped closer to Landry. She peeked around his shoulder as another shot rang out. She bit back a scream as the security guard collapsed, blood pooling around him.

As the man who shot the guard ran toward the counter, three other robbers converged on Landry, aiming their weapons at him. *Crap*. Maybe latching onto a cop hadn't been the wisest thing to do. Everly held her breath, waiting for Landry to surrender, but instead he pulled his gun and charged the men.

The bad guys tried to get a shot at Landry, but the panicked crowd made that all but impossible as people scrambled to their feet and stampeded toward the exit. Everly froze, torn between running for the door like everyone else, and staying to make sure Landry was okay.

The robbers angrily fought their way through the mob,

shoving some people and pistol-whipping others as they tried to get to Landry.

As for Landry, he strode into this sea of insanity as if he didn't even notice it. While everyone else was losing their minds—the robbers included—Landry moved with complete calm. When he finally got a clear shot, he lifted his gun and put a bullet in the center of the first gunman's chest, then did the same to the one behind him.

The third robber grabbed a teenage girl and tried to shield himself behind her. Landry darted forward before the girl could even scream, reaching around her and ripping the small machine gun out of the man's hand, then tossing him aside like he was a toy.

Everly's eyes widened as the robber flew through the air and crashed through the bank's big front window, sending glass everywhere. Everly stared in disbelief. Landry was obviously strong, but there was no way even a man his size should be able to throw another adult male that far.

The people the robbers had knocked to the floor in the melee scrambled to their feet and raced for the exit, along with the terrified teenage girl. Everly knew she should run too, but her feet refused to obey. Instead, they stayed stubbornly rooted to the floor, as if expecting Landry to come back and get her.

Landry. Where was he?

She looked around wildly, freaking when she didn't see him right away, but then she caught a blur of movement out of the corner of her eye. She turned just in time to see him closing in on the last robber. But this man seemed more ready for Landry than the first three had been.

Her heart lurched as the robber pointed his gun at Landry and pulled the trigger. The gunshot echoed in the now-empty lobby, making her ears ring. Everly ran toward Landry before she realized what she was doing.

Amazingly, Landry was still on his feet. He'd only been a few feet away from the robber when the gun went off. There was no way the man could have missed. But Landry didn't slow in the least. In fact, she swore she heard him growl as he covered the last few feet between him and the guy in the windbreaker.

The growl grew louder, and from where she stood, Everly saw Landry's lips pull back from his teeth in a snarl of anger. The gunman's eyes widened in terror. He tried to shoot again, but it was too late. Landry casually knocked the weapon across the room, then gripped the man by the throat, lifting him high into the air and slamming him hard against the marble wall.

Everly stumbled to a halt, her heart pounding. When she'd been talking to Landry earlier, he seemed sweet and charming, but now she realized he could be a little scary too. If you were a bank robber, at least.

Relieved the danger had finally passed, Everly took a step toward Landry when someone grabbed her by the hair and jerked her back. She screamed as pain shot through her scalp.

On the other side of the lobby, Landry jerked his head in her direction, his dark eyes glinting as they caught the late-day sun.

Behind her, the man let go of her hair, slipping an arm around her neck and shoulder to keep her pinned against his chest. Everly struggled to free herself, but he was too strong. She craned her neck to get a look at her captor. He was a little taller than she was, with dark blond hair and a trace of stubble on his tanned face. He might have been attractive if it wasn't for the cold, hard eyes that seemed to suck any humanity from his features. Her heart hammered in her chest as he pressed the barrel of a gun against her temple and held it there.

"Let him go and move away," the man ordered Landry in a voice as flat and emotionless as his eyes. "Drop your weapon too, or I shoot the woman in the head." He snorted when Landry stiffened. "I thought that would get your attention, cop."

Landry released the barely conscious robber, letting him fall to the floor, where he stayed. A moment later, he calmly dropped his pistol. Everly hadn't expected him to give up his weapon so easily. Cops on the TV crime dramas never did that, but it was like Landry barely cared.

That was when Everly saw the blood staining the right side of Landry's shirt just under his ribs. He must have seen her eyes widen because he smiled.

"I'm fine, Everly," he said. "And you're going to be okay too. I promise."

She didn't know why she trusted him. They'd just met, and this situation seemed impossible to get out of. But for some insane reason, she sincerely believed he wouldn't let anything hurt her.

"That's not a promise you're going to be able to keep, cop," her captor told Landry. "You've completely fucked up this job, but that's okay. Because you're my ticket out of here."

"How's that?" Landry asked.

"I'm going to take her and walk out of here, and you're

going to tell all your cop buddies, who will no doubt be here in a few minutes, to stay the hell away from me."

Landry took a step closer, then another. "I can't let you walk out of here with her."

"Like hell you can't," the robber snapped. "It's not like you have a choice. I have a gun, and you don't. And if I see a single cop following us, I'm going to kill her. Slowly."

Everly started to hyperventilate. If this psycho got her away from Landry, she'd never be seen alive again, and she really didn't want to die. But what the hell could Landry do? He didn't even have a weapon.

Her heart raced faster, and for a minute she thought she might pass out from sheer terror. She'd never been this scared in her life.

Then she heard Landry calmly calling her name, and she forced herself to lift her head and lock her gaze with his. He might seem cool, calm, and collected on the outside, but there was a fire burning in his beautiful brown eyes that belied that.

"You're going to be fine, Everly," he said softly. "But I need you to do me a favor. Can you do one small favor for me?"

As soothing as Landry's deep voice was, she was still having a hard time reining in the fear. But she nodded anyway, praying he'd somehow save her.

"That's great," Landry said. "All I need you to do is one, simple thing, Everly. I need you to close your eyes—right now."

———~~~———

Sometimes the world was such a crappy place that Cooper couldn't help but doubt the existence of a higher being. Other times, like those rare occasions when people like Becker and his girlfriend Jayna Winston found each other against all reasonable odds, he thought maybe there might be a chance. It wasn't proof, but it was reason to hope.

Then there were days like today, when things went so completely to shit in a manner that could only be called orchestrated, that he was forced to admit there simply had to be a supreme being. The world could never go this bat-shit crazy all on its own.

First, after months spent putting it off, Jayden had finally paid off their most recent bet with a check. Then, after going to the bank to deposit that check, Cooper had met a beautiful woman he was seriously attracted to while standing in line. But before he could even firm up plans for their dinner date, some assholes had decided to rob the place.

That was bad enough, but it had gotten worse when he realized there weren't four robbers like he'd thought— there were five. And the last one currently had Everly in his arms with a gun to her head, threatening to drag her out of the bank and use her for a hostage.

Cooper was pissed at himself for missing the fifth bad guy. But in his defense, the other four had been wearing the same jackets, mirrored sunglasses, and guilty expressions on their faces. This last guy wore an expensive business suit that probably cost more than Cooper's Sig Sauer service-issued sidearm. If there'd been a radio receiver in his ear, Cooper hadn't seen it. In addition to all that, right before the robbery started, the guy's pulse had been as slow and steady as it was now. That only made Cooper more determined not to let this psycho walk out of here with Everly in his arms. If he did, no one would ever see her again.

Sure as hell would have been nice to have Alex or the team's other sniper Connor Malone somewhere nearby with a large-caliber rifle. If they had been, this would be over by now.

But he didn't have any SWAT snipers on standby—there was just him. And with his Sig lying on the floor behind him, he was left with only one option when it came to saving Everly.

His boss, Gage Dixon, would shit bricks if he knew what Cooper was considering as he slowly approached Everly and the man holding her. The SWAT team commander had one hard and fast rule when it came to using their werewolf talents—never do it in public, no matter what. And with people on the sidewalk, not to mention the bank cameras, this place was the definition of public. But with the robber already edging toward the door with Everly, Cooper wasn't going to be able to follow that rule.

When he'd told Everly to close her eyes, he wasn't sure she would do it. Hell, he wasn't even sure she could hear him over the pounding of her heart. But her eyes fluttered closed, then scrunched tighter.

Good girl.

Praying that no one outside was looking his way, Cooper relaxed and let his body begin to shift.

He immediately felt the muscles of his chest, shoulders, arms, and neck thicken and tighten, his heart rate speed up, and his eyes change. He didn't have to let his eyes change. It wasn't like he needed enhanced night vision. But he knew from experience that it could be damn disconcerting to see a pair of blazing yellow eyes charging at you, and he intended to use that to his benefit.

Cooper could have taken the shift further. It would have been easy to let his fangs and claws come out, too. Hell, if it wasn't for the people and the cameras, he would have said the hell with it and shifted all the way into his wolf form. In a heartbeat, he could have been on the man holding Everly, killing him in seconds.

But shifting that far would have been stupid, not to mention unnecessary.

Cooper surged forward, feeling the power in his leg muscles propel him across the floor at a pace no human could obtain. At the same time, he let out a deep, rumbling growl as he closed the distance between himself and the guy with the gun.

The man's eyes went as round as saucers, though whether it was from hearing the growl Cooper let out, or seeing his glowing, yellow eyes, Cooper couldn't be sure. Despite being scared shitless, the bank robber managed to take the gun away from Everly's head and point it at Cooper.

Cooper dodged to the side as the gun went off, wincing as the bullet creased a line across the muscles of his right shoulder. Everly jumped, but her eyes stayed tightly closed as the shooter tried to adjust his aim so he could put the next shot through Cooper's head.

Shit. If he hit him, Cooper would be dead. Even a werewolf couldn't survive a head shot.

But to do it, the jackass had to step out from behind Everly a little more, which left the right side of his body exposed. Cooper rarely had a problem controlling the raw animal instincts that came with being a werewolf, but at that moment, the urge to let his claws slip out and rake them across the man's neck was almost irresistible.

But he controlled himself. There'd be no way to explain a wound like that, not in this environment. Instead he balled his right hand into a fist as he leaped, smashing it into the man's face. It connected with a very satisfying sound. The robber flew backward, releasing Everly. She stumbled, but maintained her balance, keeping to her feet and staying right where she was.

Cooper tucked his left arm under him as he hit the floor in a roll, then quickly jumped to his feet. The bad guy hit a lot harder, his head cracking into the marble floor with an audible thud. He was out cold, but still breathing, despite all the blood running down his face from the broken nose and jaw.

Cooper hurried back to where Everly still stood frozen.

"You can open your eyes now," he said softly in her ear.

She jumped, opening those big, beautiful eyes. She looked first at him, then at the lobby around them. Now that the last robber was down, the place was eerily silent, like the woods after a big storm.

"Is it over?" she asked.

He nodded. "Yes, it's over."

Everly threw her arms around him, squeezing so tight he could barely breathe. "Thank you."

Cooper wrapped his arms around her, closing his eyes. Even with everything that had happened, he couldn't resist her scent. "You don't need to thank me," he said when he found his voice. "I was just making sure we'd get a chance to go on that date."

She stepped back, her eyes momentarily taking in the

wound below his ribs and the newer one along his shoulder. He could practically see her fingers twitch as if they ached to reach out and check them, but she resisted the urge to mom him, instead slipping her hands down to interlock with his.

"Well, if a date is the thanks you're looking for, I can promise you one thing," she said.

"What's that?"

She stepped closer, and if they hadn't been in the middle of a crime scene, he wouldn't have been surprised if she'd gone up on her tiptoes to kiss him. And he sure as hell wouldn't have stopped her.

"That you're in for the very best date of your life," she said.

Chapter 2

ANY HOPE OF GETTING THINGS WRAPPED UP FAST SO he could meet Everly for dinner was crushed the moment Gage and Deputy Chief Hal Mason showed up with Detective Vince Coletti from Internal Affairs. It was normal for IA to do an on-scene investigation in an officer-involved shooting, but the deputy chief usually showed up only if the shit hit the fan. Cooper supposed two dead bank robbers with three more in the hospital counted as shit hitting the fan. No doubt other detectives from IA had already questioned Everly and the witnesses in the bank to get their accounts of what had gone down.

He frowned as he thought of Everly. They'd exchanged phone numbers before Gage and Mason had shown up, and even though she assured him she was fine, he'd been hoping to see her again before she left to make sure she really was okay. She'd gone through a hell of a traumatic experience in that bank. They might have just met, but he was already feeling protective.

Unfortunately, Cooper couldn't check on her until he finished with Coletti. The detective was going to keep asking his damn questions until he got the answers he wanted. They'd already spent frigging forever going over every one of his actions related to the attempted robbery and the takedown of the suspects, and it didn't look like they were even close to being done. The dark-haired IA detective was a slow note taker, and repeatedly had Cooper back up and go over certain parts of his story again…and again…and again.

"You shot the first two suspects, then threw the next one through the window?" Coletti's eyes narrowed suspiciously. "Explain to me again how that happened."

Cooper fought the urge to curse. He settled for blowing out a breath as he crossed his arms over his chest instead. They'd been going at this for nearly two hours in the small mobile command tent the team had set up in the parking lot, while more investigators pored over the physical evidence inside the bank. The paramedics and rescue workers had left a long time ago, taking the wounded customers and security guard with them. Last Cooper had heard, the guard wasn't doing so well and would likely be in surgery all night.

"Like I've told you several times already," Cooper said, "the third suspect took cover behind a teenage girl as I approached him. I couldn't shoot without risking the hostage, so I grabbed him, and in the act of dragging him away from the girl, he went flying and somehow ended up going through the window."

Coletti glanced at his notes. "I see. He just happened to end up going through the window. Like the other two suspects just happened to sustain concussions when their heads bounced off the wall or floor, right?"

Cooper caught the warning look Gage threw him. His boss probably thought he was going to tear into the IA detective for being an asshole. But while it was true Coletti seemed to take more pleasure in his job than most detectives in the department's oversight division, Cooper was smart enough to know the guy was simply trying to piss him off to see what would slip out. Cooper wasn't falling for it.

"That's exactly right." He gave Coletti his most sincere grin. "And here I was thinking you weren't paying attention the first five times I told you what happened."

Coletti didn't return the smile. He didn't get pissed either. Instead, he regarded Cooper for a long time before referring to his notes again. "What do you think I'm going to see when I watch the video from the bank's security cameras?"

Cooper had no idea what Coletti or anyone else would see on the video. Besides letting his eyes turn gold, Cooper hadn't shifted far enough for someone to figure out he was a werewolf. But they'd almost certainly see some things that would make them sit up and take notice. Like him tossing that guy through the window. Or lifting another guy off his feet and bouncing his head off the wall. Or how fast he'd moved. Cooper prayed people would dismiss those things as some kind of video glitch because there was really no good way to explain them.

He sure as hell wasn't going to say that to Coletti though. "I have no idea what you'll see, but if you find a cop to look at them with you, I'm sure he's going to point out five men trying to rob a bank. He'll likely mention that those five men had absolutely no regard for human lives. The cop you're watching with might even remark on how I kept a woman from being taken hostage and almost certainly ending up dead."

Coletti didn't say anything in reply to the jab, but just kept taking notes. After a few minutes, he looked up. Cooper expected him to start in with another round of questions. Instead he closed his notebook and looked at the deputy chief.

"I'll be recommending standard leave with pay until we complete the officer-involved shooting portion of the investigation. At least three days, perhaps a week."

No way in hell. Coletti couldn't be serious. Cooper opened his mouth to argue, but one glare from Gage halted his words.

"I'm also going to recommend that Officer Cooper undergo a complete psychological assessment as part of his formal fitness-for-duty evaluation," Coletti added. "I believe there are some additional stressors involved here beyond those that typically occur in an officer-involved shooting situation. I think Officer Cooper would be well served talking to one of the department's contracted psychologists."

This time Cooper ignored Gage. "That's bullshit, Coletti. I was fully justified shooting those suspects in there, and I'm not going to see a shrink so I can lie down on a couch and talk about my mother when I have a job to do."

Coletti leveled his gaze at Cooper, his jaw tight. "Officer Cooper, this investigation will run its course, and that includes a thorough review of the bank's security footage. Based on what you've told me so far, I'm leaning toward calling this a clean shoot. However, I have to admit I'm troubled about how you physically subdued the other three suspects. My bigger concern is the trauma you went through in that bank. Not only did you see a security guard and several civilians get shot, but you were forced to give up your weapon or risk seeing another civilian shot in the head right in front of you. I'm aware of your military background and how that ended. I'm worried about what effects these recent events could have on you. I think talking to a mental health professional would be good for you."

Cooper bit back a growl. The fact that this guy had dug around in his military record was bad enough. But the idea that Coletti actually thought he would appreciate being forced to see a shrink was even worse. He saw stuff like what had gone down inside that bank every day on the job.

Cooper expected Gage, or even Mason, to help him out, but both were infuriatingly silent.

"And if I don't want to see a mental health professional?" he ground out.

Coletti's gray eyes hardened to steel. "Then I doubt you'll be returning to duty anytime soon."

* * *

Everly hadn't had a chance to do more than exchange phone numbers with Landry before he disappeared inside the fancy tent thingy the cops had set up. She'd let a paramedic take a look at her while she waited for him to come out, then met with a detective who took her statement about what had happened in the bank. Reliving the whole experience hadn't been fun. She'd rather forget some guy had grabbed her and put a gun to her head, but the detective was only doing his job, and if her statement put the bank robber in prison, she would help any way she could. It would have been nice to have Landry there with her while she talked to the detective. It was silly, but he made her feel safe.

While she wanted to see Landry before she left, she

felt completely out of place at the crime scene. It didn't help that the other police officers kept eyeing her curiously. If she hung around much longer, they were going to think she was up to something.

She turned to leave when she saw a group of cops dressed in all kinds of dangerous-looking military gear standing over by an equally big RV. Underneath all that tactical gear, they wore the same dark blue T-shirts and cargo pants as Landry. If the clothing and relaxed, confident way they stood hadn't given them away, the word *SWAT* in big letters across the back of their vests definitely told her they were part of the city's special weapons and tactics team.

Thinking they might know Landry, Everly walked over to them. They turned at her approach, as if sensing her. She hadn't realized that one was a woman because two men had been blocking her view, but the female cop looked just as intimidating as the guys under all the tactical gear she was wearing. As for the men, Everly couldn't help noticing that all five were not only tall and well built, they were incredibly attractive to boot. Not as hot as Landry, of course, but definitely not hard to look at. Her roommate Mia would just about melt around so many big studs, even if they were a little unapproachable.

"Can we help you?" the female cop asked.

"I was wondering if any of you know Landry Cooper?"

One of the men gave her a big smile. Almost as tall as Landry, he had dark blond hair and blue eyes. "Sure we know Cooper. You a friend of his?"

Everly was hoping she and Landry would be more than friends at some point, but right now, friends worked. Especially if it meant she could hang around with the rest of the SWAT team and wait for him.

"Yes. I was in the bank when the robbery happened," she said. "We exchanged numbers, but I was hoping to talk to him before I left. Unfortunately, I think those guys would rather I leave." She jerked her thumb at the uniformed police officers keeping reporters and curious onlookers outside the yellow crime scene tape. "Could you let him know that I waited for him but had to go? I wouldn't want him to think I just bailed on him."

The female cop smiled and held out her hand. Taller than Everly, she had dark hair pulled back into a bun and brown eyes. "I'm Khaki Blake. If Cooper wanted you to hang around, you're welcome to stay here with us. We'll make sure no one bugs you until he comes out."

That had been almost two hours ago. She couldn't understand now why she'd thought the guys were intimidating. Tall, dark-haired Xander Riggs; the equally tall Alex Trevino, whose nearly black hair looked like it was perpetually tousled; wiry Remy Boudreaux with his unmistakable Cajun accent; mocha-skinned, gray-eyed Jayden Brooks; and the blond-haired Eric Becker were some of the nicest people she'd ever met. Becker, one of Landry's closest friends, was especially sweet to her. And hanging out with them helped her push aside the horrible memories of what had happened in the bank. She'd have to deal with them later she was sure, but right now, it was good simply to laugh and be thankful she was alive.

Everly sighed with relief when she saw Landry finally come out of the tent. As far as she knew, he hadn't seen a paramedic about his injuries yet, and she'd been worried. But he looked fine. Instead of coming over to join his team, he stood talking with another big man dressed in SWAT gear and an older man dressed in a traditional police uniform. She had no idea what they were discussing, but whatever it was, Landry looked angry.

"Do you think everything's okay?" she asked no one in particular. "Landry doesn't look too happy."

Beside her, Becker snorted. "The only time Cooper's happy is when he's blowing something up."

Everyone laughed at that. Everly laughed too, even though she didn't understand why anyone would enjoy working with explosives. They seemed dangerous. But the other SWAT officers she'd been chatting with for the past two hours had told her Landry worked with explosives a lot, so apparently, he didn't mind being around them.

While they'd waited, Becker entertained her with stories about Landry and some of the crazy things he'd done. If half the things Becker told her were true, Landry might be the most insane person she'd ever hung out with. But rather than dissuade her from wanting to spend time with him, the stories made Everly want to get to know him even better.

"Hey, you're still here!" a familiar voice said from behind her.

Everly turned around to see Landry walking over to join them, the corners of his sexy lips edging into a smile.

"I thought you'd already left," he said.

She smiled. "I ran into your teammates, and they let me hang out with them until you got done. I wanted to make sure you really were okay before I left."

As Landry came to a stop in front of her, she was suddenly reminded how big and muscular he was. He loomed over her by nearly a foot. She almost laughed as she had a vision of climbing up his body to kiss him. Not that she minded. Something told her it would be worth it.

He grinned. "The wound was just a scratch. The paramedics didn't even bother with it."

She found that hard to believe considering the amount of blood on his shirt. She opened her mouth to say so, but suddenly, she found herself tongue-tied as a delicious scent filled her nose. At first, she thought he was wearing a nice cologne. But she immediately dismissed that idea. She had four brothers she'd bought a lot of cologne for over the years, and Landry didn't smell like any of those. No, this scent was all his, and it was more intoxicating than any cologne, that was for sure. She didn't realize how good until she leaned in closer to get a whiff. If she could figure out how to put it in a bottle and sell it, she'd be rich.

Landry lifted a brow. He was probably wondering why she was standing there breathing him in like some kind of weirdo.

"Um," she managed, trying to gather her thoughts. What had she been going to say? For the life of her, she couldn't remember. So she said the first thing that came to mind.

"You never told me where you were taking me for dinner. I wanted to know what I should wear for our date."

Landry gazed down at her for a long moment, a slight smile at his lips, as if he knew how off kilter he had her—and that he enjoyed the fact.

"To tell the truth, I hadn't really picked a place yet," he said. "I thought I'd ask if you had a favorite restaurant, or a favorite food, then go from there."

She wasn't fooled for a second. Landry knew she was seriously attracted to him, but she appreciated the fact that he didn't let the knowledge go to his head. A lot of other men would have assumed that she'd go wherever they wanted. It was nice to know Landry was ready to make their date all about her. Still, she had to wonder how far he would be willing to go with that.

"You sure you're okay with me picking the restaurant?" she asked. "You strike me as the basic meat-and-potato type. Aren't you worried I'll pick some kind of girlie place with fondue pots and bean sprouts?"

He chuckled, a rich, warm sound that rumbled from his big, broad chest. "Are you saying you're the fondue and bean sprout kind of girl?"

She gave him a coy smile. What was it about him that made her want to flirt so outrageously? "Maybe."

Landry stepped closer, and for a split second she thought he was going to kiss her right here in the middle of a crime scene with all his SWAT teammates standing around them. She went up on her tiptoes, more than ready, but he stopped just short, leaving her hanging.

"Then it's settled," he said. "I think there's a Melting Pot over on Five Point in Arlington. Would that work?"

She laughed softly and dropped back down off her toes. She might as well stop testing him. It was clear he'd take her anywhere she wanted to go. "I'm sure it's a nice place, but I was just kidding about that stuff. I don't like fondue or bean sprouts. But if you know a place that serves authentic French food, that would be perfect."

"French, huh?" He considered that. "I think I have the perfect restaurant in mind. Tomorrow night good for you?"

"Perfect," she said, although she didn't know how she could ever wait that long. "I'm looking forward to it."

"Me too." He leaned in again, putting his mouth close to her. "Especially since you did promise me it'd be the best date of my life."

Everly's face heated at the reminder. But she had said those exact words, so she couldn't hold it against him for bringing them up, especially since her mind was probably wandering in exactly the same direction.

She smiled up at him. "Well, a promise is a promise. And I don't think you'll be disappointed."

"I'm pretty sure I won't."

His eyes caught the light of the nearby streetlamp like they had in the bank, making them almost gold, and suddenly, she was having a hard time breathing. She'd never been around a guy who had this kind of effect on her.

"I'll text you my address later," she said. "Is seven o'clock good for you?"

He nodded. "Perfect."

Even though the logistical details of their first date seemed to have been pinned down as well as they were ever going to be, Everly noticed that neither one of them moved. They simply stood there, gazing at each other, mere inches separating their lips.

Behind her, one of his teammates cleared his throat, and the trance was broken. Everly reluctantly stepped back. She turned and saw Khaki and the guys regarding her and Landry with knowing smiles.

"What?" Landry demanded.

"Nothing," Becker said, still grinning.

Landry shook his head, his mouth twitching. "Come on. I'll walk you to your car."

He fell into step beside her as she led the way to her silver Nissan Juke. She dug in her purse for her keys as she turned to him.

"Thank you," she said. "And not just for walking me to my car. For what you did in the bank. You saved my life."

"Any time," he said. "Are you doing okay? Do you need to talk to someone? About what happened in there, I mean."

Talking to him was all she needed. She smiled and shook her head. "I'm fine. I'm going to go home, take a nice, relaxing bath, and think about our date."

His mouth curved. "Okay. But if you need to talk, call me."

"I will." Everly reached up to tuck her hair behind her ear, suddenly self-conscious. "I'll see you tomorrow night."

He flashed her that gorgeous smile. "I'll be there."

―⁓―

It was nearly eleven o'clock by the time Everly let herself into the loft-style apartment she shared with Mia Barlowe. She tried to be as quiet as she could so she didn't wake up her friend, but Mia was curled up on the couch watching the local news, nervously chewing on her thumbnail. The moment she saw Everly, she turned off the TV, then jumped off the couch and ran over to hug her.

"Thank God! I've been so worried about you. I heard about the bank robbery on the news and have been trying to call you all night. When I didn't get an answer, I freaked out. Then someone posted a picture of you on

Facebook getting checked out by a paramedic. I was just about to call the hospitals." She pulled back, holding Everly at arm's length. "Are you okay?"

Everly smiled, nudging her petite, dark-skinned roommate into the apartment so she could close the door. Then she turned and took Mia's hands in hers. "I'm okay. You can calm down. I was in the bank during the holdup, but I wasn't hurt."

Mia eyed her skeptically, as if she thought Everly might be lying. "Come on. I have comfort food. You can tell me all about it while we eat."

Everly let Mia lead her into the cozy, eclectic living room they'd shared since they'd graduated from college. She almost reminded Mia that it was practically midnight, but then realized she was hungry.

She winced as she took the bottle of water Mia thoughtfully grabbed from the fridge. Her friend had obviously been freaking out in front of the TV for hours. Everly felt terrible about not calling. Then again, she did have a good reason for being distracted.

"Was it absolutely horrible?" Mia asked as Everly took a slice of lukewarm pizza out of the box on the coffee table.

"Horrible enough to make me not want to go into a bank for a while. There were five guys with guns, and they didn't seem to mind killing people. They shot the poor security guard in the back. I'm not even sure if he made it to the hospital alive."

"I read on Facebook that he's still in surgery, but the hospital seems hopeful."

Everly was glad to hear that. "What about the other people who got hurt? Anything on them?"

Mia nodded as she reached for a slice of pizza. "They all seemed to be doing okay. The guard was the worst of the bunch. The news said there was a Dallas SWAT cop in the bank at the time of the robbery. He's the one who saved everyone's life, including some poor woman one of the robbers took hostage."

Everly shuddered. "Yeah. It was *me*."

"You?" Mia's eyes widened, the slice of pizza half-way to her mouth. "Oh God! What happened?"

Everly thought about drastically editing the details of what had gone down in the bank, but Mia already knew most of it from watching the news, so she'd figure out if Everly was glossing over things. So, Everly told her everything from the moment she had met Landry until she had left him twenty minutes ago.

Mia flopped back against the couch with a sigh. "Most women would be thrilled to get out of a situation like that alive, but you come out of it with a date with a cute cop? I want your life."

Everly sipped her water. "I'm not really sure you'd say he's cute."

"He's not?"

"Not really. I'd probably go with gorgeous. Or devastating. I'd even go so far as to say he's so sexy I had a hard time not kissing him right there in the middle of the crime scene," Everly added with a grin. "But I would never call him cute."

Mia threw an unopened packet of Parmesan cheese at her, which Everly deflected as she laughed.

"You are so bad," Mia grumbled. "But I'm willing to overlook it if this new boy toy of yours has friends."

Everly was about to mention all the attractive guys

on the SWAT team when her phone rang. She quickly grabbed it, hoping it might be Landry calling to make sure she got home safely. But when she saw the name showing on the screen, any thoughts of the hunky cop disappeared.

Mia frowned at the look on her face. "Who is it?"

"My father."

Her friend grimaced. "I didn't call him, I swear."

Everly found her thumb moving back and forth between the green button and the red one, not sure what she wanted to do. She loved her dad like crazy, but he'd been treating her like she was five years old ever since she *was* five years old. She might be twenty-eight, but he didn't see it that way. He was from the old country, and sometimes, it really showed. He could be a pain in the butt when he wanted, and was overprotective to a fault. If he knew she'd been involved in a bank robbery, he'd probably insist her brothers go to the bank for her from now on.

But even if he'd heard about the bank robbery, what were the chances he knew she was there? It wasn't like he used the Internet. He didn't even have a clue what Facebook was.

She pressed the green button before she could over-think it.

"Hey, Dad. You're calling late. Is everything okay?"

"I am fine, Everly. I am more concerned about you," he said in his deep, rough voice. "Can I assume the reason you did not call was because you were hoping we had not heard about what happened at the bank? Or was it simply because you do not care if your brothers and I worry about you?"

She rolled her eyes. Honestly, why did her father

have to be so dramatic all the time? "I'm fine, Dad. I was never in any danger. You know how the news blows everything out of proportion. I didn't call because I didn't want to worry you. And of course I care that you guys worry about me."

"So the news is blowing the danger you were in out of proportion? What about this police officer who saved your life? Are they making him up too?"

She cringed. "No, Landry's real. And the part about him saving my life is true. How did you even know about that? It wasn't in the news."

"Armand and Tristan went down to the bank. They asked, and someone told them. Your brothers can be very charming when they want to be."

Everly jerked back and stared at the phone as if it had bitten her. Then she put it back to her ear, her hand tightening so hard on the small device she thought the glass cover would crack. "You sent them down to the bank to spy on me?"

She could imagine her brothers chatting up some poor female reporter, turning on the charm and laying on the French accents. It made her want to throw the phone at the wall.

"I did not send them there to spy," her father said calmly. "I sent them there with instructions to go in and get you out if they needed to, but with that very large SWAT officer there to watch over you, it wasn't necessary. What did you say his name was—Landry? I didn't realize police officers were on a first-name basis with women they rescue."

Everly didn't know which part annoyed her more. The fact that her fool brothers intended to rush into the bank unarmed and save her from a bunch of killers, or the fishing expedition her father was on. She sighed. If her date with Landry went as well as she hoped, her father was going to find out sooner or later.

"Landry was behind me in line," she explained. "We were talking and exchanged names. In fact, he was asking me out when the bank robbers started shooting up the place."

"I see. And did you agree to go out with him?"

She really needed to have a conversation with her father about boundaries. But midnight was not the time. "Yes, Dad."

Her father was silent as if considering that. "Then you must bring him by the house so your brothers and I can meet him in person. I would very much like to thank him for what he has done for our family."

Everly wanted to ask if he planned on having her brothers chaperone the date too, but bit her tongue. She didn't want to give Florian Danu any ideas.

"I'll think about it. Have a good night, Dad."

Mia lifted a brow. "Your dad already knows about Landry?"

Everly tossed her phone on the couch beside her. "Worse. He wants to meet him."

Her friend popped what was left of the slice of pizza she was eating in her mouth and grinned. "I'd pay to have front-row seats for that."

Everly could only groan.

Chapter 3

COOPER SAT IN THE CHAIR ACROSS FROM DOCTOR Hadley Delacroix's desk, watching as she jotted down notes. He had no idea what she could possibly be writing. They hadn't said more than ten words to each other in the fifteen minutes he'd been there. All she'd done was introduce herself and tell him to have a seat in the chair across from her big cherrywood desk...or on the leather couch along one wall. And there was no way in hell she was getting him on that couch.

He'd pleaded his case last night to Gage, telling him this shrink session was a huge waste of time, but the Pack's lead alpha wasn't interested in his opinion on the subject.

"With all the crazy crap SWAT has been involved in lately, it's not surprising Coletti is toeing the line on this return-to-duty evaluation and psych assessment," his boss said. "What the hell did you think was going to happen when you threw a two-hundred-pound guy ten feet through the air and into a plate glass window in broad daylight? You're damn lucky Becker was able to hack into the bank's security servers and fuzz up those videos, or you'd be looking at more than a couple days with a shrink. IA would have you down at the hospital drawing blood three times a day until they figured out what kind of drugs you're on. Just play the game, talk with the psychologist the department assigns to your case, then get your ass cleared for duty."

Play the game. *Right*. Obviously, Gage had never met this particular shrink. It looked like the last time this woman had played games was when she was three years old—and she probably hadn't liked them even then. Cooper could be charming when he wanted to be, but something told him that his werewolf charisma would be totally wasted on her.

As they sat there in silence, interrupted only by the scratching of her pen and the occasional rustle of a piece of paper, Cooper took the time to study Hadley Delacroix. She wasn't like he'd pictured. He knew that was shallow as hell, but he assumed she'd have a mousey hairdo and horn-rimmed glasses, as well as a lab coat to go with her ultra-conservative, take-me-serious outfit.

He'd been way off target. For one thing, she wasn't wearing a lab coat, and her leopard-print blouse screamed anything but conservative. For another, her fingernails were extremely long and painted a flashy color. And while he'd been right about the reading glasses, they weren't horn-rimmed. She had a seriously distinct fuck-off vibe that was hard to miss too. If Delacroix had been a werewolf, she would have been an alpha for sure.

Thank God she wasn't. That was all he and his pack needed—a shrink on the department payroll who knew the entire SWAT team was made up of werewolves.

As the minutes wore on, Cooper tried to keep his rising anger in check. He didn't have a problem with psychologists per se. It was just that he'd dealt with enough of them after getting blown up in Iraq to know they couldn't do a whole hell of a lot for most people.

They'd tried to get him to come to grips with life as a cripple when it looked like the lower half of his body was going to be nothing but a bunch of dead weight. Then, after the "miracle" had occurred and his back had healed, they'd spent months trying to medicate his nightmares out of existence with drugs he couldn't stand.

Ultimately, he never blamed the shrinks for not getting anything right with him. It wasn't their fault they didn't have a clue how to deal with a blown-up, screwed-up EOD tech, much less one who was discovering he was a werewolf.

He forced himself to think pleasant thoughts of Everly and their dinner plans, when Dr. Delacroix finally looked up and fixed him with those sharp eyes of hers.

"Why don't we start by you telling me what happened in the bank yesterday?" she said bluntly.

So much for the getting-to-know-you chitchat. "Don't you have the report already?"

She nodded. "I do. But they're just words on a piece of paper. I'd rather hear the events from your point of view instead."

"Why?"

Delacroix lifted a brow and regarded him in silence for several long seconds. "Why what?"

He rested his ankle on his knee. "Why do you need to hear it from my point of view? You've read the reports about what happened in the bank. I'm sure the one from IA was especially interesting. Maybe you've even seen the videos from the bank's security system. After all that, I'd think a person with your obvious intelligence would have already come up with plenty of opinions on exactly what happened in there, and what that says about me and my ability to do my job."

Cooper hadn't intended for his words to come out quite so confrontational, but he had to admit that after all the time he'd spent talking with the doctors from the Veterans Administration, he wasn't really a fan of sharing. In his experience, doctors liked to ask a lot of questions, only to toss you in some neatly labeled box regardless of how you answered.

Delacroix leaned back in her chair and regarded him with a look that seemed to suggest she'd anticipated his answer.

"Officer Cooper, I think you have some misconception concerning my role in this fitness-for-duty evaluation," she said calmly. "I'm not an employee of the Dallas Police Department. I'm a completely independent psychologist paid on retainer by the State of Texas to perform various forensic and mental health tasks within my field of expertise. I'm not being paid to judge your technical performance during the robbery or provide psychiatric treatment. You were just involved in a traumatic incident that required you to shoot two men and physically engage with three others. Your departmental leadership is concerned these encounters could have an adverse effect on your ability to do your job. You aren't here for therapy. My task is simply to ensure you're mentally and emotionally fit to return to your SWAT duties, as well as recommend additional resources should you need them."

Cooper couldn't help but let out a snort of laughter. "Which is a nice way of saying you're supposed to figure out if I'm insane, right?"

A slight smile curved her lips, but then it was gone, replaced with her usual professional expression. "I'm not really a fan of that word. My task is to understand what happened in that bank and determine if your reactions and emotions at the time—and now—are in line with those of other people in your profession. Anything you tell me of a personal nature is protected by doctor-patient confidentiality and won't be provided to the department. They simply get my final report concerning your suitability to return to duty."

"And if I don't feel like talking about what happened in that bank?" he asked, already knowing the answer.

She shrugged. "I certainly can't make you talk about it if you don't want to. I'm getting paid to conduct an undefined number of one-hour sessions until I arrive at a suitable determination. If you'd rather spend our sessions talking about the weather, that's fine with me. I get paid a large sum of money from the state regardless."

"But if we spend all our time talking about the weather, you won't be signing my fitness-for-duty certificate, will you?"

She shook her head. "No, I won't."

Cooper ground his jaw. This was going to suck pond water, but he couldn't see any way out. "So, what do you want to know?"

She sat up straight and picked up her pen, holding it poised over her notepad. "Instead of asking you to recount the entire event, maybe it would be easier if I started with a specific part of it, just to get the ball rolling."

He shrugged at the innocent offer, even though his instincts warned him that he was walking into a trap. "Okay. Shoot."

"Let's start with how you knew the bank was about to be robbed. It wasn't noted in the IA report, but I noticed on the video that you looked up and scanned the bank at least forty-five seconds before the first suspect pulled out his weapon. Tell me about that."

Cooper smothered a curse. When he'd walked in here, his biggest worry had been letting Hadley Delacroix poke around in his head. But now he had to worry that if he slipped up and said the wrong thing, she might figure out there was something odd about him. If that happened, how long would it take her to figure out he wasn't the only unusual cop on the Dallas SWAT team?

He took a deep breath, trying to figure out how to answer. He would have to be careful because right then, Hadley Delacroix looked pretty damn dangerous.

The moment Cooper walked into the steak house where he and his pack mates usually went for lunch, the aroma of perfectly grilled beef made his mouth water. He picked up Becker's and Jayna's scents, along with some of the other guys' wafting from the room in the back, and headed that way.

He weaved through the tables, thankful his first session with Delacroix was over. It had lasted only an hour, but he was flat worn out. That question about how he'd known the bank was about to be robbed had been the first among many. She'd let him do most of the talking, but every once in a while she'd hit him with a probing question that proved she wasn't merely focused on what he was saying. She was dissecting it. He liked to think that he'd done a good job deflecting her suspicions, but it was hard to tell. She gave absolutely nothing away, no matter what he said. He doubted even an experienced werewolf like Gage would be able to get a read on what she was thinking.

As he walked into the back room the SWAT team usually commandeered for lunch, Cooper saw that more than half weren't there. No doubt out on incidents. It was good to see the ones who were there. Knowing he couldn't work with his teammates for days, maybe even weeks, was already making him feel ostracized and out of sorts. And the grilling he'd gotten this morning at the hands of Delacroix hadn't helped.

But he forgot about all that the moment he soaked up the vibe coming off the other werewolves. This was his pack, and when he was with them, everything was right with the world.

In addition to Becker and Jayna, Xander and Khaki were there too, along with Alex, Remy, Brooks, and Carter.

Jayna was an alpha female like Khaki, but they couldn't be more different. Cooper supposed that made sense since Jayna had been a beta werewolf until a few months ago. He still didn't understand how a werewolf could spontaneously change stripes from beta to alpha, but it happened with her. While Khaki was as aggressive and assertive about stuff as any male werewolf in the Pack, Jayna was only aggressive and assertive about two things—Becker and the beta members of her own pack. Her world revolved around them.

He pulled out the empty chair between Alex and Brooks, sitting directly across from Becker. A motherly waitress appeared with a glass of his usual iced tea, setting it down in front of him and handing him a menu.

"Where's everyone else?" he asked his teammates as he scanned the menu.

He didn't know why he bothered looking at it since he already knew everything on it by heart. But he was a visual guy. He never knew what he wanted until he saw the pictures on the menu. In this case, his stomach growled when it saw the image of the half-pound burger the steak house was well known for.

"Out helping the FBI round up persons of interest related to the bombing yesterday," Alex said. A former marine, the team's dark-haired sniper was also their resident medic. "The guys on their list aren't the ones you generally send one or two unaccompanied uniformed officers after."

Cooper nodded. While the FBI might not like working with SWAT, they didn't mind letting them do most of the heavy lifting when it came to bringing in the initial wave of suspects for questioning. That way the feds got the best of both worlds. They could talk to the scary people who tended to be associated with bombings while the DPD got the bad rap for rousing people simply because they had bad reputations.

He was about to ask if they'd heard whether the FBI had any good leads on the bomber's identity yet, but Becker cut him off.

"Wait until you hear about what happened to Zak and Megan down in Galveston."

Cooper frowned at his best friend. While he loved Becker like a brother, sometimes he had an irritating way of leaving you hanging.

"What about Zak and Megan?"

He tried to keep the worry from creeping into his

voice, but wasn't sure if he succeeded. Zak Gibson, best friend and coworker of Gage's fiancée Mackenzie Stone, had been crushing on Megan Dorsey, the diminutive beta from Jayna's pack, for months now. While they made a cute couple, they had one big obstacle working against them—Zak didn't know a damn thing about the existence of werewolves. Cooper wasn't too sure how the guy would handle finding out werewolves really existed, and that his sweet little wisp of a girlfriend had fangs and claws.

"Don't worry. They're fine," Jayna assured him. She flipped her wavy, dark blond hair over her shoulder and leaned against the arm Becker draped over the back of her chair. "Things at the quaint little B&B they were staying in got a bit crazy, and they ended up getting held hostage by some criminals trapped on the island after a robbery."

Cooper felt his jaw drop. "Seriously?"

Becker nodded. "It all worked out for the best though. No one got hurt, and in the end, Zak found out Megan's a werewolf, and that we all are too."

Cooper did a double take. He looked around the table, surprised to see that no one seemed freaked out. "So, I take it he's dealing okay with it?"

Jayna smiled. "Better than okay. He's going to move into the Beta House with all the rest of us."

Huh. Cooper and the other SWAT alphas were really close—like family, but Jayna's beta pack took that to a whole new level. There were already six werewolves sleeping in the small loft they'd dubbed the Beta House located over by Baylor University's Dallas campus, including Becker. Cooper supposed bringing in a normal human wouldn't make it much more crowded—as long as they enjoyed each other's company.

But he kept those thoughts to himself. "I'm glad it's all working out for those two. If anyone deserves a happy ending, it's Megan."

Becker and Jayna lifted their iced teas in a toast to Megan and Zak's happily ever after. Cooper picked up his glass and clinked it with everyone else's.

"I just hope we can get Zak to give us details on what happened down there," Alex added as the waitress came in to take their orders. "Something tells me it's going to make for one hell of a story."

The SWAT team had been going there so long none of the waitresses even batted an eye at the crazy amount of food they ordered—Khaki and Jayna included.

"So, how did it go with the shrink?" Connor asked curiously. "Did this doctor guy make you sit on a couch and tell him about your mom?"

Connor was Cooper's age—twenty-eight—and they'd both been werewolves for four years. But Connor had only been with the SWAT team for two, so sometimes he seemed younger than his age. And when he was asking corny-ass questions like this one, he seemed even younger.

"This *doctor guy* is actually a woman, and no, she didn't ask me about my mom," Cooper said. "She spent most of the session asking questions related to all the skills I seem to have that most cops don't."

That took the levity right out of the room.

"You don't think she realizes what you are, do you?" Brooks asked.

Cooper shook his head. Someone discovering their

secret was the one thing all of them worried about. The humans who had recently come into their lives—first Mac and now Zak—might accept them, but it wasn't a given that everyone would. There were people in the world who would hate them simply because they were different. None of them ever forgot that.

"No, I don't," Cooper answered. "She's about as aggressive and blunt as any person I've ever met. If she had even an inkling of a suspicion, I think she'd confront me to see how I'd react."

"She sounds absolutely charming," Remy said in his slow Cajun drawl as he added more sweetener to his tea. "How are you going to handle her?"

"Carefully," Cooper said. "She's sharp and picks up on stuff even Coletti and the other detectives in IA missed. I have to filter every single word I say, which is hard. When I hesitate too long before answering her questions, she picks up on that too. Right now, she seems more interested in what she calls my hypervigilant tendencies and overly aggressive reactions. She's read my military record and knows I went through some stuff over in Iraq, so she probably assumes I'm dealing with PTSD. If that's where she wants to take the sessions, I'll let her."

Xander frowned. "Be careful. The last thing you want is some psychologist diagnosing you with severe PTSD. That could get you booted off the force in a hurry. Gage wants you to treat these sessions seriously, not get yourself medically discharged."

No kidding. "My gut tells me she's not interested in getting me booted from the force. It really seems like she wants to help me so I can get back on the job faster."

"All the more reason to be careful around her," Xander warned. "I hate to sound cynical, but she doesn't seem like your typical bureaucratic shrink pulling down a fat consultation fee. She might be setting you up."

His squad leader was right. He needed to keep his guard up. "I know. I'll be careful."

They fell silent as the food arrived, and the next few minutes were taken up with trying to make space on the table for all the dishes, second round of iced teas, and various condiments.

"What kind of pie do you have today?" Cooper asked as the waitress set down his cheeseburger.

"Apple. You want me to bring you a slice after you eat your burger, hon?"

"Nah, you can bring it now. I'll eat it with the burger." Cooper grinned. "Fruit is an essential part of a healthy diet, you know."

The waitress shook her head and scribbled on her order pad as Alex and Brooks asked her to add apple pies to their orders too.

"Okay, enough about this psychology crap," Becker said as the waitress left. "I'd much rather hear about Everly Danu. Where are you taking her to dinner tonight?"

Cooper chuckled at the eager faces around the table. "I asked Gage to get me into that fancy French restaurant he goes to all the time. She said she likes French food, so I'm hoping she'll like that place."

"Fancy." Connor dumped more steak sauce on his plate. "You think she's *The One*?"

Cooper snorted. "Let's tap the brakes a bit on the whole soul mate thing. We just met last night."

"But you like her, right?" Jayna asked.

"Of course I like her," he said around a big bite of his cheeseburger.

Cooper remembered a time not so long ago when most of the Pack's conversations revolved around weapons, criminals, and the various werewolves on the team getting into fights with one another. But ever since Gage had met Mac, they spent most of their time talking about women and who might find their soul mate next. Not that Cooper had a problem with it, but sometimes it seemed like the guys were starting to see stuff that wasn't really there just because they all wanted it so desperately.

"I'd be stupid not to like her," he added after he swallowed the bite he was working on. "She's attractive as hell and fun to talk to, but it wasn't like there were bells and fireworks going off when we met. Let's see where this goes before everyone decides I've met my one-in-a-billion already. It wouldn't be the first time one of us has met someone we like, only to find out it wasn't the person we thought."

They all nodded in understanding, but looked dejected. Cooper swore silently. He felt like a jerk for trashing their dreams, but sometimes it seemed like he was the only one thinking straight. It wasn't like they hadn't been involved with women before Gage, Xander, and Becker found their mates. And every one of those relationships had failed miserably—something they all forgot when the legend of *The One* started going around.

Thing was, while there hadn't been bells and fireworks, Cooper had felt something with Everly. The way he had such a difficult time talking to her when she'd first spoken to him, and the extremely protective feeling that had come over him during the bank holdup, weren't normal reactions for him. But he didn't want to tell the guys that, if for no other reason than he didn't want to jinx anything.

Cooper wondered if he'd been a bit too harsh when Alex leaned over and thumped him on the shoulder.

"Well, if it doesn't work out between you and Everly, would you mind if I ask her out?" He grinned. "She's really hot."

Cooper laughed with the others, but he couldn't deny the surge of jealousy that stirred inside. He frowned. What the hell? He'd gotten a handle on his werewolf anger management issues years ago. Maybe Everly was getting to him more than he'd been willing to admit to himself. Scary.

"What are you going to do with all this free time you suddenly have on your hands?" Brooks asked. "When you're not talking to your shrink or stalking Everly?"

He thought about that for a moment. He wasn't the kind of guy who could go see a movie or sit around his apartment reading a book—even though he did have a few graphic novels he couldn't wait to start. He supposed he could work out in the gym at the SWAT compound, but then he'd have to watch his pack mates go out on incidents without him. That would suck. No, he would need to find something else to keep him occupied.

"I thought I'd head over to the FBI forensic lab and see if they could use my help rebuilding that IED," he finally said. "The agent in charge is a friend. He'll let me nose around a bit and keep me off the entry logs."

"I won't tell you not to do it because you'd probably

only do it anyway," Xander said. "Just be careful. If Coletti or any of the DPD brass find out you're moonlighting with the FBI while you're under a fitness review, they'll have a cow."

"And if the FBI brass finds out, they'll have a whole herd of cows," Alex added. "Don't give them any more reason to hate us."

—∿∿—

Cooper parked in the main lot, then walked around to the back of the forensic lab located behind the main FBI offices at One Justice Way. Special Agent Dennis Doyle, his friend and contact at the bureau, met him at the door. Shorter and stockier than Cooper, he looked like your typical fed, right down to the conservative suit, plain tie, and perfectly polished shoes. Even though they both worked in Dallas, they hadn't met until a few years ago during a one-week explosive training seminar in Houston. Cooper had made some dry comment about the clueless instructor while they were both grabbing coffee on a break. Dennis laughed so hard he'd just about snorted the hot beverage out his nose. They'd been on each other's speed dial since then.

"Good to see you, man," Dennis said as they shook hands. "I couldn't believe it when I heard you'd ended up in the middle of a bank robbery last night. What are the chances, huh? They said you handled yourself well. The DPD giving you a commendation?"

"I wish." He stepped inside then waited for Dennis to close the door behind him. "If I'd simply shot all five suspects instead of throwing one through a window and giving the other two concussions, I would have been fine. Now IA seems to think I have some deep-seated anger management issues that can only be resolved with the help of a department psychologist. I'm on the bench until she gives me the okay."

Dennis blew out a breath. "Damn, that sucks. Now I see why you wanted to come in the back way."

"Yeah, this visit has to be completely off the books, for your sake as much as mine. You okay with me looking over the evidence, considering we'd both get jammed up pretty good if anyone knew I was here?"

Dennis led the way down the long corridor. "Yeah. Just don't touch anything without gloves on."

He grabbed some blue latex gloves from a box mounted on the wall and handed a pair to Cooper, then led him into one of the lab's many workrooms. The debris picked up after the bombing was spread out on various tables, with those portions of the device already identified arranged on a light table in the center of the room. As Cooper pulled on his gloves, he looked around at the whiteboards mounted on the walls. Streets, buildings, and the outline of a parking lot had been drawn on them, along with photos of the crime scene.

Cooper sniffed the air as he walked over to the light table, trying to identify the particular explosive residue scent saturating the room. It was definitely some kind of plastic bonded mix, but he couldn't say more than that. Unfortunately, his nose wasn't nearly as good as some of the other werewolves on his team, thanks mostly to a call back in the summer when he'd been stuck underground with nasty chemical fumes. His sniffer hadn't worked worth a crap since then. If Khaki were here, she probably would have been able to ID the exact explosive compound in seconds.

"What kind of explosive are we looking at?" he asked his friend. "Have you ID'd it yet?"

Dennis shook his head. "We don't know for sure. The techs are still working to give us that answer. But they already found enough chemical markers to make them think it's definitely high-quality stuff, maybe even U.S. military-grade C-4 plastic explosive."

Plastic explosives made for the DOD had chemical taggants added so they'd be easy to identify it they were used later in a bomb. If the FBI lab was picking up on those taggants already, this case just got really interesting.

"That can't be good," Cooper remarked.

Dennis sighed. "No, it's not. As you can imagine, the possibility of military explosives being involved has the people upstairs in a fit. This one's gonna have some seriously high visibility."

"Good to know, seeing as a DPD cop died," Cooper said dryly.

Dennis didn't bat an eye. "You know that's not what I meant. Everybody's freaking out these days worrying some fanatic wearing a suicide vest is going to walk into a shopping mall. They hear C-4 plastic explosive, and that's the only thing they hear."

Cooper spent two hours going through the hundreds of fragments with Dennis, helping identify pieces and putting them back together to make sense of them. It was like building a puzzle while looking at the backside. You had to know what you were looking at to do it right. Luckily, Cooper had lots of practice. It didn't take long for him to pick up the trademark signatures of a bomb maker who really knew his business.

"Look how minimal and consistent his insulation stripping is on these pieces of wire." Cooper pointed as he held them under a magnifying glass. "He wanted to make sure he didn't have any exposed wires that might inadvertently touch and short out the system. Take a look at the triple crimp marks on the end of this blasting cap too." He moved the magnifying glass to that portion of the wire. "Even though the cap looks like it was made recently, the bomber still took his time to seal it well so no moisture or humidity would get into it and keep it from going off properly. This isn't some good ol' boy just trying to blow something up. This guy is a pro."

Cooper moved along the table, studying one of the circuit boards with its soldered wires. *Shit.* The more he dug, the more sophisticated the bomb appeared.

"This is some of the most complicated circuitry I've seen in an IED outside of Iraq and Afghanistan." Cooper picked up one of the circuit boards on the light table to study it closely. "This part looks like a remote arming circuit, from a garage door opener or a key fob probably, while the firing circuit is motion-activated. That's some serious technology."

"Wait a minute." Dennis frowned. "You said remote arming. Are you saying the bomber was someplace close to the garage when he armed the device? And if he was, how close?"

"Five hundred to a thousand yards maximum."

"We have a ton of security and traffic cam footage from around the industrial complex," Dennis said with a grin. "If we're lucky, our bomber might just be on there."

Cooper set down the circuit board. "If I'm right about this part of the firing circuit being motion-activated, it's possible the bomber waited until he saw the target enter the garage before he armed the device."

"You mean Swanson really was the target?" Dennis asked.

Cooper shook his head. "Not necessarily. It's a large garage. The bomber could have armed the device without realizing an off-duty cop was doing a security sweep. Swanson was still an unintended target, but if you can figure out who else went into the garage around the time of the detonation, you might be able to figure out who it really was."

Dennis clapped him on the shoulder. "I think I may owe you another dinner after this one, buddy."

Cooper grinned and pulled off his gloves. "You say that now. But the last time I came over, you complained I was going to eat you out of house and home."

Dennis laughed. "This time, I'll remember to stock up."

Chapter 4

EVERLY WAS STILL GETTING DRESSED WHEN LANDRY knocked on the door. It wasn't her fault. He was five minutes early. She ran to the door in her bare feet, still trying to get the zipper up on the back of her little black dress.

"Wait!" Mia whispered as she ran after her. "I'll get the zipper while you put on your shoes. You don't want a guy thinking you're high maintenance on the first date. Spring that on him after the third one."

Everly hopped in place on one foot, dragging on her high heels while Mia did up her zipper. "I thought the third date rule had something to do with sleeping with a guy?"

Landry rang the doorbell this time, but she and Mia ignored it. There was some rule about making a guy wait at the door a certain amount of time too, Everly was sure, but she couldn't remember what it was.

"Wait to sleep with a guy until the third date?" Mia gave her an incredulous look. "When were you raised, the twentieth century?"

Everly laughed as she adjusted her dress and struck a pose for her friend. "How do I look?"

"Dazzling," Mia said. "He'd better be worthy, girl, or I'm going to send him packing."

Everly smiled at Mia over her shoulder as she reached for the door. "I don't think you have to worry about that."

She didn't know about Mia, but when she opened the door and saw Landry, she sure as heck wasn't going to send him packing. She'd expected him to dress up a little since they were going to a French restaurant, but Everly had been out with guys who thought dressed up meant putting on jeans and a clean T-shirt. It was clear Landry and she had the same definition of fancy. He looked sharp and edible in a wool-blend jacket perfectly tailored to show off his broad shoulders and muscular chest, a light blue dress shirt, and a snazzy tie. If she didn't know better, she'd think she was looking at a *GQ* cover model.

The smile Landry gave her made her wonder if he knew what she she'd been thinking—or that he'd heard her and Mia talking through the door. While both were equally embarrassing, they were also equally unlikely.

His warm brown eyes slid down her body, lingering on her bare legs before moving back up again. He must have liked what he saw, because he got the same smolder in his eyes that he had last night. After a look like that, maybe they should skip dinner and head straight for dessert.

Behind Everly, Mia cleared her throat, reminding her that yes, her roommate was still standing there waiting to meet Landry. Everly stepped back with a smile.

"Come on in. There's someone I want you to meet," she said. "Landry, this is my roommate and best friend in the world, Mia Barlowe. Mia, meet Landry Cooper."

Mia stepped forward and extended her hand, tilting her head back to look up at him. "Everly's told me so much about you, but she didn't mention how tall you are. Wow!"

He chuckled and gave her a self-deprecating shrug as he shook her hand. "It's the shoes. They add a couple inches. And call me Cooper. All my friends do."

Everly remembered the other SWAT officers calling him by his last name the other night and had meant to ask him why. "Why *does* everyone call you by your last name?"

Landry flashed her that charming smile of his, dimples and all. Everly was pretty sure she heard Mia sigh. "I spent some time in the army, and since everyone in the military wears their last name sewed on their uniform, you get used to people calling you that. There were a couple of times that I went so long without hearing anyone use my first name, I almost forgot what it was."

Mia must have thought that was funny—or she was getting punchy from standing too close to Landry—because she let out a girlish giggle.

Everly suddenly had a vision of rolling around in bed with Landry, passionately moaning his last name. Nope, that wasn't going to work.

"Mia can call you Cooper if she wants, but I'm not," she said. "There's no way I'm calling the guy I'm dating by his last name. That would be totally freaky."

Landry's mouth twitched. "If it makes you comfortable, you can call me anything you want. Except for Pookie Bear or Snookums."

Everly giggled along with Mia this time. "How about we just stick with Landry?"

"Works for me." He flashed his dimples again and glanced at his watch. "You ready to go? I made the reservation for 7:30."

"I'm ready. Let me grab my purse, and we can be on our way."

Everly headed to her bedroom, still smiling at the thought of anyone calling the big SWAT officer Pookie Bear. That name was going to be stuck in her head all night now.

Mia followed her into the bedroom and leaned against the doorjamb. "Oh God, he's hot as hell. Do you think he has any friends?"

She was about to mention the team of attractive SWAT cops she'd met last night, but then a realization struck her. "Wait a minute, I thought you were seeing that guy. What's his name—Felix?"

Mia waved her hand. "Yeah, but that doesn't mean I can't see someone else at the same time. Especially if that someone else looks anything like Cooper."

Everly shook her head. "Cooper. You're seriously going to call him by his last name? And does Felix know you have an open relationship?"

Mia smiled. "Cooper fits him. I see why all his friends call him that. And I definitely want to be his friend. As far as Felix seeing other women, he sure as hell better not be. Our relationship is a dictatorship, not a democracy."

Everly grabbed her evening purse from the bed, checking it again for the essentials—lipstick, mascara, iPhone, and emergency cab fare. She seriously doubted she'd need that last thing, but her dad had drilled contingency planning into her like a FEMA exercise.

"Girl, you're crazy," she said as she snapped her purse closed. "But I'll see what I can find out."

Mia hugged her. "You're the best! And don't worry.

I won't be coming out to check on you when you get in tonight, so feel free to let your freak flag fly as soon as you get in the door."

She laughed. "You're not just crazy. You're certifiable."

Everly walked out of her bedroom to find Landry in the long hallway leading to her art studio, studying the pictures hanging on the wall.

He gestured to the nude figure studies done in graphite pencil. "These are really good. Do you know the artist?"

"I hope so. It's me." She smiled. "And I appreciate the compliment."

His eyes widened. "You did these? They're amazing! You didn't tell me you're an artist."

"Really?" She gave him a teasing look. "I could have sworn I mentioned it somewhere in between all the shooting and you throwing that guy through the window."

"You probably did, and I completely forgot," Landry said without missing a beat. "You can tell me all over again at dinner."

Once outside, Landry led her to an olive-drab Jeep Wrangler and opened the passenger door. Wow. How long had it been since a guy had opened a door for her?

Everly was about to get in when she saw three perfectly round holes in the side of the Jeep to the front of the passenger door. She stepped closer then looked at him. "Are those bullet holes?"

He lifted a brow. "You sure you want to know the answer to that question considering you already know I'm a cop?"

She thought about that as she climbed into the Jeep. As terrifying as it was to consider, maybe what happened at the bank yesterday hadn't been that unusual for him. Not only was he a cop, he was in SWAT. She didn't know much about them, but she got the feeling from all the tactical gear they wore and weapons they carried, he was probably involved in shootings often enough that he no longer reacted the way a civilian would.

"I guess I forgot what you do for a living," she said when he got in beside her. "I suppose getting shot at sort of comes with the job."

He didn't say anything as he drove out of the parking lot and turned onto the main road headed toward the 635 loop.

Everly sat there in silence for a moment, debating how much she wanted to know about his job. "Were you in the Jeep at the time it was shot up?"

Landry gave her an appraising look before turning his attention back to the road. "No. But I was standing outside it on the driver's side. If it helps any, it's the first and only time my vehicle has ever been shot at, and the people who did it are some of my best friends now."

She stared at him, waiting for the punch line. There wasn't one. "Seriously? You're friends with people you put in jail?"

He flashed her those dimples, almost making her forget what they were talking about. "They're not in jail. They were just some people who got on the wrong side of a situation and made a few dumb decisions. Our team took them in and helped them out. Hell, Becker—the wiseass you met last night—is in love with one of them."

Everly was pretty sure her mouth was hanging open. "You're making this up, right?"

He held up two fingers. "Scout's honor—every word

is true. Trust me, the crap our team gets involved in could be in a book. It'd be a bestseller for sure."

She still wasn't sure if he was pulling her leg or not until he told her about Becker and his girlfriend Jayna, the four people they lived with, and how the bullet holes ended up in his Jeep. Everly got the feeling Landry was censoring the details to protect the people he and his SWAT team had helped. But still, it was an amazing story.

Everly was so focused on the conversation she didn't even think about where Landry was taking her until he pulled up in front of a very familiar restaurant.

She turned to him excitedly. "You got us a table at Chambre Française with only a day's notice? Mia and I have tried to get in here four times and couldn't. They're full year-round."

Landry smiled, but didn't say anything as the valet came over to take the keys. When a second valet hurried over to open her door, Everly stepped out, then stood gazing at the traditional French architecture reminiscent of Paris. She hadn't been kidding. She'd been trying to get into this restaurant since she was old enough to have enough money to afford the place. She felt like Cinderella going to the ball. She was so excited she could have kissed Landry right there. Not that she needed much of an excuse to kiss him, but he couldn't have picked a more perfect place if he'd read her mind.

"I wish I could take all the credit, but my boss did a favor for the chef a while back and the guy gave him a lifetime invitation to eat here any time he wanted, no reservations required," Cooper said. "It wasn't hard for him to help me get seating for two, though it might be in the kitchen for all I know."

"I'll take it," she told him as he took her hand, and they strolled toward the crowd waiting to get inside. "Heck, I'll wash dishes if they want me to. I don't care as long as I can eat here."

When they checked in at the front desk, Everly expected they'd have to wait forever, but two minutes later, the hostess led them to a small table in a secluded alcove near the back of the restaurant.

As soon as they sat down, a short, heavyset man wearing an apron came to their table, a welcoming smile on his face.

"You must be Landry and Everly. Gage said you'd be easy to recognize, and I see that he wasn't wrong," he said in a lightly accented voice. "I am Emile. I am so happy you chose my little restaurant for your date."

Emile shook hands with Landry then gallantly kissed the back of hers. She looked around the dining room, taking in the brocade wallpaper, gold accents, and elegant crystal chandeliers.

"I'm not so sure I would describe this place as little, but I'm truly looking forward to eating here," Everly said. "The aromas coming from the kitchen are heavenly."

The man beamed, his cheeks blushing a little. "You are too kind, mademoiselle. I promise you a dinner neither of you will ever forget. You have my word on it."

Taking their intricately folded napkins from the table, Emile smoothly opened them and draped the fine linens across their laps, then began to reposition their silverware.

"Thank you for finding us a table," Landry said. "I know it must have been difficult on such short notice."

Emile shook his head. "There is always room for my

friends, and anyone who is a friend of Gage's is a friend of mine. So, sit back and enjoy yourself. This table is yours as long as you would like to stay."

Everly expected Emile to tell them that a server would be coming by to take their order, but instead he told them he would construct a menu perfectly suited for them and cook it himself.

"I will have your drinks brought out in a moment," he added. "Bon appetit."

Then he walked away, leaving them looking at each other.

"Did he just say he was going to cook our meal himself?" she whispered.

Landry nodded. "Yeah, I guess he did. But how is he going to know what we like?"

She laughed. "Who cares? If Emile is cooking your dinner, it's going to be good."

A waiter brought a bottle of white wine, opened it, and poured two glasses without saying a word. Everly took a small sip. While she wasn't a connoisseur, she did drink wine on occasion, but she'd never had anything this good. She hoped Landry knew what he was in for when it came to the bill. But he didn't seem worried at the moment.

Landry held up his glass, the flicker of the candle on the table giving his eyes a sexy glow. "To the best date ever."

She returned his smile, gently clinking her glass against his. This was already well on the way to being the best date she'd ever had, and they were just getting started.

As they sat there, their hands only a few inches apart while they sipped their wine, their knees practically touched under the table. Everly was struck by how quiet and private their little alcove table felt, like there was no one in the restaurant but the two of them. A romantic dinner with the stunningly attractive cop who had saved her life? It was something out of a fairy tale.

"Why a French restaurant?" Landry asked softly. "You always hear people say they like Mexican, Chinese, Italian, Fusion, or Thai. But I don't think anyone has ever told me that French food is their favorite."

She shrugged as she drank more of the wine and let it roll around on her tongue. "It's because I was born in France. So opting for French is the equivalent of you eating at a barbecue place in Texas. I don't even think of it as ethnic food."

"Wow," he said, clearly surprised. "I thought I had a pretty good ear for accents, but I would never have pegged you for anything other than a Texas girl. You don't sound French at all."

"Dad moved my four brothers and me to Texas when I was very young. I think I was only seven or eight at the time, so my accent was completely gone by the time I got to middle school."

Landry looked crestfallen. "Too bad. Having a beautiful woman whisper sweet nothings in my ear with a French accent would have been intriguing."

Okay, what was a woman supposed to do after a line like that? Everly couldn't resist leaning closer and giving him what she hoped was a sexy, come-hither look.

"I think I may be able to help you with those sweet little nothings," she said in her best French accent.

At least she hoped it sounded French. She hadn't spoken more than a few dozen words in the language in years, and all of that had been around her family. For all she knew, her accent may have come off more Pink Panther than sex kitten.

But Landry must have liked it because his eyes got this seriously intense smolder. And when he tilted his head just so, the lights from the chandelier reflected back in the hottest way possible. Like those brown sugar eyes of his were lit gold from within. Damn, talk about sexy!

They were so close that Everly could feel the heat pouring off his body. Or maybe she was the one getting warmer. It was difficult to tell.

Pulse quickening, she wet her lips with her tongue. Landry's eyes followed the movement, a slightly predatory smile crossing his face. He leaned a little closer, ratcheting up the heat in the tiny alcove another few degrees. Everly parted her lips in anticipation of the kiss she knew was coming.

But before Landry closed those last few millimeters left between them, Emile appeared with their appetizers. Landry smiled and sat back. As Emile placed the beautifully arranged plates on the table, Everly reluctantly did the same.

"We will begin with a trio of pork rillettes with pickled dried apricots, Alsatian tarte flambé, and salmon trout tartare with caviar."

While they all sounded delicious, Everly was far more focused on the kiss that had almost happened than on anything the chef was saying. Considering how long she'd waited to eat at Chambre Française that should have surprised her. But she found it hard to turn her attention to the food. Landry was much more appealing.

Even though she remembered him saying something in the car about being hungry, he didn't go for the food right away either. Instead, he sat there gazing at her as if she was the most fascinating thing he'd ever seen.

"You were the only girl in a family with four brothers, huh?" he finally said. "That must have been interesting growing up."

She nodded, casually picking up one of the tartes and hoping her hands didn't shake. What had Emile said was on this one? Mia would almost certainly ask how the food had been, and Everly wouldn't even be able to tell her what they'd eaten.

"It was fun when I was younger," she said as she set the tarte on her plate. "They watched out for me and took me places and always treated me like a princess. Not to mention bought me anything I wanted, took me to whatever movies I wanted to see, and played all kinds of games with me."

Landry chuckled. "I can definitely see you wrapping men around your little finger."

Everly couldn't help but wonder if perhaps that's what he thought she was doing to him—and if it was working.

"Their attention became less endearing as I got older and started having ideas about what kind of clothes I should wear and how much time I should spend hanging out with my girlfriends. And boys, of course." She picked up her fork and cut off a small piece of the cheesy tarte. "Sometimes they could be a bit overprotective."

He raised an eyebrow. "Would they approve of the boy you're currently spending your time with?"

Everly laughed, enjoying their playful conversation. Even if she wasn't able to pay proper attention to a special meal she wasn't likely to have again anytime soon. "Yes, they're still overprotective. But I'm my own person and make my own decisions about what I do and whom I spend my time with."

"That probably doesn't make them very happy." He took a bite of the pork rillettes, his perfect white teeth practically mesmerizing. There was something so sensual about the way his mouth moved when he ate that made her think she could watch him do it all day. "Should I be concerned they may not like me?"

"No, it doesn't, but they've come to respect my independence," she said. "And you don't have to be worried about them not liking you. Since you saved my life, I think they'll give you the benefit of the doubt."

He winced. "I hadn't thought about them hearing about the bank robbery. That must have freaked them out."

There was no way in hell she was going to mention her dad had sent two of her brothers to the bank with instructions to go in and get her if needed. "They were worried, but what you did made it onto the Internet right after it happened. Once they realized I was okay, they were mostly interested in meeting you."

Everly bit her tongue. Maybe she shouldn't have told Landry that. It was their first date, and she was already talking about him meeting her family. She hoped that didn't send him running for the hills.

But he seemed to take it in stride. "I'd like to meet them too. Then I can hear all about you growing up as a rebellious teen."

She was about to tell him she hadn't been rebellious, but then changed her mind. If you asked her dad, rebellious was exactly what she'd been.

"Any discussions about whether I was rebellious or not will have to wait until at least the third or fourth time you meet them," she said with a smile. "I can't have you knowing all my secrets too soon."

His mouth quirked. "I'm willing to wait. Secrets keep things interesting."

A warm sensation settled in her stomach at the thought of spending enough time with any man as intriguing as Landry to learn all his secrets. And be able to share hers with him. Not that she had much in the way of secrets, but it was the first time she'd ever been comfortable enough with someone she was going out with to consider it—especially on a first date.

"The art you had hanging on your walls. Is that what you do for a living?" he asked as he finished the last of the rillettes.

She shook her head. "I wish. The figure studies and landscapes are my first love. I do that kind of stuff whenever I can, and even sell some of it now and then. But it doesn't really pay the bills. For that, I depend on my graphic art business. I design book covers, advertisements, postcards—promotional material, you know? When I'm not busy with that, I teach art down at the community center."

"I'd love to see more of your work."

That warm sensation she'd felt earlier burned a little hotter. She'd met a lot of guys who mentally checked out the moment she said the word *art*. Like they thought men weren't supposed to have a creative side.

Before she could say anything, Emile came over and delivered their next course—a small fish dish she completely missed the name of. Everly was about to taste it, when she realized that so far she and Landry had spent the entirety of their date talking about her. She didn't mind a man who was willing to make her the center of his attention, but she was interested in learning about him too.

"So enough about me for now," she said. "What about you? How long have you worked for SWAT?"

"Three years." Landry frowned, then smiled. "Wait. Actually, almost four. I was fortunate when I got hired with the department. A lot of the time, you have to do a year or two as a patrol officer before you can transfer into SWAT. But my boss was able to convince the brass to let me join SWAT straight from the academy. I think they agreed because I have a military background."

"Why SWAT?"

Landry was silent as he considered the question. "It wasn't the work that attracted me to SWAT as much as the environment. They have my back, and I have theirs. It's an amazing feeling knowing you can trust every member of the team with your very life. Being in SWAT is like a family."

Everly never had a job where she worked with a lot of coworkers. Artists tended to work alone or in smaller groups. But she could understand how nice it would be to know the person you were working with wasn't looking to screw you over to get a pay raise or a promotion. Even so, she had a hard time believing any group could be that loyal, and she wondered if Landry was glossing over the less-desirable people on his team. There had to be at least one or two me-first types there, right? But she wasn't about to point that out.

"Isn't it dangerous though?" she asked. "Isn't your family terrified you'll get hurt?"

He lifted a forkful of fish to his mouth. "I think my parents and brothers actually breathed a sigh of relief when I got out of the army and joined SWAT. Trust me, there's a reason I was getting hazardous duty pay while in the military. And I can honestly say it's rare when someone in SWAT ends up in the hospital. The last guy who did was my squad leader, and he walked out the door in less than twenty-four hours with hardly a scratch."

Everly found herself breathing that same sigh of relief he'd mentioned. She knew Landry was a cop and what he did was dangerous, but it made her feel better knowing the people he worked with didn't get hurt all the time.

As they finished their fish, Landry told her one hilarious story after another about the other members of his team. He paused in the middle of one about Becker when Emile showed up with their main course of stuffed pork tenderloin. Everly was sure it was as delicious as the other food he'd served them, but she was laughing so hard at the crazy things Landry was saying, she barely tasted it.

"You have a beautiful laugh," he said. "Which only makes sense since you're so beautiful."

Everly blushed at the compliment. "I bet you say that to all women on the first date."

"I've never said it on a first date before," he told her. "Actually, I've never said it to any woman before."

She would have thought that was some kind of line if she hadn't seen the blatant sincerity in his eyes. He really wasn't trying to be smooth. He seriously believed she was the most beautiful woman in the world.

Landry frowned. "I hope I didn't make you uncomfortable by saying that. If so, it wasn't my intent."

She considered that. By all rights, hearing such an
over the top compliment like that from a guy she barely
knew should have had her pulling her emergency cab
fare out of her purse and running for the exit, but it
didn't. Instead, it made her feel crazy good, like maybe
she truly was the most beautiful woman in the world.

"No, you didn't make me feel uncomfortable at all."
She smiled. "In fact, I enjoyed hearing you say it."

The smile and dimples came back—along with a
heated gaze. "I'm glad. Because it would be very difficult to sit here thinking something like that all night
without being able to tell you."

As she gazed into his soulful brown eyes, she felt
a warm flush spread across her body and settle slowly
between her legs. She wasn't sure how Landry's compliment had translated into something sexual, but somehow
it had, and like a light switch being flipped, she was suddenly turned on. Even though there was no way Landry
could know that, his gaze took on a molten look, which
only served to make her even more aroused.

From that moment on, the tone of their conversation
changed, and little flirty lines slipped into their discussions. She mentioned that she loved sleeping late on
Sunday mornings, and Landry immediately asked her
what kind of breakfast she liked having in bed. He said
something about loving to work out late at night, and she
couldn't resist giving him a sexy look, saying that it all
depended on what kind of exercise she was doing.

In between, Landry regaled her with funny stories
about his teammates, and she told him about all the ways

her older brothers tried to keep her from sneaking out of the house to go have fun when she was a teenager. But after a while, they didn't talk at all. Instead, they gazed into each other's eyes, the silence filled with an energy that made her skin tingle. She'd never felt anything quite like it before, but she had the craziest urge to get out of her chair and crawl into his lap so she could run her hands through his hair and kiss him, maybe even nibble that sexy part of his neck just below his ear. The image was so vivid she could almost feel Landry's hands yanking up her little black dress so he could get his hands on her bottom.

She stifled a moan and closed her eyes, giving her head a little shake in order to reassert control. What the heck was wrong with her? She'd never acted this way with a guy in her life.

The other courses of the meal came and went, but by now, Emile could have put a TV dinner in front of Everly, and she probably wouldn't have noticed. All she could focus on was the mesmerizing man in front of her. That, and doing everything she could to keep her butt in her seat instead of crawling into his lap. It was hard as hell though. She couldn't explain what was happening, but their date had somehow gone from a good time with an attractive man to an extremely erotic evening with a man she wanted to go to bed with. It was a little scary how turned on she was.

Right then, her thoughts weren't like any she'd ever had on a first date. Maybe not until date twenty or thirty. Because the things she wanted to do with Landry weren't something you sprang on a guy until you completely trusted him—like after ten years of marriage.

Thank God they were in a crowded restaurant, or she

had no idea what she would have done. That's when she finally broke eye contact with Landry and realized the entire restaurant was bathed in darkness and completely empty. She glanced at her watch and was shocked to see it was after midnight. When had that happened?

Landry chuckled. "I hope I haven't kept you out too late."

She shook her head. "No, not at all. I just didn't realize everyone had left. We aren't locked in, are we?"

His mouth twitched. "No. I heard Emile moving around in the kitchen."

Everly cringed. "I hate to think he stayed so late just for us."

"Me too. I'd stay here the whole night with you if we could, but I guess we should go."

"You could always come in for a drink once we get back to my place," she suggested. "I promise I won't turn into a pumpkin, and I could show you the rest of my figure studies and landscapes, if you like."

Everly was fully aware that he might take her offer of a drink as an invitation for something else entirely. To be truthful, she wasn't sure it wasn't. She wasn't the kind of woman who had a magic number of dates established when it came to stuff like this, but she'd never slept with a man on the first date. Then again, she'd never met anyone who had the effect on her that Landry did. If one thing led to another and they ended up in bed, she definitely wouldn't mind.

"A drink at your place sounds perfect. I'd love to see the rest of your art." He stood and offered his hand to her. "Let's go see if we can find Emile, then we can get out of here."

Emile was completely amazing about them leaving so late. "You cannot put a timer on romance." He smiled and even waved off Landry's credit card. "Nor can you charge it on a piece of plastic. Go and have a wonderful evening. Come back anytime you want. I'll always find a table for you."

The drive back to her apartment seemed to take forever because they hit every freaking light in town, and while Everly was practically trembling with anticipation, she played it cool as Landry led her into the building. Even so, she had to force herself not to rush as they climbed the stairs to her place on the second floor.

Everly glanced at him as she unlocked the door to her apartment. "Mia is a heavy sleeper, so we don't have to worry about waking her up."

That was a complete lie, of course. Mia was probably in her room right now refusing to go to sleep until she got a complete report on the evening's events.

Everly left off most of the lights, only flipping on the one that illuminated the hallway leading to her art studio slash office. She was going to head to the kitchen for those drinks she'd promised, but one look at his face stopped him. He didn't look like he was very thirsty right then, at least not for alcohol.

Eyes glinting in the soft glow of the overhead light, Landry placed his hands on her waist and pulled her close. Then he bent his head ever so slowly, as if he was waiting for her to stop him. Like that was going to happen.

The moment their lips touched, she reached up and weaved her fingers into his hair, moaning as his tongue slipped into her mouth. He tasted like the chocolate mousse they'd had for dessert, only sweeter.

One of his hands slipped from her waist and snuck around to the small of her back, fitting her more tightly to him. Everly could tell from the way his hardness pressed against her that he was just as aroused as she was.

The kiss went on and on, until she was dizzy and out of breath, but she didn't want him to stop. She wanted Landry to keep kissing her until she was senseless, then she wanted him to carry her off to bed and make love to her all night long. And if the hard-on she felt against her stomach was any indication, she was in for one hell of a night.

When he finally broke the kiss, she was ready to grab his hand and lead him to her room, but he shook his head as if he'd read her mind and knew exactly what she was thinking.

"I had an amazing time tonight," he whispered. "But I think I should be going."

It took her a couple seconds to process what he'd just said, then a few more to understand what he meant. Had she read the situation completely wrong? No way. She'd felt how aroused he was.

"Why?" she asked in confusion.

He smiled, gently curling the ends of her long hair around his finger. "Because I think we both know there's something special happening here. And when something special happens, I think it's a good idea to take your time. We don't have to rush anything."

That made sense, of course. But the urge to drag him into her bedroom was so strong it was like she was fighting off a living thing.

She determinedly got a grip on her sex drive. "I don't mind if we take our time."

But when he tipped her chin up and kissed her again, her resolve almost failed. If he hadn't been the one to pull back first, she wasn't sure if she could have.

"I'll call you tomorrow," he said softly.

Incapable of speech at the moment, Everly could only nod.

At the door, Landry turned to give her a grin. "By the way. Best. Date. Ever."

Chapter 5

COOPER WAS IN A REALLY GOOD MOOD AS HE HEADED for another session with Delacroix, and not even the sight of Detective Coletti coming out of the doctor's professional building could change that.

"I didn't know you were spending time on Dr. Delacroix's couch." Cooper grinned. He just couldn't resist prodding the hard ass detective. "Maybe we can arrange group therapy sessions and save the department a few bucks?"

Coletti's faced darkened, but he didn't respond as he brushed past Cooper and stomped off toward the parking.

"See you later, Vince," Cooper called. "I'll ask the doc about those joint sessions, see if there's a discount or something."

Coletti scowled as he climbed into his department-issued, unmarked vehicle. The guy looked like he was about to crack his teeth he was grinding them so hard. Cooper wouldn't have been surprised if the man flipped him the bird.

Resisting the urge to return the favor, Cooper smiled and waved. The detective squealed out of the parking lot so fast there were skid marks on the pavement. Cooper chuckled. It might be juvenile, but pissing off Coletti was fun as hell.

Okay, while sticking it to Coletti had been fun, that wasn't the only reason he was in such a good mood this morning. That had everything to do with Everly.

As she'd promised, last night had been the best date of his life. Everly was simply the most beautiful, interesting, mesmerizing woman he'd ever spent time with. It was no exaggeration to say he could have sat in that restaurant with her all night. Their conversation had flowed so effortlessly, whether they were talking about her family or the other guys on his team. He couldn't help but notice that while she'd talked a lot about her dad and brothers, she never mentioned her mom. He assumed she was out of the picture now, and Everly would bring her up when she was ready. Beyond that, Cooper couldn't remember a single time when they'd hit one of the awkward moments that typically comes up on a first date. It was like they'd been together for years.

Then there was the sexual chemistry thing going on between them. He'd been turned on almost the entire night—so had Everly. It had been damn difficult to control himself, especially when the scent of her arousal hit him like a runaway Mack truck. It had just about made him shift right there in Chambre Française. Control issues like that hadn't hit him in years, not since he'd first started going through the change after leaving Iraq. But there was something about Everly that drove him crazy.

It was even worse when they went back to her apartment. Watching her ass wiggle under that little black dress and her bare thighs flash in front of him while she climbed the stairs had been heavenly torture. He hadn't planned on kissing her the moment they walked inside, but the feel of her mouth on his, not to mention the sexy pressure of her amazing body against his hard-on had almost been the end of him. He'd come seriously close to ripping off her dress right there in the middle of the living room. And something told him Everly would have been more than willing to let him.

But he'd gotten control of himself, refusing to let a moment of temporary insanity force him into rushing this thing with Everly. It was too good to risk blowing it. So, he'd kissed her good night, then forced himself to walk out the door. His werewolf side—the part of him that only lived in the moment and never worried about consequences—had howled at him the whole way.

It was impossible not to see that there was something magical between him and Everly, no matter how much he told himself not to go there yet. Maybe he should take a page from his inner werewolf and stop overthinking things so much.

When he walked into Delacroix's outer office, he noticed that the office assistant who'd been there the day before wasn't at her desk. He heard sounds coming from the doctor's office, so he headed that way.

Delacroix was at her desk looking at something on her laptop. She was so intent on whatever it was that she didn't hear him come in. Cooper started to clear his throat, but caught himself when he realized Delacroix was watching the video of the bank robbery. It was the first time he'd seen the video, and even though Becker had blurred the images, it was hard to miss the fact that Cooper had picked up a two-hundred-pound man and thrown him at least ten feet. No wonder Coletti wanted a shrink to evaluate him. The IA detective must have thought he was on some kind of rage trip.

Delacroix's eyes locked on the screen as she watched that part of the video over and over again. It was kind of scary, like she knew exactly what she was looking at. Could she possibly have a clue about what she was really seeing?

Cooper cleared his throat as he moved over to the chair, trying to make it look as if he'd just walked in. Delacroix didn't jump like he expected. She merely looked at him, then slowly reached out to turn off her video player.

"Officer Cooper, I didn't hear you come in."

She regarded him calmly, even though she had to know he'd seen what she was watching. "Your assistant wasn't outside," he said. "I hope you don't mind that I just walked in?"

She glanced at her watch. "Not at all. You're right on time. Have a seat."

"I ran into Detective Coletti from Internal Affairs on the way in," Cooper said as he sat down. "Can I assume he wasn't here for personal reasons?"

She eyed him with that same neutral expression, and for a moment, he thought she wasn't going to answer his question. Maybe even tell him that her conversation with Coletti was none of his business.

"Detective Coletti was interested in knowing if I'd reached a conclusion concerning your fitness for duty. And before you bother to ask, I told him I hadn't. That we'd only met one time."

Cooper tried to get a read on whether the doctor was lying by listening for an increase in heart rate, a change in breathing pattern, or tenseness in the body. But it was no use. He'd been around laptops that exhibited more outward signs of emotions than Delacroix.

"I'm guessing he was hoping for a little more than that out of you," Cooper said. "He seemed pretty pissed when he shoved past me."

"Really? I hadn't noticed."

Cooper sincerely doubted that. Something told him Delacroix missed very little.

He sat back and rested his ankle on his knee. "Okay Doc, what's the topic of conversation today? You going to grill me more on how my cop instincts told me the bank was about to get robbed?"

She opened a brown folder on her desk and scanned her notes. "Why don't we talk about the real reason Detective Coletti stopped by to see me?"

The question definitely caught Cooper off guard, and it took him a moment to get his head back in the game. "Okay, I'll bite. Why did Coletti stop by?"

"Because, after watching that video a few times, Detective Coletti seems concerned about your apparent willingness to resort to physical violence when dealing with suspects versus using your department-issued weapon. He specifically asked me to evaluate that aspect of your behavior."

Cooper tried not to laugh, but he couldn't help it. "Coletti is upset that I roughed up a couple suspects? Would he feel better if I'd just shot them all?"

Her lips curved into what could only be called a smirk. "Possibly. But I'm not concerned about Coletti's opinions on your use of force. I'm far more interested in what was going through your head during those moments. I was looking at the video hoping I could pick up some kind of body language cues, but the tape is too fuzzy. Why don't you tell me what you were thinking just before you threw that man through the window? Were you angry?"

Cooper waited for his normal defense mechanism

to kick in, the one that invariably led to him saying something suitably snarky and witty. But his internal smart ass seemed to be sleeping at the moment. Maybe because Cooper realized Delacroix was simply asking the same question he'd been asking himself since the night of the robbery.

He thought back to what had happened right before he'd tossed that guy through the window. He and the other werewolves in his pack weren't mindless animals, but much of what they did on the job was a matter of muscle memory and instinct. Thinking too much about what to do and how to do it in a crisis usually got cops killed.

He forced himself to dig deep into his memory bank, trying to recall what had been going through his head at the time, and was shocked to realize Delacroix had been right—he had been angry. But it hadn't been the typical anger that normally came when someone shot at him. No, what he'd been feeling then had been werewolf rage—a seriously strong surge.

All werewolves dealt with a certain amount of rage. It came as a package deal with the fangs, claws, and muscles. Immediately after experiencing their change, every member of his pack had needed to go through a period where they'd fought for control over the animal rage inside them. For some, that fight had been tough. For others, it had been pure hell. Now that he and the other members of the Pack had learned about beta and omega werewolves, and how omegas spent a good portion of their lives trying to control that internal rage, Cooper realized there were some werewolves who would have to fight that battle for the rest of their lives.

It hadn't been like that for Cooper. Sure, he'd felt the

anger, the rage, and the pure adrenalin rush that always hit alpha werewolves really hard right after their change. But at the time, he'd been flat on his back and partially paralyzed, so all he could do was lie there and deal with it. By the time his back had healed, he'd gotten a pretty good handle on his inner werewolf. That was why he'd never had a problem handling a full wolf shift, something that had taken other members of the Pack years to master, and something many of them still couldn't do.

"Well?" Delacroix prompted when he didn't answer. "Were you angry?"

Cooper nodded, hoping he wasn't screwing himself by admitting it. "Yeah, I guess. I hadn't really thought about it too much, but I was."

At least Delacroix didn't start scribbling frantically in her notes. Instead, she regarded him thoughtfully. "Because the man shot at you?"

That wasn't it. Hell, he'd been shot at so many times he barely noticed it anymore. But that probably wasn't something he should tell a psychologist.

He could count on one hand the number of times he'd even come close to losing control like he had at the bank, and in every one of those times, one of his pack mates had been in danger. Except this time, none of his mates had been around. But Everly had.

Crap. Now that it'd finally dawned on him, he felt like an idiot. And more than a little scared. He'd started losing control because Everly—a woman he'd known for a grand total of ten minutes—had been in danger.

The idea that Everly might be anything other than *The One* for him was harder to support by the minute.

Of course, he couldn't say any of that to Delacroix.

Yeah, Doc, I'd just met this woman standing in line a couple minutes before the robbery started, and knowing she was in danger pissed me off so much I threw a two-hundred-pound guy out a plate glass window. But it's all good because she and I are destined to be together.

So instead, he went along with what he assumed Delacroix wanted to hear.

"I'm sure that was part of it. I can't imagine many people like getting shot at. But the thing that really ticked me off was the way that guy was spraying his submachine gun around in that crowded bank. Like he didn't care who he killed. Which is stupid, I know. They obviously didn't care who they killed. I knew that the moment they shot the security guard in the back."

She wrote a few words in her notes. Probably: *He's full of crap.* "Anything else?"

"It also didn't help that the jerk tried to hide behind a teenage girl," Cooper added. "I'm not sure why, but that infuriated me. I couldn't shoot, not without hitting the girl. So I grabbed him and tried to yank him away from her. I guess I threw him harder than I thought."

Delacroix didn't react to that admission one way or the other. She simply asked him about the guy he'd thumped against the wall, then the jackass who'd been holding Everly hostage with a gun to her head.

"I could see on the video that you and he were speaking to each other, but there was no sound. What was he saying to you?" Delacroix asked.

Cooper caught himself just before a growl slipped out. Just thinking about the man who'd threatened Everly made his gums and fingertips tingle. He wanted to drive straight down to the county jail right now and tear the guy apart.

"The guy wanted to use her as a hostage, a shield. He thought if he walked out of the bank with her in front of him, the police would let him get away. That I would let him get away. I told him that wasn't going to happen."

"You didn't think the man would release her if you let him go?" Delacroix asked.

Cooper shook his head. "I knew I'd never see her alive again if I let them walk out that door."

"So, you just rushed him without a weapon?"

It wasn't like Cooper could tell her that he'd had all the weapons he needed, so he nodded. "It didn't seem like I had much of a choice."

Delacroix didn't say anything for a while, content to sit there and scribble more notes on her pad. When she was done, she looked up and took off her reading glasses. "You seem a bit more relaxed today. More open."

He shrugged, as surprised as she apparently was that he was saying any of this in the first place. All he could think was that being with Everly last night had put him in a chatty mood. If he kept up like this, people were going to think he and Becker had switched bodies.

Cooper gave her a smile. "Maybe I'm just in a good mood."

"Mind if I ask what put you in such a good mood? Yesterday you were extremely upset about being suspended during the investigation and resented our mandatory sessions. What changed?"

He considered making up something, or simply refusing to answer. But he knew Delacroix would keep digging until she figured out what he was hiding. Besides, it wasn't like he had anything to hide.

"I went out on a date last night."

Delacroix set her glasses on the desk and sat back in her chair. "It must have been some date because you seem like a different person than you were yesterday."

Cooper couldn't help smiling. Maybe he was a different person today. It was one thing accepting the concept that theoretically, there was one perfect woman for you out there in the world. It was completely different once you actually met her—and he was pretty sure he had. There couldn't be any other explanation for the way he'd been acting and feeling since meeting Everly. It was like anything was possible now.

"It was a pretty amazing date," he admitted to Delacroix. "In fact, I think I may have stumbled over that rare, one-in-a-billion woman I'm meant to be with."

———

Cooper was still smiling when he left Delacroix's office. Mostly, because she'd implied it wouldn't take many more sessions before they were done, and he could get back on the job. But also because talking about stuff— even if he had to hide the dangerous details of being a werewolf—was kind of cool. Since he'd joined the Pack almost four years ago, he'd somehow become the person everyone came to for guidance and advice, or to just plain vent. It felt nice to finally be able to talk to someone about what he was thinking or feeling. He never imagined he could talk to a total stranger about anything personal—like why the date last night with Everly had been so amazing from others he'd gone on— but he could, so he wasn't going to overanalyze things.

He glanced at his watch as he walked to his Jeep and saw that it was barely noon. If he wasn't suspended—well, technically he was on paid leave, but it was a suspension as far as he was concerned—he would have headed to the SWAT compound. He supposed he could go home and start on the new graphic novel he had. Hell, he might even want to clean up his place, just in case he wanted to bring Everly over. He should probably go grocery shopping, too. He lived off fast-food restaurants and delivery pizza most of the time. The only stuff he kept stocked in his place was beer, soda, and junk food.

He climbed into his Jeep, planning to hit the H-E-B store on the way home for some food Everly might like, but the mere thought of her had him reaching for his cell phone.

She answered on the second ring. "Hey, Landry! What's up?"

Cooper grinned at the sound of her voice, imagining her standing in front of an artist's easel, cell phone in one hand, a paint-smeared brush in the other, and a big smile on her face.

"Nothing much," he admitted. "I just wanted to call and tell you I had a great time last night."

She laughed, and he almost groaned at the sound. "Me, too. I haven't been on a date that fun in…well… ever. I can't wait to see you again."

"Same here."

"So, what are you up to today? Nothing dangerous, I hope."

That's when Cooper realized he'd never told Everly about the whole paid leave and fitness-for-duty evaluation. He wasn't sure he wanted to tell her. He was kind of embarrassed about it. But it was stupid to hide it from her. It was bound to come up in conversation at some point, especially since he didn't have a clue how long this suspension crap was going to last. The sessions with Delacroix might be going well, but Coletti could drag out his investigation as long as he wanted.

"Actually, I'm not doing too much of anything right now. Since I was involved in a shooting at the bank robbery, the department has me on paid leave until they finish the investigation. About the only thing I have on my calendar for the next couple days is my sessions with a department-appointed psychologist, and I just finished today's. I kind of have a lot of free time on my hands right now."

"That sounds like a pretty crappy way to treat a cop who saved so many people," Everly said. "But their loss is my gain. You want to get together and do something?"

He could think of a thousand things he wanted to do with her. "I'd love to, but I didn't mean you had to blow off work."

She laughed. "Don't be silly. I work for myself, which means I can take time off whenever I want. So if you want to get together and hang out, I'm game."

"It's hard to say no when you put it that way," he said with a laugh.

"Good. Because my schedule is wide open this afternoon."

"Do you have something special in mind you'd like to do?" He didn't care what they did as long as he got to spend time with her.

"Surprise me."

A thousand ideas popped into his head, but he got the sensation Everly wasn't interested in the typical date stuff.

She seemed like the kind of woman who would appreciate doing something a little different. He knew just the thing.

"I'll pick you up in twenty minutes then. And wear something casual. Shorts and a T-shirt are fine. And tennis shoes. No flip-flops." He had an ulterior motive for suggesting shorts. Anything to give him a chance to get another glimpse of those perfect legs. But she didn't need to know that. "Oh, and bring a change of clothes so we can go out to dinner later."

"What exactly are you planning?"

"You said to surprise you. See you in twenty."

Grinning, he thumbed the red button on his phone then hit the speed dial for Becker. He needed his friend to get some gear ready if he was going to pull off what he had planned.

Forty minutes later he pulled his Jeep into the gated SWAT compound and parked in his usual spot.

"What are we doing here?" Everly asked as he led her toward the admin building.

She'd hounded him the entire drive over, trying everything to get him to tell her what they were going to do. But he'd resisted. He wanted the pleasure of seeing her eyes light up when she found out what he was up to.

"You'll see soon enough," he said, giving her hand a tug. "Come on. There're some people I want you to meet."

He held open the door of the admin building, his gaze caressing her long legs as she walked in ahead of him. Everly might be an artist, but it was obvious from the tone in her legs that she exercised a lot.

The first floor of the admin building was essentially a big open space with enough desks and chairs for the entire Pack, except for Gage. He had a private office. It was your typical bullpen setup, but he and the other guys had jazzed it up with posters, a TV, and a slick paint job.

Becker and Alex were leaning back against one of the desks, while Jayna swiveled in an office chair. All three looked up at their approach.

"Everly, you already met Becker and Alex," Cooper said. "And this is Jayna Winston. For reasons none of us understand, she's Becker's girlfriend."

Jayna laughed and got up to give Everly a hug. "Eric told me all about what happened in the bank. I'm glad you're okay. But let me warn you now, you probably shouldn't believe half the stuff Cooper tells you. These guys all make up stuff."

"Only to make it more interesting." Becker grinned.

Jayna gave him a look. "Uh-huh."

Everly smiled. "So I probably shouldn't have believed Landry when he told me that you were one of the people who helped shoot up his Jeep?"

Cooper had about half a second to cringe before Jayna burst out laughing. "Actually, that one you can believe. His Jeep wouldn't have those holes in it if it wasn't for me."

"That's okay," Cooper said. "It looks better with the holes in it anyway."

Everly didn't look convinced, but her lips curved up at the corners all the same.

Becker pushed away from the desk. "You guys ready?"

"Ready for what exactly?" Everly asked. "Cooper wouldn't tell me."

"I told you—it's a surprise." He took her hand and fell into step beside Becker and Jayna. "Everyone else still out providing security for the warrant and search teams?"

"Yeah," Becker said as they walked past the volley-ball courts and steered away from the shoot lanes toward the cluster of training houses in the rear of the compound. "The FBI, ATF, and the DPD are checking out every possible source of military grade explosives in the state. I don't know exactly what they're looking for, but anyone with a connection to military weaponry seems to be on their radar. They have us stretched so thin that Gage has us going out in teams of two and three. Xander even had to cover a warrant search this morning completely on his own. You need to get your ass off paid leave and get back here."

Cooper shook his head. "I'm trying, man. I'm trying."

Beside him, Everly eyed the single-story training building in the very back corner of the compound as they approached. The place had no doors or windows, and almost everything inside was cheap and replaceable. This was one of their facade houses, nothing but the shell of a building that they could set up to do any kind of training they needed. One day it might be set up to look like a meth lab, the next it could be reconfigured as a residential hostage scenario.

But today, the only thing he needed the building for was its sturdy flat roof and outside walls. He led Everly inside and up the steps to the roof. Becker and Jayna hung back to give him time to spring his surprise on Everly.

When they came out on the roof, her eyes widened as she took in the harnesses, ropes, and gloves. She turned to him. "Are you going to teach me how to rappel?"

At least she hadn't freaked out and run screaming down the stairs.

"You told me to surprise you." He hesitated, trying to

figure out what she was thinking and failing miserably. "Want to try it?"

She walked over to the edge of the roof and cautiously looked down. There was a low parapet along the edge of the roof, but he followed her anyway, just to make sure she didn't fall. She took hold of his hand, then peeked over the edge, blanching a little. After a moment, she took a step back and looked at him.

"I'll give it a try," she said. "But I have to warn you. I don't do well with heights."

"Don't worry about it." He smiled. "It's completely normal to feel a little queasy when you look down. But trust me, after a while you won't even remember how high you are."

She peeked over the edge again. "If you say so. What do we do first?"

"Let me get you into a harness and set up the ropes. Then I'll teach you everything you need to know."

He led her over to a collection of straps, buckles, and rings on the rooftop, then had her stand in the middle of one. Kneeling down, he slowly began to get everything situated. The position made it damn hard to concentrate. It was impossible to miss the delectable scent coming off her body, or the way her cute little belly button kept making an appearance whenever she stretched and her T-shirt slid up. The urge to lean forward and kiss her toned stomach was hard to resist.

The temptation got even worse when he started positioning the leg straps around the top of each thigh.

"Would you like to do this part?" he asked, hoping she didn't notice how turned on he was getting. "These two pieces need to snug up tight around your thighs."

"You'd better do it," she said, and he swore he saw a little smile tease her lips. "I wouldn't want to mess up and do something wrong. Safety first and all that."

"Safety first," he agreed.

He placed the straps around the top of each thigh, carefully moving the material of her shorts around so he wouldn't get it bunched up under the straps. He tried to stay professional whenever his hands came into contact with the bare skin of her legs or the cloth-covered junction between her thighs, but there was only so much he could do. To say that he was inside her personal space at the moment was an understatement.

But Everly didn't seem to mind. She simply stood there patiently while he got each strap perfectly positioned and pulled tight. In fact, it was entirely possible that she enjoyed the process. Her heart was definitely beating faster, and the scent of arousal pouring off her just about made him drunk. When he brought the main waist strap around from her back and cinched it down in the front, it would have been so easy to pop open the button on her shorts. Just a little flick of his fingers, and he'd have an even better view of that sexy midriff.

He glanced at Everly to see her looking down at him with heavy, almost sleepy, eyes. Was she thinking the same thing he was?

Cooper firmly shoved those thoughts aside. Everly could get hurt out here if he didn't focus on what the hell they were doing. He took a deep breath and stood, then checked her harness to make sure everything was cinched properly.

"Aren't Jayna and Becker rappelling?" she asked as he handed her a pair of heavy leather gloves.

He shook his head as he went to work on his own harness. "They'll come up after the first time you do it. They don't want you to get distracted or feel rushed."

Once they were both ready, Cooper spent some time showing her how the rappelling rope went through the carabiner, and how she could position the rope behind her to stop the rope from sliding through the ring, or hold her arm out to the side to let it slide through. Then he held one end of the rope and had her lean back while they were both still in the center of the rooftop, letting her learn to trust that the carabiner would keep her from sliding down the rope until she held her hand in the proper position. He knew Everly was nervous because he could hear her heart beating even faster than when she'd been aroused earlier. But she still paid attention to what he was saying, asking smart questions and responding properly when he gave her directions. Soon enough, she was so focused on the technical part of what they were doing that she relaxed.

He grinned. "You're doing great. You ready to start?"

She smiled back and nodded. "Just stay close."

"Always," he told her.

Cooper attached the end of two ropes to the heavy metal rings mounted in the center of the roof then locked the ropes into their harnesses before slowly backing them toward the edge of the roof.

"Stand up straight and tall until you get to the edge of the roof," he instructed. "Then let a little rope slide through the ring with each step."

Beside him, Everly licked her lips and moved carefully to the edge of the roof until she was standing right on it. She glanced behind her at the ground fourteen feet below. "Okay, now what?"

"First, stop looking down. You can worry about the ground when you get there. Right now, I want you to keep your attention on me and what I'm saying."

She obediently looked at him, and he was a little stunned at the blatant trust he saw in her eyes. "I can do that," she said with a nod that made her ponytail bounce in the cutest way. "You're kind of easy on the eyes."

"Nice to know." He chuckled. "Keep your arm in the stop position, then try to lean backward off the roof."

She frowned, like she thought he was crazy, but then she did it. Her brow furrowed even more. "I can't. The rope won't let me."

He smiled. "That's exactly why I asked you to do it. I wanted to show you that you can't fall if you put your right arm behind your back. Even if you slip going down the wall, just put your arm behind you, and you'll stop. Make sense?"

"Yup. Arm out to slide down. Arm back to stop."

"Okay. Now for the hardest part. To get the angle necessary for the rope to slide through the ring properly, you have to let out enough of it to stand out almost perpendicular from the wall. That can be scary the first time because you really have to commit, and it will feel like you're hanging in space."

Everly started to look at the ground, then snapped her eyes back to him. "Can you show me what you mean?"

"Sure thing. Just watch what I do." He slowly let the rope slide through the ring a little bit at a time, keeping his legs locked until he was leaning straight out from the edge of the roof like a gargoyle. Then he looked at her. "Your turn. Just take your time, and remember that I'm right here to talk you through it."

Everly kept her eyes on him and tipped back like she'd been rappelling for years. She didn't bend her knees like a lot of first-timers did, instinctively trying to hug the wall so she wouldn't hang out in space. She didn't even look down that much.

"That was easy enough," she said. But while she might look calm, her heart was still racing. "What's next?"

He gave her an appraising look. "Are you sure you've never done this before? Because you're a natural."

She laughed and shook her head. "No! Are you crazy? I'm an artist, not a daredevil. If you weren't right beside me, I wouldn't be doing it now."

Cooper liked the hidden implication in those words. Unable to resist, he leaned close and kissed her. Everly kissed him back. Damn, who knew that rappelling could be so sexy?

"Okay, we're past the hard part," he said as he pulled away to give her space to work. "Now we just hop down the wall, letting out a little rope each time. Ready?"

She nodded, then took a deep breath and pushed away from the wall with her feet. She swung out and down about two feet, touching lightly against the wall beside him.

"Perfect." He grinned. "Let's do it again."

And just like that, Everly was rappelling down the wall. By the time her feet hit the ground, she was giggling like a kid. Clearly, she'd enjoyed herself.

"Can we do it again?" she asked excitedly.

"We can. But don't get careless." He unhooked her from the rope. "And don't forget what I taught you."

She nodded and turned to run back inside and up the steps to the roof. Cooper followed, finding Everly properly hooked in by the time he caught up. But she still patiently waited while he checked her gear, then strapped in himself. Jayna and Becker set up two more ropes, and within a few minutes, all four of them were bounding down the wall and covering a lot more distance with each hop.

But after the fourth time, Everly grew bored with the one-story building. "Can we do something higher?"

He jerked his head at the two-story facade next door. "How about that one?"

She considered that, then turned and pointed at the three-floor structure he and the rest of the Pack used for most of their rappelling and freestyle climbing work. "How about that one instead?"

He lifted a brow. "You sure? That one is a lot higher."

"I'm sure." She smiled. "If you promise to go down right beside me."

Like he'd be anywhere else? "Becker and I'll get the ropes untied from upstairs and meet you and Jayna on the other roof."

She and Jayna were off like a shot for the climbing tower, laughing all the way there.

Becker chuckled as he started coiling up the ropes on the ground. "I think you've created a monster."

Cooper let his gaze follow Everly until she disappeared inside the three-story building. "Yeah, I think maybe I have."

When Becker didn't say anything, Cooper turned to see his best friend smiling at him. "It didn't take long for you to figure it out, huh?"

Cooper didn't have to ask what Becker was talking about. "No, it didn't. I think I knew it when I woke up this morning." He grinned. "But don't worry. Your record of pegging Jayna as *The One* for you in under thirty seconds is still safe."

"Hurry up!" Jayna shouted from the roof of the climbing tower. "Why are you two just standing around down there?"

Cooper motioned toward the building with his head. "Come on. We'd better get up there before they decide to rappel using their shoelaces."

They spent the rest of the afternoon rappelling down the climbing tower. And even though it was hot as hell out, Cooper couldn't remember ever having more fun. The best part of the day was when he and Everly went down the tower together, her in the traditional style while he used the Australian technique, where he went down the building facing forward. That meant he and Everly got to look into each other's eyes all the way down. Except for when they stopped halfway so they could kiss. Then he let his eyes close for a while because he was in heaven. Damn, he could have done that all day.

Around five o'clock, Alex came out with some bottles of water and Gatorade. "I figured none of you would think about dehydration, so I decided I better do it for you."

Cooper winced when he saw Everly down a whole bottle of water, then a Gatorade. He should have brought something along for them to drink. Werewolves got dehydrated like everyone else, but it took a lot longer than a few hours out in the Texas sun. Everly, on the other hand, had to be exhausted after all the trips up the stairs and down the walls. Besides, it was getting late. They needed to go back to his place and clean up before they went out to dinner.

They were heading over to his Jeep when Alex stuck his head out of the admin building. "Just in case I don't see you before Sunday, make sure you're at the church before noon."

Cooper nodded. Crap, he'd almost forgotten about the wedding. Gage and Mac were getting married in two days. Maybe he'd better write it down on a piece of paper and stick it to his fridge. Between getting put on leave and meeting Everly, he hadn't even thought about the upcoming nuptials.

He glanced at Everly as he started the engine. "I know it's short notice, but my boss is getting married on Sunday, and I was thinking maybe you'd like to come to the wedding with me?"

She put the cap back on the nearly empty bottle of Gatorade. "You sure they won't mind if I show up at this late date? I don't want to mess up seating charts and meal counts—stuff like that."

He chuckled. "Between all the people Gage and Mac know, there are probably going to be two hundred people at the reception. Trust me, you don't have to worry about upsetting any seating charts or menu plans—there aren't any. It's one of those the-more-the-merrier things."

Everly smiled. "Well, in that case, I'd love to come with you. Do you think we can bring Mia? She'd hate to miss out on a chance to meet all the single guys on the SWAT team."

That was fine with him. Who knew? Maybe Mia would turn out to be *The One* for someone in his pack.

Chapter 6

LANDRY'S APARTMENT WAS THE TYPICAL BACHELOR pad, complete with a comfy looking couch, a ridiculously huge flat-screen TV mounted on the wall with a Blu-ray player on a shelf underneath it, and the requisite surround sound system. But there were also framed posters hanging on every available wall, as well as a big bookshelf stuffed full of the largest collection of comic books and graphic novels she'd ever seen in one place. She wandered over to take a closer look at the posters and realized they weren't reprints of comic book covers, but original paintings. Her artist's eye told her they were expensive too. Landry had spent some serious money on them.

"Water okay?" Landry called from the kitchen.

"That's fine," she called back.

She could definitely use another bottle, she thought as she picked up a thick graphic novel from the stack and flipped through it. She'd gotten quite a workout rappelling. She'd never done anything that crazy in her life. Her heart might have been racing a thousand miles an hour as she'd stood on the edge of the roof and looked down at the ground below, but bounding down one wall after another with Landry beside her had been exhilarating. No wonder he liked it so much. Of course, she would never have been able to do something like that if Landry hadn't been there. It was insane, but when they were together, she felt fearless and protected. Safe.

And aroused as hell. She couldn't believe how turned on she'd gotten when Landry helped her into the rappelling harness. From the way her whole body hummed at the casual feel of his hands on her inner thighs, you'd think a guy hadn't touched her in forever. The memory of how close his mouth had been to her pussy while he kneeled before her was enough to make her wet all over again.

And the kisses while they'd been rappelling? If she could have figured out how to do it safely, she would have jumped him right there on the wall.

"I see you found my collection," Landry said, coming into the living room.

Everly turned to see him gesturing to the book in her hand with the bottle of water. She glanced down at the cover featuring a bunch of shambling zombies and the title *The Walking Dead* inked in lurid red across the front.

"Yeah, it's cool," she said. "I don't think I've seen so many graphic novels in one place."

He smiled. "Thank you for not calling them comic books."

She made a face. "Anyone can see these aren't comic books."

He shook his head. "You wouldn't believe the flak people give me for reading them."

She laughed, carefully placing the book back on the shelf. "Actually, I can believe it. I can't tell you how many times people ask me when I'm going to get a real job after I tell them I'm an artist."

"You know what they say. Haters gonna hate." He chuckled as he handed her one of the bottles. "You want to hit the shower first? I have some extra towels in the linen closet in the bathroom. I think there's even some fruity bodywash I bought by accident a while ago."

"Maybe you better go first. It will take me longer, and that way you don't have to stand around sweaty for so long."

Not that she minded him all sweaty or anything. On him, it was sexy as hell.

"Okay. Feel free to grab something to eat while I'm in the shower, if you want," he said. "I have to warn you though—I don't have a lot of variety. It's mostly chips and junk food."

She smiled at the almost sheepish look he gave her. Like he was embarrassed he didn't have any girlie food in his place. It was adorable. It also confirmed he didn't have a lot of women stay over. She and Landry might have just started dating, but she already felt proprietary about him.

Everly headed into the kitchen as he sauntered across the living room.

"I'll keep the bathroom door open a crack in case you want to talk," he said over his shoulder. "No peeking."

She halted in mid-step, leaning back so she could see down the hallway. Just to check if he'd left the door open. Of course, he had. And the view was drool worthy. Luckily, he was facing away from her, so he didn't catch her staring as he stripped off his T-shirt and dropped it in the hamper. What could she say? She was an artist. God had made her curious about the human form. And Landry was just about perfect. His back was broad and defined, and his shoulders were thick and powerful. If the models in art school had looked like him, she never would have graduated.

Everly's breath hitched as he reached down to unbuckle his belt. Face coloring, she hurried into the kitchen. As much as she wanted to stay and enjoy the show, she'd be mortified if he looked over his shoulder and caught her.

She heard him turn on the shower as she opened the cabinet beside the built-in microwave.

"Do you like Mexican?" he asked over the spray of water. "There's this place that has great food and killer margaritas."

"That sounds perfect," she said.

She closed that cabinet and opened another. Wow, he hadn't been kidding about the junk food. All he had were bags of chips and cheese in a can. How the heck did he stay in such amazing shape eating this stuff?

She tried the fridge next, thinking she might have better luck there. But all she found was beer, soda, bottled water, and jars of two-hundred-year-old condiments.

In the bathroom, Landry turned the shower off. Everly closed the fridge. She knew men could clean up fast, but that was ridiculous. He'd been in there for less than five minutes.

She walked into the living room in time to see Landry come out of the bathroom. He had one towel wrapped around his waist and was drying his hair with another. She stopped and stared again. It wasn't her fault. While his back had been amazing to behold, his front was downright godlike.

His chest was broad and muscular, his abs looked like they'd been chiseled from stone, and there was a little happy trail of hair leading from his belly button downward until it disappeared into the towel wrapped around his waist. The urge to walk over and pull that towel away and see what he was hiding down there was almost irresistible.

She took the top off the bottle and downed half the water, afraid she'd give in to the urge if she didn't give herself something else to do.

Cooper finished toweling off his hair, then casually draped the damp towel over his shoulders. Did he know she'd been checking him out?

The smile curving his mouth as he came toward her made her think he had.

Everly's pulse quickened, sure he was going to pull her into his arms and kiss her. But then she realized his bedroom was on the other side of the living room, and he was heading there so he could get dressed. Honestly, she could get so goofy sometimes.

She forced herself to focus on the wolf-head tattoo on his chest with the word *SWAT* underneath, hoping it would distract her. It didn't. The water droplets running down his chest and abs had to work hard to get past all that muscle in their race to the towel at this waist. Her fingers itched to reach out and wipe them away, but she controlled herself. If she put her hands on him right now, she didn't think she'd be able to let go. She was already aroused—and they weren't even touching.

"Shower's all yours," he said softly, coming to a stop in front of her. "I put some extra towels and the body-wash on the counter. Sorry I don't have much in the way of shampoo selection. I usually buy whatever's on sale."

She tried to answer, but couldn't tear her attention away from his bare chest and abs long enough to get the words out. Not only were all those muscles drool-inducing up close, the faint round scars that dotted his pecs and stomach were strangely fascinating. They reminded her of the bullet holes in his Jeep, but that was obviously impossible. Nobody could get shot that many times and live. They didn't even look like they'd been stitched up. It was like someone had poked him with an ice pick then let the wounds heal on their own. The funny thing was, the scars weren't ugly. If anything, they added to his overall perfection.

She reached out to trace her fingertip along one of the scars when Landry's soft voice stopped her.

"All-in-one shampoo and conditioner good for you?"

She jerked her finger back and mentally shook herself until her head was back on the same planet as her body.

"What? Oh! Don't worry about it. I brought my own shampoo." She wet her suddenly dry lips. "I'd better get into the shower, or we'll never get out of here."

"I'll be waiting." His mouth curved. "Feel free to leave the door open a crack if you want to talk."

Everly picked up the weekender she'd brought with her, almost stumbling as she walked toward the bathroom. Her legs felt weak, like she'd pushed herself too hard rappelling and succumbed to heat exhaustion. But she didn't feel ill. She felt fantastic.

She stepped into the bathroom, leaving the door open a few inches. As she rummaged in her bag for her toiletries, she tried to make sense of this crazy attraction she felt to Landry. It was more than just physical. When she was around him, she felt a sense of bliss unlike anything she'd ever experienced.

She stripped off her shorts and T-shirt, then stepped into the walk-in shower and turned on the water. She gasped as the spray hit her breasts. Yikes, her nipples were super sensitive. Being turned on for most of the day would do that. Unable to contain her curiosity, she slipped her hand between her legs to run her fingers over her folds. She was wet all right, and if she hadn't been in Landry's shower with him right outside the partially open door, she would have touched herself until she came.

If she was this excited from seeing Landry in a towel, she could only imagine how much more aroused she'd be when she saw him completely naked. She stifled a moan and reached for the shampoo. Not even her imagination was that good.

———

When Everly came out of the bathroom, she found Landry standing by the bookcase flipping through a graphic novel. He'd traded in his towel for a sexy pair of jeans, black work boots, and a skintight T-shirt. From where he was standing, he would have gotten a good view of her standing half-dressed in front of the mirror as she put on her makeup. If he'd peeked, of course.

Everly liked to think he had…at least a little.

"Ready to go?" she asked as she walked over to him.

Landry glanced at her, his eyes catching the light and reflecting gold. But while the flash disappeared a split second later, the heat and hunger lingered. The way he looked at her was almost predatory, and she was more than happy to be his prey.

"You look beautiful," he said softly.

Everly looked down at her flirty boho dress. It was cute, comfortable, and swirled around her legs when she walked. But the real reason she'd picked it was because it was prewrinkled. She could shove it in her tote bag and no one would ever know it.

She opened her mouth to thank him, but she completely lost her voice. In the few moments it had taken her to glance down and back up again, Landry had moved all the way across the living room and was now standing in front of her. And that hungry look he'd had before was now ravenous.

"Thank you," she finally said, her voice barely above a whisper. He was so close she could feel the heat pouring off his big body. "I'm glad you like the dress."

He leaned in even closer, his mouth now only an inch or two from hers. "I wasn't talking about the dress. I was talking about you."

She opened her mouth to thank him again, but instead, leaned in to kiss him. He met her halfway, his lips coming down on hers.

Everly heard people talk about a kiss taking their breath away. She'd always thought that was crap—or poor technique. But when Landry's other hand slid down to cup her ass through the material of her dress while his tongue had its way with hers, she actually went light-headed. But there was no way in hell she was going to stop kissing him. She didn't care if she passed out. So, she wrapped her arms around his neck and gave as good as she got.

Landry buried his other hand in her hair, holding her captive as his mouth ravaged hers completely. She responded in kind, pushing her tongue back against his, determined to give him as much pleasure as he was giving her.

Her body was on fire, the almost constant throb she'd felt between her legs all day erupting into a rapid drumbeat. Her tender nipples stiffened even more, and she knew Landry could feel them against his chest. She was aware of his arousal pressing against her. He wanted her as much as she wanted him.

Landry's hand glided over her ass, searching for the hem of her short dress and sneaking underneath. She moaned against his mouth. It looked like they weren't going out to dinner after all. That was okay. She could make do with Doritos and cheese in a can if it got her into bed with him.

But as he pushed her back against the bookshelf, she thought maybe the bed would have to wait until later as well.

His fingers were moving up her thigh to the edge of her panties when a ringing sound echoed around them. Everly tried her best to ignore it, but the ringing came again, more insistent this time. It was immediately followed by a knock that made Landry jerk back with what sounded like a growl.

Everly didn't blame him. She wanted to scream herself. Who the hell knocked on a door after already ringing the bell twice? Didn't they know she was trying to have sex here?

"I'll get rid of them," Landry said in a husky voice, his eyes glinting gold in the light again.

If she hadn't been so turned on at the moment, she might have thought more about how he was doing that, but right then, she didn't care.

When Landry unlocked the door and jerked it open, she thought he was going to punch the person on the other side. If so, Everly would have helped hide the body.

But the moment Landry saw the man standing there, his whole demeanor changed. "Jim? Holy crap, is that you?"

The man grinned. Shorter than Landry, he was thin with graying hair cut military style. "Yeah, it's me. Who the hell do you think it is?"

Landry chuckled. The next thing Everly knew, he and Jim were locked in a man-hug and slapping each other on the back so hard they were going to leave bruises.

"Damn Coop, did you get bigger?" Jim asked, pulling away to eye Landry. "You were always tall, but you look like you've put on a good four inches and added a ton of muscle since I've seen you last."

"I've added a few pounds of muscle here and there," Landry said. "But what the hell happened to you? You look like shit."

Jim laughed and slapped Landry on the shoulder, not offended by the frank words. "Army years are like dog years, you know that."

Landry shook his head, but didn't say anything. Instead, he turned and motioned her forward. "Everly, I want you to meet the man who saved my life in Iraq four years ago—Sergeant Jim Wainwright. Jim, Everly Danu."

Jim smiled and extended his hand as he stepped into the small foyer. "Nice to meet you, Everly. If you've gotten this guy's attention, you must be special. All he ever did when he was back in EOD was work, work, and work some more."

Everly laughed. She had no idea what EOD was, but

assumed it was the job Landry did when he was in the army. "Well, he's still all about work. We met in the middle of a bank robbery."

Jim looked at Landry. "You're shitting me."

Landry shook his head. "It's a long story, but enough about that. What I want to know is why the hell you didn't tell me you were coming into town. Are you in Dallas doing a VIP detail?"

First EOD, now VIP. She was going to need a military acronym guide.

"Nah." Jim stuck his hands in his pockets. "I'm out of the army now—I bailed about three weeks ago. I'm in town job hunting. I had your address, so I figured I'd stop by and see you." He glanced at Everly. "Probably should have called first, but I didn't think about it."

"You don't need to call first. You're always welcome," Landry said. "Why the hell would you get out of the army now? No one bails on a military retirement with less than six years left to go. Crap man, you had a good shot at making sergeant major. Why the hell would you just walk away?"

Jim snorted. "Life in EOD isn't what it used to be, not with deployments starting to slow down and the battalions sending all their techs on every field training exercise they can find just to keep them occupied. There's way better money to be made in the contractor world than staying on active duty anyway."

Landry frowned. "I'm glad you told me you got out. I would have been worried as hell if I tried to email you at Fort Bragg, and it bounced back as undeliverable."

Jim glanced at her again before looking at Landry. "I stopped by hoping we could go out to dinner, but that was before I realized you had company. I'll give you a call later once I find a job and get settled. I'll let you know what my new email is."

Landry didn't say anything, but Everly could see he was torn. She knew he wanted to spend the night with her, but he clearly wanted to hang out with Jim. The guy had saved his life. While she didn't know Jim, she felt like she owed him a huge debt for saving the man she was falling for so fast.

"We were just about to head out to a Mexican place for dinner," she said impulsively. "You should come with us."

Jim shook his head. "Thanks, but I don't want to intrude."

"You're not intruding," Everly insisted. "I'd love to hear all the stories you have about Landry. He hasn't told me much of anything about the army. In exchange, I'll tell you how he saved me from bank robbers."

Jim hesitated. "You sure I won't be a bother?"

"Of course you won't." She smiled and grabbed her purse from the couch. "Come on, we need to get to the restaurant before it gets too crowded. You can follow in your car or come with us. Whatever works for you."

Jim nodded. "Okay. I'll follow you guys."

As Jim walked out, Landry took her hand.

Thank you, he mouthed.

Everly smiled. It wasn't the evening she'd envisioned. That one had involved her and Landry getting naked. But their white-hot romance could handle a little time on simmer for one more night at least. Something told her that Jim needed a friend right now, and she was okay if that friend was Landry.

—∿∿—

Landry hadn't said a word since they'd dropped Jim off at the Doubletree Hotel near Love Field twenty minutes ago. Everly understood why. Dinner with Jim had been…well, *emotional* was the word for it, she supposed.

It started out lighthearted and fun when Landry and Jim had explained all the acronyms they'd thrown at her earlier. It turned out EOD was short for Explosive Ordnance Disposal, which was a long-winded way of saying Landry and Jim had been in the army's bomb squad. A VIP detail was when an EOD team was sent to work with the Secret Service or the State Department to provide bomb search expertise for protection of high-level American and foreign dignitaries, like the president.

Everly couldn't believe Landry had failed to mention the fact that he'd worked security details for people like George Bush, Dick Cheney, Colin Powell, and some well-known foreign big shots. Landry had immediately downplayed his part in what he said was a huge, complex operation, saying that EOD's only job on VIPs was to search any area where the protectee would be for bombs and explosives. But still, it seemed like a big deal to her, and she told him so.

As they ate, Jim regaled her with stories about all the crazy things he and Landry had found while working VIPs together. She'd laughed so hard she could barely eat.

But then, Jim's stories had turned more introspective and somber. Maybe that had to do with all the beer he'd been drinking. Or maybe, it was simply because it was hard to talk about their work without thinking about friends who hadn't made it back from Iraq and

Afghanistan. Neither of them would get into specifics, and Everly hadn't pried, but as they talked, she realized why Landry hadn't mentioned his time in the army on their first date.

If half the stories about what he'd done for those six years were true—and something told her they were—EOD made SWAT look positively safe by comparison. Landry had been on at least three deployments she had counted, plus a lot more trips overseas for something they called TDY. She knew it had something to do with temporary assignments, but hadn't bothered to ask what it actually meant. She'd quickly figured out that military acronyms were stupid, and as long as she got the general gist of what they were talking about, she didn't bother digging any deeper. The bottom line was that Landry and Jim had spent a lot of time in really dangerous places doing really dangerous things.

Something had gone horribly wrong on Landry's last deployment in Iraq though. From the hushed way Jim said the names of the people who'd been with them, Everly knew a lot of their fellow soldiers had been killed. And while Jim wouldn't go into detail, she knew Landry would have died too, if Jim hadn't risked his life to save him. She wanted to know what had happened, but neither could seem to talk about it, so she didn't push.

Everly had watched the news, waved flags for Veterans Day parades, and knew people who had family members in the military. But hearing Landry and Jim talk about it and the price people paid, it suddenly felt a lot more real.

By the time they finished dinner, Jim had switched

from beer to hard alcohol. He downed so many whis-
keys that Everly was surprised he was still upright and
able to talk coherently. Then again, maybe Jim drank
like that all the time. But from the way Landry frowned
at his friend, she didn't think so.

When they'd left the restaurant, Landry refused to
let Jim drive, saying they'd drop him off at his hotel
and that he could take a cab to get his car tomorrow.
Fortunately, Jim hadn't fought Landry on the issue.

"Give me a call, and we can get together again
while you're in town," Landry said when they got to
the Doubletree.

Jim's eyes teared up, and for a moment, Everly was
sure he was going to cry. Instead he man-hugged Landry
tightly, mumbling how good it'd been seeing him again
but that Landry had Everly, and he didn't want to be a
third wheel. Everly had felt her own eyes well up.

"Jim, you're not a third wheel. You guys are friends
who haven't seen each other in a long time—I get that. I
don't need Landry all to myself," she said, adding with
a smile, "just the parts you're not interested in."

Jim had laughed, then squeezed Landry on the shoulder and told him he'd call. As Everly watched him make
his way to the hotel's entrance, she got the feeling he
walked like a man who wasn't quite sure where he was
going. But was it thanks to all the alcohol he'd consumed, or something else entirely?

"You want a beer or something?" she asked Landry
as they walked into her apartment.

Mia wasn't around, but Everly kept her voice low in
case her roommate was sleeping. She turned on only one
light, which left the living room in deep shadows cast

by the glow of the streetlamp coming through the living room window.

Landry hesitated. "No, thanks. I'll take a bottle of water, if you have it."

She grabbed two bottles from the fridge, then carried them into the living room. Handing one to Landry, she sat down on the couch beside him.

"You okay?" she asked. "You've been quiet ever since we dropped Jim off."

Landry took a swig of water, then put the cap back on the bottle. "I guess. Jim and I have talked on the phone, and emailed a few times since I got out of the army, but…" He shook his head. "He's changed so much since the last time I saw him."

She kicked off her sandals and curled her legs under her. "When was that?"

Landry sighed and leaned back against the cushion. "Four years ago as he was dragging my partially paralyzed ass out of a burning building in Iraq. But he's changed so much since then that I barely recognized him today when I opened the door. He's gone gray and gotten thinner. He looks like he's the one who got screwed up over there—not me."

Everly stared. A few hours ago, she'd almost begged him and Jim for details about what had happened, but hearing Landry using such succinct words to describe something as awful as that… The thought of him being hurt so badly made her feel like she couldn't breathe. Part of her didn't want to know any more, but the other part needed to hear it.

She sat there silently, hoping he would tell her, but dreading it at the same time.

"I fell for a stupid trap I should have recognized," he said finally. "My team and I blew up an IED—improvised explosive device—in an old abandoned building outside this city called Samarra in Iraq. Standard operating procedure is to check to make sure the IED is completely destroyed after you blow it and that the area is safe. As the team leader, that was my job. But there was a second bomb waiting for me when I went into the building. I didn't realize it until it was too late, and I couldn't get out in time."

Landry's voice was flat and emotionless, like he was reading a book he'd read a hundred times…or reliving a movie that had been playing over and over in his head since that day. Everly almost told him to stop, that she didn't want to hear any more. Yet something told her he wasn't telling her the story because he thought she wanted to hear it. He was doing it because he needed to say it out loud.

"I was hit really hard," he continued. "Broken back. Bleeding out from a half dozen wounds. Choking to death on smoke from the fire the blast had started. I was sure I was dead. Then Jim showed up and dragged me out."

Tears filled Everly's eyes, but she ignored them, letting them pool up and run down her face. She couldn't in her darkest nightmares imagine having to live through what he was describing. He hadn't said a single word about the pain, but she knew that it must have been beyond horrible.

Landry swallowed hard. "The bomb going off was a signal to the local insurgents to launch an assault. Bullets were flying everywhere, but Jim ignored them and dragged me all the way back to the safe area where our vehicles were set up. He and the other members of my team cut me out of the bomb suit and plugged up the holes in my body, then got me on a spine board and called in a medevac bird. And the whole time, Jim was right in my face telling me over and over that I wasn't going to die. Turns out he was right."

Thank God. "What happened after you…got better?"

"It took a while before I did, and by the time the army realized I was actually going to be able to walk again, they'd already medically discharged me." He blew out a breath. "To tell the truth, I wasn't in the right frame of mind to stay anyway, not after everything that happened. Finding the SWAT team was a godsend. After getting blown up, there was no way I could ever go back into EOD work full-time again."

Landry turned to look at her then. Everly quickly tried to wipe the tears from her cheeks before he could see them, but he lifted one big, gentle hand and softly did it for her. His touch was so tender she almost started crying again.

"I'm sorry to dump all this depressing crap on you," he said softly. "But I've never been with anyone I trusted enough to talk about it until I met you. I never even realized how much it's been weighing on me, not until I saw Jim tonight. Thank you for listening."

She reached out and took his hand, giving it a squeeze. "Of course. I'm glad you feel comfortable enough with me to talk about it. I've never had to deal with anything like what you went through, but I know what it's like to have stuff inside your head you can't talk about."

Landry lifted her hand to his lips and pressed a kiss to it. "Like your mom, you mean?"

Everly blinked. "How do you know about my mom? Did you do a background check on me or something?"

He smiled. "No. I just guessed. Since you didn't mention her even once in all the time we were at dinner last night, it wasn't much of a leap. I figured you'd tell me about it when it seemed like the right time."

Everly relaxed against the cushions embarrassed she'd accused him of doing something as under-handed as a background check. She shouldn't be surprised he'd picked up on the fact that she hadn't mentioned her mom. She'd already figured out he was amazingly perceptive.

"It's not like it's a big secret or anything," she said quietly. "It happened a long time ago, so I don't think about it that much now."

He lifted a brow as if to say that was a bunch of BS.

She sighed. "Okay, maybe I do think about it."

Actually, she thought about it every day.

"What happened?" he asked.

She took a deep breath. "When I was little, we lived on a big farm in the French countryside. I don't really remember much about it, but my parents had a huge winery. Dad grew the grapes and made the wine, and Mom took care of the business side. She and I were in the house one day when a worker Dad hired came in and attacked Mom."

"Oh God," Landry breathed. "How old were you?"

"Seven."

She bit her lip, digging through the few memories she had left of her mom—and that day. It had always made her mad that she could barely remember her mother, or what had happened.

"I only remember bits and pieces," she said. "I was helping Mom bake a pie when he came into the house. He was angry about something, and Mom pushed me down behind the kitchen counter and told me to stay there. I can't remember much after that. I don't know exactly what he did or how she died. All I know for sure is that he killed her, then left without ever looking for me."

"Did the police catch the man and find out why he'd done it?" Landry asked.

She shook her head. "Dad told me that the police found the man dead several days later, but they didn't say who had killed him or why he murdered my mother. But once Mom was gone, Dad couldn't live in the house anymore. It was too hard for him. Too hard for all of us. So…he sold the farm and the winery and moved us here."

"I'm sorry you lost your mom," Landry said gently.

"Me too." She wiped a tear from her cheek. "The worst part is that I was so young when it happened. I barely remember her at all. I mean, I have photos of her, but it isn't the same thing. Sometimes, it feels like I lost her twice."

Another tear escaped, and this time, Landry wiped it away.

He put his arm around her, and she rested her head on his shoulder, sad at the reminder of her mother's death, but glad she had told him. They talked some more about what she did remember about living in France—the farmhouse, playing hide-and-seek with her brothers, running through the vineyards in a yellow sundress, stomping around in a vat of grapes. The memories made her cry all over again, but in a good way.

"I should probably get going," Landry said softly against her hair.

Everly wanted him to stay the night, but after having dinner with Jim and talking about what Landry had gone through in Iraq, not to mention what had happened to her mother, she wasn't in the mood to pick up where they'd left off at his apartment. She suspected he wasn't either.

"Landry, do you think Jim might have a drinking problem?" she asked as they walked to the door. "It could be why he looks so much different than you remember him."

She expected Landry to deny his friend had a drinking problem. The guy had saved his life, after all. But Landry surprised her.

"As much as I hate to say it, yeah." He sighed.

"Was he already drinking a lot before the accident in Iraq?"

She hated to even ask because she didn't want Landry feeling guilty, but seeing his best friend broken and bleeding must have been horrific for Jim.

But Landry shook his head. "Jim drank for years before seeing me get blown up. I don't think it was a big problem back then, and it never interfered with his job, but he could always knock 'em back. Hell, if you ask around, most people will tell you that EOD actually stands for Every One Drunk. But seeing me get screwed up may have pushed him in that direction. Unfortunately, what happened to me wasn't the worst situation Jim had to deal with on that deployment to Iraq."

"What do you mean?"

"You heard us talking during dinner about those

other soldiers in our unit who died, right?" At her nod, he continued. "He feels responsible for their deaths."

Everly listened in shock as Landry described what happened in Samarra after he'd been injured and mede-vacked out of Iraq. From what Jim had told him, he had responded to a large IED call along with five other members of his unit. A device had gone off in the safe area while Jim had been downrange, and three EOD techs had died.

"I saw a copy of the final report," Landry added. "There were implications that someone had made a poor decision in selecting the safe area where all the other team members had been waiting, but the conclusion was that the deaths were due to hostile action, something that couldn't have been foreseen or prevented. Yet the offi-cial report didn't stop the rumors. EOD techs are people, and people talk. The conspiracy theory is that someone screwed up badly. Most people think it was Jim because he was the senior EOD tech there."

Everly didn't really understand the details of what had happened. She just knew Jim had been blamed for it. "Do you think he did something wrong?"

"Definitely not," Landry said firmly. "Jim is the best tech I've ever worked with. Hell, he's forgotten more than I'll ever know. If someone screwed up, it wasn't him. Unfortunately, not everyone knows him as well as I do. I imagine he's had to put up with people whispering behind his back ever since the accident."

"No wonder he drinks," Everly muttered.

Landry shook his head. "Seeing your friends and teammates die, and knowing people blame you for it is bad enough, but then there's the guilt of surviving when those you were responsible for didn't. Jim is probably dealing with some PTSD. He's going to need help whether he wants to admit it or not."

She noticed Landry didn't mention he'd gone through some traumatic ordeals of his own. No doubt he was dealing with serious issues from his past as well. But at least he'd been surrounded by his friends on the SWAT team. And now, he had her. It didn't sound like Jim had anyone.

"If Jim gets a job in Dallas, maybe we can convince him to get help," she said.

Landry regarded her for a time, then reached out and pulled her into his arms for a long, languid kiss.

Regardless of the serious discussion they'd been having for the past few hours, all it took was his lips to make her feel better.

He pulled away to rest his forehead against hers. "Do you know how amazing you are, Everly Danu?"

That made her feel even better.

Chapter 7

COOPER PULLED OUT HIS PHONE TO CALL HIS FRIEND Dennis the moment he came out of Delacroix's office. Now that he was allowed to suit up and get back in the game, he wanted to figure out where the FBI was on the bombing case. He still didn't understand exactly why Delacroix had done it, but she'd signed off on his fitness-for-duty evaluation, and he sure as hell wasn't going to look a gift horse in the mouth.

He hadn't even known he and Delacroix had a meeting this morning until he'd left Everly's last night and saw a voice mail on his cell phone saying she could slip him in at nine o'clock the next day if he was available.

Cooper would have rather headed over to Everly's place this morning just to see what she looked like with her hair all tousled and sexy from sleeping, but Becker and the other members of the Pack needed him to get his ass off suspension. They were running themselves ragged covering all the search warrant details plus their normal workload. If meeting with Delacroix on a Saturday morning would get him closer to that, he was there.

Cooper left Dennis a message, saying he was off suspension and to give him a call, then climbed in his Jeep. He was still surprised at how well the meeting with Delacroix had gone. He'd walked into her office to find her watching the bank video again, this time going over the section where he'd charged the guy holding Everly and knocked him out.

He'd almost groaned, expecting their session to be like the previous one, with her asking him why he'd done what he had in that part of the video, and what he had been thinking about at the time. But instead, he and Delacroix had spent the first thirty minutes talking about last night's dinner with Everly and Jim. At some point, the conversation got around to all the stuff that had gone down in Iraq—both to him and Jim. It still wasn't easy to talk about, but now that he'd already had the conversation with Everly, he could get the words out at least.

He'd been on the verge of asking Delacroix how he might approach Jim with his concerns about the drinking, but then right out of the blue she told him she was going to sign off on his FFD paperwork.

"If you continue to come in and see me on an as-needed schedule completely outside the department's purview, I'll sign off on your paperwork right now," she said. "You can be back on duty by lunch."

He'd been so frigging surprised, it had taken a minute for him to answer. "I'm eager to get back on the job and all, but why now? What changed your mind?"

She looked at him for a long moment before answering. "Officer Cooper, I'm going to be completely frank. You're still carrying a truckload of baggage from your time in the army, and it's likely to take you a lifetime to get over it."

Well, that was depressing.

"But at least you're aware of the baggage, and you're facing it head-on," she continued. "More importantly, it's obvious your SWAT teammates play an important role in your life. Simply put, they're your bedrock.

Suspending you and keeping you away from them is actually counterproductive to the steps you need to take to move forward. That's why I'm recommending that you return to duty. It's where you belong."

He sure as hell wasn't going to argue with that. "You know Coletti will have a cow over you closing this review so quickly, right?"

Delacroix smiled—one of the few times he'd seen her do it. "I'm sure he will. But in this matter, I work for the Dallas Police Department, not Internal Affairs. The DPD tasked me with determining if your reactions at the time of the bank robbery were in line with those of other police officers and to assess your overall mental stability in regard to future performance. I've done both of those tasks to my satisfaction. When Coletti viewed the video, all he saw was the violence and what he assumed to be out-of-control rage. I think we both know that while you were certainly angry, you never lost control of yourself or the situation for even a second. What he construed as rage was simply you using the abilities you had available at the time."

Cooper stared hard at Delacroix, trying to figure out what the hell that little line had meant. Was she dropping a hint that she knew what he was? If so, she wasn't giving anything away. No increase in heart rate or breathing pattern, no tension in her muscles— nothing. Maybe she hadn't been hinting at anything.

"You don't think I'm a risk to the public then?" he asked.

"No." She leveled her gaze at him. "I believe you are fully capable of doing your job, far more capable than most."

Okay, that one was damn hard to ignore. But how could she know he was a werewolf? And, if she did, what was he going to do about it? He obviously couldn't shut her up if she intended to tell people.

But as he sat there thinking about the possibility of Delacroix knowing his secret, he realized there weren't any alarm bells going off. If she were a threat, he would have picked up on it. And right then, he wasn't feeling threatened.

Finally, he went with his gut and decided he was just reading too much into a few random comments. But that didn't mean he wasn't concerned about one thing she'd said.

"These other sessions you want me to come in for?" he asked. "If I'm cleared for duty, why should I come in at all?"

"Like I said before, Officer Cooper, you've got some things you need to work through. I'm simply offering my help. Whenever you need to talk, give me a call, and I'll find room in my schedule. You talk—I'll listen."

"I thought you didn't do general therapy," he pointed out.

"I do it when the right case presents itself."

He'd sure as hell like to know what made his the right case. He only prayed it wasn't because she knew what he was and was hoping to be the first psychologist in history to have a chance to climb inside a werewolf's head and muck around a bit.

But again, it just didn't feel that way to him, and ultimately, he decided to accept the offer at face value. It wasn't like he had much of a choice. Not if he wanted to get his ass off suspension.

Cooper had just cranked the engine and was wondering if he should share his concerns about Delacroix with

Gage, when his cell rang. He checked the screen then thumbed the green button.

"Hey Dennis, thanks for calling back. Anything new on the case?"

His friend sighed. "Our lab confirmed the bomb was made with military grade C-4 explosives. Unfortunately, the chemical markers the DOD laced into the mix aren't helping us much. All the DOD can say for sure is that the batch of explosives used to make the bomb is part of a shipment of several tons that was supposed to have been consumed in Iraq a few years ago."

Cooper swore. The military layered different chemicals into their bulk plastic explosives so that forensic labs could track the stuff back to the ammo plants that produced it, all the way down to lot numbers and shipment dates. But when the lots were measured in tons, that information didn't do any good.

"We're working to track down anyone who might have a connection with moving stolen military explosives, but it's a long list of suspects," Dennis said. "And that's only here in the Dallas area."

"I'm guessing these suspects don't go out of their way to keep their contact information up to date with the FBI?" Cooper said drily.

Dennis snorted. "No, they don't. But we're not putting all our eggs in that basket. Like you suggested, our techs went through the videos taken by the cameras in the parking garage around the time the bomb went off. Depending on how large of a window we go with, we're looking at fourteen possible targets. We're checking out each to see if any stand out."

"What about the security and traffic camera

positioned around the industrial area?" Cooper asked. "Any luck locating somebody with a record?"

"That part is going slow," Dennis said. "We're looking at somewhere north of four hundred vehicles, even more people to identify and check out. That's a big job, and we can't say for sure if we're wasting our time or not. The area has a lot of gaps in their camera layouts. Our bomber could have driven out through any of those gaps, and we'd never even know it."

Dennis didn't say anything for so long Cooper thought he'd lost the connection. Then his friend finally spoke. "We need a break in this case, Cooper, or this guy might get away with killing that cop."

⁓

Jayna and her petite friend Megan might not like to shop for clothes, but they clearly liked pizza, Everly thought as she sat across from them at a table in Grimaldi's and watched them tear into the pies like they hadn't eaten in a week. When they'd ordered the two large pizzas, Everly was sure they were going to end up with enough food for another meal and then some, but now, she realized she might have to grab a second piece or both pizzas would be gone before she finished her first slice. She found it hard to believe two women— especially one Megan's size—could pack away this much food. There was a table full of big college-aged guys in the corner, hanging their heads in shame right at that moment.

"Tell me you two don't eat like this all the time," Everly said. "Because if you do, and don't gain any weight, I'm going to be really mad."

Jayna laughed. "No, we don't. All that shopping was exhausting. I never knew buying a dress could be so hard."

Now it was Everly's turn to laugh. "Just remember, you're the ones who called me."

"I know." Jayna grabbed another slice of pizza. "It seemed like a good idea at the time since Mac and Gage are getting married tomorrow, and we still didn't have anything to wear."

Everly thought Jayna was using the whole I-need-a-new-dress-for-the-wedding scenario as an excuse to go shopping and hang out together. Like anyone really needed an excuse to do either. She'd been floored when she realized Jayna was serious.

"I haven't worn a dress since I was five years old and don't know a thing about what to wear to a wedding," Jayna admitted. "I've never even been to one."

Everly had been planning to spend the morning working on a book cover for a local romance author she knew, but since the wedding was tomorrow, she decided helping Jayna and Megan shop for dresses definitely constituted a clothing crisis. So, she'd shut down her computer, picked up Jayna and her friend in front of their apartment complex, and headed for one of her favorite malls. The Shops at Park Lane had a ton of cool stores, so they'd have no problem finding something.

As she bit into a slice of pizza, Everly realized she'd been a bit too optimistic. It had taken over three hours to find them something suitable for a wedding and something they'd agree to wear. Because Jayna hadn't been kidding—she hadn't worn a dress since she was a little girl. She wasn't even comfortable in one. Every time she'd try one on, she pulled and yanked on it. Megan had only been marginally easier to deal with. They'd gone into every single women's clothing store in the big open-air mall—some more than once.

In the end, she'd helped Jayna and Megan find two perfect dresses for the wedding—and one for herself. It had taken a little work to get them comfortable with the idea of wearing outfits that showed a little cleavage and flashed a little leg. Even now, between inhaling pieces of pizza, Jayna frowned at the shopping bag by her chair.

"Don't even say it, Jayna," Everly warned. "You're going to look fabulous in that dress."

"Are you sure?" Jayna bit her lip. "It's not too revealing?"

It was hilarious to see a woman as attractive as Jayna, who was obviously very confident in every other way, be so timid about a dress. "Trust me, it's not too revealing. Showing a little cleavage is completely acceptable. And I can guarantee that Becker will absolutely love you in it."

Jayna didn't look convinced. "I don't know. Eric loves it when I wear yoga pants. I don't think he likes women in dresses. I'm sure he won't like the high heels either. Maybe…"

Everly was all about a comfy pair of yoga pants, but there was no way Jayna was wearing those to the wedding. "Jayna, there's not a man alive who doesn't love the way a woman's legs look in a pair of heels. There will be drool—guaranteed."

Megan perked up. "Drool. Really? I like the sound of that."

Everly couldn't help but smile. Megan was such a joy to be around. In some ways, she seemed so young—like when she was shyly talking about how much she cared for her boyfriend Zak. Other times—like when she was talking about growing up on the streets as she and Jayna had done—she seemed much more mature. *An old soul*, her father would say.

"How long have you and Zak been seeing each other?" Everly asked.

Megan couldn't be more than twenty-one, but Everly got the feeling she must have been dating Zak for a while. Their relationship sounded pretty serious.

Across from her, Megan fingered the small silver dolphin pendant attached to a fine chain around her neck. Everly had caught Megan playing with the pendant throughout the morning, and every time she did, she smiled. Like the jewelry reminded her of something—or someone—very special.

"We met about three months ago, but didn't go on our first date until three weeks later," Megan said. "He just moved into the loft a few days ago."

Everly was pretty sure her jaw dropped because Megan and Jayna burst out laughing.

"Yes," Megan said as she tried to control her giggles. "Zak and I are sleeping in the same bed in a small apartment with five other adults."

Everly waved her hand, even though she was shocked to learn there were actually that many people living in one apartment. "I don't care about that. From first date to cohabitating in two months? Wow. I'm not judging or anything, but I don't think I could move that fast."

The words were out of her mouth before she realized she might have offended Megan. That hadn't been her intent.

But Megan didn't look upset. "I get that. If you'd

asked me four months ago whether I would ever do something as crazy as have a guy move in with me after having known him for less than ninety days, I would have said you were insane. But then I met Zak, and everything changed."

Everly wasn't cynical about love and romance, not by a long shot. But she'd dated enough guys to know love at first sight was something that only happened in romance novels. Not that she would ever say that to a woman as idealistic as Megan.

"Still, I'm not sure I could ever fall for a guy that fast," Everly said tactfully.

"Really?" Jayna put a half-eaten slice of pizza on her plate and wiped her hands on a cloth napkin. "So you're saying you're not falling head over heels for Cooper?"

Everly opened her mouth to say no, that she liked Landry a lot, but they were taking it slow. Then she stopped herself because it would be a lie. They really weren't taking it slow at all. They'd seen each other every night since the robbery at the bank. The only reason they hadn't slept together already was because Jim had shown up and put a damper on the evening last night. The feelings she had for Landry were stronger than anything she'd ever felt for another guy. Was she falling for him?

She was so focused on the question that she didn't realize Jayna and Megan had fallen silent until she looked up and saw them regarding her with broad smiles.

"Ding, ding, ding." Jayna laughed. "I think someone just figured out that she's falling in love."

Everly shook her head. "Whoa, wait a second. How did we get from falling head over heels to falling in love? The two things are completely different."

"Are they?" Jayna gave Megan a knowing smile. "Let me ask you a simple question. I want you to answer without thinking about it for even a second. Just close your eyes, and go with your first instinct, okay?"

Everly wasn't sure where the heck this was going, but she closed her eyes. "Okay."

"Remember—don't think, just answer," Jayna reminded her. "If Cooper walked over here right this moment and said he loved you, what would you say?"

The first thought that popped into Everly's mind was that Jayna's question was silly, but then she stopped herself. Because that really hadn't been the *very* first thing. Before she'd started thinking too much, her first thought was that she'd say, *I love you, too*.

Her eyes snapped open. "Oh my God!"

Jayna grinned. "Don't feel obligated to answer the question because you already did."

Everly sat there stunned, not able to talk. Heck, she could barely breathe. "How is this even possible? I've only known Landry for three days. I can't be in love with him yet."

"Why not?" Jayna asked.

"I don't know. It's just…" Everly was at a loss for words. "I barely know him."

"What do you want to know?" Megan asked. "What his favorite color is? If he sings in the shower? How he voted in the last election? Whether he wears boxers or briefs? Whether he wants kids right away or if he'd rather wait? Would the answer to any of those questions change the way you feel about him right now?"

Everly's head swam with confusing emotions. She

couldn't be in love. She and Landry hadn't even slept together yet!

"I know you're feeling pretty overwhelmed right now. I get that," Jayna said. "I've been there. The same thing happened when I met Eric. Everything hit me so fast. Like you, I tried to deny it at first. Then I tried to run away from it. Ultimately, it didn't matter. Love happens whether we're ready for it or not. It's just a matter of how much time you want to waste running from the obvious. You're in love with Cooper, as insane as that is. The reason you're feeling so confused right now is because your heart already knows—it's your head that's taking a while to catch up."

Everything Jayna said was absolutely true. "Wow," she murmured as it all sank in. This was really happening. "I've fallen in love with a man in what, seventy-two hours? That has to be a record in any place but Hollywood and Vegas. Even Megan took longer than that."

Megan laughed. "Don't go running off to call *Guinness* just yet. It might have taken Jayna a while to realize Eric was the one for her, but he knew in ten seconds. Which is a good thing, or he probably would have shot her."

Everly's eyes widened. Landry had told her that Becker helped Jayna and her friend out of a little trouble, but he hadn't mentioned that little nugget. "Did he really come close to shooting you?"

Jayna shook her head with a laugh. "Nah. He was too busy stuffing me in a packing crate to shoot me."

"Okay, now I have to hear the whole story," Everly said.

But as Jayna explained how she and her friends had

become involved with Becker and the rest of the Dallas SWAT team, something struck Everly as unusual.

"Doesn't it seem odd that all of these love-at-first-sight relationships seem to revolve around the SWAT team?" she asked. "Even Megan and Zak are together because of their interaction with the team."

Jayna and Megan exchanged looks.

"Nah," Jayna said. "Pure coincidence, I'm sure."

Everly sipped her iced tea while Jayna and Megan finished the last of the pizza, then they grabbed their bags and headed to Everly's SUV.

"So, what's the plan for tonight?" Megan asked as she climbed in the back of Everly's little Juke. "You and Cooper going out again?"

Everly started the SUV and swung the wheel toward the mall's exit. She would have liked to sit down with Landry and tell him how she felt about him. Or drag him into bed and rip off his clothes. Both sounded fun. But she couldn't do either of those things—at least not until later tonight.

"I wish," she muttered. "But I promised my dad this morning that I'd bring Landry over tonight to meet him and my brothers."

Jayna glanced at her as she turned onto Highway 75 heading south. "You aren't worried about Landry and your family not getting along, are you?"

Everly shook her head as she checked her side mirror before merging with the traffic. "I'm not worried at all. I know they're going to love him as much as I do."

How could they not?

Chapter 8

"SO, HOW'S EVERYTHING GOING WITH EVERLY?"
Alex whispered to Cooper as they slowly moved through
the woods toward the rear of the shabby ranch house.
Remy and Brooks, along with three DPD uniformed
officers, were stuck with the crappy task of approaching
the front of the house with Dennis and his FBI partner.

Remy and Brooks would be the ones knocking on
the door—and that was plenty dangerous enough—but
if what they'd been briefed about the guys living in this
place was right, there was a good chance that some bad
folks were likely to be hauling ass out the back door of
this place pretty soon. And they were almost certainly
going to be armed. He and Alex were back here to keep
those guys from getting away. One of Dennis's informants claimed they were the men who'd provided the
explosives for the bomb, so the feds really wanted to
talk to them.

"Great," Cooper whispered back. "We almost blew
off dinner plans last night so we could hang out at my
place, but then an old friend from my army days showed
up, and we ended up going out with him."

Alex paused for a moment, sniffing the air. No doubt
making sure no one had snuck around behind them. His
eyes shifted to yellow-gold, and his nose tilted up a little
as he tested the air. A few moments later, the flash of
color disappeared, and he looked at Cooper.

"That was pretty cool of her to hang with your army buddy."

"Yeah. She's amazing like that."

Cooper smiled as he remembered those late night kisses at her place just before he'd dragged his butt out of there.

"Damn, I never thought I'd see it," Alex said as they reached the edge of the woods and took a knee, waiting for a signal from the front of the house. "Dry and wry Landry Cooper walking around with a big-ass grin on his face. Everly must seriously be *The One* for you."

"I wasn't sure in the beginning, but I think she has to be," Cooper admitted. "Because I can't imagine feeling like this for another woman."

"I'm happy for you, guy," Alex said. "If any of us jerks deserve a shot at cosmic happiness, it's you."

Cooper snorted. "Because of all the hard times I went through in the army?"

Alex flashed him a grin. "Hell no. I just figure you deserve a reward for the all the time you've spent playing Doctor Phil for Xander, Khaki, Becker, and everyone else who goes to you for help. If you're going to be handing out advice about love, you might as well get some yourself." He glanced at Cooper out of the corner of his eye. "You are getting some, aren't you?"

Cooper shook his head. How the hell did a guy like Alex ever get laid? "Since we're talking about love advice, let me provide a little before you come and ask me for it."

Alex regarded him with amusement. "This I have to hear."

"It's simple. If you're lucky enough to find the

woman you're meant to be with, don't talk. Just give her a smoldering look with that furrowed brow, flash her a shot of your abs every time she looks at you—maybe even smile—if you can figure out how to do it without looking like you're in pain. But don't talk, because every time you do, her opinion of you is going to drop like a rock."

Alex grinned—and it did kind of look like he was in pain—but before he could respond to Cooper's jab, a voice over their earpieces interrupted.

"We have a visual through the front windows," Dennis said calmly over the radio. "All four brothers are inside the house. No indication they know we're here yet."

"Does that mean we don't have to worry about them shooting at us until we knock?" Remy asked sarcastically.

"Probably," Dennis replied without missing a beat. "Just remember, Jackson Burke owns the property, so his name is the one on the warrant, but his oldest brother Jed is the one you have to watch out for. He's the guy my informant fingered as running this operation, and he's the one with a sheet as long as my arm. He's been charged multiple times for aggravated assault—once against a police officer—and armed robbery. He's been in and out of prison most of his adult life, and the next time he's in front of a judge, he's looking at a three-strike sentence."

"So he knows that if he goes to prison again, it's probably going to be for life," Cooper added. Dennis had shown them photos of the four brothers, so they'd be able to ID them on sight. "That means there's no reason for this guy to play nice."

"Great," Remy drawled. "So, it's almost guaranteed this is going to turn ugly?"

"I hope not," Dennis said. "I really need these guys to talk to me. They may be the link to the bomber who killed Officer Swanson."

"This informant of yours," Brooks said. "He actually saw explosives on the property?"

Cooper knew exactly why Brooks was asking. The past couple days, everybody involved in this case—FBI, ATF, DPD, Homeland Security—had all been pushing hard on their sources and informants. Suddenly having somebody claim to have seen explosives at a ranch just inside the Dallas County line, north of Ferris on I-45, seemed a little too convenient. Wouldn't be the first time an informant had sold his handler a piece of bogus info because they knew the cops were desperate.

As the minutes stretched out and Dennis didn't say anything, Cooper got a funny feeling in his gut. "Dennis, answer the question. Your informant saw explosives, right?"

His friend sighed—and Cooper's stomach dropped. "He didn't see explosives, but he did see boxes with military markings. Some were the right size and shape to hold the C-4 blocks we're looking for."

Cooper heard his teammates grumbling over the line. They weren't hiding the fact that they felt like they'd been played.

"Dennis, you're sending us in against four shoot-first bad guys on the off chance the boxes your informant saw might hold explosives," Cooper said. "With guys like this, our mere presence is going to lead to a confrontation, all over a weak-ass tip on some *military-looking boxes*?"

Dennis hesitated again. "It's the best tip I've got. And it's why I asked for as many of you guys as I could get—because I knew this could get ugly. But I wouldn't ask you and your guys to go in if my gut wasn't telling me there was something here."

Cooper glanced at Alex, who nodded. But Brooks was the senior SWAT officer present—and the one going through the front door. He was the one who had to give the word.

"Brooks?" Cooper prompted.

"We know all about going with your gut," Brooks said. "We're going in."

Cooper heard Brooks and Remy approach the front of the house just as the shooting started.

"There are only two shooting out the front," Brooks said calmly over the radio. "Cooper, Alex—you can expect company any second."

As if on cue, the back door burst open and two men raced out, carrying pistols and hauling ass for the woods to the left side of the house.

Cooper called out the obligatory, "Stop—Dallas Police!" But that didn't slow the two men down at all. Why the hell would it? The idiots already knew the men outside the house were cops. That's why they were running in the first place.

"Two suspects just came out the back heading for the woods," Cooper said into his mic. "Jed is one of them."

"Don't let him get away!" Dennis shouted. "Go after them."

Cooper switched off his mic. He didn't want anything he said—or growled—over the next few minutes to make it onto the official recordings that were made of all police channels. In his ear, he could still hear Brooks making the occasional comment as he and Remy smashed their way through the front of the house and began seriously screwing up the two brothers who'd been dumb enough to stay behind to give their siblings a chance to escape.

He glanced at Alex as the two fleeing men disappeared into the woods. "Apparently, the FBI thinks we should chase those men who just ran off."

Alex snorted. "Good thing we have your FBI friend here to tell us what to do. I would never have thought of that."

"I guess we should go get those guys then," Cooper said. "Before they get away."

Alex shrugged. "We could give them a few minutes head start. Might make it more sporting. There's nothing in the direction they headed but woods, field, and barbed-wire fence."

Cooper considered that. "Better not. If Dennis came back here and saw us standing around, he might think we don't take this stuff seriously."

"Yeah, you're right," Alex agreed. "But if the two brothers split up, you can have Jed. That way I won't get in trouble if I end up having to damage the other one."

That didn't seem fair to Cooper, but Alex was already running toward the far tree line.

They kept their pace slow until they were a few hundred feet into the woods, just in case one of the other officers or feds might look their way. But once they were under the cover of the trees, he and Alex immediately put on the speed.

Cooper felt his leg and ab muscles tighten and tingle as

energy poured into them. His fangs and claws instinctively slipped out at the thrill of the chase, and he had to force himself to retract them. They needed Jed Burke alive and talking—preferably not ranting about seeing a monster with glowing eyes, sharp fangs, and vicious claws.

He glanced at Alex to see that his fellow werewolf was having a little more trouble with that. The former marine's eyes were blazing, and his fangs protruded nearly an inch over his lower lip. He and Alex were close in age, and both had gone through their change about the same time, but Cooper had been able to shift fully into a wolf within a year of his change, while Alex still couldn't do it. Cooper could keep his fangs and claws in check, no matter how tense or excited he got. Alex, on the other hand, was on the edge of control right now, and he probably didn't even know it.

That was how the werewolf thing worked. Control wasn't only about maturity and experience. It was about personality, acceptance of the rage inside you, and in some ways, pure dumb luck. Having seen what a full omega werewolf was like when the SWAT team had fought several of them a few months ago while saving Jayna's pack, Cooper was now of the opinion that some alphas in his pack had a little omega in their blood. It definitely explained why some had a harder time than others when it came to controlling their inner wolf.

Up ahead, the trail left by the Burke brothers split off. As arranged, Cooper went after Jed. He couldn't trust his nose completely to track the man, but the idiot was running so hard and was so out of control, it didn't take much to follow. Jed was crushing plants and leaving deep boot prints everywhere he went.

A minute later, Cooper picked up the sounds of thudding footsteps and labored breathing. Then he caught a glimpse of Jed's red hair and plaid shirt between the trees. While he might be trim and wiry, the poor guy clearly hadn't worked on his cardio while he was in prison because he was huffing and puffing the whole way.

Cooper slung his M4 over his head and across his back, picking up speed.

Jed whipped his head around, his eyes widening in shock. He recovered quickly enough, pointing his weapon in Cooper's general direction and snapping off three shots. The bullets never came close, but the move gave Cooper a good look at Jed's weapon. It was a large frame Beretta. It didn't have more than fifteen rounds in the magazine—one more, if Jed had kept a round chambered. And he'd already fired three.

Cooper wasn't worried about getting shot. A werewolf could handle anything but a direct hit to the head or the heart. But sometimes a shooter could get lucky—and even if he didn't—Cooper didn't want to show up at the house with blood pouring out of him.

So, he spent the next few minutes toying with Jed. He alternated charging him then darting behind a tree, with racing toward him, only to veer away at the last moment to slip off into the deeper forest.

As Cooper had hoped, Jed freaked at the sight of a cop moving way faster than any big guy in full tactical gear should be able to. He stumbled blindly in first one direction, then another, before tripping and slamming into the ground hard enough to knock the air out of his lungs.

But then Jed came up shooting wildly in Cooper's direction, completely forgetting he'd been popping off rounds for the past minute. When the upper receiver of the automatic locked back after he fired the last round, he looked at the weapon in confusion, like the gun had purposely betrayed him.

Growling, Cooper closed the distance between them. He didn't think Jed had another magazine, but he wasn't going to wait and see.

Jed tossed the empty gun aside and pulled a Buck knife from his belt, opening it with a flick of his wrist. "You might as well pull your gun and shoot me now, you fucking pig! No way in hell am I going back to prison."

As if wanting to give Cooper added incentive, Jed advanced, holding his knife low. He moved like someone who knew what he was doing with a blade, keeping one hand up like a shield while taking short, tight slashes and jabs at Cooper.

Unfortunately for Jed, his knife skills weren't really going to help him now—not against someone so much stronger and faster than he was. Cooper waited until the man jabbed the point of the four-inch-long blade toward his stomach, then reached out and got a grip on Jed's wrist faster than the man could see.

Cooper twisted Jed's arm, throwing the guy over his hip and slamming him to the ground hard. Getting the knife out of Jed's hand after that simply took a little pressure. Jed released the weapon with a cry of pain.

Jed struggled as Cooper cuffed him, then tried to run when Cooper dragged him to his feet. Cooper let go, shaking his head as Jed ran smack into the trunk of a nearby tree. While the guy was recovering from that,

Cooper walked over to pick up the gun and knife the guy had tossed, and slipped them into a cargo pocket.

Then he dragged Jed to his feet again and started toward the house.

"I'm not going back there!" Jed shouted, digging the heels of his boots in the dirt. "You'll have to carry me if you want to take me in."

Cooper shrugged. "Have it your way."

Tossing the two-hundred-pound idiot over his shoulder in a fireman's carry, he started heading back the way he'd come. Alex's idea of letting the bad guys get a head start didn't seem nearly as funny now as it had before.

Cooper got back to the house just as Alex was shoving his guy in the back of one of the DPD cruisers. Cooper pushed Jed in the other side, then slammed the door. The two other Burke brothers were sitting stone-faced and pissed off in the back of the second cruiser. There was no sign of Brooks and Remy, or Dennis and his partner.

"Where's everyone else?" Cooper asked, cursing his screwed-up nose for about the thousandth time.

Alex looked around, his eyes flashing as he shifted slightly, while testing the air with his nose. "Brooks and Remy are in the house with the uniforms. I think Dennis and his partner are in the barn."

Cooper frowned. "The barn? Did Brooks and Remy clear it yet?"

"No," Brooks said in his earpiece. "He said he'd stay out of there until we did."

Cooper was off and running toward the broken down barn before Brooks even finished talking. He only slowed long enough to snag his demo bag out of the backseat of the SWAT team's SUV, then raced for the barn. Of course Dennis wouldn't wait for someone else to clear the place first. He was too damn impatient for that. The idiot better hope that impatience didn't get him killed.

The main doors in the front of the barn were still locked with a heavy steel chain, so Dennis and his partner obviously hadn't gone that way. Cooper sped around to the back of the building, cursing when he saw the door that had been kicked in. Dennis might be a friend, but he was also a frigging moron.

"Dennis, wherever the hell you are—stop!" Cooper shouted as he cautiously stepped inside the barn.

He tried to pick up any smells that might make him think this place was booby-trapped, but it was worthless. He tensed, ready to charge headlong down the dimly lit hallway when Dennis's head poked around the corner. His partner—whose name Cooper couldn't remember for the life of him—appeared beside him.

Dennis frowned. "What the hell's wrong?"

"What the hell is wrong?" Cooper strode down the hall and grabbed both men by their tactical vests, dragging them back around the corner to stand with him. "I'll tell you what the hell is wrong. The two of you running around a barn that belongs to people you think are selling military weapons and explosives on the black market. Didn't you think that if their illegal shit is in here, it might be booby-trapped?"

Dennis looked like he was about to argue—no man liked being called out in front of a coworker—but one look at Cooper's pissed-off expression changed his mind. At least he had the decency to look chagrined.

"I didn't really think about it," he admitted. "I mean, Karl and I walked this far down the hallway without anything happening."

Cooper bit his tongue. "I could say something about human mine detectors, but I'm not that insensitive. How far down the hallway did you get?"

"Just a few feet," Dennis said. "It's hard to see in there, but the hallway opens into a larger room at the front of the barn—where the big main doors are."

"Stay here," Cooper ordered.

Not waiting for a reply, he walked slowly around the corner and knelt down. He let his eyes shift, taking in the pitch-black, dusty space. He couldn't see anything, but that little tingling running up and down his back told him something was wrong. He let his eyes shift back to normal and reached into his demo bag for the small can he always kept in there. He popped off the cap and was just lifting it when Dennis's voice distracted him.

"What's that?" Dennis asked.

Cooper looked over his shoulder to see Dennis peeking around the corner.

He swore. "It's a can of didn't-I-tell-you-to-stay-behind-the-wall."

"I am behind the wall. Most of me, anyway," he added. "Seriously, what's in the can?"

Cooper didn't bother to answer. It would only prompt more questions. Instead, he popped the top of the can, then pointed it in the right direction and pressed the button on the top down hard, shooting a long line of solvent string all the way down the dark corridor.

"You're shitting me," Dennis grumbled. "You yank us out of the hallway so you can play with Silly

String? Um…Cooper, why is that stuff hanging in midair like that?"

Cooper frowned at the long piece of dayglow pink string hanging magically two feet in the air at the far end of the hallway, then turned and looked at his friend.

"That's the trip wire you and your partner almost walked into. You know—the one that's probably hooked to an explosive device of some kind."

It took nearly three hours to clear the barn, even if Cooper ultimately found only two devices in there—the trip wire in the hallway attached to a homemade grenade hidden inside the wall, and a device attached to the main door. That one had been slightly more complicated since it was designed to set off a big cluster of black powder-filled pipe bombs if a small switch outside the barn wasn't flipped before trying to swing either of the big doors open.

Dennis was damn lucky, and he knew it. If either device had gone off while he and Karl had been in there, they'd be dead. Cooper was pretty sure neither one of them would let their curiosity get them into trouble again.

Cooper and his teammates were still looking around the interior of the barn's main room when Dennis came in. He'd gone out to the cruisers to talk to Jed and his brothers because they weren't finding anything in here. The back rooms were empty or full of fifty-year-old crap that hadn't been touched in forever, and the main area didn't seem to be hiding anything suspicious, either. It looked like a good old boy's home garage, complete with toolboxes galore, car parts everywhere, a busted up Chevy big-block V8 engine sitting in the middle of the floor, and a big chain hoist attached to the roof beams.

"None of the Burke brothers are talking," Dennis said, frustration clear in his voice. "They claim there's nothing here to find."

"Then why the booby traps?" Alex asked sarcastically.

"To protect their tools, or so they claim." Dennis shook his head. "Look, at any other time, these guys would be looking at serious jail time just for shooting at us. The improvised devices in the barn would be the icing on the cake. But right now, my bosses are looking for people selling military explosives, not a bunch of rednecks building homemade pipe bombs. My informant swore there were military explosives here, and we haven't found squat."

Cooper and the others were about to walk out when Alex stopped by the engine block on the floor. "What the hell? What am I smelling over here?"

Dennis looked at Alex like he was on crack. "What does anyone smell in an old barn? Crap?"

Brooks and Remy moved back to the engine and started sniffing, ignoring Dennis, who was saying he couldn't smell a damn thing. Cooper joined them, even though his nose wasn't much better than Dennis's at the moment.

"It's coffee," Remy said suddenly.

Brooks nodded. "It's faint, but I smell it too."

Remy, Brooks, and Alex dropped to their knees, looking for a trap door. But everything around the engine sounded just as solid as the rest of the barn.

Cooper looked around, frowning as he realized the

gears of the hoist were shiny with fresh oil. "Wait a minute. Why is the hoist so well taken care of, but that engine block looks like it hasn't been worked on in twenty years?"

His teammates stopped and looked at each other.

"Shit," Remy muttered. "We're not smelling coffee around the engine—we're smelling it under the engine. That big hunk of metal is a cover, like a rug over a trapdoor to a cellar. It just takes a hoist to move this particular rug."

"Get that chain around the engine," Dennis said excitedly. "Let's move it out of the way!"

"Forget that," Brooks said. "Get out of the way."

Cooper had half a second to wonder if maybe he should point out that there was an FBI agent standing right in their midst who had no idea they were were-wolves. But before he could, Brooks grabbed the big old V8 engine with those equally big hands, jerking the thing up and tossing it to the side.

Dennis gaped. No doubt wondering how even some-one as big as Brooks had picked up an engine that easily weighed over six hundred pounds. Fortunately, the fed was more interested in the metal manhole cover Brooks had uncovered.

Brooks and Remy pulled the cover away, revealing a dark hole. The smell of coffee coming from it was so strong even Cooper could smell it. Apparently, Dennis could, too.

"What the hell is going on with the Starbucks coffee-house aroma?" Dennis asked.

"Coffee throws off scent dogs." Alex grinned. "There's something down there that the Burke boys don't want a dog picking up on. Drugs, maybe. Or—hopefully—explosives."

Cooper reached into his demo bag and came out with two high-intensity light sticks. Ripping them out of their foil packages, he popped the glass vial inside, then gave them a shake and dropped them down the hole. They fell about a dozen feet before bouncing off something and coming to a stop.

Cooper went down on one knee and stuck his head in the hole. He could easily see the wooden and metal military-style boxes bathed in the green glow coming from the sticks.

"We have boxes," he announced.

Giving the guys a grin, he hopped on the metal rungs set into one side of the concrete-lined hole and slowly moved down them. He didn't think there was much chance of running into a booby trap down here, but he took his time anyway, checking out each rung of the ladder carefully before putting his weight on it. This time, Dennis didn't follow until he looked up and gave the all clear.

Taking out his flashlight, Cooper shined the beam around the twelve-foot-square space. The floor was concrete too, solid and completely dry. And all around the small room stacked to the ceiling were military shipping crates and ammo boxes. He saw labels identifying M4 carbines, matching rifle ammunition, hand grenades, claymore mines, anti-tank rockets, and in one corner, a single, easy-to-recognize, wire-bound box.

He was pulling back the closure wires on the lid when Dennis joined him. "Is that what I think it is?"

Cooper lifted the lid and saw exactly what he expected to see nestled in their aluminum foil outer bags—green rectangles one inch thick by two inches wide by almost eleven inches long. The words in yellow on top were clear and distinct. *Charge. Demolition. M112.*

"It's C-4 explosive," he confirmed.

Dennis took out his notebook and compared the lot number on the blocks of explosive with the numbers written down. "It's a match. This stuff is from the same lot the lab techs said was used to make the bomb."

Cooper frowned at the half-empty box of explosive charges.

"Why the hell don't you look happier?" Dennis asked. "This is the frigging break we were looking for. For all we know, Jed Burke is the person who planted the bomb in that parking garage."

Cooper shook his head. "Yeah, it's a break. But you don't seriously believe the person who made those low-tech piece of shit devices in the barn also made that complex work of art—the IED you have in your forensic labs—do you?"

Dennis hesitated, his brow furrowing. "Okay, maybe not. But even if Burke didn't make the device, he and his brothers provided the explosives to the man who did. Once we put pressure on them, one of those assholes is going to crack and give up the buyer."

"Maybe," Cooper said.

Dennis swore as he put his notebook away. "What the fuck is up with you? Can you at least be happy we have a solid lead?"

Cooper jabbed a finger at the box. "How many blocks of C-4 do you see in there?"

Dennis looked confused, but then leaned forward to count. "Fifteen."

Cooper locked eyes with him in the green glow. "A case of C-4 comes with thirty blocks. The bomber used three to make that bomb at the industrial area. That's a lot of explosive still left unaccounted for. Enough for another four bombs, the same size as the last—or one really big device that's four times as deadly."

Dennis didn't say anything. Probably because he was trying to figure out what the chances were that some *other* psycho had bought the explosives, instead of their psycho. He must not have liked the odds, because his shoulders slumped in defeat.

"Shit," Dennis muttered, summing up the situation perfectly.

"Yeah," Cooper agreed. "Shit."

Cooper and his teammates hung out at the Burkes' ranch for the rest of the afternoon along with the crime scene teams, ATF, DPD Bomb Squad, Army Criminal Investigation Division, and a dozen other organizations and offices who rolled on the scene to get their fingers in the pie. While they waited, Dennis and Karl took a run at Jed and his three brothers back at the FBI. Dennis called to report that none of them talked. And once the lawyers got involved, no one would be talking for days, not without grants of immunity and other legal BS that would take forever to iron out. Dennis might like to think they'd finally gotten a break in the case, but in a lot of ways, it didn't seem like they were any closer than they'd been before.

In between, Cooper thought about Everly. Damn, that woman was on his mind about every waking minute. She'd texted fifteen minutes ago, saying she was looking forward to seeing him that evening, and hoped he wouldn't mind if they stopped by her dad's house on the way to dinner so her family could meet him. He texted back telling her he didn't mind at all. Funny thing was, he meant it. Granted, he hadn't met a girlfriend's parents since high school, but Everly was obviously close with her family. If meeting them was important to her, it was important to him.

After texting Everly, he called Jim's cell, but it went straight to an out-of-service message. Cooper frowned. That was weird.

He Googled the phone number for the Doubletree Hotel where he and Everly had dropped him off the night before. Since Jim would be out hitting interviews, Cooper figured he'd just leave a message, but the woman at the front desk told him there was no Jim Wainwright registered there.

"When did he check out?" Cooper asked.

He heard clicking on the other end of the line as the woman tapped her computer keyboard. "I can't find Jim Wainwright's name anywhere in our system, sir. Are you sure he was staying here?"

"I dropped him off there last night. So yeah, I'm sure he was staying there."

More clicking. "I'm sorry, but I'm still not finding anything, sir."

Cooper thanked the woman and hung up. Maybe Jim had already found a job and checked out early. While that made sense, it didn't explain why his name wasn't in the computer.

Cooper shoved his phone in his pocket. He hoped Jim would call and tell him what the hell was going on because he didn't like the uneasy feeling churning in his gut right then.

Chapter 9

EVERLY ALMOST LAUGHED AT THE EXPRESSION ON Landry's face when he saw all the cars in front of her Dad's two-story house—a dozen parked bumper-to-bumper in the long driveway, spilling onto the street.

"I thought we were meeting just your father and brothers," he said, a hint of alarm on his handsome face.

She took his hand and tugged him along the walkway toward the front door. "You are, but my three oldest brothers—Armand, Claude, and Giles—are all married and have big families. Armand and his wife have six kids, and usually use two minivans to keep the noise to a minimum. Then there are all my cousins. They moved here about ten years ago. They show up with their families whenever my dad cooks a big meal."

"We're having dinner?" He frowned. "I thought we were going out for dinner."

Everly stopped in front of the door, turning to smile at him. "We are. Don't worry. I already told Dad that we're not staying. If someone tries to convince you otherwise, just point them in my direction."

She closed the distance between them until they were only a few inches apart. His masculine scent was almost overpowering up close, and the urge to pull his head down for a kiss was just as strong. But she resisted. She had no doubt that several of her relatives were probably watching them through the big living room window.

She didn't mind kissing Landry in front of them, but she didn't want to make that first impression more complicated than necessary.

"There are going to be a lot of names coming at you in there, but I don't expect you to remember any of them," she said. "I'll point out my brothers, and of course, my dad—Florian. Beyond that, just smile, nod, and shake hands. My brothers will try to crush your hand when they shake, but that obviously isn't going to be a problem for you. Oh, and my sisters-in-law are huggers. But that just means they like you. It's when everyone stares at you that you know you have problems."

Landry chuckled. "So, this is basically a test, huh?"

She moved another step closer, letting her breasts press into his strong chest as her fingers entwined with his. "For them—not for me. You've already won me over."

Everly thought he was going to kiss her, but then he tilted his head to the side. "I hear giggling coming from inside. I guess we're being watched."

She hadn't heard anything, but didn't doubt that her nieces and nephews were watching. They probably thought the idea of their aunt having a boyfriend was quite hilarious.

"Shall we go in then?" she asked.

Everly didn't bother announcing herself as she led Landry inside. The kids had probably let everyone know they were here.

As she expected, the whole extended family was in attendance, and they immediately crowded into the foyer to meet Landry. It was hard not to laugh as they all charged forward and gathered around them, but Landry slapped on a smile and greeted each person she introduced. It was like working a reception line at a wedding, but once Everly got Landry through her cousins and their kids, she finally had a chance to introduce one of her brothers.

"Landry, this is Tristan. He's the youngest of my brothers."

And my favorite, she almost said. But, of course, she couldn't—even if it was true. That didn't mean she didn't like her other three brothers. It was just that they seemed so much older than Tristan—in temperament, if not in years. Of all her brothers, Tristan was the one she hung out with the most, even if he was ten years older than she was.

"Nice to meet you," Landry said, extending his hand. "Everly has told me a lot about you."

Tristan chuckled as he shook Landry's hand. "Oh, I doubt that. But that's okay. I'm just glad to finally have a chance to meet the man who saved her life." Her brother smiled at her. "As you can imagine, my little sister is very precious to me—to all her brothers. It's fortunate you were in that bank at the right time."

Everly resisted the urge to cringe. She hated when her brothers called her their *little sister*, like she was still seven years old. And *precious*? What the hell was she, a ring of power? Her tall, good-looking brother could be such a dweeb.

"I'm glad I was there too," Landry said. "I haven't known Everly nearly as long as you have, but she's very precious to me as well."

Funny how hearing Landry call her precious didn't seem nearly as corny.

Even so, she was about to remind Tristan that while

she was his little sister, she could still post old photos of
him as a goofy teenager all over the Internet. But before
she could threaten him, her father walked into the living
room followed by her three older brothers.

The room fell silent as the patriarch of their family
came out wiping his hands on a dish towel. He still had
a few traces of flour up near the tops of his forearms,
meaning he'd probably been making fresh pastry crust
for a dessert. Her father was magic with desserts.

He wiped off the last of the flour dust and handed the
towel to his youngest granddaughter, Phoebe, asking
her to run it back to the kitchen. Then he came closer,
studying Landry openly. Her dad was over sixty, but
looked younger thanks to few gray hairs and an unlined
face. He was still tall and broad-shouldered, too. He
wasn't anywhere near Landry's size, of course, but she
could tell by the way he was eyeing her new boyfriend
that he was deciding if he was a man worthy of his
daughter. She could have told him that Landry was.

"Landry, this is my father Florian, and my other
three brothers—Armand, Claude, and Giles." She
pointed out each of her brothers as she introduced
them. But unlike Tristan, none of them extended
a hand in greeting. They simply stood there behind
Dad—waiting.

"You are a very large man, Officer Cooper," her
father finally said in his thick accent. "I can certainly
understand now how you were able to deal with those
bank robbers while protecting my daughter at the
same time. Her mother would have approved as much
as I do."

Everly blinked. Her dad had always been blunt

to the point of rudeness with the guys she'd brought home, but he'd never mentioned her mother to any man she dated. That had to be a good start.

"I wish I could have met her," Landry said softly. "From what Everly tells me, your wife must have been an amazing woman."

Her father glanced at her, surprise clear in his blue eyes. He might never have mentioned her mother to any of her boyfriends, but neither had she.

He smiled at Landry. "Yes, she was an amazing woman. Speaking of my wife, where are my manners, I haven't even welcomed you into our home. The place is nearly a perfect replica of the farmhouse we had in France, with a few improvements. Come. I'll show you around."

Everly followed in shock as her dad led Landry toward the kitchen. He'd never given her previous boyfriends a tour of the house either—first date or not.

The rest of the family must have decided the drama was over because everyone went back to talking and laughing. That was a relief. The hum of conversation made it hard to hear what her dad was saying to Landry though. She glanced at Tristan and saw him smile. She smiled back.

Up ahead, Landry and her dad had stopped in the hallway outside the kitchen. Her father was describing the Italian marble there, and Landry was nodding politely. Armand, Claude, and Giles stood directly in front of her and Tristan, making it hard for Everly to even fit down the hallway.

Her father turned and pointed at the monstrously large mirror that had been mounted in their home since they'd built the place. As far as Everly knew, her family had brought the overly ornate thing with them from France. She hadn't really cared that much for it. The gaudy thing seemed more like it belonged in the Palace of Versailles than in a simple American home.

"I brought this mirror with me from France," her father said. "It was made in the mid-fifteen hundreds. It is priceless, to my family at least."

Everly reached Landry's side just as he turned and glanced at the mirror, the silvered glass reflecting that familiar flash of gold in his eyes. But he looked away before she could truly appreciate it. She'd never seen his eyes reflect in a mirror before. The late afternoon sun coming through the kitchen windows must have bounced off the mirror and caught the color at just the right angle.

Figuring she'd better tell her dad they needed to be leaving so he wouldn't try to cajole them into staying for dinner, she turned back to him, but the words died on her tongue. Her father and all four of her brothers were suddenly looking at Landry like they'd rather shoot him where he stood than share a meal with him.

Her stomach clenched.

"Dad?" she prompted.

Her father's features hardened. "You were wrong to bring this man here, Everly. He needs to leave—now."

The house was so quiet Everly was sure she could hear a pin drop—if anyone was dumb enough to drop one. Landry threw a quick, confused glance in her direction, but she couldn't offer any explanation because she was just as baffled as he was. He hadn't done or said anything in between her father pointing out the antique mirror, and now, to make them dislike him. Why the sudden cold shoulder?

"Look Dad, I don't know what the issue is, but if you want us to leave, that's fine," she snapped. "We're out of here."

She grabbed Landry's hand and started for the front door, her face red with embarrassment as the rest of her family stared at them. How could her father humiliate her like this? She only thanked God Landry didn't complicate the situation by making a scene and demanding to know what her dad's problem was.

But then her brothers circled around, stepping between them and the front door. There was a hatred in their eyes she'd never seen before. This was like something out of a nightmare. Had everyone in her family completely lost their minds?

"Get out of the way," she demanded.

Armand lifted his chin. "Can't do that, Ev."

Everly clenched her jaw. They were spoiling for a fight.

"You aren't leaving with Officer Cooper, Everly," her father said sternly from behind her and Landry.

The angry fire that had been building in the pit of her stomach a moment ago became a raging inferno. She spun around to glare at her father. "I most certainly am leaving with him."

"No, you are not," her father said firmly. "He's not the man you think he is, and I don't want you seeing him again."

This was why she hated bringing guys to meet her father. It invariably turned to crap. No one was ever good enough in his eyes. He'd been rude to a lot of her boyfriends before, but this time he'd crossed the line.

"I'm twenty-eight years old, Dad," she shot back.

"You don't get to tell me who I can see anymore. You haven't been able to do that for a long time."

Her father didn't blink. "I most certainly can. You will not see him again. I forbid it."

She would have laughed if anything about the situation had been funny. What was this, the fifteenth century?

Everly wanted to scream. Either that or walk over and smack her dad for being so blasted archaic. She'd almost died in that bank robbery, and instead, stumbled across the most amazing man she'd ever met. Hell, a few hours ago she'd admitted to Megan and Jayna that she was in love with Landry. And now, her dad thought she would stop seeing him because he forbid it? That was never going to happen, and she needed to make that abundantly clear to him and everyone else in the room.

"I'll see whoever the hell I want, Dad. And if you don't like it, too damn bad."

Tightening her grip on Landry's hand, she turned and headed for the door again. For a moment, she thought she might have to shove her brothers out of the way, but they must have seen the determination on her face because they stepped aside. Apparently, they weren't willing to get into a fight in front of everyone. That didn't stop them from glaring daggers as she pushed past them.

Ignoring them, she yanked open the door and walked out on her family. Considering the way she felt right then, she wasn't sure she would ever walk back in.

"I'm sorry about that," she said to Landry when they got to his Jeep.

"It's okay."

"No, it's not," she insisted.

Landry sighed as he helped her into the seat. "What the hell happened in there anyway?"

She turned and looked back at the house. Tristan was standing in the doorway, staring at them, his face expressionless. He was the last person on earth she'd ever expect to turn on her.

"I have no idea," she told Landry softly.

He didn't say anything, but just walked around to the driver's side and climbed in beside her.

They didn't bother going out for dinner. Everly didn't know about Landry, but she was way too angry to sit in a crowded restaurant with a knife and fork in her hand. She probably would have stabbed someone. So instead, they stopped by a Chinese restaurant and grabbed some takeout, then went back to her apartment.

As they sat on the couch eating spicy chicken, brown rice, and fortune cookies, Landry let her vent about her overprotective father and controlling brothers. Just thinking about her dad imperiously declaring that he forbid her to ever see Landry again made her so mad she wanted to pick up something and break it.

Fortunately, Landry kept her away from the dishes, glasses, and other breakable items, and let her talk it out. He was also smart enough not to try to *fix* anything like most guys would. Probably because he knew she wasn't in the mood for that kind of advice. Or maybe, because he instinctively knew this wasn't something that could be fixed. Not this time. Her family had tried to control the people in her life since she was a child. But this time, they had gone too far. Instead, Landry nodded calmly as she alternated out loud between wanting to go back to her father's house to have it out with him and dragging Landry off to Vegas for a quickie wedding so she could irritate her father even more.

After she was done with her rant, Landry pulled her into his arms and kissed her until she forgot what it was that had her so crazy in the first place.

"Everly, sweetheart, they're family," he said when she sat back. "Are you really ready to turn your back on them?"

"Until they stop trying to control my life?" She nodded. "Yes. I'm serious. I'm done with them."

The impact of how harsh those words truly were hit her then. She might be furious with her family, but that didn't keep the tears from welling in her eyes.

Landry cupped her face in his big hand, gently wiping a tear from her cheek with his thumb. "Hey, it'll be okay. We'll figure out some way to get through this."

She wanted to believe him. "I hope so. But I need you to believe me when I say this. I want my family to like you, but if they don't, that's their problem, not ours. I'm not going to let them come between us. You're too important to me."

He looked at her for a long moment, then kissed her again. She melted against him, sighing as his tongue teased hers. It was crazy, but even after the night she'd had, it took only a few of his kisses to make her forget everything but the need to be with him.

Still kissing him, Everly swung her leg over his to straddle his lap. The move made her skirt slide up her thighs, and inside his jeans, his erection pressed against the silky material of her panties. Nice to know she wasn't the only one who was aroused.

His hands slid up her bare thighs, pushing her skirt

even higher and making her shiver. She undid the first few buttons of his shirt and was just nibbling her way down his scrumptious chest muscles when she heard a key in the door.

Everly wasn't so turned on that she didn't remember her roommate had a date tonight. Or that Mia sometimes invited Felix in afterward.

She quickly straightened her skirt as Landry reached for the buttons on his shirt. He had just enough time to get two done up before Mia walked in. Everly tried to look composed—well, as much as she could, straddling a hunky guy's lap as his hard-on pressed insistently against her suddenly wet panties.

She needn't have bothered. Not only was Mia alone, but she didn't even seem to notice them as she tossed her purse on the coffee table and flopped down in the chair adjacent to the couch. One look at her face told Everly that her roommate was pissed about something.

"What's wrong?" Everly asked, starting to climb off Landry's lap.

Mia motioned her back down. "Stay there. No reason for both of us to be sexually frustrated."

When Everly lifted a brow, Mia sighed.

"Felix and I got into it downstairs because he's upset that I'm going to the wedding tomorrow."

Mia having a disagreement with her boyfriend was as common as days that ended in *y*. "What, is he scared you're going to find some hot groomsman and dump him?"

Mia laughed. "He should be considering all the big, hunky cops who are going to be there. But no, he doesn't like me going to weddings because he thinks it might give me bad ideas. As in—maybe I'll want us to get married."

Everly tried to work through the logic of that, but couldn't. Then again, it was guy logic, which was basically an oxymoron.

"So I take it you and Felix are over?" she asked.

"Yup. That means my social calendar is suddenly wide open in time for tomorrow." She flipped her jet-black curls over her shoulder with a flick of her hand. "So Cooper, if you have any hunky, available friends coming to the wedding, feel free to point them out."

"I'll do that." His mouth quirked. "If I can figure out what constitutes hunky."

"Just find me a few about your size and build. I'll do the rest on my own." Sighing, Mia stood and grabbed her purse. "You guys don't have to stop what you were doing on my account. I'm going to bed so I can get my beauty rest. I need to look good if I'm going to be back on the market. Feel free to stay as late as you want, Cooper."

Landry chuckled. "I'd like to stay," he said to Everly as Mia went into her room and closed the door. "But I have to get up early tomorrow and let the caterer and florist into the compound so they can set up stuff for the reception."

Everly did a double take at that. "Gage and Mac are having their reception at the SWAT compound?"

He grinned. "Yeah. But trust me, you won't even recognize it as the same place. They're bringing tents and flowers and decorations. It's going to be amazing, I promise."

Everly would have to see that to believe it. The

SWAT compound didn't look like any wedding venue she'd ever seen.

She ran her hands down his chest, toying with a button on his shirt. "Just because you have to get up early, doesn't mean you have to leave yet." She gave him a flirty smile. "In fact, there's no reason you couldn't spend the night."

A hungry glint came into his eyes, and she felt her breath hitch. She got all warm and tingly when he looked at her that way. It was like he wanted to eat her up. Heat pooled between her thighs at the thought.

"It's tempting, Everly. God, you have no idea how much." He took a deep breath. "But I think it would be better if we didn't rush into anything tonight, not after everything that happened at your father's house."

She opened her mouth to tell him that was silly, that she was over it, but she knew in her heart he was right. She was still pissed off about the fight with her father. It probably wasn't a great idea to jump into bed with a guy for the first time right now.

"Who knew there could be a downside to dating a mature, intelligent guy?" she grumbled, flicking a button on his shirt with her finger.

"Tell me about it." He caught her hand and pressed his lips to her palm. "I'll be here at ten to pick you and Mia up for the wedding."

"We'll be waiting." Everly climbed off his lap and walked him to the door. "You're good, right? With what we talked about earlier, I mean."

Landry wrapped her in his arms, gently resting his forehead against hers. "I'm good. I don't want to come between you and your family, but I'm not going to let them come between us either. No way in hell."

Everly hadn't realized how tense she'd been until she felt the weight fall from her shoulders at his words. She'd been worried he'd think she wasn't worth all the drama.

She went up on her tiptoes to kiss him, trying to tell him without words how much he meant to her. And how much she appreciated his willingness to say the hell with her dad, her brothers, and all their stupid crap.

She could have stood in the doorway kissing him all night, but she knew she had to let him go home, if for no other reason than so he could hurry back to pick her up for the wedding.

She smiled. "I'll see you tomorrow."

"I'll be here." He leaned in and snagged another quick kiss. "Don't worry about your family, okay? They're not the ones I'm crazy about—you are."

Everly watched him go, returning his wave before he disappeared down the steps at the end of the hallway.

Going back into her apartment, she closed the door and leaned against it with a sigh. Her family might not like Landry, but she thought he was about as perfect as a man could be.

Chapter 10

LANDRY SHOWED UP AT EVERLY'S DOOR PROMPTLY at ten the next morning looking incredibly yummy in a dark suit and another splashy tie. Damn, he really should be a model. He gave her a kiss, then stepped back to take in her short floral-print dress, sky-high sandals, and streak of temporary light blue color she'd put in her long hair on one side to match her outfit.

"You look amazing," he said.

She smiled. "So do you."

And if they didn't have a wedding to attend, Everly would have dragged him off to her bedroom right then.

They got to the church an hour before the ceremony, which turned out to be a good thing since the pews were already filling up. There were hundreds of cops, firefighters, city officials, federal agents, and journalists from every paper and television station in Dallas, along with friends and family galore. Even so, Everly could easily identify the SWAT officers. They were all so damn big and muscular that they stood out in the crowd.

While the ceremony was beautiful, the reception at the SWAT compound was like something out of a fairy tale. Landry was right. Everly barely recognized the place. Several huge pavilion tents surrounded with tall ferns and palms, decorated with potted plants and fragrant flowers, had been set up to provide separate seating areas, as well as block the hot Texas sun. And right in the middle, next to the volleyball court, was a huge dance floor and DJ booth with twinkling lights and strobes. Everly could hardly wait to get Landry out there.

Off to the side, there were a dozen big grills manned by chefs. Everly had never thought of serving steak, burgers, hot dogs, and chicken at a wedding, but it smelled delicious.

She turned to Landry to find him smiling at her, the sun glinting off his brown eyes and making them the color of whiskey. She smiled back. This was going to be an amazing night. She could feel it.

He took her hand. "Come on. I'll introduce you to Mac and Gage."

Because there were so many guests at the wedding, the receiving line that usually took place right after the ceremony had been relocated to the reception. The line moved surprisingly quickly though.

"Gage, Mac, this is Everly Danu," Landry said when they finally stood before the newlyweds. "Everly, my boss, Gage Dixon, and his wife, Mackenzie."

Mac smiled warmly, pulling her in for a hug. "It's so great to finally meet you, Everly. You and Cooper make such a perfect couple. Like you were made for each other."

Blushing, Everly glanced at Landry to see if he'd overheard, but he seemed occupied with whatever Gage was saying—something about finally having one of his guys meet a woman "without having to worry about somebody ending up shot or sent to jail over it."

Everly turned back to Mac with a smile. "Would it be too soon in our relationship if I admit I've been thinking we're made for each other, too?"

Mac laughed. "Definitely not. When you meet the right guy, you know it."

Everly silently agreed.

Congratulating Mac on her marriage, Everly wandered over to join Mia, while Landry finished up with his boss. Mia was staring in slack-jawed appreciation at all the hot guys walking around, so Everly took pity on her and pointed out the ones she knew—Xander, Trevor, Alex, Remy, Brooks, and Becker.

"Alex, Remy, Trevor, and Brooks are all single, in case you're interested," she added with a grin.

"Oh, I'm interested, girlfriend." Mia let out an audible sigh of appreciation. "What the heck do they feed these SWAT cops—whole cows? They're huge!"

Everly laughed. She'd had the same thought that night of the bank robbery when she'd met Landry's teammates. It was hard to believe so many big, fit, hunky men could all work in the same place.

When Landry joined them, he introduced them to the rest of his SWAT teammates as well as quite a few officers in the Dallas Police Department. Everly had to work hard to keep from laughing as Mia's eyes shined a little more with each sexy SWAT hunk they talked to.

First was Zane Kendrick, another six-foot-four stud with just the slightest hint of an accent. British, Everly thought, though she couldn't imagine how a British guy had ended up on an American SWAT team in Dallas.

Then there was Max Lowry, a younger guy with the most amazing blue eyes that seriously sparkled with mischief the whole time they talked to him. She thought Mia was about to walk straight up and kiss him at one point, and Everly wouldn't have blamed her. The guy pulled off sexy and adorable in a way Everly had never seen before.

Landry introduced them to another SWAT officer named Connor Malone, who had a blond surfer look going on complete with tanned skin, hazel eyes, and a great smile. But unfortunately for Mia, Connor seemed completely captivated by one of Mac's bridesmaids. He looked up long enough to say hello, then went right back into the flirty conversation he was having with Mac's old college roommate.

After that, she, Landry, and Mia wandered over to get something to eat. Landry was piling way too much BBQ on her plate when Everly saw the cutest thing she'd ever seen in her life—a sweet pit bull mix wearing a collar that matched Mac's wedding colors walking around the grill area like she owned it.

"Who is that little cutie?" she asked Landry.

He turned to see who she was talking about and smiled at the dog—who was politely declining to eat a big piece of hamburger three kids were offering her. Everly watched in amazement as the beautiful dog accepted the same burger when Alex came over and held it out himself.

"That's Tuffie," Landry said. "We picked her up at a crime scene a few months ago. She'd been badly hurt, but Alex and our other medic, Trey Duncan, nursed her back to health. She hangs out with us at the compound during the day, then comes home with a different one of us each night."

Tuffie must have heard them talking about her because she turned and smiled at them.

Everly smiled back. "Oh my God, she's adorable!"

The compliment only made Tuffie wag her tail and grin even more.

Plates in hand, they walked into the main pavilion to grab a seat.

"How about over there?" Everly suggested, catching sight of Jayna and Megan at a table off to the side.

Landry nodded, and they made a beeline through the crowded tent. While he headed back to the bar area for drinks, Everly introduced Mia to her new friends.

"So, how did Becker and Zak like your new dresses?" she asked Jayna and Megan.

Jayna grinned. "Let's just say you were right, and there was drool involved."

"I knew it," Everly said.

"Well, we owe it all to you," Jayna said to Everly, then looked at Mia. "She convinced us to buy the dresses, even though they're way more glamorous than we usually wear. But she was totally right. They're perfect. I thought I was going to have to beat Eric off with a stick this morning so we wouldn't be late."

Everly laughed, then looked at Megan. "What did Zak think of your dress?"

Megan blushed. "I tried it on last night with the heels and everything so he could get the full effect. He…um…really liked the look. In fact, we didn't go to bed until nearly five this morning." Her color deepened. "I've been wearing this dress since ten o'clock last night."

Everly's mouth fell open. She couldn't imagine Megan being so naughty, but she supposed it was the shy ones you had to watch out for.

They were still laughing when Khaki joined them with a plate of barbecue and enough wine coolers for all of them.

"Cooper asked me to drop these off for you," she said as she set two bottles in front of Everly and Mia.

Everly looked around. "Where'd he go?"

Then she caught sight of him, along with the other SWAT guys and Zak, out on the sand-covered volleyball court with their jackets and shoes off. A moment later, Gage ran out to join them.

"Just remember you and your groomsmen rented those tuxes," she heard Mac shout above the rising tide of laughter. "If you mess them up, you're buying them."

Gage waved in acknowledgment, then served the ball. Everly laughed as the guys flew around the sand, smiling and goofing like teenagers as they played a volleyball game in the middle of the reception.

"They're like a bunch of kids, aren't they?" Khaki said. "They'd rather run around half-dressed playing a game in the sand than sit in their suits."

"Probably so," Everly agreed. "But they look damn good doing it."

In between watching the game, she, Mia, and the other women talked about shopping, hot guys and their silly games, dating, and weddings. It was like Everly had known Khaki, Jayna, and Megan as long as Mia. There was a bond developing between them unlike anything Everly had ever experienced. She couldn't believe how quickly all of Cooper's friends had made her feel welcome. Like she was family. She hadn't ever felt so accepted by people she'd just met.

Which was why it wasn't surprising Everly found

herself telling them about what had happened at her father's house.

"I feel like my father and brothers betrayed me," she said. The same anger she'd felt last night threatened to consume her again, and she forced it down. "I finally meet this great guy, and they hate him. My father seriously ordered me never to see Landry again. I'm not some fifteen-year-old dating a bad boy. Landry's a cop, for heaven's sake."

She would have said more, but fell silent as three cute guys came over and sat down at the table with them.

Jayna smiled. "This is Cooper's girlfriend, Everly Danu, and her friend Mia Barlowe. Ladies, our roommates— Joseph Garner, Chris Hughes, and Moe Jenkins."

Everly blinked. When Jayna and Mia said they lived with a group of friends, she hadn't expected them to be a group of guys. None of them were as big as Landry or the other SWAT guys, but they weren't wimpy either.

Moe's perfect brown skin and bulging muscles made him look like a model—or a superhero. Chris had a serious Captain America thing going on and the most charming Southern accent. And Joseph, the oldest of the three, had blue eyes that positively twinkled. Everly nudged Mia, knowing her friend had a thing for blond-haired, blue-eyed cuties, but her roommate had already locked gazes with him. A moment later, they got up and left, ostensibly to get something to drink, even though her wine cooler and his bottle of beer were almost full.

Everly laughed. "I think Mia just found a date for the rest of the day."

"Or longer," Jayna agreed.

Moe and Chris effortlessly joined in the conversation,

and Everly learned they not only lived in the same loft as Jayna and Megan, but they all worked together at a horse rescue and rehabilitation center outside of Dallas. She was about to ask how they'd all managed to get a job at the same place when Landry, Xander, and Zak joined them, their shoes and jackets back on, all traces of sand gone from their clothes.

"I hope you don't mind that I played a few games of volleyball," Landry said as he sat next to her. "Gage is going to be gone for two weeks on his honeymoon, so he won't have a chance to play for a while."

She smiled. "I don't mind at all. You looked good out there. I never knew watching you run around in a shirt and tie could be so much fun."

He leaned in and gave her a kiss. "You liked that, huh?"

"Yeah," she said softly. "It would have been even nicer if you'd had less clothes on, but I made do."

His eyes smoldered. "I'll have to see what I can do about that later."

The words sent a quiver of anticipation rushing through her. "Promises, promises."

As they sat there and chatted with everyone else, Landry rested his hand casually on her thigh. Just being close to him like this, her hip almost touching his, his lips occasionally grazing her neck and jawline as he kissed her, made her heart beat faster and her breathing ragged. She could barely focus on what anyone was saying much less speak.

Instead she focused on Landry and watched his lips move as he talked. Of course, that made her think of all the other things he could be doing with that sensuous mouth. Doing them in public would only get them arrested, so she'd have to be satisfied with fantasizing. While she was slowly getting turned on, she could have happily sat there with Landry all night and done nothing but talk. The sun had started to set, and now that the hot Dallas day was finally cooling off, Gage and Mac went out and had their first dance together as husband and wife. She and Landry stood with the rest of the guests to watch, then took to the floor when the newlyweds invited everyone to join them.

Everly couldn't remember dancing so much in years, or having so much fun. But she and Landry didn't sit down once over the next few hours. Everly caught sight of Connor and the bridesmaid he was crushing on dancing beside them before the couple disappeared. Then Jayna, Megan, and Khaki dragged their guys onto the floor, and a little while later, she saw Mia and Joseph.

Half a dozen songs later, Mia stopped by long enough to let her know she was going to take off with Joseph and his friends, and that Everly should feel free to bring Landry back to their apartment because she'd be out until very late.

Mia flashed her a smile. "In fact, I might not be back until morning."

While the dance floor was filled to capacity most of the night, it felt like she and Landry were the only two people out there. It didn't seem to matter to him whether the songs were fast or slow, and it sure didn't matter to her. She loved being in his arms.

"You dance very well," she murmured as one slow song faded into another.

This one was a soft country tune, so she and Landry weren't doing much more than rocking back and forth.

But he even did that well, and with a perfect, sensual rhythm that matched her thumping heart.

"I think that might have something to do with you." His mouth quirked. "I don't usually dance, but I like doing it with you."

She smiled. It was difficult to miss the big hard-on in his slacks that had been rubbing up against her tummy for the last hour. Still, she couldn't help teasing him. "Really? What's so special about dancing with me?"

He slipped his hands to her waist, letting his fingers spread wide along the top of her ass as he pulled her firmly against his erection. Then he leaned down until his mouth hovered right above her ear. "Dancing with you is special because it has me thinking about all the ways I'm going to make love to you later, starting with ripping off your dress and taking you up against the wall like an animal."

Everly's breath hitched. That admission, not to mention the way Landry's warm breath tickled her ear, made her pussy spasm. It was entirely possible she could come simply from wiggling her thighs together, especially if he kept talking dirty.

He stood straighter, moving her through a little two-step around the floor. "I didn't upset you, did I? Saying something like that out loud, I mean."

She responded to his leading touch instinctively, keeping her feet moving with his, even though her knees were weak.

"Not at all. I did ask, and you only said what you were thinking." She gently pressed her hip into his cock as they kept dancing, silently letting him know she was fully aware how excited he was. "And to be completely

honest, they're the same thoughts I've been having too.
Except in my mind, I'm the one ripping off your clothes
and pressing you against the wall, while I drop down to
my knees in front of you."

A growl slipped from Landry's throat. He did that a lot,
she noticed. It was unbelievably sexy. The lights strung
up around the dance floor caught that gold reflection in
his eyes. And that little sparkle was damn sexy, too.

She licked her lips, ready to ask in her very best
coy voice if he minded she'd said something like
that out loud, but she didn't get a chance because
Landry's mouth came down on hers, his tongue slipping between her lips and doing its own kind of slow
dance with her tongue.

Everly didn't realize they'd stopped dancing until
she found herself standing there in the middle of the
floor, both arms draped around Landry's strong neck
and holding on tight as her knees turned to Jell-O.
Landry had one hand in her hair, the other resting on
the curve of her ass. Everly didn't know how close they
were to having sex right there until she felt his fingers
wrap around hers, which were at the moment trying to
undo the buttons of his crisp, white dress shirt.

"Maybe we should take this somewhere else?" he
suggested in a husky voice.

She nodded, not trusting herself to speak.

Landry took her hand and led her toward the parking lot where his Jeep was parked. Thank God no one
stopped them to talk. If they had, Everly probably would
have done bodily harm to them. She was done waiting.
They'd been getting closer and closer to this moment
since the second they'd met. First Landry's friend Jim

had gotten between them, then her stupid, overprotective family. This was finally going to happen, and she wasn't letting anything interrupt them this time.

When they reached his Jeep, Landry opened her door, but before she could climb in, he pulled her into his arms and kissed her. In a heartbeat, his big, strong hand was on her bare leg, and he nudged her into the vehicle. Then with a groan, he dropped to his knee and pressed his mouth to the tender skin of her inner thigh, right above her knee.

She gasped in surprise. The part of her that vaguely remembered where they were told her that making out in the parking lot of the SWAT compound was crazy. But then she found herself helping, grabbing the hem of her skirt and yanking it higher, exposing her legs all the way to her panties. Tangling the fingers of her other hand in Landry's silky hair, she impatiently urged his mouth higher.

He let out another one of those growls she loved and complied, his warm mouth moving along her inner thigh. When he finally got to her pussy, she was going to scream for sure.

She didn't care. She was so hot for him that she was ready to let Landry have his way with her right there in the parking lot.

But then the sound of laughter from nearby intruded, and Landry jerked upright. Hands trembling, he carefully pulled down her dress and helped her back into a straight and upright position on the seat. A half-second later, a couple walked by. Landry waved at the police officer and the woman with him before turning back to Everly. He looked as excited as she felt.

"Let's get out of here before we do something crazy," he said.

"Sounds good." She grabbed the seat belt and clicked it into place. "But crazy is good too," she added when he climbed in beside her and started the engine. "So don't make me wait too long, or I'm going to attack you right there in the driver's seat."

———————

Everly still didn't know how they made it out of Landry's Jeep, across the parking lot, through the lobby, up the stairs, and into her apartment without anyone calling the cops. They had their hands all over each other the entire way. Once they got through the door and slammed it shut behind them, the clothes started flying.

She kicked off her high heels as Landry grabbed the hem of her dress and yanked it over her head. She could have pointed out that undoing the zipper first was usually a good idea before taking it off, but his method worked much faster—and was a whole lot sexier.

When she stood there in nothing but her bra and panties, Landry took a step back and gazed at her with appreciation. The look of pure, hungry lust on his face was the most empowering sensation she'd ever experienced. She felt like a complete and total goddess.

He reached around for her bra, but she batted his hands aside and went for the buttons on his shirt.

"It's not fair for you to wear so many clothes when I'm practically naked," she said.

Unfortunately, her hands were shaking so much she could barely find the buttons much less undo the little suckers. Thankfully, Landry came to the rescue. He shrugged out of his suit jacket and let it fall to the floor, then ripped open his shirt, scattering buttons everywhere. That was so sexy.

She yanked her bra off, showing him that she could be wild too. She would have stripped off her panties just as fast, but Landry came at her in a rush, trapping her between the door and his muscular chest. She reveled at the feel of her hard, tender nipples pressing into his warm skin, moaning as he dipped his mouth down to nibble her bare neck and shoulder. His teeth were sharp, but God, he knew how to use them, teasing her and nipping at her in a way she'd never felt before.

She was so dizzy from what he was doing, she could barely think straight, so when she heard a tearing noise, it took her a moment to realize what it was. Landry's hand came out from between them, and she caught a glimpse of her tattered panties before they went flying across the room. A smart part of her mind tried to remember where they ended up, so she could grab them before Mia came home. But then Landry's hand slipped between her legs, and she said the hell with her panties.

Landry nipped teasingly at her neck as his nimble fingers slid inside her. She was wetter than she'd ever been in her life. Lifting his head, he took a step back, keeping her pinned against the door with his gaze as he looked deep into her eyes and slowly fingered her pussy.

Everly wanted to wrap her arms around him and hold him close as he pleasured her, but she couldn't make herself move.

"Oh God," she moaned as he moved faster. She reached one hand up to grab his shoulder to steady herself, the other down to cover those beautiful fingers manipulating her pussy. "You're going to make me come so hard if you keep doing that."

His eyes flared gold in the light as he gave her a lazy grin. "I know. That's why I'm doing it."

Just when she thought she would pass out from how good it felt, he slipped his fingers out and found her clit, making perfect little circles. It took mere moments for the first wave of her orgasm to hit her like a speeding truck, and then all she could do was throw back her head and scream as her climax rushed through her.

Everly would have collapsed if he hadn't been holding her up, especially when he kept his fingers moving slowly over her clit, dragging another orgasm out of her on the heels of the first.

Landry waited until the last tremors faded before taking away his fingers. She thought for a moment he was going to say something, but instead, he pulled her naked body against him and kissed her hard. Her mouth responded of its own accord, kissing him back even though her mind was too scattered to do much beyond stand there and hold on to his shoulders for dear life.

When she could think clearly again—as clearly as she could after back-to-back orgasms—she realized that Landry was still wearing his pants. For some reason, that seemed terribly wrong, considering she was completely naked.

With a moan, she pushed Landry away. Then, while he was confused by why she'd done that, she got her hands on his belt and spun them around so he was the one with his back to the door now. That got his attention, especially when she put a hand in the center of his chest and held him there.

She lifted a brow. "Where do you think you're going?"

He chuckled, relaxing against the door. "Well, now that I have your dress off, I was going to see about moving forward with the next part of that fantasy we talked about earlier," he said. "You know—the part that involves me taking you up against the wall like an animal."

She liked the sound of that so much she almost relented and let him drive. But then she remembered how hard he'd made her come and decided she owed him a little something first.

"Don't worry," she murmured as she reached for his belt. "We'll get to that part of your fantasy soon enough. But for now, let's spend time on mine. You know—the one that involves me on my knees in front of you."

That stopped him from any further protest. In fact, he helped her yank open his belt and work his pants down his legs. Once she pushed them past his muscular thighs, she didn't even bother getting them off. She simply let them puddle around his ankles as she dropped to her knees and reached for the straining material of his underwear. Her mouth watering, she slipped her fingers into the waistband of his boxer briefs, pushing them down to slowly reveal his extremely large, extremely aroused shaft.

She got his underwear down to mid-thigh, then promptly forgot about it as all of him filled her view. She let out a sigh of pleasure. He had the most beautiful cock she'd ever seen in her life. It was long, thick, and heavy, and even as she watched, a little pearl of essence appeared at the tip.

She leaned forward to wrap her lips around the head, moaning at how good he tasted. Circling his shaft with her hand, she moved it up his length at the same time her mouth started down. When her hand and mouth met in the middle, she wasn't sure who moaned louder— her or Landry. Now that she had him in her mouth, she wanted to take him as deep as he could go. And she wasn't going to let him go until he exploded.

Everly had never shied away from going down on a guy. In fact, if it was the right guy, it could be downright fun. But with Landry it was so much more than that. She was actually getting turned on from feeling him pulse and throb against her tongue, not to mention hearing him growl and groan in pleasure.

She wiggled closer, her mouth and hand moving faster as she tried to make him come just as intensely as she had. When she felt him get even harder and throb even more, she knew he was about to climax. But before she could get him there, he slipped his hand in her hair and gently pulled her off his cock.

"Hey, you were getting close," she complained. "I was having fun."

Cooper chuckled. "I'm sure you were. But what I have in mind is even more fun."

Landry kicked off his shoes and pants then made quick work of his underwear before bending to pull something out of the back pocket of his slacks. She immediately recognized a condom packet.

As she watched him roll the condom down over his large cock, Everly was glad condoms came in different sizes. She had some in her bedroom, but they might be too small. She would need to get some bigger ones.

When he was done, he looked at her. "But you never said that your fantasy involved you making me come, just that you wanted to rip down my pants and drop to your knees in front of me. And that part, you most definitely did."

Tugging her to her feet, he grasped her waist and lifted her up in one smooth motion. She instinctively wrapped her legs around his waist and draped her arms around his neck as he turned and pressed her back against the door. She felt the head of his cock against her and knew exactly which part of his fantasy they were going to be working on next.

"Is this the part where you take me up against the wall like an animal?" she asked coyly.

He smiled as he moved his hands under her ass and lifted her so he could wedge the head of his cock against the entrance of her pussy. A moment later, he slid her down on his shaft, eliciting a long moan from her. But rather than sheathing himself completely inside, he stopped after only a few inches.

His smile turned devious. "Oh, this is most definitely the part where I take you up against a wall—this wall, as a matter of fact."

Everly squirmed around a little, trying to slip farther down on his length. But it was no use. He was so strong he could probably hold her here all night.

"Something tells me that with you doing the taking, this position might become my very favorite."

Landry's mouth quirked, as he let her slowly slide the rest of the way down his long, hard shaft. "Is that right?"

She opened her mouth to answer, but as she moved down on Landry's cock, all she could do was gasp—and then gasp some more as she kept going. Was it possible that he might be too big for her?

Finally, when she thought there was no way she could handle any more, she felt him slip all the way in. She tightened her legs around his waist and dropped her head to his heavily muscled chest, panting. It felt so good, she didn't want them to move, and yet she couldn't resist experimenting a little, squeezing and relaxing her inner muscles while Landry held her comfortably against the door.

"I definitely think this could be my favorite," she whispered. "This feels so good, and you're not even moving yet."

He flashed her a grin and pressed her harder against the door, burying himself deeper still. "Then I guess I should start moving so we can find out what you really think."

He didn't wait for her to respond. Instead, he held her steady against the door, then pulled back a little and shoved himself deep inside again. She gasped as her body tremored and her pussy spasmed. Everly tried to clench down tightly on Landry's cock, keeping him from slipping out again.

No matter how hard she squeezed, she couldn't prevent Landry from sliding out again, or from thrusting in. She gasped again, almost sobbing at how good it felt.

With each pump of his hips, Landry moved faster, slipping nearly all the way out, then plunging back in over and over. Everly tightened her arms around him, and when the trembling inside her threatened to make her scream, she bit down on Landry's strong, muscular shoulder.

That earned her a deep, sexy growl, and more powerful thrusts.

She came harder than she ever thought possible. Her climax was one long, continuous orgasm that hit her like waves on the beach, each wave cresting in time with his thrusting.

She screamed into Landry's shoulder, sure she'd pass out if this kept up any longer.

Then Landry groaned, his hands squeezing her ass cheeks hard as he thrust deep inside her and pinned her against the door. He held himself there, his mouth coming down on her neck, his teeth nipping her. She could feel heat flooding her pussy even through the condom.

She was practically dizzy as Landry repositioned her in his arms and carried her to the bedroom, his shaft still hard and ready inside her. She couldn't imagine she'd be able to make love to him again so soon.

But apparently, her pussy had other ideas because it was already quivering at the thought of what her man was going to do next.

Chapter 11

COOPER WORE ONLY HIS SUIT JACKET AND PANTS home the next morning because his dress shirt had been a ragged mess, along with Everly's equally shredded panties. Thank God no one saw him or that probably would have sparked a lot of questions he didn't have time for. He still had to shower and change before work. The guys wouldn't appreciate him coming in covered in Everly's exquisite feminine scent and reeking of sex. He, on the other hand, thought the combination was delectable as hell.

He showered off and got his uniform on as fast as he could, then went into the kitchen to grab something to eat. As usual, there wasn't a whole lot there, so he made do with a bag of Doritos and a can of Cheddar 'n Bacon Easy Cheese. Thank God that stuff couldn't go bad, or he'd never get his daily allowance of dairy.

He glanced at his watch as he shoved chips and cheese in his face. It was official—he was late. Damn, he hadn't been late for work in…well…ever.

At least he wouldn't be the only one showing up late. Werewolves couldn't get drunk or hung over, but they could sure party hard as hell. When he and Everly had left the reception last night, most of his pack had still been there, wooing all the single ladies at the wedding. Cooper doubted any of his teammates had gone home alone. Hell, some of them probably hadn't gone home at all.

He grinned as he sprayed cheese on another chip. Last night had been the best of his life hands down. While it had seemed over the last week like the fates were conspiring to keep him and Everly out of bed, last night proved the wait was definitely worth it.

Neither of them had slept a wink. Every time he thought they were both worn out and couldn't possibly go again, he'd catch a whiff of her arousal or see some naked body part. His cock would harden for her all over again.

The best part was Everly was as hungry for him as he was for her. Every time he found himself reaching for her, it was to find her reaching for him. There was nothing she wasn't up for, as long as it meant they were in each other's arms.

Besides up against the wall, they'd made love in her bed, on the floor, on her dresser, on the island in the kitchen, and on the vanity in the bathroom. He quickly learned the *where* didn't matter. Being inside her was all that was important. He would never get enough of her. He knew that now with a certainty.

Yeah, he had it bad for Everly. So bad that he wasn't sure how he'd found the strength to drag himself out of her bed and leave this morning. If the other guys who'd found their *Ones* felt like this all the time, how the hell did they get any work done? Never mind that. How the hell did they even come to work? All he could think about was being with Everly.

He sprayed a mountain of gooey processed cheese on top of a Dorito, capped it with another triangular piece of crispy goodness, and then shoved the whole thing in his mouth.

As he crunched his way through breakfast, a nagging

voice in the back of his head reminded him that everything with Everly wasn't all cupcakes and rainbows. There was her dumb-ass family to deal with. He still couldn't understand how her entire family had gone from nice and cordial to get-the-fuck-out in the span of thirty seconds.

What, did they think he had a few bodies buried in the backyard of his apartment complex? That would have made sense if they would have treated him shitty from the get-go. But they'd been relaxed and chill around him the first ten minutes he'd been there. Then her father had shown off that antique mirror, and it had all gone to shit—without explanation. Hell, he'd even checked to see if his fly had been open.

With the way her brothers had lined up to block the door, he'd thought for a minute that things were about to turn violent. Fortunately, Everly was too bullheaded and stubborn to let anybody tell her what to do. Her spunk was just one more thing he loved about her.

He froze with a red-orange chip halfway to his mouth, realizing what he'd just thought. Holy crud, he loved her. *I love her!*

Cooper said those three little words out loud a few times, arranging them into different phrases and enjoying the way they sounded as they bounced off the walls of his small apartment. It had been one thing to think she was *The One*, but to finally realize he was in love with her, well, that was another. He'd never felt anything like this for another woman, and it felt frigging epic.

He wondered how long he should wait to tell her— he didn't want to freak her out or anything, but everyone knew women liked to hear it—when he realized that at some point, he would have to say those other three little words.

I'm a werewolf.

Cooper couldn't remember a time when he didn't play it cool, even when he was getting shot at or blown up. But the thought of standing in front of Everly and telling her he was a werewolf—and possibly having her reject him—filled him with a dread like he'd never felt in his life.

Sharing their secrets hadn't been a big deal for Xander and Becker, but that was because the women they'd fallen for happened to be werewolves too. It had been damn near catastrophic for Gage. Mac had flipped out and almost revealed their secret to the whole world. Would Everly handle it any better?

He liked to believe she would. She seemed like the most stable and even-keeled woman he'd ever met, but he was scared. You never knew how someone would deal with a piece of information like that. If she lost it, it wouldn't be just his ass that was devastated. The Pack would be in trouble as well.

Maybe he shouldn't tell her at all. Did she really have to know everything about him for them to be happy?

Cooper gnawed on that for a good long while, along with some more chips. When he looked down, he realized he'd eaten the whole bag. Hell, the can of cheese was spewing air now.

Tossing them in the trash, he washed his hands then guzzled a bottle of orange soda. He'd just grabbed the keys to his Jeep when his cell rang. "I have sucky news and god-awful sucky news," Dennis said without preamble. "Which do you want first?"

"Good morning to you too, sunshine," Cooper said. "Most people start by saying, hey, how are you, but if you insist on being all about the job, let's start with the sucky and work our way up to the god-awful sucky part."

"Jed still isn't talking," Dennis said. "But his youngest brother Jackson is. Turns out he was at the house when our bomber showed up there. Unfortunately, he couldn't see the guy because Jed didn't want to spook the buyer."

"That does suck."

"Yeah, but while Jackson didn't see anything, he did eavesdrop on the conversation. And this is the part where things start to really suck."

"What do you mean?" Cooper asked.

"Jackson overheard a lot of words of a military flavor. He didn't know what half of them meant, but our profilers are sure the bomber is somebody with a military background, maybe even active duty."

"Shit."

Cooper sat on the edge of the couch. He felt like someone had just let all the air out of his happy balloon. The idea that there was a soldier out there responsible for setting off a bomb that killed a fellow cop was fucked up. It was like fate was forcing him to take sides between the two halves of his life—military and law enforcement. No matter what, it was going to end badly.

"Yeah, I thought you might say that." Dennis sighed. "You ready to hear more?"

"No, but we might as well get the rest of it out of the way," Cooper muttered. "I can't imagine how it could get any worse than it already is."

"It does," Dennis said. "At six o'clock this morning, there was another bombing at the industrial area. This one directly targeted the main lobby of a defense firm called Soldier Support Systems Incorporated—Triple S-I for short. No deaths, but the people who arrive at that hour got hurt pretty bad."

"*What?*" Cooper shot to his feet. "Why the hell didn't you lead with that?"

"Don't blame me—you said to start slow. Besides, I'm telling you now. That's why I called in the first place, to ask if you'd be willing to come over to the industrial area and poke around with me. We've already got a field team out there collecting evidence, but I wouldn't mind your take on the situation."

Cooper agreed, but not before cussing his friend out for being a complete shithead. Then he hung up and called Xander.

"I already heard," Xander said the moment he answered. "Get over there, if they want you, and let me know if you need any help. Try not to step on any FBI toes, huh? We're trying to rebuild some bridges here."

Cooper didn't have a problem finding the defense firm that had been hit by the bomber. It was surrounded by emergency vehicles—unmarked federal sedans and SUVs making up the majority. News vans and crime scene gawkers filled the nearby parking areas to over-flowing, and some enterprising guy with a food truck had shown up. The guy was going to make an ass load. The line already stretched a hundred feet.

Triple S-I looked more like an ordinary office build-ing than anything associated with the Department of Defense. Other than the big military icon on the side of the building, there was nothing that even suggested what kind of work the company did.

Cooper ducked under the crime scene tape and made his way to the front entrance. The building used to have a row of big picture windows and glass doors along the front, but the bomb had blown out the glass and most of the wall.

As he made his way through the debris to get inside, he breathed in the overwhelming odor of hydrocarbons that always hung in the air after an explosion. Back in the day—before he'd been blown to shit in Iraq—he used to love the smell. Now it only reminded him of the pain that came from being temporarily airborne.

Glass was scattered across the tile-covered lobby. It was everywhere—stuck in the walls, the furniture, even the ceiling. He winced at all the blood. There were spatters and puddles here, there, and everywhere. The only saving grace was that the bomb had gone off before most of the employees had come to work. If it had been later, a lot of people would have gotten killed. It probably wasn't a coincidence that the garage bomb had been set to go off around the same time. No doubt Dennis would be working that angle.

Since the device had blown into the lobby instead of all over the grass and pavement outside, the FBI had chosen to set up a temporary collection area in a conference room off to the side of the bomb scene. They'd move everything to the forensic labs later, but right now, they were hoping to get lucky and stumble over something that would wrap this up fast and tight.

Even though he was in uniform, Cooper flashed his badge as he walked into the conference room. The female agent glanced at it, then handed him a pair of gloves.

Every inch of the big table in the center of the room was covered with metal and plastic fragments. Dennis wasn't there, but there were three other feds looking at evidence with magnifying glasses and writing down notes. They glanced up as he snapped the gloves on and walked over to the first table, but didn't say anything.

He surveyed the twisted bits of metal, melted hunks of plastics, and random pieces of glass and wood from the lobby. He immediately found the key fob circuit board rigged to initiate the device. Beside it was a rudimentary, delay arming circuit. He picked it up with a frown. It looked like something a twelve-year-old would make from an old Radio Shack hobby kit.

While everything indicated this bomb had been made by the same guy, the design was poor and the work rushed. The first device had probably taken him months to make. This one had taken hours.

Cooper set down the arming circuit and slowly moved around the table. The fed there gave him a look that said he'd checked and hadn't found anything, so Cooper didn't have to. Cooper ignored him and looked anyway.

He frowned as something caught his attention. It was a bent piece of metal from a dog tag. He picked it up to study it more closely with a magnifying glass. There were a few letters stamped into it. Twisted, smeared, and impossible to read, but letters nonetheless.

"Hey, you find something?"

Gut twisting, Cooper lifted his head to see Dennis coming into the room, an expectant look on his face.

"What?" he asked, stalling.

"Did you find anything? You were standing there with a really serious look on your face, so I thought you'd made a big discovery."

Cooper opened his mouth to tell Dennis about the dog tag, but nothing came out. He gave himself a mental shake and tried again. If the FBI could recreate the name or social security number on that tag, it would almost certainly lead them directly to the bomber, he was sure of it. Then why were his werewolf instincts shouting at him to keep his damn mouth shut?

He knew it was crazy, but he'd spent the past four years of his life trusting those instincts, and they'd never let him down before. So he pushed down the human side of himself that was telling him he was being a dumb-ass and gave Dennis a shake of the head.

He set the piece of dog tag on the table. "Nothing worthwhile beyond the fact that it's the same bomber and that he made this one in a big rush."

Dennis nodded. "Pretty much the same conclusion my guys are coming up with. Didn't hurt to have you take a look anyway. I'm going to talk to Arnold Braun, Triple S-I's owner and CEO, and see what he has to say. Want to join me?"

Cooper stripped off his gloves and followed him out of the room.

Dennis led the way back through the lobby and into an area filled with a maze of cubicles, until they reached a big corner office in the back of the building. The gray-haired man seated at the fancy walnut desk was on the phone when they walked in. Thanks to his keen were-wolf hearing, Cooper could hear the person on the other end of the line giving Triple S-I's CEO a rundown of the

injuries sustained by the employees who'd already been
taken to the hospital.

When he was done, Arnold Braun dropped the phone
back in its cradle with a heavy sigh. Dennis introduced
himself, then Cooper. While Braun answered their
questions, he was too upset to be much help. Cooper
wouldn't have been surprised if the man broke down
and started crying.

"Why would someone attack my company like
this?" he asked. "We're not a weapons developer. We
don't even have any security-related contracts. We
handle minor support contracts for our deployed forces,
like food, supplies, construction, and administration
services. Nothing controversial. We feed and shelter
people, do the little things so the soldiers can focus on
their work. Why would someone bomb us and hurt so
many innocent people?"

Dennis didn't have the answer to that question, and
neither did Cooper.

"Did you or your employees get any emails or threats
from service members or people who recently got out of
the military?" Dennis asked.

Braun shook his head. "No. I go out of my way to hire
as many former military men and women as possible. I
like to do whatever I can to help those who've served."

Dennis nodded. "Can I get a list of the employees
who typically arrive early for work, and maybe arrange
to meet with the senior ones?"

Cooper knew exactly where Dennis was going with
that. If there was someone pissed at an employee, it was
most likely going to be a supervisor. Dennis might be
completely wrong, of course, but it was a good place to

start, especially if one of those supervisors turned out to be on the list of people who'd been in the parking garage around the time of the first bombing.

"I'll have my assistant get it for you," Braun said. "As far as meeting my senior people who come in early, I'll arrange that, but it might take a little time. Most of them are at the hospital right now, either getting their own injuries tended to or helping others who were hurt."

The meeting with Braun ended shortly after that, and Cooper spent the rest of the day at the crime scene helping collect evidence and move it to the FBI lab facilities. Before he left for the day, he got Dennis to promise he'd call once the FBI had the meeting set up with the senior members of Triple S-I. He wanted to be in on that.

As he pulled out of the parking lot and onto the main road, he tried to understand for about the hundredth time that day why he'd lied to one of his best friends about something as important as that dog tag. He didn't like the idea that he was protecting a killer—even if it was a fellow soldier—no matter what his inner werewolf demanded he do. Hopefully, Dennis and his forensic team had already found that scrap of dog tag and were tracking it back to the person responsible for the bombings even now. That didn't do much to calm the confusing twist of emotions roiling through his gut, but it was something.

Cooper was so distracted with those thoughts that he didn't realize he was on his way to Everly's until he pulled into the parking lot of her apartment complex. His mouth curved. His inner werewolf might be wrong about concealing evidence, but it was right on target when it came to Everly. She had a way of making him forget everything but her, and right now, he could use a little work-related amnesia.

Cooper was still thinking about Everly as he strode up the sidewalk. As sweet as the distraction was, it was why he didn't notice the tingle in his senses that normally alerted him something was wrong. By the time he heard rapidly approaching footsteps, the attackers were already on him.

He spun around just in time to see Armand Danu swinging a baseball bat at his head. *What the hell?*

Cooper blocked the bat with his left forearm, but the bone cracked under the blow. It hurt like a son-of-a-bitch, but he couldn't think too much about the pain because Giles, Claude, and Tristan converged on him too, swinging and bashing with three more baseball bats, like they were trying to kill him.

He kept one arm up to protect his head and face, but that left his back and ribs exposed, and they weren't shy about taking advantage of his vulnerability. His first instinct was to draw the Sig .40 at his belt, but he clamped down on that thought. He didn't know what the fuck was going on here, but he couldn't just shoot Everly's brothers.

A bat came down hard across his back, cracking ribs and hurting like hell. The pain brought on an involuntary shift, and Cooper felt his fangs and claws start to extend. He retracted them with a snarl. The werewolf inside him might want to rip the four men apart, but he didn't. But just because he didn't want to kill them didn't mean he was going to stand here and let them beat him to a pulp.

He caught the bat that Giles was swinging in a pretty

good imitation of Babe Ruth. The business end smacked hard into his palm, cracking a few bones and tearing some ligaments. The stab of pain made him grit his teeth, but he held on and jerked the weapon away from Giles, then reached out and grabbed him by the arm, tossing him into the shrubs a couple yards away. He could have easily smashed the jackass into the nearby building, but he knew Everly would be upset with him if he did—even if these shits deserved worse than that.

He turned to see Armand coming at him, ready to tee off. Cooper stepped into the man's swing, lifting his left arm and letting his upper ribs and lat muscles absorb the brunt of the impact. It still fucking hurt like hell, but without the added force of a full-arm extension behind it, the blow didn't do a lot of damage.

Cooper clamped his left arm down, trapping the bat beneath it, striking out with the heel of his other hand at the same time. Armand went flying back with the force of the blow, air whooshing out of his lungs.

Cooper tossed Armand's weapon aside just as Tristan came in swinging at his head like a madman. *Shit.* Not even a werewolf would survive an impact that hard.

His hold on his inner wolf slipped a bit, and even though he fought it, Cooper couldn't stop the low growl that erupted from his throat. At the same time, the muscles of his shoulders and arms began to twist and flex. If he didn't end this shit soon, his body might shift solely in order to protect itself.

While Tristan's swing was aggressive, it was also out of control. Cooper easily ducked under it and came up with his hand around the youngest brother's throat. Claude tried to dive at him, but Cooper lashed out with a roundhouse kick to the man's chest, sending him to the ground.

For the first time since the assault had started, he was blessedly clear of his attackers.

Cooper tightened his grip on Tristan's throat, lifting him two feet off the ground and giving him a shake. "What the fuck is wrong with you people? Are you seriously trying to get yourself killed?"

He didn't expect Tristan to answer since he was gasping for air at the moment, but before he could put Everly's youngest brother back on the ground, he sensed movement off his right shoulder. He looked up, expecting more trouble—and found it. Armand and Claude stood there holding two large caliber pistols pointed right at his head.

"Let him go, or I'll shoot you where you stand," Armand ordered.

Cooper ground his jaw. He dropped Tristan none too gently, feeling a perverse sense of pleasure when the man stumbled backward and fell on his ass. Then he turned to face Armand and Claude. He let his legs start to shift, feeling the power trembling through him as he prepared to strike. This was no longer a game—if it ever had been one. A head shot would kill a werewolf. Period. The end. He wasn't going to let that happen.

He moved a bit to the left, putting Armand between him and Claude. He didn't want to kill Everly's two oldest brothers, but if they pulled the trigger, he'd be forced to move. He liked his odds of ducking Armand's first shot. And before he could get off a second, Cooper would be on him. Claude would be forced to hesitate for a fraction of a second or risk hitting Armand. That would give Cooper all the time he needed to reach him too.

He waited, listening for the sound to start everything and end it—for some of them. But the sound never came. The two men just stood there, their weapons pointed at Cooper. Apparently, they weren't ready to kill him in cold blood. So, what exactly were they doing?

"Seriously, guns?" he finally asked as Tristan slowly climbed to his feet. "Don't you think you're carrying this overprotective brother thing a little far?"

"This was a warning. Stay away from our sister," Armand said, as if Cooper hadn't spoken. "Or the next time we come back, we'll kill you."

Cooper stared at Everly's oldest brother, his inner wolf telling him the man was speaking the truth. Even so, he had the craziest urge to tell Armand he could have just called him with the threat. Or texted. This was the twenty-first century, after all.

Wisely, he let that urge pass without comment.

A moment later, the four brothers turned as one and walked away. Cooper watched them go, wondering what the hell had just happened. Was this some kind of French thing he didn't understand?

The Four Brothers Stupid drove out of the parking lot in one of Armand's minivans. The irony of four toughs escaping justice in a frigging minivan was not lost on Cooper. He chuckled, which only reminded him he'd just been beaten by four grown men with baseball bats. He hurt all over. He'd heal, but they'd busted up a few bones and bruised up a lot of real estate.

That was about the time he realized he was bleeding all over the sidewalk. *Shit*. So much for spending the night with Everly now. He'd better bail and call her, saying he had to work late. He'd be more presentable by tomorrow. That would also give him time to come up with a convincing explanation about any scratches and bruises that might remain. He sure as hell didn't want Everly finding out he'd gotten in a fight with her brothers. She'd blow a gasket for sure.

Cooper was about to head to his Jeep when Everly walked up onto the sidewalk from the parking lot, her arms full with grocery bags.

"Was that my brothers in Armand's minivan?"

She looked over her shoulder, standing on her toes to get a better look at the road exiting the apartment complex. When she turned back around, she was close enough to see his face and reacted exactly how he expected—she freaked.

"Oh my God!" She dropped her bags where she stood and ran over to him. "What happened?"

Cooper gave her a smile. Or tried to, anyway. His jaw didn't feel like it was working quite right. "It's nothing," he said.

Her eyes widened. "Nothing?" She looked over her shoulder at the parking lot again, then back at him. "Oh, hell no! My brothers did this, didn't they?"

"It was a misunderstanding—" he began, but she cut him off.

"Misunderstanding! Landry, they beat you up!" She lifted a gentle hand to his face, her eyes bright with fury. Muttering something that sounded like, "I'm going to kill my brothers," she dug her cell phone out of her purse. "I'm calling the cops. I'll have those idiots arrested and put in jail until they're a hundred."

Cooper gently took the phone away from her and slipped it back in her bag. Then he took her hands in his and held onto them tightly.

"You can't call the police on your brothers," he said. "I'm a cop, and they came at me with weapons. If you have them arrested, they'll go to jail for a long time. No joke, Everly. They'd be looking at decades in prison."

She opened her mouth then closed it. Finally, she nodded. "Okay, I get that. And even though I'm so mad right now I want to scream, I really don't want my brothers in jail."

"Exactly." He brushed her hair back from her face. "I'm going to head home so I can fix myself up. I'll call you later, okay?"

Everly's eyes widened. "Hell no, that's not okay. There's no way I'm going to let you go home and take care of yourself. You'd probably do something stupid and medieval like trying to cauterize your cuts with a hot butter knife. We're going up to my apartment where I can take care of you."

Cooper would have preferred to deal with his injuries on his own. The last thing he needed was for Everly to notice that his cuts and scrapes had magically closed by the time they reached the second floor. But what could he say? She was so damn cute when she was feisty.

"Okay," he agreed. "I'll come upstairs with you on one condition."

She gave him a sharp look. "What's that?"

He motioned over his shoulder. "We go back and pick up your groceries first. I saw a bag of Doritos in there."

Chapter 12

"MIA ISN'T HOME?" LANDRY ASKED. HE WAS SEATED at the kitchen table while Everly collected what little she had in the way of first-aid supplies from the bathroom. Well, at least she had some antiseptic spray. Unfortunately, Everly didn't have any medical gauze, but hoped her makeup remover pads would work in their place.

She had nearly lost her mind when she saw Landry standing there covered in blood. She'd just been daydreaming about how much fun they'd had the day before, laughing and dancing at the wedding, then making love all night. When she'd seen all the blood, every romantic image in her head evaporated in a wave of fear and anger.

"Mia went out with Joseph again. Something about going dancing with the Scooby Gang," she murmured distractedly as she walked into the kitchen and piled her stuff on the table.

She couldn't help looking at the police belt he'd hung over the back of the chair. The holstered gun seemed so much bigger now that he wasn't wearing it. Her idiot brothers could have gotten shot attacking him.

Landry smiled. "Mia and Joseph really seem to have hit it off. Maybe we should find out where they went and join them."

Everly gave him her best *are you kidding me?* frown.

He still had dried blood crusting on a cut along his jaw-line. The outside of his left arm was covered in more blood from elbow to wrist, and a rip across the back of his SWAT T-shirt told her he'd been hit there too. And he was suggesting they go out clubbing. She should have learned from growing up with four brothers that men were stupid.

"Why haven't you taken off your shirt like I asked?"

He shrugged, wincing a bit as he did. "No need to do that. Like I said, it's just the scratches you see."

She pinned him with her gaze until he relented with a sigh.

"Fine. But I'm sure it looks worse than it is."

When he yanked the dark blue shirt over his head, it took everything Everly had to not cringe in horror. "I'm going to find all four of my brothers as soon as I get a chance and remove their balls with a pair of rusty scissors." She swore as she cataloged his injuries. "I can't believe they did this to you."

She'd known Landry hadn't wanted to take his shirt off because he was trying to hide the damage underneath. She wasn't stupid. She'd seen those baseball bats lying outside. She knew what that meant. But she never imagined her brothers could do something like this. They'd always been protective of her since her mother had died, but this was insane.

Landry had big purple-red bruises and welts already coming up along his rib cage on the left side, several places on his back, and even on his right shoulder. Two of the ones across his back were so bad they were bleeding. Well, they had been bleeding, but they weren't now. She couldn't imagine how hard her brothers had hit him to do this.

"Maybe we'd better take you to the hospital," she said. "I think this is way beyond the antiseptic spray and Band-Aid stage."

Landry laughed as he craned his head around, looking at himself. "Nah. I've beaten myself up worse playing volleyball. Just clean me up, and I'll be fine. Trust me."

She doubted that. But she'd learned a long time ago that you can't simply talk logic into a man. It was a foreign language. So she grabbed some paper towels, soaked them in the sink, and then gently washed the blood off his left arm.

She'd known Landry was tough, but she was amazed by how he could sit there and chat about Mia and Joseph the whole time she worked. It had to hurt.

After she got most of the blood off, she was relieved to see the impact point on the outside of his forearm wasn't nearly as bad as she'd originally thought. With all the blood, she was sure there'd be a nasty gash big enough to park a small car in. But there was just a thin, shallow line, no more than an eighth of an inch deep. It was hard to believe it had bled so much.

Still, it was blood. Worse, it was Landry's blood. And that made her queasy. So as she moved to the other cuts and bruises, applying antiseptic as she went, she distracted herself by asking him about her brothers' attack and what the hell they were going to do about it.

"I guess all we can do right now is avoid them and hope they realize I'm not going to hurt you," he said. "And we're not splitting up just because they want us to."

Everly liked the sound of that. She decided then

and there that if her brothers came at Landry again, she'd have them arrested—if they lived through the encounter. She glanced at the gun holster.

She wiped dried blood from the long red welt that lay directly across his spine. Even though he didn't seem phased by her ministrations in the least, she still worked carefully, applying just enough pressure to get the blood off and using the fingers of her free hand to protect those parts of the welt she hadn't reached yet, so she wouldn't tug on the wound. "You had a gun. Why didn't you draw it on them?"

Landry didn't answer right away. When he finally spoke, his voice was extremely soft. "Everly, a gun isn't a prop. If you pull a weapon on someone, it's with the intent to shoot. And I was never going to shoot your brothers."

She nodded, realizing that had been a foolish question. And as furious as she was with her brothers, she didn't want them to get hurt. Well, maybe have their balls kicked in, but not shot.

Everly finished up his back and moved in front of him to wash off the blood along his jawline. She couldn't get the chair close enough though. And when she tried to stand and lean over to do it, Landry chuckled.

"Here, let me help you," he said, putting his hand on her waist and tugging her closer until she was straddling his lap.

She had to lift up the hem of her flowy dress to make it work, but yup—sitting like this definitely made tending to the cut on his jaw much easier. Of course, sitting on him like this was also a bit distracting. The position was more than a little sexual, especially with her dress hiked up the way it was. For a moment, she wondered if Landry had that in mind when he pulled her onto his lap, but that was just silly. There was no way Landry could be in the mood, not after getting beaten with baseball bats. She stuffed her overactive imagination back in its box and did her best to pay attention to her patient.

She tilted his face to the side and gently patted the dried blood from his jawline. Like the other cuts she'd cleaned, this one wasn't nearly as bad as she'd thought. It was probably still going to leave a scar, but at least it wouldn't need stitches.

Everly was just running her pad down Landry's neck to get a few spots she'd missed earlier when she noticed that his eyes had taken on a languid, relaxed look. If she didn't know better, she'd think he was enjoying what she was doing. But then another, more alarming thought struck her. What if he was going into shock or something?

She lifted his chin to look into his eyes. "Hey, are you okay?"

He smiled, his eyes going from languid and relaxed to smoldering in the space of a heartbeat. "I'm very okay. But I think you've gotten me about as clean as you're ever going to."

Reaching out, he took the pink-tinged makeup pad out of her hand and set it on the table. Then he grasped her waist and pulled her higher on his lap. The move spread her legs open a little wider, causing her dress to ride up even more. Something hard poked her through her panties, and she glanced down to see a very obvious bulge in his uniform pants.

She lifted up a little. "Hey! You shouldn't be getting

excited. You just got beat up by four guys swinging baseball bats. You should be resting."

His laugh was husky as he tugged her back down on his lap, putting her panty-covered pussy in firm and interesting contact with that bulge of his. She wiggled around, trying to get into a more comfortable position, preferably one that didn't put so much pleasurable pressure on her clit.

"You should have thought about that before you climbed on my lap and started wiggling around," he pointed out with that sexy grin of his.

"I didn't climb on your lap. You pulled me," she said. "And I am not wiggling."

He raised an eyebrow. That's when she realized she was wiggling. Well, gyrating was a better word for it. But that wasn't her fault.

She forced herself to stop then stabbed him with a glare. "Landry, I'm serious. I don't want to hurt you."

He lifted a hand and gently cupped her face. "Everly, you could never hurt me."

She was just grasping the deeper meanings behind those few simple words when his finger dipped under her chin and tugged her forward. Then his mouth was on hers. He kissed her softly at first, then with more passion. It quickly became obvious that Landry was just fine—and very aroused.

Everly tried to kiss him back as gently as she could. She was serious about not wanting to hurt him. But once Landry's tongue slipped inside her mouth and started playing Twister with hers, that willpower soon turned to mush. She buried the fingers of both hands in his hair and yanked him forward, returning his kiss with an almost violent desire. She nipped at his lips then sucked on his tongue, moaning as she let herself go wild. She didn't know what it was about Landry's kisses that drove her so crazy, but it was like the taste of his tongue was an aphrodisiac. One little kiss, and she was ready to rip off his clothes.

She was pleased to see that she seemed to have the same effect on him. He groaned deep in his chest until he let out that growl she found incredibly sexy. Then he clamped his hands firmly around her hips and rocked her in a slow, sexual rhythm on his hard-on.

Good thing she'd worn a dress today. With nothing between her clit and that bulge in his pants but some ultrathin cotton, Landry would be able to make her come without them ever taking off their clothes. The pressure on that most sensitive spot was absolutely perfect.

As the tingling between her legs grew, she moved her hips faster in quick, little circles that soon had her breathing harder and harder.

Suddenly light-headed, she dragged her mouth away from his to suck in a breath. That was when she realized that he'd slid her dress all the way up to her hips. He held it bunched there, and now that they weren't kissing, he could see exactly what she was doing down there.

She almost blushed at how wanton she looked grinding on him like this. But she didn't, because she felt completely comfortable being as naughty as she wanted.

Everly clutched his shoulders, her breath coming in quick pants as her orgasm approached. She was going to come just from grinding on him. It was like they were crazy teenagers in the back of a car at a drive-in movie theater.

The circles she made with her hips got smaller and tighter, becoming more twitches than grinds as she rounded the corner of the last turn and raced for the finish line.

She looked up and saw Landry gazing down at her with those beautiful, light-reflecting eyes of his. She was going to come as he watched her playing with herself. This had to be the hottest thing she'd ever done.

She was seconds from exploding when Landry stopped her.

Everly gasped as his grip tightened on her hips. His hands were so damn big and strong that she couldn't move an inch. He held her pressed against him so that the tingle in her clit kept going and going, but he refused to let her wiggle enough to finish. The sensation built and built until she thought she would scream. Then it built some more—and she did scream. Well, not really a scream, but definitely a whine of frustration.

That's when Landry took pity on her and yanked her quivering pussy down hard on his uniform-covered erection.

Bam! That was all it took. She was so close to the edge that she fell over with only that single nudge.

"Oh God, I'm coming." She moaned as she shook and trembled through one long, enormously intense orgasm.

She clamped her hands on his shoulders and held on tight, lifting her feet completely off the floor so her pussy was pressed as hard as possible against him. Then she groaned, screamed, and gyrated on his lap.

Luckily, Cooper kept his hands on her hips, or she probably would have fallen off. When the climax finally slowed to a body-shaking shiver, she fell forward and collapsed against his chest. She'd never come that hard—even with the aid of modern technology. And she still had all her clothes on. How crazy was that?

Everly closed her eyes, reveling in the aftershocks of her orgasm. Without a doubt, Landry Cooper had ruined her for every other man—and sex toy—on the planet. Not that there were ever going to be any more of either. She had no need of anyone or anything but Landry now.

She could have fallen asleep right there on Landry's big muscular chest without any trouble. But he scooped her up in his arms and got to his feet, holding her close. She rested her head against his shoulder as he carried her to her room. Between last night and tonight, she'd had more orgasms in the past twenty-four hours than she'd had in years. She couldn't wait to return the favor.

Landry lowered her to the floor beside the bed and pulled her dress over her head. Her bra disappeared just as swiftly. She had to admit she was seriously impressed with how good he was at getting her clothes off. Then he sat her down on the edge of the bed and urged her onto her back so he could reach down and carefully slid her wet panties over her hips and down her thighs.

The sensation of her warm, wet panties sliding down her legs was a serious turn-on. But not nearly as much as the sudden realization that she was once again completely naked in front of Landry.

This is getting to be a habit, she mused as he gazed down at her with blatant, hungry heat in his eyes.

. "Do you just like to see me naked in front of you all the time, or what?" she asked with a laugh.

"That's a rhetorical question, right?" he asked with a chuckle as he nudged her back on the bed a little more.

Everly thought at first he'd scooted her over so he could climb in. But then he spread her legs nice and wide and plunked himself down on his stomach right between them. She knew what he was going to do even as he pressed a warm, soft kiss to the inside of her thigh mere inches above her clit. Her whole body hummed in anticipation at what was coming. Oh yeah, Landry could get to her like no one she'd ever been with.

Thank God he didn't tease her—he'd done enough of that out in the kitchen. Instead, he trailed his mouth gently along the inside of her thigh until his lips hovered above her clit. Then he flicked out his tongue and swirled a little circle around that most sensitive part of her anatomy. She'd been a little worried she might be oversensitive from her most recent orgasm, but that definitely wasn't the case.

"Mmm," she breathed. "That feels so good."

He chuckled as much as he could, considering his mouth was kind of busy. Then he stopped and looked at her with a smile. "And I'm just getting started."

He dropped his head again, and this time his whole mouth closed over her clit, his tongue slowly lapping back and forth over her. While he did that, he slipped one long finger inside her. Not thrusting, but just teasing and tracing the inside of her pussy. Like he'd secretly found a map of her most sensitive spots. Hell, some of them she hadn't even known about, not until he started caressing them.

He worked her slowly, letting the pleasure grow a little at a time. Mostly, he kept his tongue focused on her clit, but every once in a while, he moved lower, letting it dip inside her, both to pleasure her there, and to keep her from exploding too quickly.

Everly lay back on her elbows and enjoyed the view as Landry went down on her with calm, confident laps of his tongue. She'd thought he was a good kisser, but at this he was a master.

Part of her wanted to climax this way with his mouth buried between her legs. But she'd already had one incredible orgasm out in the kitchen. Now, it was Landry's turn. Besides, she'd been dreaming about having him inside of her all day, and she didn't want to wait any longer.

She reached down and grabbed his hair, giving a little tug. When he looked up, she made a little come-hither motion with her finger. "Get up here. Now."

He must have realized she wasn't messing around, because he gave her pussy one more lick, then sat back on his heels. "Can I take off the rest of my clothes first, or would you prefer I come up there just as I am?"

She laughed, thumping him lightly on the shoulder with her foot as she scooted farther back on the bed to make more room for him. "You'd better get naked unless you want me ripping those pants off you myself."

He got to his feet, mouth quirking. "I'd better do it. You have some pretty long fingernails. They might hurt me."

Everly doubted that.

She watched as Landry unlaced his big SWAT boots and took them off. She hadn't realized until now that he had another smaller handgun attached to the inside top of the left boot. But she forgot all about it as he slowly unbuckled his belt and started working his pants off. Even though she'd seen him completely naked the other night, she still got a thrill seeing the big reveal.

He was built absolutely everywhere—and she did mean *everywhere*.

He moved to her nightstand and found one of the condoms there. She was going to have to remember to get a bigger box the next time she went shopping. They were going through them really fast.

As Landry climbed in bed, she spread her legs wide, giving him all the encouragement he needed to slide between them. He carefully placed his arms on either side of her body, moving slowly as if he was afraid he'd hurt her. She might be a lot smaller than he was, but he was the one all battered and beat up. She eyed the big bruise on the left side of his rib cage. Surprisingly, it was already looking less purple than it had a few minutes ago. But it still looked like it was painful.

"You sure this isn't going to hurt you?" she asked.

Landry settled comfortably between her thighs, the head of his very thick cock teasing the opening of her pussy. He lifted a brow, obviously amused at the question.

"I'm pretty sure pain is going to be the last thing on my mind," he said. "In case you didn't know it, most people tend to think of sex as kind of pleasurable."

She laughed, about to remind him to go slowly and not overdo it, but then he slowly slid his hard shaft into her, and all rational thought disappeared.

She moaned his name, her legs wrapping around his waist, pulling him in even more. She couldn't imagine how she could take all of him as it was, but it felt so good trying.

Landry's mouth came down on hers at the same time he slowly pumped in and out. She tried to squeeze him tighter with her legs so he'd stay buried deep inside her, but he paid no attention, instead plunging his tongue into her mouth and pulling almost all the way out before driving back into her, pressing her ass deep into the mattress with every thrust.

Some part of Everly knew she shouldn't put her hands anywhere near his back since that was where he'd been thumped the worst. But it was hard to remember that as Landry's cock began to drive her crazy. All she could think about was grabbing hold of him and never letting go.

She'd been close to coming before he'd even slid into her—his mouth had made sure of that—so it wasn't surprising when she felt those wonderful tingles deep inside, warning her another amazing orgasm was on the way. She pulled her mouth away from his and gazed deep into his eyes, intending to tell him how good he was making her feel. But the words were trapped inside her, the pleasure she was experiencing making intelligent speech impossible. All she could do was whimper with each thrust as her climax began to build.

Finally, one single word slipped out.

"Harder!" she gasped.

He responded, slamming his cock into her and pinning her to the bed. Then he dipped his head and buried his face in her neck as he began to thrust so hard it made the bed shake. She couldn't breathe, but she didn't want to breathe right then. All she wanted to do was scream and come around him.

She heard a sound above her screams, and she recognized it as Landry's deep, sexy voice. He was saying her name over and over again against her neck and shoulder as he nibbled her there. Hearing him say her name with more love and emotion than she'd ever heard from any other man in the world did something powerful and amazing.

The wave of pleasure that washed over her was almost painful in its intensity. Her whole body shook violently as every muscle contracted and locked tight at once. She screamed so loud it tore at her throat, but she didn't care. She wanted this sensation to keep going until she exploded from the pleasure.

Landry grunted as he rammed his cock into her one last time and held it there as he poured himself into her. His body bucked and spasmed, and she knew in her heart that she was bringing him pleasure to match her own. And with Landry, knowing she was making him feel good too was the most important thing in the world.

God, she loved him. Not just for the pleasure he could bring her, but for reasons that were too big for her to understand. All she knew was that they were supposed to be with each other like this, locked together at the heart—forever.

Afterward, Everly should have wanted to do nothing more than cuddle up to Landry for some well-deserved sleep. She'd barely gotten any sleep last night, and even though she grabbed a quick nap this morning after Landry had left, she was still tired. The funny thing was, right then she didn't feel like sleeping at all. In fact, she felt crazy alive, like her whole body and mind was buzzing with excitement. She knew she was never going to fall asleep.

Well, they could always make love some more. Gauging the look on Landry's face, this wouldn't be a problem for him. Or she could spend a few hours doing something else she loved, something amazingly creative.

She was up and out of the bed the second the idea entered her head. Grabbing Landry's hand, she dragged him out of bed, pulling him toward the door.

"Where are we going?" he asked with a laugh.

He didn't resist, but instead, let her pull him down the hall and across the living room toward her art studio.

"I want to sketch you," she said as she led him into the room and turned on the lights.

She'd chosen this room as her studio because it had great natural light, but now that the sun was down, she would have to make do with artificial light instead. That was okay. Landry had such a spectacular body, he'd look good in any light.

Now that the urge to draw him was on her, it was like she couldn't get started fast enough. She threw a big canvas drop cloth in the center of the hardwood floor, both to give him something to lay on and to give her some textures to work with. Then she quickly pushed him down until he was lying on his side, his head cradled in the palm of one hand like he'd done in her bed.

She tweaked the pose a little, positioning his legs just so, then mussed up his hair a bit more. Landry didn't have a clue what she was doing, but he was a good sport, staying exactly the way she instructed and chuckling as she raced for the easel on the far side of the room. She had to move everything around so she faced in his direction, but since she was using only graphite pencils instead of paint, it didn't take long.

Everly put her biggest pad on the easel then grabbed a soft pencil and drew superfast figure studies of Landry's incredibly perfect body. And with him as a model, her pencil flew across the paper. She filled one sheet of the pad, then tore it off, and started another.

She did figure studies of her friends and neighbors all the time—except they had clothes on. Tracing the basic outline of the human form, with no interest in details, was one of her favorite things to do. But it felt different now. She hadn't felt this energized with her pencil in forever.

Maybe it was the great sex she'd just had, or maybe it was the fact that she didn't get a chance to draw nude guys too often. Hell, to be truthful, she'd never had a chance to draw a nude guy who looked like Landry because muscled Adonis types rarely volunteered at the art school she'd gone to.

Then again, maybe it was the fact that she was naked too. She'd never drawn in the nude before. It was refreshing. Maybe she'd have to do it more often.

Whatever the reason, the drawings practically jumped onto the page. She filled sheet after sheet with his beautiful body, posing him different ways, then moving her easel to get him from different vantage points.

It was as she sketched him from the back that she realized his bruises were much smaller than they'd been after the attack. She swore that at least two or three had disappeared completely. She stopped drawing and walked over to take a closer look. Crap, she could barely see the big welt he'd had across his back a few hours earlier.

"Is something wrong?" Landry asked over his shoulder.

She shook her head and ran her hand down his back. Even the worst of the bruising was already lightening.

When she got a bruise, it could take days, sometimes a week, to get to that point.

"Nothing," she said. "I just noticed how fast your bruises are healing."

He didn't answer right away. "Yeah. I know. I've always healed quickly. It's probably why I dealt with my injuries as well as I did when I got hurt in Iraq."

That made sense, she supposed. She wished she could get rid of bruises that fast. Every time she walked into a piece of furniture, she was forced to wear yoga pants every day or use concealer. She healed as slow as a tortoise compared to Landry.

She repositioned Landry again then went back to her drawing pad. As she drew picture after picture, he asked her about art school, what she liked to draw, how and where she sold her works. It was so nice having a person besides Mia she could talk to about her art. Her dad and brothers acted like it was a waste of time.

She tightened her grip on her pencil. Thinking about her brothers only reminded her of how mad she was at them. Regardless of what Landry suggested about simply ignoring them, Everly knew she would have to talk to them soon. If they thought they could chase her boyfriend off by beating him up, they were stupid. And wrong. If they thought she would let them do something like that to Landry again, they were even dumber. She didn't care if they were family. If they tried anything like that again, she'd have them arrested. They needed to be fully aware of that in a way they'd understand.

Everly pushed thoughts of her stupid brothers aside, refusing to let them ruin this evening. She focused on the beautiful naked man in front of her, positioning him in different ways and having fun sketching him. The fact that he was having so much fun posing for her only made it better.

It was as she put Landry in a standing pose, turned at the hips like a Greek god glancing back at her, that she realized his cock was hard. Now that would definitely add a little more interest to her next drawing.

"Sorry about that," he said. "But standing in front of you naked for the last couple hours is kind of a turn-on for me."

Everly laughed. She'd been aroused for most of the time they'd been in her studio too. She knew without reaching down to check that she was wet, and there was no way Landry could have missed her tight, hard nipples.

She'd never gotten sexually aroused drawing nude models in college, but that was because none of them were as hunky as Landry.

"Don't be sorry." She reached down to wrap a hand around his erect shaft. "It's nice knowing I can get you worked up just by being naked."

At her touch, his cock jumped and got even harder. Landry completely abandoned his pose to turn around and kiss her. A minute later, they were on the floor with the canvas drop cloth under them, her body on top of his, his hard cock throbbing in her hand. For about the hundredth time, Everly couldn't help but wonder at the luck that had befallen her. She'd walked into the bank that day on a whim and stumbled over the most perfect man she had ever met. She couldn't imagine ever being happier.

Chapter 13

A LOW RUMBLING SOUND WOKE EVERLY UP. AT first, she didn't know what it was until she heard it again. It was Landry's cell phone. He had some kind of rumbling ringtone.

She opened her eyes and groaned at the sun streaming through the window and at the clock on the bedside table that told her they'd only been asleep for forty-five minutes. It was Landry's fault. He'd kept her up making love all night. Okay, maybe it wasn't all his fault. She'd been more than willing to participate. She was replaying a few of the evening's memorable moments in her head when the serious tone in Landry's voice caught her attention. She rolled over to see him standing by the bed, his phone to his ear.

"Is he okay?" Landry asked, the worry in his voice unmistakable.

Everly tensed, fearing that one of his SWAT teammates had been hurt on the job. But then his next question confused the heck out of her.

"Has he been arrested yet?"

She tried to get his attention, but Landry held up his finger and asked several more questions before he hung up and grabbed his boxer briefs.

"What's wrong?" she asked, getting out of bed.

He motioned her back down. "It's Jim. He got drunk and got in a fight at a bar down near the airport. He'd be in jail already, but the responding officer found my business card in his pocket and figured that maybe this was something I'd want to handle."

She jumped out of bed again, running for her dresser and clean clothes. She could tell that Landry was upset, and she didn't want him to deal with Jim on his own. She half expected him to say she didn't have to go with him, but instead, he leaned over and kissed the top of her head.

"Thanks," was all he said.

There wasn't too much traffic yet, so it didn't take them long to reach the bar the police officer had told Landry about. The parking lot was almost empty, making the black and white patrol car sitting there stand out like a sore thumb.

She saw Jim the moment they walked into the small bar. He was sitting at a table near the back, pretty much passed out. The uniformed officer was standing near the bar with another man that Everly assumed was either the owner or the bartender on duty. The cop approached her and Landry.

He motioned to Jim. "Is this guy a friend of yours?"

Landry nodded. "Yeah."

The cop—Officer Warwick, according to the name tag on his uniform—explained Jim had gotten drunk and in a fight with some locals when the owner tried to tell him the bar was closing and that Jim couldn't drink anymore.

"You need to get this guy some help," the officer said in a soft voice as he handed Jim's car keys to Landry. "A couple locals took these from him when he tried to leave. He's been here since seven o'clock last night.

The owner said your friend should probably be dead from all the alcohol he put away. People don't last long drinking like that. He knows your friend is a veteran so he's not going to press charges, but I can't guarantee he'll be so lenient if this happens again."

"Tell him thanks," Landry said.

He paid the owner for the half dozen broken chairs, two tables, and the mirror behind the bar that Jim had smashed with a beer bottle. Then he gave the owner a business card.

"If you need help with anything, call me. I owe you."

The man nodded and slipped the card in his shirt pocket, then went behind the bar to finish cleaning up.

Jim didn't say a word as Landry helped him up from the table and guided him toward the door. They put him in the back of the Jeep then climbed in the front seats. Everly frowned in confusion when Landry asked Jim where he was staying. How could Landry not remember? They'd been there a few nights ago.

Jim mumbled something about a hotel behind the Doubletree about four or five blocks down the road. She gave Landry a questioning look, but he didn't say anything as he started the Jeep, a grim, disappointed look on his face.

Everly stared in disbelief when they got to the motel. It definitely wasn't a Doubletree. Actually, she couldn't see the name at all, but it kind of looked like a place someone might rent by the hour. Why would Jim make them think he was staying at the Doubletree instead of here? Was he hurting for money that badly? Why hadn't he said anything? She had no doubt Landry would have helped him, and she would have too.

Jim pointed them toward a room at the end of the building. Landry practically had to carry Jim inside and dump him on the bed. Everly waited outside. Jim seemed like a proud man. This wasn't something he'd want her to see.

She tried not to eavesdrop, but she could hear Landry asking Jim what the hell was going on with him. Jim was surprisingly coherent for a man who had obviously drank as much as he had.

"I was just letting off a little steam, that's all."

"You're full of shit," Landry ground out. "Jim, you need to get some help. Drinking like this is going to kill you."

"You're such a fucking hypocrite," Jim shot back. "When you were a tech, you drank like a fucking fish. How many times did I tell you to shower before PT because you reeked of alcohol? And now, you want to call *me* a drunk. Go fuck yourself!"

Everly turned and walked back to the Jeep, tears stinging her eyes. She didn't want to hear any more.

Landry came out five minutes later. He cranked the engine and drove out of the motel parking lot without saying a word. Everly wanted to ask him if he was okay, but didn't. He obviously wasn't okay. He was upset. If he wanted to talk about it, he would. She wouldn't push.

But he didn't say anything the whole way back to her apartment. As upset as he was, though, he still walked her to her apartment and kissed her good night—or good morning, in this case.

"I had an incredible time last night," he said. "Thanks for coming with me to get Jim. I know that wasn't easy for you to see."

"It wasn't, but I'm glad I came if it made things a

little easier for you." She reached up to brush back an unruly piece of hair that had fallen over his forehead. "You coming over tonight after work?"

His mouth curved, but the smile didn't quite reach his eyes. "Definitely. There's nowhere else I'd rather be."

Landry kissed her again then left. Everly watched him go, wishing she could say something to make everything better. She couldn't believe how much she hurt for him. Maybe because it seemed like he wasn't capable of hurting for himself.

～～

Cooper knew he probably should have gone back to his place to shower. He hadn't had more than an hour of sleep in the past two days. But the idea of being alone with his thoughts for even that long convinced him that would be a shitty idea. That was why he headed to the compound instead.

The moment he walked in the door of the admin building, Dennis called his cell saying he'd set up a meeting with all the people from the defense firm targeted by the bomber. The CEO would have everyone there in an hour.

"Take Alex and Remy with you," Xander said from his desk when Cooper hung up. "And keep me in the loop about what's going on."

Damn, sometimes it was really nice having coworkers who could overhear a person's phone call from forty feet away. It definitely cut down on a whole lot of repeated conversations.

Cooper, Alex, and Remy made it to Triple S-I with ten minutes to spare. If not for the big pieces of plywood put up to replace the blown out glass, the place would have looked almost respectable again.

Dennis came over and brought them up to speed on where they were with the case as soon as they walked in the conference room.

"Things are finally looking up. With this recent bombing, Jed and his brothers are looking at life in prison, maybe the death sentence, for being part of a terrorist conspiracy. They're looking to cut a deal, so we're bringing in a sketch artist tomorrow for them to work with. With any luck, we'll find this sick fuck soon."

Cooper hoped so. He, Alex, and Remy moved to stand in the back of the room as Arnold Braun came in with the company's corporate officers. Dennis joined them at the big conference table and asked the standard questions: Did any of them have dealings with a distraught member of the military? Did they know someone who had a grudge against the company? Did anyone know someone in the military who died under circumstances that someone might think Triple S-I was involved in? Did any of them have connections to a soldier who had been recently deployed?

They each gave the same answer to each question—no. There didn't seem to be a reason for these people to be targeted by the bomber. Few of them even dealt with service members in the course of their everyday jobs. They mostly moved paperwork—and money—around.

Cooper was starting to think all of this was a waste of time when another man in a suit walked in. Braun introduced the late arrival as Ryan North, former captain in the U.S. Army. The CEO said something about why North had been late, but Cooper didn't hear any of it.

All he could hear was his own heartbeat pounding in his ears.

Cooper had never met North because he'd arrived in Iraq the day Cooper had left. North had been the inbound commander of his EOD unit, the one he'd missed by mere minutes when he'd been blown through a brick wall and flown back to the States four years ago.

A sickening feeling churned in his gut, as his heart beat faster. His inner wolf shouted at him that there was no way in hell that North working for the company targeted by the bomber was a coincidence.

As far as Cooper knew, North had quietly left the army after serving his initial officer obligation, his reputation marred by the death of three of his men. But while he'd been the commander of the EOD unit when those men had died, he'd only been a wet-behind-the-ears lieutenant back then. No one expected him to know what the hell he was doing.

Unlike Jim, who'd been the senior and most experienced tech on the op. Jim was the one who'd been forced to live with the rumors, whispers, and innuendoes, saying he was to blame for his fellow soldiers' deaths every day of his life since it happened.

The sick feeling in Cooper's stomach got worse as he considered all the other coincidences in this case. Like Jim walking away from the army and EOD, then showing up on his doorstep a few days after the first bombing and drinking like a man desperate to make certain memories go away that night at dinner. Like Jim getting drunk in that bar last night after the second bombing.

Oh, fuck no. Cooper told himself that he had to be wrong. But his gut told him he wasn't. Ryan North was the bomber's target, and Jim was the man trying to kill him.

The bottom fell out of Cooper's world then. For the first time since he'd been lying paralyzed in that burning building in Iraq, he felt powerless and unsure of what to do next.

A part of him refused to believe Jim was involved. There had to be another explanation. Jim was an EOD tech, and techs risked their lives to defuse danger, not blow up people. Jim would never do anything like this.

But another part of Cooper whispered that maybe he didn't know Jim as well as he thought he did. The Jim that Cooper knew now was different than the Jim he used to know all those years ago. Something bad had driven his friend to get out of the army and out of EOD and start drinking so much. And it wasn't too hard to figure out that *something* had been the accident that had killed three of their friends. An accident everyone believed Jim was responsible for.

Even then, Cooper had a hard time accepting Jim would go after someone with a bomb. Would the alcoholic he knew now willingly hurt people—kill people—in a crazy attempt to get revenge?

"Cooper, you okay, man?" Alex whispered from beside him.

Cooper glanced at Alex to see him and Remy gazing at him with concern. "What?"

"Your heart is racing like crazy, and your face is so pale it looks like you've seen a ghost."

Cooper hadn't realized he'd let his emotions get away from him like that, but he wasn't surprised that his pack mates had picked up on it. They were attuned to one another like that.

"Did someone say something that caught your attention?" Remy asked, jerking his head at the conference table.

Cooper shook his head. He forced his heart to slow to normal and took a few deep breaths. "No. I was just thinking about Everly."

Remy grinned. "Must be nice having a woman who can get your heart racing just by thinking about her."

Alex didn't say anything, and he didn't smile. He regarded Cooper for a moment then turned his attention back to the discussion going on at the table.

Cooper wondered if Alex suspected anything. Maybe. But it wasn't like his friend knew about Jim, or Cooper's suspicions.

Cooper turned his attention back to the group at the front of the room, listening to North talk. He wasn't sure what he expected the man to say, but ultimately, North didn't say much. While North freely admitted to being in the army a few years ago, he claimed to have no idea who was behind the bombings. He didn't even offer up any of his fellow soldiers when Dennis prompted. If North thought someone was after him, wouldn't he say?

The next hour in the conference room was pure hell, as Cooper tried to figure out what he should do. In his heart, he wanted to believe that Jim, a man who had saved his life and was as dear to him as any member of his pack, could never be the bomber. But his head told him it wasn't his job to protect Jim. It was his job to protect the people in the city who were put at risk by leaving a killer on the streets.

And stuck in the middle of all this was Dennis, a

good friend and FBI agent who deserved to know about Cooper's suspicions.

In the end, he couldn't say anything to Dennis. Not until he looked in Jim's eyes and really knew for sure. So, when Dennis asked what he thought about the group of potential targets after the meeting, he remained noncommittal.

Dennis sighed. "Okay. Well, now that we've established who was in the parking garage and in the building yesterday morning, we can start looking at everyone these individuals know, and see if someone sticks out. Since North is the only one with ties to the military, we'll start with him."

After Cooper dropped Alex and Remy off at the compound, he hauled ass straight for the cheap motel where he and Everly had dropped off Jim that morning. Jim wasn't there, and the guy at the front desk had no idea if he was coming back.

Cooper sat in his Jeep in the parking lot and agonized over what he should do. He took out his phone to call Dennis, but then shoved it back in his pocket. First he had to find Jim, and then he'd figure out what to do with him.

He drove to the bar by the airport where he and Everly had picked him up, on the off chance Jim had gone back there. He hadn't. So Cooper got back in his Jeep and went to every place that served alcohol in the same general area. He asked around, talked to the bartenders and the waitresses, left his business card with anyone who would take it.

By the time he got back in his Jeep after the last dive bar, he was mentally exhausted. He cranked the engine and pulled out of the parking lot to head for the highway. Suddenly, he needed to be with Everly. Because when he was, everything was right with the world. And after the last few hours, he could use some of that in his life.

Chapter 14

"HE'S NOT GOOD ENOUGH FOR YOU, EVERLY, AND HE'S dangerous to be around," her father said in that stern voice he used when he was on the verge of losing control and headed for a rant in his native French.

She'd called her dad a little while after Mia left to go out with Joseph and the Scooby Gang again, knowing he was the one who had sent her brothers over to her place with the baseball bats. She didn't know why she thought she'd be able to talk any sense into him.

"Dad, I don't care what you think about Landry or whether you think he's good enough for me," she snapped. The conversation hadn't degraded into a shouting match yet, but it was getting there. "I decide who's good enough for me, not you."

She could practically see him shaking his head on the other end of the line. "Everly, you are too young to realize how foolish you are being. I'm doing this for your own good. You must walk away from this man. While you still can."

Everly wanted to scream. She should have known he'd go there. He always did. Next he'd tell her to be a good girl, and do as she was told. Yeah, well, she'd stopped doing as she was told a long time ago.

"Dad, I can see this is an exercise in futility, so I'm going to make this as simple and as clear as I can," she said. "Tell my idiot brothers that if they try to beat up

Landry again, I'll be the one who presses charges, not him. And since he's a cop, they'll all go to jail for a very long time."

"Everly…" he began, as if talking to a child.

"Tell them. If they harm even a hair on his head, I'm having them arrested."

Everly hit the red button with her thumb, wishing she had an old-fashioned phone so she could have slammed it down. God, her father was infuriating. But she'd done all she could. If her brothers ended up in jail now, it was their own stupid fault. She didn't want that to happen, but she wasn't going to stand by and do nothing the next time they hurt Landry.

She tossed her cell phone on the desk and glanced at the clock on the wall of her studio, wondering if Landry was on his way. It was after five, so he might be. But she knew he didn't work a job with standard hours, and as much as she wanted to, she wasn't going to call and check on him. He'd get here when he got here.

Of course, saying she wouldn't sit around and count the minutes until Landry showed up sounded mature, but it was nearly impossible to actually do. Not when all she could think about was the amazing evening she'd had with Landry last night.

She'd come to several important conclusions today while she was working. One was that she needed to call her dad and get a few things straight with him. That hadn't gone as well as she'd hoped, but she had a good feeling the other was going to go much better. In the midst of wondering how she'd ever gotten lucky enough to meet a guy like Landry, she decided it might be time to talk about their future together and that little subject known as love.

Yes, it was early in a normal relationship to be batting that word around. But this magnetic pull between
her and Landry was anything but normal. It was flat-out
magical, and she had no doubt that he felt it too. All it
took was one look in his eyes to know he felt exactly
the way she did. She was going to tell him she loved
him tonight, and something told her he was going to
say the same in return. Since they'd have the apartment
to themselves, it would make it easier to have a semi-
serious talk with her man.

Everly smiled as she read through her email. She
wasn't the only one falling fast for a guy. Mia and
Joseph were giving her and Landry a run for their
money. Everly had never known Mia to be exclusive
with anyone so quickly, but she and Joseph had been
together almost 24-7 since the wedding. Everly didn't
think she'd ever seen Mia happier. When her friend
wandered in this morning after being out with Joseph
and his friends all night, she'd kicked off her shoes and
told Everly that Joseph was every girl's dream. Then
she sent a text to her boss saying she wouldn't be able
to make it into work—apparently that passed as official
notification where she was employed—and fell into bed
with all her clothes on.

Everly was still reading through her emails and orga-
nizing her thoughts about what she wanted to say to
Landry, wondering if this was a conversation better to
have before or after sex, when he knocked on her door.

She closed her email program and hurried into the
living room to open the door. Landry stood there looking as handsome as always in his uniform, but also
more exhausted than she'd ever seen him. She promised

herself that she'd get him into bed early tonight—and not just so they could make love. He needed to catch up on some sleep.

After giving her a long, knee-weakening kiss, he hung his holster on the back of the chair in the kitchen, then collapsed on her couch, while she grabbed two bottles of water from the fridge. When she curled up on the couch next to him, he took the bottle she held out and swigged half the water.

"Long day?" she asked.

"Yeah. There was another bombing yesterday morning." He sighed. "No one was killed, but more than a dozen people got hurt."

"Is the FBI getting close to catching the guy?"

He hesitated then nodded. "They should have him in custody soon."

Talking about the bombing was obviously upsetting him, so she didn't press for details. Every time some psycho set off a bomb, he was probably reminded of what happened in Iraq.

"You want to go out for dinner?" she asked, changing the subject. "Or I could just make something, if you feel like staying in."

Landry's mouth curved into a grin as he reached out and grabbed her, pulling her laughing onto his lap. She ended up straddling his thighs with her hands on his shoulders.

"So, does this mean you're not hungry?" she asked, leaning forward to kiss him.

He nipped at her lower lip, giving it a little tug. "Oh, I'm hungry, all right. But not for food."

She moaned. "In that case, I think I'm famished."

Grabbing hold of his T-shirt, Everly tugged it out of his cargo pants and yanked it over his head. She took in his beautiful muscled chest, noting that the heavy bruise on his left side was completely gone. He wasn't kidding when he said he healed fast, she thought as she kissed him again.

Cooper was just undoing the buttons on the front of her sleeveless dress when he suddenly jerked his head up to stare at the door. She didn't even have a chance to ask him what was wrong before it slammed back against the wall. A moment later, her brothers stormed in.

Landry had her on her feet and pushed behind him so fast she barely realized they were off the couch. But that sure as hell wasn't where she stayed. She moved around the coffee table, ready to flay her brothers alive. Not just for having the gall to show up here again, but for kicking in the door. The wood around the lock was completely shattered.

"You're paying for that door, Armand," she shouted. He was always the ringleader of these little interventions.

"Did he bite you?" Armand demanded, ignoring her threat as he took in her partially undone buttons.

Everly was so furious right then that she could barely compose a rational thought, but hearing her oldest brother say something so incredibly stupid broke through the red haze of anger around her and gave her back the gift of speech.

"No, but he was about to," she said, angrily doing up the buttons. "And I'm still hoping he will—once I throw the four of you the hell out of my apartment."

Landry came around beside her, trying to get between

her and her brothers, but she refused to put him in the middle of this. Not that it mattered. Her brothers only had eyes for her, and right now, they were looking at her like she was insane.

"You want to be one of them?" Tristan asked.

The look of stunned surprise on her youngest brother's face flabbergasted her.

"What the hell are you talking about? One of what, a SWAT officer?" she asked him. "I'm pretty sure it takes more than a night in bed to get into SWAT, but I'll let you know in the morning, if you're really that interested."

"You've always been naive, Everly," Armand growled. "But even you can't be blind to what this man really is. You must have seen his true nature at least once. None of them can hide what they really are, not for long."

Everly was so confused she wasn't sure whether she should ask for clarification or simply kick them out now. She opted for the former, since they would probably walk right back in now that they'd busted the lock on her door.

"Okay, you've made me curious," she said. "What do you think Landry is—beyond the best thing that has ever happened to me, I mean?"

Armand's lips twisted into a disapproving frown. Everly wondered if he knew how much he looked like their father when he did that.

"I never wanted you to hear this, but if you won't trust us, then you leave me no choice," Armand said. "This *creature* standing at your side is a monster—a werewolf. And he wants to turn you, make you a spawn of the devil, like him."

Beside her, Landry tensed. He probably thought her

brother had lost his mind and was a danger to everyone in the room. Werewolf? Was that honestly what her father had told her brothers? They clearly believed him. It was so ridiculous, she actually laughed.

Armand didn't think it was nearly as funny. Muttering something in French, he reached behind his back.

Landry moved faster than she would have thought possible, putting himself between Everly and her brothers again before she could even blink. The next thing she knew, Armand was coming at them with a knife.

Everly screamed, but it was too late. Landry must have thought her brother was going to attack her, and by the time he realized his mistake, Armand had plunged the knife in his chest.

For one horrible moment, time stood still. Then Landry's eyes flashed a deep gold, and he shoved Armand so hard that her oldest brother flew across the living room the same way the robber had in the bank lobby a few days ago.

Giles and Claude took several steps back, pulling pistols from behind their backs and aiming them at Landry.

Everly ignored them. Instead, she took Landry's arm, turning him to face her and praying she'd been wrong about what she saw. But she hadn't been wrong.

She choked back a sob as Landry yanked the knife out of his chest and dropped it to the floor with a heavy clunk. Blood sprayed everywhere.

"Oh God, what have you done, Armand?" Everly screamed.

Tears flooded her eyes so much she could barely see. But she didn't need to see Landry clearly to know it was bad. There was so much blood.

Landry must have been as stunned by the speed and violence of Armand's attack as she was. He just stood there looking down at his bloody chest in confusion, oblivious to the trauma. There was no pain on his face either. Instead, an expression that could only be described as sadness filled his eyes. She gripped his shoulder in one hand to keep him from falling, then pressed the other to the wound, desperate to stop the bleeding.

"Don't just stand there!" she shouted at her brothers. "Call for an ambulance."

They didn't move.

Dammit! If she wanted to get Landry help, she would do it herself. And since there was no way she could depend on her brothers to put pressure on his wound, Landry was going to have to do that himself. But when she took her hand away to put his in its place, her eyes widened. The bleeding had already stopped. She watched, stunned, as the edges of the horrible wound closed up in front of her eyes.

That was impossible. Armand had stabbed him in the chest with a knife big enough to go more than halfway through him.

"Landry?" she asked softly.

The sorrow in his eyes tore at her heart. "I'm so sorry, Everly. I didn't want you to find out like this."

She shook her head, even more confused. But Landry didn't say anything else. He only stood there, tears welling in his eyes.

"Find out what?" She took his hand. "Landry, please talk to me."

Out of the corner of her eye, she saw Armand get up and move to stand near Giles and Claude. Both of her other brothers still had their weapons out and pointed at Landry.

Behind her, firm hands came to rest on her shoulders, and she glanced back to see Tristan standing there.

"We tried to tell you, but you wouldn't listen," he said. "This man you think is the best thing that has ever happened to you is a werewolf—a monster. Stabbing him was the only way Armand could get you to see that."

Everly shook her head, her thoughts suddenly too scattered and broken to piece together. "I don't understand. How can he be…?"

"A werewolf? Or alive?" Tristan asked with a shrug. "I don't know why he's a werewolf—he simply is. And he's alive because evil cannot be killed so easily, even with a knife through the chest."

She stared at Landry's chest. The wound had closed almost completely now, and there was a fine line of pale pink scar tissue already forming around the edges. She thought about the bruises and cuts she'd tended last night, about how they were already gone, barely twenty-four hours later. No normal human healed that fast. And yet, her mind rebelled. Werewolves were the stuff of folktales and horror movies. They weren't real.

But when she looked at Landry's face, she realized her brother's words weren't as shocking to him as they had been to her. He wasn't even denying it. He simply stood there waiting, silent as a graveyard, a defeated expression in his eyes.

Doubt crept into her heart, then fear. So many things she'd overlooked flooded her mind. The way Landry had responded in the bank, knowing what was going to happen long before anyone else. The way he'd thrown one bank robber around like a toy, and held another two feet off the floor with one hand. Then there was the gunshot wound he'd gotten, the one she couldn't even find now. And she couldn't forget the growls he sometimes let out.

The images closed in on her, collapsing all at once and threatening to crush her under the weight of too many strange facts. Could her brothers possibly be telling her the truth?

She locked eyes with Landry. "Tell me my brothers are lying. If you tell me, I'll believe you."

Tristan's grip tightened on her shoulders. "Everly…"

"No! I want to hear it from him." She shook off her brother's hands then turned back to Landry. "Is it true?"

He was silent for so long she thought he wouldn't answer, but then he nodded. "I'm not a monster like they say, but the rest is true. I am a werewolf."

Most of his words were drowned out as her heart exploded in her chest, but she heard the part that mattered. Something inside her tore loose, racking her body with unbelievable pain. It felt like she was dying one heartbeat at a time.

"Everly we tried to tell you…" Tristan began, but his words trailed off when she jerked her head to pin him with her angry glare.

"How could any of you possibly know something like this?" she demanded, fresh tears in her eyes.

Tristan glanced at her other brothers before answering. "It's the antique mirror in Dad's house. It was made by people who spent their entire lives hunting werewolves. The mirror reflects their savage nature in the glow of their eyes."

Oh God. Landry's eyes.

All the times she'd seen that flash of color she'd thought it was simply the light reflecting in a funny way. God, she was so stupid. But her ignorance didn't explain why her father would have a hideous mirror that identified werewolves in his home. Or why he'd been parading her friends and boyfriends past that thing since she was a teen. He'd even done it to Mia the first time she'd brought her roommate to visit.

"Why does Dad have something like that in his house?" she asked.

"Because Landry is the same kind of monster that killed our mother, Everly," Armand answered, his voice softer and more pain-filled than Everly had ever heard it. "And Dad swore he would never let someone he loves be killed by one of these monsters again. So, he found people who knew how to fight these creatures, and they gave him the mirror."

After learning that Landry was a werewolf, Everly thought there was nothing left that could shock her, but she was wrong. What Armand had just said made a lie of everything she thought had happened to their mother.

"I thought Mom was killed by one of the farm-hands," she stated.

Armand nodded. "She was. He was a drifter Dad hired. But he was also a werewolf. The man became infatuated with Mom, and when she said she wasn't interested in him, he turned into a beast and ripped her apart."

Everly turned her gaze on Landry again, trying to imagine him doing something like that. She liked to think he couldn't, but then again, what did she really know about him? She'd seen him attack those men in the bank. Maybe he was more of an animal than she realized.

"Why didn't anyone ever tell me what really happened to Mom?" she demanded of her brothers.

Armand sighed. "Because you already knew it. You were there and saw the whole thing."

"No, I wasn't." What was he talking about? She remembered that day like it was yesterday. "Mom pushed me behind the kitchen counter. I didn't see anything."

Armand shook his head. "No, she didn't. That might be what you want to remember because the truth is too painful. When we got to the house, we found you standing in the kitchen beside Mom's body, blood all over you and still trying to scream. But you'd already screamed yourself hoarse. You—"

"That's enough, Armand," Tristan cut him off. "She doesn't need to hear any more."

But Everly already heard enough. She suddenly remembered the sensation of something warm and wet hitting her face that day—her mother's blood. Just like that, the rest of the memories came rushing in like a tidal wave of fear and pain. She remembered her mother telling her to run, but being too frightened to move, then her mother screaming and begging the farmhand for her life and Everly's. And above everything else, she remembered the horrible, awful growls so similar to the ones Landry made.

Everly clamped her hands over her ears. She didn't want to remember any more, but she couldn't stop the sounds or the memories. They played repeatedly in her head, and she watched her mother die right in front of her, over and over again.

Stifling a sob, Everly turned and ran for the door. She heard angry voices and the sounds of a struggle behind her, but she didn't stop.

She didn't even realize she'd grabbed her car keys until she squealed out of the parking lot. She hit the road in front of the complex moving way too fast and almost spun in a complete circle, but she didn't care. She had to get away from there.

She didn't know where she was going, so she just drove. Now that she knew what had happened to her mother, it seemed like a dam burst in her head. With every mile that passed, she saw more and more details of her mother's murder, and it terrified her.

Equally as terrifying was the realization that she'd been so wrong about Landry. How could she not have known he was a monster? She'd been with him almost constantly for nearly a week. They'd made love, for heaven's sake!

Part of her wanted to believe this was all a crazy misunderstanding, that her brothers were wrong, and that Landry wasn't a monster. That he would come after her and make all of this okay.

But that wasn't going to happen. Her brothers were right. Landry was a monster. And she was never going to be okay again.

She hit the 635 loop, then Interstates 20 and 35 in an almost random fashion, but what she was really doing was driving in a big circle around Dallas. Her mind spun in circles just as large and traffic-filled as the highway, but she kept going. She needed to think.

She vaguely remembered stopping to get gas at a deserted station where she normally never would have stopped, then made another circle around the city, followed by another.

At three in the morning, she finally found herself in front of Landry's apartment.

What the hell was she doing here? But she knew the answer to that question. She needed answers, and Landry was the only one who could give them to her.

Landry opened the door before she even knocked, relief on his face. "Everly, thank God."

He made as if to put his arms around her, but she held up her hands. "Don't touch me. I'm only here to ask you a few questions. That's all. You just keep your distance."

Pain filled his eyes, but he nodded resignedly and stepped away from the door, then moved all the way to the far side of the living room and waited. He'd changed out of his uniform into jeans and a T-shirt.

Everly closed the door quietly behind her, but didn't move away from it. Now that she was here, she wasn't quite sure what to say, or even how to start.

"I was scared when you ran out like that," Landry finally said. "I wanted to go after you, but your brothers wouldn't let me. They said I'd hurt you enough already."

She nodded, realizing for once, her brothers had been right. If Landry had followed her, she probably would have lost her mind.

"I never knew I buried all those memories of my mom's death," she said. "Not until I saw you survive that knife wound. Until I learned what you are."

Landry didn't say anything. Then again, what could he say?

"Were you bitten against your will?" she asked.

She had to know if he was a werewolf because he'd

wanted to be a monster. Or was it something that had
been done to him? She didn't know why that was important, but it was.

He shook his head. "It doesn't work that way. People
who become werewolves are born with a gene that pre-
disposes them to it. If we go through a traumatic, violent
event, we change into a werewolf. We don't run around
biting people to make more."

A stupid part of her was relieved she didn't have to
worry about becoming a werewolf from all the times
he'd nibbled her neck. The memories of how good
things had been between them made her want to cry for
all they'd lost.

"Was it Iraq that did it to you?" she asked after a
moment, mostly to keep her mind from going places she
didn't want it to go.

"Yeah. I broke my back in three places, crushed my
spinal cord completely, and had five pounds of frag
shoved through me. I should have died that day, but the
wolf inside wouldn't let me. It healed me."

Even though he was a monster, she felt thankful for
that. Despite what he was, the idea of something happening to Landry made it hard to even take a breath.

"I want to see the wound," she said. "From where my
brother stabbed you."

He seemed hesitant, like he no longer wanted her to
see his body, even though she'd already seen all of it—
more than once. She knew it so well she could draw him
from memory.

But he finally lifted the T-shirt to expose his torso.
Everly tried not to gasp when she saw the smooth, light
pick scar on his chest.

"Did it hurt?" she asked.

He dropped his shirt down. "When Armand stabbed me? Yeah, it hurt like hell. But not as much as the way you're looking at me now. That's much worse."

The pain in his voice made her want to run across the room and put her arms around him. But she firmed her resolve. "Would that knife have killed you if Armand had stabbed you in the heart?"

Landry didn't answer right away. He probably thought she was looking for information on how to do a better job on him next time. She wasn't, but she didn't know how to explain why she wanted to know that small bit of information. She just did.

"Yes," he said. "A few inches in the wrong direction, and I wouldn't be here now."

The thought made her queasy, and she leaned back against the door for support. "Why did that other were-wolf kill my mother?"

That one seemed to surprise him. "I don't know. We aren't all the same, regardless of what your brothers told you. What do you remember about the attack? If you don't mind talking about it, I mean."

There was nothing she wanted to talk about less, but when she opened her mouth to tell him that, she found herself recounting what she recalled.

"I remember blood—a lot of blood. And my mom screaming." She took a deep breath. "The werewolf was so angry. He kept shouting at my mom as he attacked her."

"It sounds like an omega werewolf that went out of control," Landry said.

She frowned. "An omega?"

His mouth twisted sardonically. "I'm no expert on this—unlike your family, apparently—but there are three types of werewolves. Alphas, who are big, strong, fast, and in control. Betas, who aren't as big, or as strong, or as fast, but who have much stronger pack instincts. Then there are omegas. They're as big and strong as alphas, but have almost no social skills. They tend to be loners, and that can make them dangerous. They can sometimes lose control and hurt people."

Everly tried to wrap her head around the fact that there was a whole other world out there—a world where monsters came in different flavors. She didn't have to ask to know that Landry was the first type—an alpha. "So when this omega got angry at my mom, he lost control?"

Landry nodded. "Probably."

She searched her memory of that day, but her recollection of the werewolf was fuzzy. She mostly remembered him growling a lot. And the fact that he had big teeth. Even knowing what she did now, that seemed insane.

"Did he really have fangs and claws, or am I imagining that?"

It was Landry's turn to frown. "Are you sure you want me telling you this? Tristan implied it might not be good for you to push so hard to remember. There's a reason your subconscious suppressed those memories."

"Tristan doesn't have a right to decide what I get to know about our mother's death, or when I get to know it. None of my brothers do," she said sharply. "This monster that killed my mom. Did it have fangs and claws, like I remember?"

Landry ran his hand through his hair, looking torn.

"Yeah, he did. Alphas and betas are better at controlling it, but with omegas, the claws and fangs come out anytime they're upset."

She considered that fact. It was terrifying to know there were monsters with claws and fangs in the world—and that Landry was one of them. She still couldn't reconcile that fact.

"Show me," she ordered.

"Show you what?" he asked.

"I want to see what you really look like."

Maybe then she would really believe what he was. Despite the flare of gold in his eyes, his superhuman strength, and ability to heal faster than a normal person, part of her still didn't want to believe he was a monster.

On the other side of the room, Landry looked at her as if he regretted ever having opened the door and letting her in. But now that she was here, there was no going back.

She took a step toward him. Now he was the one moving away from her. That hurt, but she had to know.

"I want to see the claws and the fangs," she said.

When she took another step closer, he edged around the couch, putting it between them. "I don't think that's a good idea, Everly. Considering what you're dealing with right now, seeing something like that could do more harm than good."

He was saying that to protect her, exactly like her father and brothers had done. But she didn't need protection anymore. She needed the truth.

"Let me decide that," she said. "I think you owe me this much, don't you?"

The anguish in his eyes was almost enough to make

her take back the words. But she resisted. She needed to see Landry in his true form.

"I never wanted things to be this way, Everly," he said softly. "I'd planned to tell you about what I am when the time was right. When you were ready."

"I am ready," she insisted.

No, she wasn't. Her heart was beating so fast she thought it might burst out of her chest.

"Everly, please don't ask me to do this."

"Show me, damn you!" she shouted.

She thought Landry would refuse yet again, but then his eyes turned that golden color she'd thought was so beautiful before. Even now, she was mesmerized by it. But then the fangs slowly came out. Easily an inch long and unbelievably sharp, they gleamed in the light. Curved claws followed, extending beyond his fingers like edged weapons.

Just like that, she was transported to that day twenty years ago, watching as an enraged werewolf ripped her mother apart. But this time, she saw every detail of the killer's face. The glowing eyes, the flashing fangs, the deadly claws. All the same characteristics that Landry possessed.

"I can't do this," she whispered.

Whirling around, she yanked open the door with a trembling hand and raced out of the apartment. She couldn't believe she was stupid enough to have come here in the first place.

Landry let her go. She had no idea what she would have done if he'd followed her. Now that she'd seen what he looked like, she wasn't sure how she would ever be able to look at him again. How could she ever have fallen in love with a monster to begin with?

Chapter 15

COOPER WANDERED INTO THE ADMIN BUILDING AT the compound a little after seven the next morning. For the second time in his life, he was late for work. Not that he could give a damn. He had more important things to worry about. Like how fucked up last night had been. How the hell had everything with Everly gone to crap so fast?

When she'd run out of her apartment in tears, his first instinct had been to chase after her. But of course, her asshole brothers had moved to block the doorway, telling him he'd done enough damage and to leave their sister alone.

"The only reason you aren't dead already is because you saved Everly's life during that bank robbery," Armand told him. "But if you go after her again, we will kill you."

It had taken everything in him not to rip those four jerks to pieces. But he restrained himself, partly because they were right. He had caused enough damage already.

So, he'd stood there glaring at them for fifteen minutes until they finally left. He'd thought about putting out a BOLO on Everly's car, but then realized that was stupid. What the hell would he do if a cop found her and pulled her over? If she was still in the same emotional state she'd been in when she left her apartment, the officer would probably take her into police custody for her own good. He hadn't wanted that, so instead, he prayed she'd be okay.

In the middle of the night, when she'd shown up at his place, her eyes red from crying and full of fresh tears, he'd wanted nothing more than to wrap his arms around her and never let her go. But she couldn't even stand to be near him. Things had just gone from bad to worse after that. Why the hell had he agreed to shift in front of her? That had to be the dumbest thing any werewolf had ever done.

He had followed her that time, but at a safe distance so she wouldn't see him, just to make sure she made it home okay. Then he'd sat in his Jeep a couple blocks down the street for the rest of the night, both to make sure she didn't go out again and to figure out how to fix the mess.

He hadn't come up with anything. All he'd done was berate himself for not telling her his secret earlier. Not that it would have helped. What kind of cruel fuck was fate to let a werewolf fall in love with the one woman on the planet whose mother had been killed by one of his kind?

So much for love conquering all and her being *The One*. Then again, maybe she was *The One* for him, and he'd just fucked it up. The folktale only said every werewolf had that one perfect soul mate out there. It didn't say they were guaranteed to be together. Quite obviously, he was so good at fucking things up that he'd even screwed up a fairy-tale romance.

Unfortunately, even though Everly was completely sickened by the mere sight of him now, Cooper was still head over heels in love with her. Nothing that happened last night had changed that one bit. If anything, it only made him want to protect Everly and keep her safe even more than before. That meant for now he needed to stay away from her. At least that way, one of them would be happy.

For the short term, this was the best he could come up with. Beyond that, he had no idea what he was going to do. It was strange. He was the one all the guys in the Pack came to when they had a problem. But now that he had a problem, he couldn't think of a single good piece of advice to give himself.

Becker looked up from his computer and did a double take when he saw him. "Whoa, dude. I know you and Everly can't keep your hands off each other, but good God, mix in a nap now and then. You look like shit."

The rest of his squad was all staring at him from where they sat at their desks.

"Becker's right, man," Alex agreed. "You look like one of the zombies in the comic books you read."

Any other time, Cooper would have laughed and flipped his pack mates the bird, but today all he did was let out a snort as he pulled out his chair and sat at his desk. *Shit.* He'd had his share of bad days before, but they were nothing compared to this. The woman he loved thought he was a monster, and one of his best friends was probably a killer. He should be out looking for Jim, not sitting here pretending his life wasn't in the toilet.

At the desk across from his, Becker sat back and swigged coffee out of a mug with the words *Either You're SWAT Or You're Not* on it. "Jayna and I are doing dinner and a movie Friday night with Zak and Megan. You and Everly want to come?"

Cooper's hand stilled on the mouse, the cursor hovering over the email icon on his computer monitor. It

suddenly struck him that he and Everly weren't going
to see any more movies, or go out to dinner, or kiss, or
make love. He swallowed hard and took a deep breath.

"Cooper?" Becker said. "What's wrong?"

He opened his mouth, but nothing came out. He cleared
his throat and tried again. "Everly and I broke up."

Shit, even saying the words hurt.

"Broke up?" Alex sat forward at his desk. "I thought
she was *The One*?"

Cooper clicked on the email icon with more force
than necessary. "Yeah, well, I guess sometimes that's
not enough."

"What happened?" Khaki asked.

Cooper didn't want to rehash last night, but for some
reason, he ended up telling them everything, from how
her family knew he was a werewolf to her brothers beating him up with baseball bats, then stabbing him last
night, and finally, to Everly running out.

"I don't think she's ever going to get past the fact that
I'm the same kind of creature that killed her mother," he
said quietly.

He knew Khaki and the guys would have hung out
with him the rest of the day and talked if he'd wanted
them to, and he might have taken them up on it, if the
calls hadn't suddenly started rolling in.

"We've got a domestic dispute on Randel," Alex
announced when he hung up. "Guy holding his girlfriend and her sister hostage."

Cooper got up to head out with the rest of the squad,
but Xander pulled him aside.

"Maybe you should sit this one out," his squad leader
said. "You had a tough night."

Cooper snorted. "Yeah, well, something tells me they aren't going to get any easier. I can't sit on the bench every time an incident comes in."

"I know," Xander said. "But you can today."

Maybe Xander was right. He wasn't at his sharpest right now. If he didn't pick up a scent or hear a bad guy coming, it could end up getting one of his teammates killed. Besides, he needed to look for Jim anyway.

Xander turned to catch up with the rest of the squad, but Cooper stopped him.

"This stuff Everly's brothers said about the magic frigging mirror and hunters out there who spend their whole lives killing werewolves? Did Gage ever tell you anything about them?"

Xander shook his head. "No. But maybe that's because he's never heard of them."

Cooper wasn't sure what worried him more—the thought that there might be hunters out there looking to kill him and every other werewolf, or the idea that Gage might not know anything about them.

————

When he left the SWAT compound, Cooper had every intention of going from one cheap motel to another looking for Jim, but instead, he found himself at Delacroix's office. It was barely after eight thirty, and she didn't come in until nine, so he stood outside her office door and waited. He wasn't exactly sure why he was there or what the hell he was going to say when she got there.

My girlfriend dumped me because she found out I'm a werewolf, and I really need to talk to someone?

Yeah, probably not.

He was just thinking he should go when Delacroix showed up, a cup of coffee in one hand and a stack of folders clutched in her arm. She took one look at his face and told him to come in.

"Sorry to show up without calling first," he said as she unlocked the door.

"No worries. My first patient doesn't arrive for an hour." She gestured to the chairs in front of her desk. "Have a seat."

Cooper did, then waited for her to do the same. She folded her forearms on the desk, pinning him with that sharp gaze of hers.

"So, what's on your mind?" she asked.

He didn't answer because he wasn't quite sure what to say. It wasn't like she was a drinking buddy. He wasn't going to cry in his beer and sob about Everly dumping his ass. He was a dumb shit to even come here.

"Maybe this wasn't such a good idea," he mumbled.

"You came here because you obviously need to talk," she said when he started to get up. "So, talk."

He dropped back down into the chair with a sigh. Oh, what the hell? "Remember that amazing woman I told you I was dating? The one who seemed to fit me so perfectly?" Delacroix nodded. "Well, about the time I realized I'd fallen in love with her, she decided to bail. I'm not dealing with it too well."

Delacroix frowned. "I'm sorry things didn't work out between the two of you. There aren't many people out there who could handle the world in which you live, you know. It's not for everyone."

Cooper regarded Delacroix for a moment. Did she mean because he was a cop, or a werewolf? He still couldn't get a read on how much the good doctor knew.

"I guess not," was all he said.

"Just because you broke up doesn't mean there's no way for you two to get back together. Have you talked to her about what's coming between the two of you?"

Cooper had spent most of last night and this morning asking himself that same question. If this had simply been about him being a cop, the answer would have been easy. But it wasn't about him being a cop. It was about him being a werewolf. And while he would have gladly walked away from his job on the force for Everly, he couldn't walk away from being a werewolf.

"I wish there was, but I just don't see it," he said quietly.

It hurt like hell to admit that, but it was true. He and Everly were never going to get back together.

The emotionless mask Delacroix normally wore slipped a little at that. She actually looked sad. "I'm sorry. As hard as it is for you to talk about what happened between the two of you, I have the hour free, and I'd be more than happy to listen."

Cooper sat back in the chair, but didn't say anything. He'd already talked to his pack mates. Why rehash everything with a complete stranger? It wasn't like he could tell Delacroix the real reason he and Everly had broken up. But he could tell Delacroix about how much more amazing his life had been with Everly in it…and how he felt now that she was gone. And if a few tears misted his eyes, he and Delacroix both did their best to ignore them.

Chapter 16

EVERLY WASN'T COMPLETELY SURE WHAT DAY OF the week it was. But she'd heard Mia calling into work this morning to tell her boss she was taking another day off because her roommate still wasn't feeling well. That meant it must be Friday. Two days since she'd broken up with Landry. It felt more like two hundred.

Poor Mia had missed work three days in a row now, the last two to babysit her. Mia was so sweet. Everly didn't really need a babysitter. She wasn't twelve, and she wasn't sick. Yet she didn't know why she was so devastated. She'd broken up with guys before and it had never been like this. It felt like a piece of her heart was missing.

She'd crawled into bed the moment she came home from Landry's apartment two days ago and hadn't gotten out since. She vaguely remembered Mia bringing her something to eat now and then, but she didn't remember what.

She had cried like a banshee that first day after everything had fallen apart with Landry. She'd tried to stop it, told herself to get a grip and stop being so dramatic. But none of that self-cajoling crap had worked. She kept thinking of Landry and the anguish on his face when she'd turned her back on him.

That was how Mia had found her, curled in a ball on her bed and crying like a madwoman. Her friend had immediately thought something had happened to Landry, that he'd been hurt—or worse. She'd tried to tell Mia that wasn't it, but the mere thought of Landry being injured—or dead—had made her start crying all over again.

Mia had lain with her in bed for hours, refusing to leave her side until she calmed down. When she had, Mia asked what happened, but Everly couldn't talk about it. So, she'd only told her friend that she and Landry had broken up.

Everly rolled onto her other side now and bunched the pillow under her head. She wished it could be that simple. She wished she could walk away from him like it was nothing, but that was impossible. She'd been in love with Landry—there was no denying that. She'd been thinking of making a life with him—of marriage and kids. Now she couldn't even think of him without seeing the vicious, bloodthirsty monster that had killed her mother.

She felt so stupid. Why hadn't she seen this coming? He was too perfect right from the start. She supposed that was the allure monsters like him used to get close to people. But if Landry was a monster, why was she lying in bed feeling like her heart had been torn out, instead of thanking her brothers for saving her life?

Outside her room, the door of the apartment opened, and she heard Mia talking softly to someone. For a crazy moment, her heart leapt at the thought that it might be Landry. But deep down, she knew better. He wasn't coming back. She had burned that bridge with a flamethrower.

"I have to go grocery shopping anyway," Mia said to

whoever it was. "Since I'm guessing you probably had something to do with why she's been crying her eyes out the past two days, maybe you can do something to fix this."

Everly didn't bother to look up as she heard a man's heavy footsteps approaching her bedroom. It obviously wasn't Landry. He was much lighter on his feet than that, even if he was huge. Like a predatory animal, she supposed.

Whoever it was knocked on her door, then opened it. "Hey Everly, it's me." Tristan's voice was soft. "Mia mentioned on the phone that you were feeling a little under the weather. I thought I'd come over and see how you were doing."

She didn't bother rolling over to look at him. "I'm fine. You've met your brotherly obligation, so you can leave. Go home and tell everyone I'm just peachy now that you've chased away the big bad werewolf."

Everly felt the bed dip as her brother sat down on the other side next to her. She ground her jaw in frustration. She had no interest in seeing anyone right now, especially any of her brothers.

"What do you want, Tristan?" she asked, still not looking at him.

"I just want to make sure my little sister is okay. I know what you saw the other night scared you. But Landry is gone now, and he's not coming back."

Even though Everly already knew Landry was never coming back, it still hurt like hell to hear the words spoken out loud. For some reason, it infuriated her even more that Tristan was the one saying it. Of all her brothers, he'd always been the one on her side, no matter what.

She rolled over and looked at him, ready to lay into him for having the nerve to come here and even utter Landry's name, but the words stuck in her throat at the stunned expression on her brother's face. She supposed she did look a fright. Two days of crying could do that to a girl.

Tristan leaned closer, putting his hand on her forehead like he was checking her for a fever. Then he pushed up her top lip to look at her teeth. She smacked his hand away.

"What the hell are you doing?" she asked as he reached for the collar of her sleep shirt and tried to pull it down. She smacked his hand away again. "Stop that!"

"I'm trying to see if he bit you," he said, reaching for her collar again.

She held up a finger in warning and glared at him. "You touch me again, and I'm going to punch you in the nose. No, Landry didn't bite me, you idiot. Why would you think he did?"

Her brother shrugged. "You look horrible. Your nose is all red and puffy, and your eyes are bloodshot. I thought…I thought you were turning into a werewolf."

God, her brother was a moron. "I'm not turning into a werewolf," she snapped. "My face is red and puffy because I've been crying, and my eyes are bloodshot because I haven't slept for two days. Besides, you can't turn into a werewolf from getting bitten. You need to have the werewolf gene already in your blood, and then go through a life-threatening, traumatic event for it to turn on. The biting stuff is a fairy tale."

Tristan's eyes narrowed suspiciously. "How do you know all that?"

Just thinking about the last conversation she had with Landry brought tears to her eyes. "I know because I went to talk to Landry the night you stabbed him. I drove around town for hours and ended up at his place."

He sucked in a sharp breath. "Did he hurt you?"

"No, he didn't hurt me," she said, getting more and more ticked off by the second. "All we did was talk about what he is. I had questions, and he answered them. Then I left. I haven't seen him since."

Tristan sagged with relief. In silence, he looked around the room, taking in the pile of used tissues on the nightstand and those that had fallen to the floor, then the pillows she'd thrown against the far wall when she got angry for not being able to forget about Landry. Finally, he swung his gaze back to her.

"Dad told me once that sometimes if a woman spends too much time with a werewolf that he can get into her blood. Do you think that's happened to you—that Landry got into your blood? If it is, you don't have to worry," Tristan added, holding up his hands in a gesture his stupid ass probably thought was calming. "According to Dad, women have been falling prey to this werewolf glamour for millennia, but like any addiction, it passes with time. What you're feeling isn't real."

If Everly had a knife right them, she would have stabbed her brother. But she didn't have a knife—at least not in her bedroom.

"God, you're an imbecile," she snapped. "Doubly so for listening to Dad. Landry is not in my blood, Tristan. He never was."

Her brother frowned. "How do you know? He could be, and you're just confused."

She shook her head at how thick her youngest brother was—and he was the brightest one. "I know he's not in my blood because he's in my heart. And that's ten times worse!"

Tristan's eyes widened, a look of pure terror crossing his face. "You're in love with him?"

Everly fell back onto the pillow, all the fight gone. Besides, this was a meaningless argument. "I was, but it doesn't matter now. He's a monster with claws and fangs, and every time I look at him—every time I even think of him—I see the creature that murdered Mom. I can never get past that, no matter what my heart wants. So, you can go home and tell the others that I'm safe from the big bad werewolf. He'll never come near me again. Which is exactly the way you all wanted it, right?"

Not waiting for a reply, she rolled over and curled into a ball again. The tears she'd thought had finally dried up after two straight days of crying spilled onto her cheeks. Dammit, she really didn't want Tristan to be here when she lost it again.

"Just go," she told Tristan. "I'm done talking about Landry with you."

He hesitated, and she thought she was going to have to say something awful to get him to leave, but then he stood and left the room, quietly closing the door behind him.

Everly held off for another few moments just to make sure he didn't come back, then she gave into the agonizing pain in her heart and cried all over again.

In the motel parking lot, Cooper cut the engine of his Jeep and glanced at the long list of fleabag motels he'd scribbled on the notepad, most of which he'd already scratched out. In an effort to get Everly out of his head, he'd thrown himself into his work. In this case, that meant spending every minute of the past two days trying to find Jim.

Cooper didn't have any idea what he was going to do when he found his friend, but he had to at least look. The alternative was walking into the FBI field office and telling Dennis that he thought Jim might be the bomber. Cooper really didn't want to do that, not until he looked his best friend in the eye and knew without a shadow of a doubt that Jim had set those bombs.

He knew he was being stupid, and that his breakup with Everly was almost certainly messing with his judgment. But no matter how bad it appeared, he couldn't force himself to turn his back on Jim. Soldiers didn't do that to each other. Especially when that other soldier had saved your life.

Cooper got out of his Jeep and headed to the front office of the motel, passing another rusty sign announcing they had rooms available. Empty rooms in a fine establishment like this? Shocking.

Before going inside, he checked his cell phone to make sure he hadn't missed any calls. Xander was under the impression that Cooper was "helping" Dennis with the bombing case, so he was giving him a lot of free time. But if something big came in, Xander would expect him to come running. Cooper was cool with that. Anything to keep his squad leader from figuring out what he was really doing. Xander would lose his mind if he found out Cooper was hiding evidence from the FBI.

Even though he was in his SWAT uniform, he still flashed his badge at the heavily bearded guy behind the counter who was staring at the TV on the wall. The office smelled like two-hundred-years' worth of beer and cigarettes. The smell was so bad it made Cooper wish his crappy nose was even worse.

The man turned his head enough to see the badge. When he realized Cooper wasn't likely going to rent a room, he turned his attention back to the TV.

Cooper pulled out a photo of Jim he'd printed at the office. One he'd shown around Dallas hundreds of times in the past few days.

"Is this guy staying here?" he asked, hoping he could get the man to unglue his eyes from the TV long enough to look at the photo. "He's older than in the picture, so he has some gray hair and wrinkles around his eyes now."

The man's gaze flicked to the picture, then back to the TV.

"Room nineteen on the back side of the building," the man grunted without taking his eyes off the screen and the frigging infomercial on vacuum cleaners. "There ain't no numbers on some of the doors, so you have to count the rooms as you go."

Cooper thanked the man and headed for the exit, his heart thumping a little harder at the thought of finally talking to Jim.

"Hey!" the man called from behind the counter.

Cooper turned back just in time to catch something flying at him. He opened his hand to see a room key attached to a beat-up piece of plastic.

"Don't break down the door," the man said as the announcer on the TV demonstrated how useful the vacuum was at picking up marbles—since that was what everyone dropped on the floor all the time.

Cooper nodded and left the office. It took a few minutes to locate room nineteen. You had to find at least two room numbers before you could establish a pattern and start counting doors. But a few minutes later, he was standing in front of a room he was sure was the right one, mostly because even his crappy nose could smell Jim's scent wafting through the cracks around the door. Jim's rental car was parked a few spaces from the room.

Cooper knocked, tensing as footsteps approached the door. This could go bad in so many ways. Jim could be drunk off his ass and belligerent to boot. He might realize why Cooper was here and try to run. Hell, his friend might even pull a gun and try to shoot his way out of this situation. All of those scenarios were likely to end up with Jim dead, and Cooper really didn't want his friend's blood on his hands. This week had been shitty enough already.

He braced himself as the door opened, ready to protect himself, if Jim came out shooting.

But he didn't come out shooting. In fact, he didn't come out at all. He merely stood there, looking like he'd just come back from a job interview, if the tan pants, button-down shirt, and conservative tie were any indication. Cooper took a quick sniff, waiting to be bowled over by the odor of booze, but he didn't smell any alcohol on his friend. And rather than looking crazy and belligerent, Jim seemed surprised to see him.

"Hey. What the hell are you doing here?"

Cooper peeked past his friend into the motel room. It definitely wasn't much—dirty walls, dirty carpets, and dirty beds. But the place wasn't trashed, and the suitcase lying at the foot of the bed looked organized and clean. A suit jacket was hanging on a chair over by the room's desk, and Cooper could see an electric razor sitting on the vanity by the bathroom. One look at Jim's face showed that his friend had just shaved.

Cooper had spent the last two days building an image in his head of how Jim would look when he found him, and this wasn't it. Not even close.

"Coop, you okay, buddy?"

"Yeah, I'm good," he said. "I thought I should come find you since I haven't heard from you in a while."

Jim frowned as he motioned Cooper inside the room. Cooper stepped in and closed the door. The scent of stale cigarettes immediately assaulted him. There was a plastic sign on the wall stating this was a non-smoking room, but it looked like someone had used it to put out their cigarettes.

"Don't take this the wrong way, Coop," Jim said as he turned to face him. "If you'd said you were worried I was lying dead in a pool of my own vomit, I might have believed you. But I was your supervisor long before I was your friend. I know bullshit when I smell it. Why did you really come looking for me?"

Cooper thought about claiming he'd simply been worried about Jim's drinking problem, but why the hell screw around? Jim had given him an opening. He might as well use it. But this was a lot harder to bring up than he'd thought. Outside of his pack and his biological family, there weren't many people in the world more important to him than this man—except Everly, of course.

"I came to talk to you about Ryan North."

Jim frowned. "Ryan North, our former commander, the one who ran our EOD company into the ground? Why the hell would you want to talk to me about that piece of shit?"

"Because somebody tried to blow him up—twice. Both times at the DOD contractor offices he works at here in Dallas. I'm helping the feds find the bomber."

"And you think I might have some idea who...?" Jim's voice trailed off, his eyes widened. "Holy shit! You tracked me down because you think I'm the one who tried to kill him?"

"Did you?" Cooper asked bluntly, still trying to sense whether Jim's reactions were legitimate or not.

"Of course not!" Jim snapped. "I didn't even know that dickhead lived in Dallas. Why the holy hell would you even think something like that?"

"Because I'm having a hard time believing it's a coincidence that North is being targeted by an extremely skilled bomb maker at exactly the same time you show up in town looking for a job," Cooper said.

"That's your problem then." Jim let out a derisive laugh as he leaned back against the desk. "If the only requirements necessary to make it into your suspect pool is knowing how to make a bomb and being in Dallas, then maybe I should point out that there are about thirty or forty different local, state, and federal bomb techs working in this city—and that includes you. Can I assume *you're* on the suspect list?"

"Funny, but no, I'm not," Cooper said. "Because unlike you, I don't have a motive. I never even met Ryan North, and I certainly don't have as much reason to hate him as you do."

Jim rolled his eyes. "Spoken exactly like a person who has never had to work with him. Everyone who's ever met the guy hates him. Besides, hating a guy isn't a reason to kill him. For example, I'm starting to hate your ass right now, but that doesn't mean I plan on killing you."

"Maybe because I never fucked up and got a bunch of our friends killed, then let you take the heat for it," Cooper pointed out.

Jim went deathly still. "You asshole. I can't believe you went there. Yeah, I was pissed the investigation team was made up of a bunch of desk jockeys who didn't know a damn thing about field operations. I always thought more of the blame for what happened should have been laid on North's shoulders, but that's not how it worked out. I got over it." He looked Cooper straight in the eye. "And I didn't try to kill North."

Cooper studied Jim, looking for some sign that his friend was lying. Elevated heart rate, change in breathing pattern, nervous tick—anything. Cooper wasn't as good at picking up on this stuff as some of the other werewolves in his pack, but he could do it. And Jim wasn't putting off any signals that indicated he wasn't being entirely honest. He was tense and more than a little pissed off, but he wasn't lying.

It hit Cooper then that he might have been wrong about Jim. Before coming here, he'd been so sure his friend was the one behind these bombings, but now, he didn't know. It just didn't feel right. Then again, Cooper wasn't so sure how much he trusted his gut these days. After all the crap with Everly, his head wasn't exactly screwed on straight.

While he didn't want to keep going down this road,

he didn't have a choice. There were still some questions he needed answers to.

"Where were you last Monday morning at 0530?" he asked.

Jim glared like he was some kind of frigging monster. Cooper's gut clenched. He was getting that look a lot lately.

"You're seriously going to ask me these questions?" Jim demanded. "Doesn't our friendship mean a damn thing to you?"

Cooper ground his jaw. "Our friendship is why I'm here talking to you instead of arresting you. Now just answer the fucking question."

Jim stared at him for a long time. Muttering a curse, he turned and opened a leather-bound notebook on the desk and flipped through a few pages. "I was having breakfast at the IHOP off 360 because I had an interview at 0630 at Lockheed Martin for an analyst position. About eighty people saw me at the restaurant, including the waitress."

Cooper felt himself relax. "What about this past Monday at 0600?"

"I was over at Lockheed again, waiting around for hours, only to be told I'm not the kind of person they were looking for. And before you ask, I spent the rest of the day drinking. Remember, you picked me up the next morning?"

Cooper walked over to look at Jim's calendar. He had appointment times, names, addresses, and phone numbers listed for just about every defense contractor in the area. It shouldn't be too hard for the FBI to verify his story.

He took a deep breath then let it out slowly. He'd never been so happy to be wrong in his life. Not that Jim was likely to forgive him, but Cooper could deal with that.

"Look, I know this isn't going to mean much now, but I'm sorry I ever doubted you," he said. "Unfortunately, there's one more thing I need you to do, so you can be completely in the clear on this one."

"What's that?" Jim asked suspiciously.

Cooper pulled out a business card and set it on top of the calendar. "I need you to see the FBI agent in charge of the bombing case and tell him everything you told me."

Jim snorted. "You're shitting me, right? Why the hell do I need to talk to the FBI?"

"Because the FBI has a composite sketch of the person who bought the explosives used to build the bombs, and it looks a little like you. Not a lot, I'll admit, but it's in the ballpark."

Cooper had seen it when he'd stopped in to see Dennis before going from motel to motel. As sketches of suspects went, it wasn't great, since the guy who'd bought the explosives from the Burke brothers had been wearing sunglasses and a ball cap at the time. But Jim was nondescript enough for the FBI to think it might be him.

"They've also got a list of every military person Ryan North has ever had a run-in with," Cooper added. "Something tells me that your name is on that list. Pair that with the fact that you rented a car from the airport only a few days before the first bombing, not to mention that you're hopping from one motel to another like a criminal trying to hide out, and you start looking like a really good suspect. I'd rather you go talk to the FBI now, rather than wait for them to kick in your door."

Jim picked up the card and stared at it for a long time, then tossed it down with a sigh. "Fine. I'll stop by tomorrow between interview appointments."

Cooper frowned. "Tomorrow might be too late. I can go with you right now, if you want."

Jim pinned Cooper with a glare. "I liked you so much better when you were just a bomb tech, you know that? I'll stop by and see your FBI boyfriend today then. But it will have to be this afternoon. I have two places to drop off my résumé before the weekend. And no, I don't want you to come and hold my hand."

Cooper ignored the barb. "Fine. Dennis will probably be working until at least 1800 hours. Just call his cell if you need to. It's on the card."

Jim didn't say anything. Then again, there wasn't anything more that needed to be said. Cooper tried to apologize again before he left anyway, but Jim wasn't in the mood to listen.

He swore as he walked back to his Jeep. In the past week, he'd not only lost the woman he loved, but one of his best friends. On the upside, Jim wasn't the bomber. That was something at least.

Everly sat on her stool in front of her easel, gazing at the sketches she'd done of Landry a few days ago. It was pure torture, but she couldn't make herself stop. She gently ran her fingers over one picture, pretending she was touching the real thing. He was so damn mesmerizing to look at, even in her simple line drawings.

She'd dragged her miserable butt out of bed a little while after Tristan left, deciding she'd wallowed long enough. She'd showered off, eaten a little something, and then come into her studio, figuring she should actually get some work done. Since then all she'd done was look at the sketches she'd drawn of Landry and think about how amazing she felt when they were together. She was seriously thinking maybe Tristan was right about Landry putting something in her blood—like a werewolf curse or something. And if she didn't get past this overwhelmingly horrible feeling soon, she might start looking for a witch who could remove the curse. After all, if werewolves existed, why not witches?

She was trying to convince herself to put away the sketches of Landry when the doorbell rang.

Everly groaned. No doubt it was Tristan coming back with more unhelpful advice. Or worse, what if her brother had told their father that his one and only daughter had fallen in love with a werewolf? He was so crazy he might show up with a priest to do an exorcism.

She reluctantly slid off the stool and walked out of her art studio and through the living room. When she got to the door, she peeked out the peephole.

But to her surprise, it wasn't her father or her brothers. It was Jayna. Her long, blond hair was down and she flipped it over her shoulder as she waited.

Everly sighed with relief, but then frowned. She'd never told Jayna where she lived, which meant Landry must have. Had he sent her here to convince her to take him back?

She hesitated, torn between letting her friend in or

not. Then she yanked open the door before she could change her mind.

"Hey. Eric told me what happened," Jayna said. "I wanted to come over and see how you were doing. I thought maybe you might want to talk."

Everly opened her mouth to say she didn't feel like talking, but stopped herself. She felt closer to Jayna than anyone—even closer than she felt to Mia in some crazy way. So instead, she nodded and stepped back to let Jayna into the apartment. Besides, talking to Jayna about Landry had to be better than being alone with her own thoughts right now.

"Do you want something to drink?" she offered.

Jayna shook her head as she sat down on the couch. Everly collapsed on the other end, curling her legs under her.

"So…" Jayna said. "You broke up with Cooper because you found out he's a werewolf, huh?"

Everly stared at her friend, sure her exhausted and confused mind had twisted Jayna's words. She couldn't possibly have heard right? "Wh-what?"

Jayna held up her hands. "I'm not judging, and I'm not taking sides. I'm your friend, no matter what. Eric didn't go into any details, but he did tell me that your mom was murdered by an omega, and that you witnessed it, so I understand why you feel the way you do about werewolves."

Everly finally gained control over her vocal cords enough to spit out two words this time. "You know?"

Jayna slowly nodded. "That Cooper is a werewolf? Yeah. "

Everly stared at her. "And you're okay with that?"

she blurted out. "He has claws and fangs and glowing eyes. My brother stabbed him in the chest, and he pulled the knife out like it was nothing. The wound healed in hours. Jayna, he's a monster."

Jayna regarded her thoughtfully. "A monster, huh? Is that what you thought he was when he saved your life last week in that bank? Or when he refused to retaliate against your brothers even though they stabbed him?"

Everly didn't answer. She couldn't.

"Was Cooper being a monster when he helped Eric save my friends and me from Albanian mobsters?" Jayna persisted. "How about a couple months before that when he crawled through a maze of pitch-black tunnels filled with homemade explosives to save a kidnapped little girl? Or before that when he was shot multiple times trying to protect Mac from a low-life thug who wanted her dead?"

Everly's heart seized in her chest at the thought of Landry getting shot, but that had nothing to do with him being a werewolf. She wanted to explain that it was more complicated than that, but she couldn't find the words.

Jayna pushed her hair behind her ear with a sigh. "Look. I'm not saying Cooper's an ordinary man. We both know that's not true. And I'm not making light of what happened to your mother. What I am saying is that just because he has claws and fangs, that doesn't make him a monster. The werewolf who killed your mother was a monster. For all you know, he could have been a cold-blooded killer before he became a werewolf."

Everly knew all the things Jayna was saying were true because she'd had those same thoughts swirling through her head for two days. But it didn't matter that Landry was a good man. Every time she closed her eyes and thought of him changing into that monstrosity, she almost lost it.

"How did you figure out Landry was a werewolf?" Everly asked. Anything to distract herself so she'd stop picturing him with claws and fangs. "Did he turn into one in front of you?"

Jayna shook her head. "No. Once you know what a werewolf smells like, you can pick one out of a crowd at a couple hundred feet away, if the wind is right."

Lack of sleep was obviously affecting her ability to think clearly because what Jayna was saying simply didn't make any sense. Everly had been extremely close to Landry—multiple times—and she hadn't noticed anything unusual about the way he smelled. Except that he smelled good.

"I don't understand," she said. "Landry doesn't smell any different than anyone else."

Jayna gave her a small smile. "Of course he doesn't, not to a regular human like you. But it's very easy for a werewolf to recognize another werewolf. The scent is unmistakable to us."

Apparently, she was beyond being surprised. The only thing that shocked her was that it had taken so long to realize what Jayna had been driving at this whole time.

"You're one of them too, aren't you?" she breathed.

Jayna's eyes flashed a glowing, emerald green. Then, as fast as it appeared, the glow was gone. Everly gasped.

"Yes, I'm a werewolf," Jayna said. "By the way, Megan is too. Are you going to run out on our friendship like you ran out on Landry?"

Everly felt her face heat. As shocking as it was to hear that sweet, tiny Megan was a werewolf, it didn't keep her from feeling the sting of Jayna's words.

"That's not fair!" she cried. "I didn't want to leave Landry, but every time I think of him with claws and fangs, all I can see is my mom screaming in pain as that creature tore her apart. That's never going to go away."

Tears ran down her cheeks—again. Everly wiped them away with an angry swipe of her hand. *Dammit!*

Her expression softening, Jayna moved across the couch to put her arms around her. "Hey, it's okay."

No, it wasn't okay. Nothing about this was okay. But instead of telling Jayna that, Everly wrapped her arms around her friend and sobbed harder. Jayna didn't complain, but simply held on to her and let her cry it out.

"I'm sorry for losing it like that," she said when she could finally talk.

"It's not your fault," Jayna murmured. "I should never have said what I did. It was cruel and vicious, and you didn't deserve it."

"Maybe." Everly sniffed, wiping the last traces of tears from her cheeks as she pulled away. "But it was true, too. I did run out on Landry, and it's killing me inside."

Jayna's lips turned up at the corners in a sad smile. "When two people are meant to be together like you and Cooper, being apart is supposed to be hard."

Everly snorted. "How can we be together if seeing him brings back memories so bad I feel like crawling under the covers and hiding? I wish I could get them to go away."

"Because that's not the way memories work," Jayna said. "Bad ones don't go away, not if you keep running from them. At some point, you have to turn around and face them. If you don't, you'll be running the rest of your life. And you'll end up running away from everything that's good and right."

Everly chewed on her lip. "That sounds like the voice of experience."

"It is." Jayna took a deep breath. "When I was seventeen, my stepfather tried to rape me. I got away, nearly killing him in the process. It wasn't until later that I realized I really didn't get away that night. In my head, I was trapped in that bedroom with my stepfather for five years, running away from almost everything and everyone. I couldn't be with another man without seeing my stepfather's horrible face, and every time I thought about him, I could smell the cheap booze on his breath and feel his hands ripping at my clothes."

Everly shuddered at the thought of Jayna being attacked like that—and by someone who was supposed to be family. "How did you learn to forget?"

"You don't forget—ever." Jayna smiled. "But with the right person to support you and give you the strength to believe in yourself, you figure out that you have it in you to face the memories and move forward."

Everly sighed, marveling at how smoothly Jayna had drawn the conversation around to her and Landry. "I'm guessing that for me, the right person would be Landry?"

"Of course it is, you dope." Jayna snorted. "Why the hell do you think you're feeling so crappy? I wasn't kidding when I said you two are meant to be together— you're soul mates."

Everly lifted a brow. "Soul mates?"

"Don't look at me like that," Jayna scolded. "I'm

not being melodramatic, and I'm not kidding. You and Cooper are more than in love—you're bonded to each other. In the werewolf world, you're *The One* for him, and vice versa. You two can no more walk away from each other than you can walk away from yourselves. You feel like crap because you're denying yourself the one and only thing you really need. When you're with him, you'll be strong enough to face the memories of what happened to your mother. You'll be strong enough to face anything."

Everly didn't miss the emphasis Jayna had placed on *The One*. "You make it sound like Landry and I are somehow magically connected."

"You are," Jayna said.

Tristan had been right. Landry really was in her blood.

"But if Landry and I are connected like this, how could he have let me walk away from him?" she asked. "Didn't he know it would feel like this?"

Jayna looked at her like she was crazy. "How could he have known? It's not like he's ever felt this way about another woman. That's what being *The One* means—as in the one person in the world a werewolf is meant to be with because she or he can accept them for what they are. And as for how he could have let you walk away, it's because he loves you too much to stop you. He wants you to be happy, and if that means letting you go, he's ready to deal with the pain that comes with it. He's as miserable as you are right now."

Fresh tears started in her eyes again. Knowing Landry was feeling the same kind of anguish she felt, but was staying away because he thought that was what she needed to be happy made her heart hurt so much she could barely breathe.

"What am I going to do?" she whispered.

Even if she could face Landry again, he might not take her back. What if he thought helping her get past her psychological issues was more trouble than it was worth?

Jayna took Everly's hands in hers and gave them a squeeze. "It's not that complicated. You get changed and go see Cooper. Then figure out together what you need to do to get the two of you back on track." She smiled. "After that, everything else is doable."

Everly wasn't too sure of that, but she didn't resist as Jayna dragged her toward her bedroom. Jayna made it sound so easy. Something told Everly that getting back together with Landry was going to be the hardest thing she'd ever had to do. Maybe even harder than walking away from him in the first place.

Chapter 17

EVERLY PULLED HER CAR INTO THE FIRST FREE SPACE in Landry's apartment complex. It was probably a little early for him to be home from work, but his place was on the way from her apartment to the SWAT compound, so she figured she'd stop there first and check. If not, she'd head to the compound.

She could have simply called and found out where he was, but the fact was, she was too scared to call. What if he saw her name on the call screen and didn't answer? Or what if he did answer, and she couldn't figure out what to say? No, this was something she needed to do face to face.

She grabbed her purse and got out of her car, groaning when she realized she was so rattled she hadn't even parked straight. What the hell did it matter? She probably wouldn't be here very long. Regardless of what Jayna said about Landry being as hopelessly connected to her as she was to him, she wasn't going to delude herself into thinking their conversation would be all sprinkles and rainbows. It was going to take a long time to repair the damage that had been done to their relationship.

She looked around as she crossed the parking lot, but didn't see Landry's Jeep. That didn't mean anything. The parking area wrapped around three sides of the complex, so he could be parked anywhere.

Everly hesitated when she got to the entrance to the

building. Maybe she should have taken Mia up on her offer to come with her for moral support.

"You want me to come with?" Mia had offered when Everly told her she was going to see Landry. "I could sit in the car and wait for you, if you want?"

Everly had thanked her, but told her that she could do it alone. Now, she wasn't so sure. She squared her shoulders anyway and walked inside.

Her steps slowed as she approached Landry's apartment again. She had no idea what she was going to say to him. On the way over, she'd tried to rehearse something. Most everything she came up with started with some variation of *I'm sorry*, but none had sounded good enough to really use.

She took a deep breath and reached out to ring the bell, but stopped when she saw that the door to his apartment was already partially open. That was so like Landry. He probably hadn't bothered to push it all the way closed.

Everly almost rang the bell anyway, but then realized it would probably be a waste of time. If a werewolf's nose was as good as Jayna had said, Landry probably already knew she was out here, hesitating like some criminal. So why the heck was she still standing here? If she was going to do this, she would have to walk in his place first.

She pushed open the door and walked in, closing it quietly behind her. She was about to call out his name when she heard a noise coming from Landry's bedroom. She walked across the living area and into the room. She took in the big bed with the covers hastily tossed up over the pillows before she caught sight of movement to the right. Someone was leaning into the closet. And it wasn't Landry.

Whoever he was, he must have sensed her behind him because he stopped whatever he was doing and jerked up, spinning to look at her.

Her eyes widened when she saw that it was Jim. He gave a start, almost falling back into Landry's neatly organized SWAT and police uniforms. If he hadn't thrown one arm out to grab the edge of the closet with one free hand, he would have.

Everly stared at the green rectangular block in his other hand. She didn't know what it was, but she saw the word *Demolition* written on it.

"Everly," Jim said in a tone of voice that didn't do a thing to help her relax. "What are you doing here?"

What was *she* doing here? What was *he* doing here?

She would have asked, but then she caught sight of the duffel bag in the closet. It was unzipped, and there were more of those green blocks inside. Why would Jim put something that looked like a bag of explosives in Landry's closet?

Alarm bells rang so loudly in Everly's head she could hardly think. She backpedaled as Jim took a step toward her.

"Everly, this isn't what it looks like," he said.

When someone said, *this isn't what it looks like*, it was always exactly what it looked like. Heart pounding, Everly turned and ran for the front door.

Jim's footsteps were loud behind her as she ran into the hallway and raced for the stairs. She only had to make it to her car. Then she could call the cops.

Everly didn't make it to the top of the stairwell

before Jim caught up and gave her a shove in the back.
She barely avoided flying headlong down the flight of
steps, but didn't avoid the concrete support column off
to the side. She lifted an arm to protect her face, but
still hit the column so hard that every ounce of air in
her lungs exploded. The pain was immediate, intense,
and everywhere.

The impact stunned her so much, she couldn't even
scream. Then Jim was dragging her down the stairs
toward the parking lot, and there wasn't a damn thing
she could do to stop him.

Cooper sat on the workout bench in the small weight
room the SWAT team had put together in the training
building. It could hold only about six or eight of his
teammates at a time, but it had a lot of weights, and
right now, that was all he cared about.

"One more set," he announced, wiping the sweat out
of his eyes, then dropping back on the bench and wrapping his hands around the heavily loaded barbell.

Brooks didn't say anything—one of the benefits of
working out with him—as he took up point at the head
of the bench to spot him again.

Cooper lifted the weights off the rack with a growl.
The thick bar flexed and bowed, but he ignored it as he
slowly lowered the bar to his chest and let it rest there for
a moment before shoving up with an explosive grunt. He
held the four-hundred-and-twenty-five pounds at arm's
length for a second and let it come back down before
doing it all over again. He didn't cheat the exercise by
letting the weight bounce off his chest each time it came

down, either. He was here for the burn, not the number of reps he could do.

He'd come back to the compound after seeing Jim, relieved that he didn't have to worry about his friend being involved in all this bomber crap anymore. But without Jim to focus all his attention on, he was left with only one other person to fixate on—Everly. He couldn't even remember how many times he'd almost headed out to his Jeep so he could drive by her place and make sure she was okay. He'd controlled himself, but only because he knew Everly would freak out if she caught him snooping around. She'd made it pretty fucking clear she didn't want to have anything else to do with him. Hell, now that she knew a knife to the heart would kill him, she'd probably send those psycho-ass brothers after him to finish what they'd started.

"Dude," Brooks said. "You might want to put more weight on the bar because this obviously isn't enough."

Cooper looked up to see Brooks grinning at him. That was when he realized his arms, shoulders, and chest muscles were burning like hell. He racked the weights and sat up. "How many reps did I do?"

Brooks shrugged as he came around to take his turn. "I don't know. I got tired of counting—around forty."

Cooper stood and moved around the bench into the spotter position. "Yeah, sorry about that. I'm a little preoccupied."

Brooks laughed in that deep, rumbling voice of his. "You think?"

Cooper was going to mention that he liked Brooks better when he wasn't talking so much, but he didn't get the chance because Alex walked in.

"Hey Cooper, you have some visitors at the gate."

Unless one of them was Everly, he wasn't interested. "I'm not really in the mood to talk to anyone. See if you can get rid of them."

Alex snorted. "I think you might want to reconsider. They have guns."

Cooper frowned. Who the hell would be bold enough to come to the SWAT compound toting weapons? There were only four people he could think of who would be that stupid—Everly's brothers. Swearing under his breath, he strode out of the weight room. Alex and Brooks followed him to the front gate, clearly intending to give him backup if he needed it.

Tristan, Armand, Giles, and Claude were waiting on the other side of the chain-link fence, looking pissed off as hell.

"Where's our sister?" Armand demanded, his hand resting on the butt of the pistol tucked in the front of his belt.

A twinge of panic zipped through him. "I haven't seen her in two days. Is she okay?"

The four Danu brothers looked at one another questioningly, but it was Tristan who answered him.

"We went to see Everly, hoping to cheer her up, but Mia said she'd left for your place over two hours ago. When we went over there to make sure she was okay, we couldn't find her. We found her car though."

A part of Cooper's mind wondered how the brothers had even known where he lived, but he brushed that off as unimportant.

"What do you mean, she's not there?" Cooper growled. "Did you search around the apartment complex?"

Tristan nodded. "She's not there."

Cooper threw Alex a quick look. "Open the fence."

Not waiting for a reply, he turned and ran to his Jeep. Brooks fell into step beside him, jumping into the passenger seat without a word. Figuring Alex would want to come too, Cooper paused just long enough for him to lock the gate and hop in the back.

Alex grabbed onto the roll bar as Cooper sped away from the SWAT compound. "What's wrong?"

"I don't know that anything is wrong." Cooper glanced in the rearview mirror and saw Armand's minivan chasing them. "But my gut has been shouting at me all day to go check on Everly, and I've been ignoring it."

Fifteen minutes later, he squealed to a stop in a space only a few down from Everly's car. Behind him, Armand stomped on the brakes and brought the minivan from hell to a smoking stop a few cars farther down. The Brothers Stupid jumped out and immediately headed for his apartment. Cooper, Alex, and Brooks caught up before they took two strides.

"You just going to keep it running like that?" he asked as he raced ahead and bounded up the stairs three at a time.

"It's a frigging minivan," Armand shouted back. "Who the hell would steal it?"

There was that, Cooper agreed.

He was so desperate to get into his apartment he probably would have kicked in his own door, but someone had already done it. Everly's brothers no doubt.

"Sorry about the door," Tristan said.

Everly's brothers piled in after Cooper, looking around his apartment like they expected her to jump out from behind the couch. His nose immediately told him she'd been there—and so had Jim.

But how had they gotten in his apartment? Neither had a key.

Suddenly, it all came together in one sickening punch to the gut. Jim promised he'd go see Dennis, but instead, he came here. Cooper wasn't sure why Jim had broken in, but he could think of only one reason his friend would have had blown off meeting with Dennis—because he really was the bomber. *Shit.* He didn't know how Jim had been able to lie to him so convincingly, but his friend had played him for a fool. How the fuck could he have been so wrong? Because he'd been desperate to believe anything his friend had told him, not to mention so messed up about Everly that he hadn't been thinking straight.

But why the hell had Jim grabbed Everly? Since her car was here, and she wasn't, it only made sense that she'd gone with him. And Cooper's gut told him she hadn't gone willingly.

"Shit," he swore.

Armand glared at him. "What is it? Where's Everly?"

"I don't have time to explain," Cooper said.

Understatement there. Now that Jim knew Cooper was on to him, it was reasonable to assume his friend wouldn't waste any more time going after Ryan North. If Cooper found the former EOD company commander, he'd find Jim. And if Everly wasn't with him, Cooper would make Jim tell him where she was. And if Jim hurt her, Cooper was going to kill him, friend or not.

He turned to head for the door, but the Brothers Stupid blocked his way, their faces set like they thought

he was full of shit. If they didn't move, this time he
would hurt them.

"Cooper, something's not right here," Alex said.

Yeah, no shit. He opened his mouth to say as much
when Brooks interrupted him.

"Cooper, we're about to have company." And from
the tone in his voice, that company wasn't friendly.

Before Cooper could move, Dennis and his FBI partner, along with three more FBI agents and four DPD
uniformed officers burst into his apartment, guns drawn
and aimed at him.

Cooper stared. "What the hell, Dennis?" While he
was pretty sure they wouldn't shoot him, he definitely
decided he didn't like the feeling of being on this end of
a gun. "Do me a favor and point those fucking guns in
another direction, would you?"

"No can do, Cooper," Dennis said.

Weapon still trained on him, Dennis walked over and
pulled Cooper's gun out of the holster. Then he leaned
down and yanked out Cooper's backup piece as well.

"What's going on Dennis?" Cooper asked again. He
was on the edge of losing his patience. He was wasting
valuable seconds with this shit when he needed to be out
there looking for Jim. The mere thought that Everly was
in danger had him spinning like the Tasmanian Devil on
caffeine. "I'm in kind of a rush, so I don't have time to
hang around and chat."

"That's too bad Cooper, because I can't let you leave
until I look around your place and ask you a few questions," Dennis said.

Cooper's eyes widened. "You're searching my apartment? What the hell for?"

Dennis regarded him with a look that could only be called disappointed. "Do you own a solid black duffel bag?"

The question took Cooper completely by surprise. "Um, yeah. It's one of my work bags. It's in the closet in my bedroom. Why?"

"Wait here," Dennis ordered as he walked past Cooper to head that way.

"Oh shit," Alex muttered.

Before Cooper could ask Alex what the hell that was about, Dennis came back out of the bedroom, the duffel bag in one hand and a block of C-4 in the other.

Cooper stared. What the hell?

"And we're fucked," Alex said.

"That's not mine," Cooper told Dennis.

He realized how incredibly stupid that sounded even as he said the words. How many perps had used that exact same line with him?

But Dennis didn't seem to be listening anyway. He handed the bag to his partner, then holstered his gun and took out a pair of handcuffs. He read Cooper his rights as he pulled his hands behind his back and snapped the metal around his wrists.

"Dennis, you know this is insane, right?" Cooper asked.

"All I know is that we got an anonymous tip a couple hours ago from someone who said they saw you carrying a black duffel bag possibly filled with explosives into your apartment. And what do you know? The C-4 that I found in there is the same lot used in the bombings."

"That's bullshit," Cooper snapped. "That C-4 isn't mine."

But now he knew what Jim was doing in his

apartment. One of his best friends in the world was framing him, not only for the bombing, but murdering a fellow DPD officer. Jim must have grabbed Everly because she saw him do it.

Dennis looked for a minute like he wanted to believe him, then his mouth tightened. "Maybe not, and if it isn't, we'll get it all straightened out at the FBI office."

Everly could be dead by then. "I don't have time to go straighten this shit out. Someone very important to me is in trouble. I need to find her—now!"

"Not going to happen, buddy," Dennis said, nudging Cooper toward the door.

Cooper tensed, balling his hands into fists so he could break the cuffs. He'd probably end up getting shot a few times, but as long as they didn't hit him in the head or the heart, he'd be fine.

Tristan locked gazes with Cooper then nudged his oldest brother. "We can't let them arrest Landry," he whispered. "He's the only one who can find Everly."

Armand looked at Tristan incredulously. "You believe him?"

Since pushing Cooper toward the door wasn't working, Dennis gripped his arm and tried to drag him. Cooper dug in his heels.

"Yes," Tristan said softly. "Landry loves Everly as much as we do. More, if that's possible."

Armand looked at the cops, then at Cooper. "You'd better be right about this," he said to Tristan.

Then before the feds or cops could stop him, Armand drew back his fist and punched Dennis.

There was a single second of stunned silence, then it

was a free-for-all as Alex, Brooks, and Everly's other brothers jumped into the fray and started swinging.

The fight would end with her brothers and his pack mates getting arrested for sure, but they were willing to risk it so he could save Everly. He wasn't going to let their sacrifice go to waste. Cooper just prayed nobody started shooting.

Lifting his shoulders, Cooper snapped the links between the handcuffs, then turned and ran into the bedroom. He leaped for the big window beside the bed, twisting in mid-air so his shoulder hit the glass first. The window shattered, the noise echoing in his ears as he hit the ground two floors below.

He rolled to his feet and hauled ass around the building, heading for his Jeep. But then he skidded to a stop. There were four cop cars right behind his vehicle. He was never getting out of there.

Armand's minivan, on the other hand, was still sitting in its space all nice and lonely with the engine still running.

Cooper dashed across the parking lot and jumped in, squealed out of the parking lot, and headed for the Triple S-I office and Ryan North, praying Jim didn't get there first.

———

Everly had barely been aware of where they were going when Jim had grabbed her on the stairwell. By the time she'd come out of her impact-induced fog, she'd been taken to some kind of self-storage place and tied to a chair with a thick length of rope. She didn't know where they were, but the sounds of jets passing over told her that they were close to the airport. Jim was on the far side of the room, leaning over a table, a soldering iron in his hand.

"Don't bother screaming," he said quietly. "No one will hear you, and it will only make me jump, which would probably get us both blown into a big pink mist."

Between the block of explosives Jim had been holding back at Landry's apartment and the disgusting visual he'd just provided, it wasn't hard to figure out what her kidnapper was doing—he was making a bomb.

Besides what she'd seen on the news, Everly hadn't known much of what was going on with the bombing case, except that Landry had been helping the FBI, and that he didn't like to talk about it. But she never would have dreamed in a million years that Landry's friend was the bomber.

"Why are you doing this?" she asked softly.

Jim didn't say anything for so long that Everly thought he was going to ignore her. But finally he put down the soldering iron and turned to look at her.

"Did Cooper ever tell you about how our friends got killed in Iraq?" he asked.

She nodded, trying to remember exactly what Landry had said, and what it had all meant. "He said that a secondary device had blown up in the safe area while you were dealing with the first bomb. He told me that the final report said the deaths were the result of hostile actions."

"He got some of it right." Jim snorted and turned to pick up a pair of pliers. "I did go downrange to work on an IED, and a secondary device did kill our friends, but that's about all the official report got right."

Jim stopped, his brow furrowing as he leaned closer to the device he was making. Everly wondered if it was wise to keep him talking. She had no idea what he had planned for her—and would prefer if she never found out. Better to keep him talking.

"Then what happened?" she prompted.

Jim let out a short laugh. "I left four of the unit's soldiers and our commander—Lieutenant Ryan North—in a good safe area while I headed downrange. But the LT decided to move the safe area to a place with better shade so it would be more comfortable. He moved to the same place that another EOD team had used just a week before, something the insurgents hoped we'd do. It was a trap. An IED was planted there, and that's how those three guys died. The enemy didn't kill them—Ryan North killed them."

Everly could see how he might think that. "Couldn't it simply have been a stupid mistake on his part?"

Jim threw something down on the table with an oath so loud it made Everly jump, practically knocking over the chair she was tied to. "If that was the case, why'd he tell the investigation team I put them in that location? And why did he pay off the only other survivor of the explosive to say the same thing?"

Everly stared. Landry hadn't said anything about that—obviously, he hadn't known. "North paid someone to lie to cover up what really happened?"

Jim's hands were shaking so badly he had to grip the edge of the table to steady them. "Yeah—Specialist Neal Christian. Of course, I didn't find that out until a couple months ago when Christian called me and told me what he'd done. At the time, all I knew was that two people I trusted lied about me and destroyed my reputation, my career…my life."

Maybe it would have helped if she had grown up around a military family and could understand how these people thought, but right then, none of this was making any sense.

"All of that just to cover up a mistake?" she asked. "That's insane."

"That's because it was never about covering up a mistake," he said bitterly. "It was about making sure Ryan North stayed in Iraq."

Okay, that was even more insane. "Why would anyone in their right mind want to stay in Iraq?"

Jim started pushing small silver tubes inside lengths of larger steel pipe. "Because North had gotten himself sent to Iraq so he could help some people win service contracts from the army. He never spent any time learning how to be a good EOD tech. He was more interested in working deals with all those contractors over there. He figured that by helping to get bigger contracts and sweeter deals, they'd give him a little something on the side."

Jim kept working on the bomb, running wires from pipe to pipe as he gestured at a cardboard box full of papers on the floor. "Of course, I didn't know any of this until Christian brought me that box of stuff there. Turns out Christian couldn't live with what he'd done any longer, but he was too much of a coward to do anything about it. He drove down to see me, dropped all this shit in my lap, then walked out and hung himself a few days later. That's when I knew I had to do something. If I didn't, North would get away with everything."

Everly frowned. "If you have all that evidence, why didn't you take it to the police or the army?"

Jim laughed again, and there was a really scary edge to it this time, like he was close to losing it. "Because the police don't care about why a bunch of soldiers died in a foreign country, and the army only wants to bury crap like this. No one was ever going to do anything about North unless I did. That's when I decided to get out of the army and kill him. A bomb seemed like the most appropriate way for him to go."

The cold, emotionless way Jim said it convinced Everly more than all the bomb components scattered about the table that he was flat-out insane.

"Do you have any idea how hard it actually is to kill a particular person with a bomb?" Jim asked almost conversationally. "If you just want to go out and kill anyone who wanders by, it's easy, but if you're aiming for a particular person? Well, that's hard as hell. I showed up in town last week assuming I'd get my explosives, build a simple car bomb, kill North, and then find a new job here in Dallas within a couple days."

Jim never stopped working on the bomb as he talked. "But then I found out that North lived in a fancy condo apartment, with secure parking, guards on the doors, and cameras everywhere. I had to give up the idea of getting a bomb onto his personal vehicle. There was no way to get into his condo without a hundred people seeing me. And the parking garage where he works is even worse." He shrugged. "I thought I'd come up with a perfect plan to get him as he drove into the garage near his office, but then that cop showed up out of nowhere and set off my bomb too early."

Jim started yanking on the wires he was twisting together so hard that Everly flinched every time he moved. This crazy guy was going to kill himself if he wasn't careful, and he'd end up taking her with him.

"The second bombing attempt was rushed, I admit," Jim continued. "I couldn't get close enough to the entrance to his office because of the cameras, so I ended up putting it as close as I could. It wasn't close enough though."

Jim leaned over and picked up a piece of black material from the far side of the table. She couldn't see what it was, but he attached the bigger metal pipes to the material.

"But this time is going to be completely different," he said softly as he worked. "This time, I won't have any problems getting close enough."

Everly shuddered. She definitely didn't like the flat, dead look Jim got in his eyes as he said that last part.

"Why were you at Landry's place?" she asked, trying to keep him talking. "Why were you putting those explosives in his closet?"

Jim laughed. "Because Cooper is too damn smart for his own good—always has been. He started getting the idea in his head that I was involved in all this. I got him off my case, but only for a few hours. He wanted me to talk to the FBI today, and I don't have time for that. North has a reservation in a couple hours at the fancy restaurant in his condo building. It's one of the rare chances I'm going to have to get close to him, and I couldn't have Cooper showing up and getting in the way. So I dropped an anonymous tip to the FBI telling them that Cooper is storing explosives in his apartment. He's probably been arrested by now."

Everly gasped. The thought of the FBI arresting
Landry and treating him like a criminal made her so
mad she wanted to scream. "How could you do that to
Landry? My God, you saved his life!"

Jim glanced at her. "Don't worry about your boyfriend. I'm sure the feds will let him go at some point,
especially after I kill North. But until then, at least he
won't be in the way."

He adjusted something on the bomb, then lifted the
black material off the table and held it up. Her heart began
to race when she realized it was a vest.

She watched in horror as he slipped his arms into it and
settled the weight on his shoulders. He must have liked the
way it felt because he smiled. Oh God. If he was wearing
explosives strapped to his chest, it was because he didn't
plan on living through the next attack on Ryan North.

"Why did you kidnap me?" she asked.

"It was a spur-of-the-moment thing," Jim said. "I
never would have done it if you hadn't shown up at
Cooper's place. But now that I have you, it's sort of ser-
endipitous. I could use your help."

"How?" she asked, even though she didn't want
to know.

Jim smirked at her. "That restaurant I mentioned?
Well, it's kind of fancy, and a guy walking in there alone
might attract attention. But with you on my arm, I'll be
able to waltz right in."

She shook her head. "I'm not going to help you
kill anyone."

He laughed. "Sure you will. Or I'll go down to the
FBI field office and figure out where they're holding
Cooper, then blow *him* up instead of North."

Everly's heart skipped a beat. She didn't know if a werewolf could be killed by a bomb, and she wasn't ready to find out. Considering how much Jim hated North, she didn't think he'd make good on his threat, but she wasn't sure. Jim had said the one thing that would get her to do anything he wanted.

"If I help you get into that restaurant, you'll let me go and won't try to hurt Landry, or anyone else, right?" she asked.

"Of course I'll let you go," Jim said. "I have no interest in killing anyone but North."

If she went along with him, maybe she'd be able to alert someone at the restaurant and stop the bombing before it started. But as she watched him slip a suit jacket over the explosives vest, she wasn't sure her plan would work. When he buttoned the single button on the front of the jacket, you couldn't see anything that indicated Jim was wearing a bomb. What was she going to do, shout out that he was a bomber right in the middle of a crowd?

Jim arched a brow in her direction, like he wanted her to tell him how good he looked. Everly only glared at him. He might have been a great EOD tech and Cooper's friend, but that had been a long time ago. Now, he was nothing more than a cold-blooded killer.

Chapter 18

COOPER PULLED ARMAND'S MINIVAN INTO THE guest parking area of the luxury condo complex on North Pearl and looked up at the tall building. It was ten stories high with lots of glass, immaculate landscaped trees and bushes around the first floor and pool, and a monthly maintenance fee alone that was more than Cooper's total rent. It wasn't the Ritz-Carlton, but it was in the same neighborhood, and as a management-level drone in a small DOD contracting firm, this place should have been out of Ryan North's price range. Cooper only hoped Jim was here, and that he had Everly with him. If Cooper struck out, he wasn't sure where to look next.

Cooper had gone straight from his apartment to Triple S-I, praying there wouldn't be any cops or feds hanging around. Because he had no doubt there was a BOLO out on him already, and if anyone saw him, he was screwed. But there hadn't been a cop or fed in sight.

Unfortunately, North wasn't in his office. Recognizing him from the investigation, Arnold Braun's secretary had told him that North had gone home already, getting ready for an overseas trip to handle some contractor work. Cooper had left a few minutes later with North's home address, doubting it was a coincidence that the man was leaving the country at the same time Jim was trying to kill him. The theory that North believed he was no more a target than any of the other senior company officials was starting to look a little bogus. Then again, as Cooper looked at the expensive place where North lived, he started to think there were a lot of bogus things going on with the former EOD officer. Something told Cooper that if North left the country tonight he probably wouldn't be back.

Cooper flashed his badge at the doorman, and like magic, a bigger man in a slightly more expensive suit showed up.

"Is there a problem officer?" the man—obviously security—asked, taking in Cooper's SWAT uniform and probably wondering why the holster at his hip was empty.

"I hope not," Cooper said. "Have you seen a man about forty or so, gray at the temples, medium height, about a hundred-and-ninety pounds? There may have been a beautiful woman with long, golden brown hair with him."

The doorman immediately looked at the security guy with a look like, *I fucking told you so*, and then turned back to Cooper.

"Yeah," the doorman said. "They were heading to the restaurant on the tenth floor. The woman smiled, but she didn't look like she was enjoying herself. Is there a problem with them?"

At least Everly was with Jim. "Was the man carrying a bag or package of any kind?"

"No." The security guy frowned. "He didn't have anything with him. What is this about, officer?"

Cooper ignored the question. "I'm guessing you don't pat down your guests before they go up to the restaurant?"

When the guard shook his head, Cooper headed for the doors. "Which way are the elevators to the restaurant?"

Cooper ran through the lobby, looking at the

green-tinted glass of the atrium roof above him and
the view of the trees and shrubs that grew right up to
most of the big windows of the ground floor. It was a
beautiful place. Hopefully, it wouldn't get messed up.
Hopefully, he'd be able to stop Jim before anything like
that happened.

There was a crowd waiting for the elevators. *Shit.* He
didn't have a lot of time. Cooper swerved and shoved the
door leading to the stairwell. He sprinted up the flights
to the tenth floor. As Cooper slowly pushed open the
heavy metal door at the top of the landing, he realized
the shit had hit the fan. He could already hear screaming
and shouting.

Cooper slowly stepped out of the stairwell. Across
from him, both sets of elevator doors were wedged open.
Now he understood why there was such a huge crowd
downstairs waiting for elevators. Jim hadn't wanted
anyone interrupting him.

Cooper swore as he walked into the restaurant, past
the hostess table and over to a partition separating that
area from the rest of the restaurant. He really wished
Dennis hadn't taken his weapons. He felt frigging naked
going into a situation like this.

He poked his head around the wall and immediately felt his whole body tense as his claws and fangs
extended on their own.

Twenty terrified customers, chefs, and waitresses
huddled against the far wall of the restaurant, their eyes
as big as saucers. Ryan North stood on one side in front
of the panoramic windows, holding a Glock on Jim and
Everly, who were standing near the other end of the panoramic windows. Jim held Everly in his arms, using her

as a shield. There were tears in her eyes, and her heart was beating a hundred miles an hour. She was scared, but she was holding it together.

Cooper frowned in confusion. Jim didn't seem to be holding a weapon, but North and the rest of the customers in the restaurant where obviously freaking out. Then Cooper saw the one thing he would have never in his life expected to see on Jim—a suicide bomb.

The vest was tight-fitting and partially hidden by the sports jacket Jim had on, but Cooper could see at least six pipe bombs attached. No doubt there were more in places he couldn't see.

Jim held a controller in his left hand, his thumb already pressing down on the top button. That definitely wasn't good.

"Go ahead, Ryan," Jim taunted. "Shoot me. The bomb goes off as soon as my finger comes off the trigger."

Fuck. This was about as bad as it got.

Jim already had the button pushed on a dead man's switch, and Cooper seriously doubted there'd be a way to return the system to the safe condition. Jim had walked in here planning to die—why have a safety switch?

Cooper took a deep breath to calm himself, forcing his claws and fangs to retract. The animal inside him wanted out so badly, wanted to run to Everly's side and protect her no matter what. But there was nothing a werewolf could do to solve this problem. Cooper was going to have to do it all on his own.

He exhaled loudly then walked around the dividing wall and into the restaurant.

"That was pretty fucked up the way you stashed those C-4 blocks in my bedroom closet, Jim," he said as casually as he could as he approached his friend—and the woman he loved. "The damn feds tried to arrest me."

Jim stared at him stunned, but it was the look on Everly's face that almost stopped Cooper in his tracks. Her eyes widened, and her heart began to pound even faster. Damn, she seemed more terrified of him than she was of Jim and the bomb strapped to his chest. God, that hurt like hell.

He pulled himself back to the here and now just in time to hear Jim telling him he should leave.

"You know I can't do that, Jim," Cooper said. "Why don't you just let Everly and all these other people go, then I'll help you get that damn vest off, and we can get the hell out of here?"

Jim shook his head violently and ranted about all their friends being dead, about North murdering them and how wrong it was for their former commander to be walking around free—hell, to be walking around at all. About how he'd put the dog tags from one of the soldiers North had gotten killed in that IED attack. As much as Cooper hated admitting it, the man he used to know and love as a brother was gone.

"If you won't let everyone go, what about letting Everly go and using me as a hostage instead?" Cooper asked.

Jim was so busy running down the list of all the atrocities North had committed he didn't even hear Cooper. He wanted revenge, and he didn't care if had to die to get it. Unfortunately, he was going to take Everly and everyone else in the restaurant with him.

Everly was so terrified it hurt Cooper down to his bones. She wouldn't even be here right now if it weren't for him. If he could go back to the bank that day and do it all over again, he would never have asked her out.

He'd known for days there would never be a happily ever after for them. That knowledge took so much out of him that it was hard to think about anything but how miserable he was without her. The one woman in the world who was *The One* for him just happened to be terrified of werewolves. He'd found his *One*. They simply could never be together.

But none of that was important now. All that mattered was saving her life. If he could do that, in some small way, it might repay her for all the pain he'd brought her.

Cooper looked at Jim, considering the vest he wore and the trigger in his hand, then the window behind his friend. Ten stories was a long way down. But the fall wouldn't be the thing that did him in. No, the bomb going off would take care of that. He'd survived an IED blast once before, but that time he'd been in a bomb suit and nearly ten feet away when the device had gone off. This time, he would be much closer.

What the hell? Once an EOD tech, always an EOD tech. It was almost a given that someday he'd get blown into a big pink mist.

Jim was ranting so loudly now that Cooper doubted he was even aware of what the hell was going on around him. It didn't help that North was pleading for his own worthless life in between calling Jim a psycho.

Cooper locked eyes with Everly.

"I love you," he said, even though there was no way she could hear him over the bedlam.

Then he growled and let his body partially shift like he'd done in the bank a few days ago. The moment his muscles twisted and hummed into life, he ran toward his best friend and the woman he was supposed to spend the rest of his life with but never would.

Jim had lied to her. Everly had helped him get into the restaurant, but the moment he'd seen Ryan North sitting by himself at a table near one of the windows, he forgot his promise to let her go. He forgot the promise that he wouldn't hurt anyone but his former commander too.

Instead, there was a whole restaurant full of people trying to hide behind a few pieces of furniture, and Jim was using her as a human shield as he taunted and shouted at North. She'd been too terrified to try to free herself, afraid she'd jostle his hand and set off the bomb.

But then Landry had strolled in, and her panic level had shot through the roof. How the heck had he found them? More importantly, what the heck did he think he could do here? Jim was slipping closer to the edge by the second. Now that Jim had North in front of him, she was surprised he hadn't already released the bomb trigger and killed them all. Landry couldn't do anything here except get himself killed. She shook her head, trying to silently tell him to get away while he still could. She would have shouted at him to run, but she was afraid if she did, it would set Jim off.

She'd known after talking to Jayna earlier that she still loved Landry, but it wasn't until that moment when she realized they might both die, how incredibly stupid she had been. Yes, the werewolf inside him scared her, but it was something she knew she could have come to accept given time. But now, it didn't seem like there was going to be any more time for them, and Everly was furious with herself for wasting the last two days she could have been with him.

Then Landry's eyes caught hers, and she saw him mouth those three little words that people throw around so casually. But with Landry, she knew there was nothing casual about it because in the next breath, he released a growl and darted toward her and Jim in a blur.

Everly opened her mouth to scream for him to stop. But before she could even make a sound, Landry slammed into Jim. There was a tug on her shoulder, then both Landry and Jim flew past her, smashing through the big window behind her. She was so shocked it took a moment to register what happened. When she figured it out, her heart seized in her chest. Screaming, she spun around and ran toward the broken window, even though she knew it was too late.

She'd barely taken two steps when an explosion rocked the building. The sound of breaking glass seemed to last forever, then a huge ball of black smoke rolled upward past the shattered window.

Everly rushed to the window, grabbing the frame as she leaned out. Her stomach spun as she looked down. She expected to see both Landry and Jim lying lifeless on the pavement below, but all she saw was the broken glass of the lobby atrium. Smoke rolled up through the opening, keeping her from seeing anything. She strained her eyes anyway, hoping to see Landry getting to his feet, but she didn't.

She wasn't sure why she expected him to be alive. It was impossible to believe that even a werewolf could survive the impact with a glass roof from this high up, not to mention falling through it, and then an explosion.

That didn't stop her from whirling around and shoving past a confused North and running for the elevators. She had to find Landry.

—⁓—

Cooper had clamped his hand around Jim's as he slammed into him, doing all he could to keep the man he once considered his best friend from lifting his thumb and blowing all of them to pieces—at least until they were through the window and far enough away for Everly to be safe. He barely felt the impact as they hit the window. He'd been moving too fast, and his mind had gone numb. Only one thought existed in his head— let Everly live through this.

Jim tore at his hand as they fell, but Cooper hung onto the bomb trigger silently counting the milliseconds until they were far enough away from the only perfect thing that had ever stepped into his life. The air whistled in his ears, and the sensation of weightlessness was almost a comfort. He expected it to last only a few seconds so he didn't bother to look down. Why should he worry about what was coming when he couldn't do anything about it?

One moment he was falling, the next he and Jim smashed into something that shattered under them. It took a nanosecond for Cooper to realize it was glass, not pavement. They'd hit the roof of the atrium.

Shit.

He must have landed on one of the aluminum framing pieces that held up the glass of the atrium. While the glass beneath Jim shattered, whatever was under Cooper didn't. He heard and felt things inside him break as he bounced on impact. Then, as Jim was ripped out of his arms, Cooper felt himself slide down the inclined glass roof and keep right on going.

Cooper went only a couple feet when the blast hit him, breaking the glass out from under him and flinging him off the atrium roof into the air.

He was immediately transported to that day more than four years ago when another blast had shoved him like this. Except this time, he didn't have all those images of regrets and things left undone running through his head. He had gotten far enough away from Everly, and she was safe. He had no regrets and had left nothing undone this time. He'd met and spent an amazing week with the love of his life. A man couldn't ask for more than that.

Frag from the bomb and glass thrown by the blast wave sliced through him, but only for the barest fraction of a second. Then he was spinning uncontrollably toward the ground rushing up to meet him.

Cooper tried to twist around, flailing against unresisting air as he attempted to get his feet under him, but he hit something that definitely wasn't the ground before he could. It yielded then snapped under him, altering his trajectory and bouncing him against the glass wall of the building.

He had a moment to realize he'd bounced off a tree branch before he hit more, ricocheting back and forth, like a pinball in an old-fashioned arcade game. Every impact slowed him down, but it also hurt like hell as smaller branches stabbed into him like tiny knives, and larger ones slammed into him like baseball bats. Things were cracking and snapping inside him like a fucking bowl of Rice Krispies.

He gave up any thought of getting his feet under him and settled for getting his arms up to protect his face and head. He'd hated his old army bomb suit, but he would have killed for one right about then.

Cooper held his breath, his body tense as he waited to hit the next branch, but it didn't happen. Instead, he slammed hip-first into the ground. Agony exploded through him as he felt bones break. Pain unlike anything he'd ever experienced rushed through him.

Shit.

If he was feeling pain, did that mean he was still alive? The answer to his question was a black sheet slowly pulled over his head.

Chapter 19

THE ELEVATORS WERE MOBBED WITH TERRIFIED people trying to get down from the restaurant level, so Everly headed for the stairs. She ran down the steps so fast she almost fell. It didn't help that her eyes were so full of tears she could barely see. She almost stopped half a dozen times, convinced that she really didn't want to see what she knew she'd find downstairs.

How had everything gone so wrong? The conversation with Jayna had finally made her realize how badly she'd treated Landry, a man who had never done anything but save her life over and over, loving her the whole time. But when she'd tried to fix her mistake, it seemed like fate had decided to conspire against her, teasing her with a glimpse of the man she could have had, then taking him away in the most horrible way. Seeing him go through that window with Jim had taken a part out of her soul she doubted she could ever get back, especially if Landry was gone.

That thought brought even more tears to her eyes, but her feet kept moving of their own accord, bringing her to the ground floor much faster than she would have thought possible. She ignored the door that led outside, reaching out to shove down the bar on the door that led into the lobby instead.

The area that Jim had practically dragged her through fifteen minutes earlier was in chaos now. Glass was still falling from the atrium roof, and thick, hazy smoke filled the space. People ran across the open area screaming and crying.

Everly ignored everything but the broken body lying partially in the reflecting pool in the center of the atrium. She couldn't tell for sure if it was Landry or Jim from where she was. Knowing there was only one way to find out, she slowly walked toward the body. She didn't want to know, but she had to. Could a werewolf survive something so awful?

When she finally got close enough to see, she immediately knew two things. One, the body there wasn't Landry's. And two, if it had been, not even a werewolf would have survived that kind of damage.

Everly turned away from the mangled body, praying the horrific image wouldn't be seared into her mind for the rest of her life. Fighting the urge to be ill, she turned her head left and right looking for Landry. But he was nowhere to be found.

Afraid to hope, she scanned the lobby again when she caught sight of something lying on the sidewalk outside the building. It was shrouded in the shadows of the nearby trees, and it wasn't moving, but Everly knew it was Landry. She had no idea how he'd ended up outside, and she didn't care.

She headed for the exit and hit the door at a full run, then sprinted around the outside of the building, almost slipping on the sidewalk she was moving so fast. She slowed as she approached Landry's unmoving figure.

Every instinct in her body screamed to throw herself down beside the man she loved, but suddenly she was having a hard time taking those last few steps.

He looked so...hurt. And there was blood all over the pavement.

"Landry," she whispered softly.

Her heart plummeted as she slowly closed the distance between her and Landry. Dropping to her knees beside him, she placed a hand on his shoulder and gently turned him on to his back so she could see his face. Common sense told her she might be hurting him worse, that he might have a broken back, like he had in Iraq. But something told her that werewolves didn't work that way.

Her breath hitched at the slashes across his chest and arms. But they weren't bleeding much at all now. Was that good or bad?

Everly cupped Landry's face, tenderly wiping away a smudge of blood from his cheek with her thumb. He had a cut on his forehead too.

"Landry?" she said again, a little louder this time.

But he still didn't move.

She would have tried to feel for a pulse, but she was too afraid of what she'd find if she did. Tears ran freely down her face as her heart tried to tell her it was over.

Then she heard a soft groan.

Pulse skipping a beat she leaned close. "Landry. Can you hear me?"

The groan came again. Then his eyes fluttered, and the edges of his lips curved up. "I must be in heaven," he whispered. "Because only angels are this beautiful."

Laughing, Everly kissed him. It wasn't much of a kiss really, since there was more crying on her part than smooching, but Landry responded, his mouth opening and his tongue slipping out for a quick taste of her lips.

Then he closed his mouth, and she could feel him trying to physically pull back.

Everly lifted her head, alarmed. "Oh God! Are you okay?" She groaned, realizing how stupid the question was. "Of course, you're not okay. You just fell ten stories while getting blown up. You shouldn't even be alive. I'm going to make sure they have an ambulance on the way."

She started to stand, but Landry grabbed her hand, stopping her. "I'm fine," he said, and then winced. "Well, I'm not quite fine. I broke a few bones in that fall, and I think I have a bunch of glass and bomb fragments in me that Alex or Trey are going have to dig out. But all that can wait. There's something I need to say to you first."

Everly wasn't sure whether she was relieved to hear he was okay or terrified there were fragments inside him. But the serious look on his face made her sit back on her heels.

Everly heard sounds coming from the front of the condo, mostly those of people shouting and running away from the building, but also the distant wail of approaching sirens. In another minute, people would be coming around to this side of the building.

"I'm sorry," he said softly, gazing at her with eyes crystal clear, even though he had to be in pain.

"Sorry about what?" She took his hand in hers and held it tightly. "You saved my life again. What do you have to apologize for?"

"I'm sorry that I brought all those horrible memories of your mother's death back to the surface. I'm sorry that I pulled you into the middle of this mess and almost got you killed. And more than anything, I'm sorry that

I'm a werewolf instead of the normal human you could have been happy with."

Everly recoiled as if he'd slapped her. Except the sting she felt wasn't to her face. It was to her heart—her very core. Landry had just apologized because she'd made him feel as if his werewolf half wasn't worthy. Suddenly, she felt about two inches tall. Landry might be the one with claws and fangs, but she was the one behaving like the monster.

Choking back a sob, she threw herself forward, wrapping her arms around his shoulders and burying her face in his neck. Considering how injured he was, she knew it probably wasn't comfortable for him, but she had to be close to him. He must have felt it too, because he wrapped one arm around her.

"Don't you apologize for being what you are ever again," she rebuked him as she squeezed for all she was worth. "I'm glad you're a werewolf, do you hear me?"

"I hear you," he said in her ear. "I'm just not too sure I understand you."

"If you weren't a werewolf, you'd be dead right now." The thought brought fresh tears to her eyes, and she pressed her face tightly against his neck. "I'm glad you're a werewolf because I never want you to leave me."

He cupped her shoulders and pushed her up. "What are you trying to say?"

She smiled at him, tears streaming down her face. "That I love you, you big idiot. I know it took me a while to figure it out, and I'm sorry about everything I put you through as I was wrapping my head around this whole werewolf thing. But now that I have everything straight and know what I've found, I don't want to lose it."

He regarded her for a long time. "What about what happened to your mother? What about your father and brothers?"

She brushed his hair back from his forehead. "I'm never going to forget about what happened to my mom, but with you there to support me and give me strength, I can face the memories and move forward."

"You don't even have to ask," he said. "I'll be here for you as long as you want me to be."

"Good." She smiled. "Because my mom would want me to be happy, and you make me happy. As for my dad and brothers, well, they'll just have to deal with it. Though I don't think they'll have too hard of a time, considering you threw yourself out a ten-story window to save me this time. But if they do have a problem with us being together for the rest of our lives, they're going to have to deal with me, and I don't think they want to do that."

Cooper took her hand and tugged, pulling her back down and wrapping his arms around her. "For the rest of our lives," he whispered, giving her a kiss. "I think I could get used to the sound of that."

—∽∾—

Everly had sat in the ambulance with him for a while as Trey painstakingly pulled out pieces of metal and glass from various parts of his body, but Cooper could tell she was having a hard time with it. So when she'd mentioned something about needing to talk to someone, he hadn't asked too many questions.

That had left him alone with Trey, the clink of debris falling onto the surgery tray, and his own dark thoughts.

"You had to do it, you know," Trey said suddenly, breaking the silence filling the back of the ambulance.

"Do what?" Cooper asked, even though he had a good idea exactly what his teammate was talking about.

"Kill your friend." Trey grasped the corner of a piece of glass sticking out of his arm and pulled it out. "He didn't leave you a choice. If you hadn't done what you did, Everly would be dead and so would a lot of other people."

Cooper nodded. On some level, he knew Trey was right. But it didn't change the fact that the man who had saved his life all those years ago was dead at his hands. He wasn't sure he'd ever get past that.

The back door opened, and Xander stuck his head in the ambulance. "With what North and the other witnesses in the restaurant are saying, plus your friend from the bureau, I think I might be able to keep the FBI from taking you in for resisting arrest and obstructing a federal investigation," he said to Cooper. "But I doubt Gage is ever leaving town after this."

"Well, that's one less thing to worry about," Trey said when Xander closed the door. He shoved a pair of forceps between two of Cooper's ribs and pulled out a shard of green-tinted glass almost two inches long. "Now we just have to hope he can get Alex, Brooks, and Everly's brothers out of jail."

Cooper couldn't stop a hiss of pain from slipping out as Trey took another piece of glass from his side. *Shit.* They hurt a lot more coming out than they had going in. Then again, he didn't actually remember them going in, so maybe he was wrong about that. He was just glad Trey could sense where the fragments of metal and glass were without the aid of an X-ray. It was already going to be

hard enough explaining how he'd survived the bomb blast
and the fall from the tenth floor. It would be worse if he
had to go for major surgery to get bomb debris out of him.

Cooper ignored the stunned looks from the two paramedics standing beside the ambulance when he stepped
out fifteen minutes later. His T-shirt still had blood on it
and rips in a dozen places, but at least he didn't look like
a human pincushion anymore. That was certainly going
to start a few new rumors about the Dallas SWAT team.

He immediately scanned the parking lot looking
for Everly. He found her by Dennis, talking in a soft
voice as she signed a piece of paper. He and Dennis had
spoken for about five minutes when the FBI agent had
first arrived at the scene. The conversation had been cool
to put it mildly. Cooper had burned a bridge there, and
something told him he might never be able to rebuild it.

Dennis took out his cell and put it to his ear on the
opposite side of the big bruise already forming along his
jawline thanks to Armand's punch. He nodded at whatever
the person on the other end of the phone was saying, while
reading the piece of paper Everly had just given him.

Cooper had no idea what that was about, but before
he could walk over and ask, he heard someone calling
his name. He turned and saw North walking toward him.

"Damn, I always heard you were one tough son of a
bitch, but tackling a bomber out a ten-story window and
walking away with a couple scratches? That's something else." North grinned and stuck out his hand. "I
just wanted to thank you. That crazy fuck Wainwright
would have killed me and everyone in that restaurant if
you hadn't stopped him."

Cooper didn't stop to think. He simply stepped

forward and punched North so hard the bastard flew backward through the air and landed on his ass.

"Don't even say his name, you piece of shit," Cooper growled. "You know exactly why he tried to kill you, and if there hadn't been other people around, I probably would have let him."

North cradled his jaw and looked around, his gaze going first to Cooper's SWAT teammates, then to the uniformed cops, and finally to Dennis and the other FBI agents on the scene.

"Did you see what he just did?" North shouted. Or tried to anyway. His jaw wasn't working too well.

Dennis walked over and reached down to help North to his feet. "Nope. Didn't see a thing." He turned North around and jerked his hands behind his back, then snapped on a pair of cuffs. "Ryan North, you're under arrest for conspiracy to defraud the federal government, contractor fraud, illegal shipment of weapons-grade technology, tax evasion, and federal racketeering."

Cooper probably looked pretty silly standing there with his mouth hanging open in shock as his FBI friend led an equally stunned North away. What the hell had just happened?

Everly laughed softly as she placed a fingertip under his jaw to close his mouth.

"Did you have something to do with that?" he asked.

She nodded. "Jim talked a lot while he was building that suicide vest. He told me that North was involved with corrupt contractors in Iraq and paid off an EOD tech named Christian to hide the truth about what happened during that accident over there. Christian had a change of heart and collected a whole box of evidence against North, which he gave to Jim. While you were with Trey, your FBI friend sent some people over to the storage unit where Jim took me to check it out. Apparently, there was a lot of dirt on North."

"Dennis decided to arrest North without even looking at the evidence first?" Cooper asked.

That wasn't the way the FBI normally worked. They preferred to have all their ducks in a row before they moved on anyone.

"I think he would have rather waited until he'd gone through all the evidence first," Everly said. "But when I mentioned what you said about North planning to fly out of the country tonight, he realized he couldn't wait."

Cooper watched as Dennis put North in the backseat of a car, then got in and drove away. It wasn't the crime Jim had wanted the man punished for, but it might help Jim's soul find some kind of peace, knowing North would be in jail for a very long time. Maybe it would even help Cooper's.

"You okay?" Everly asked, putting a hand over his heart and resting it there.

Even through the bloody clothes he had on, her touch felt good. Comforting. Right.

"I'm good. Now that you're here." He placed his hand on top of hers. "It's possible I didn't remember to tell you this before, what with me having just jumped out of a window and all, but I love you like crazy, and I know how lucky I am to have you in my life. It's more than I could ever ask for."

She blinked her eyes to keep the tears that filled them from falling, then went up on her toes to kiss him. "I think we're both lucky. Jayna came to see me, and if everything she told me is true, it's not every day two people who were meant to be together forever find each other."

He smiled. "She told you about *The One*, huh?"

Everly nodded. "She was trying to explain why being apart from you was so hard on me. After she told me about it, everything made sense, and I knew I couldn't be without you anymore."

He leaned down and kissed her, not caring that there were dozens of people watching. He was so engaged in the kiss that he didn't sense Xander standing there until his squad leader tapped him on the shoulder.

"You going to get cleaned up before heading to the police station?" Xander asked, gesturing at his blood-stained and torn clothing.

Everly looked at him in alarm. "Police station? I thought everything had been taken care of, and they weren't going to arrest you?"

Xander laughed. "They're not. Cooper always comes out of crap like this smelling like a rose. No, we need to go to the police station and see if we can get Alex, Brooks, and your brothers out of jail. I can probably talk Alex and Brooks out of there, but I don't know what to do with your brothers. If they need to post bail, it's on Cooper."

Everly turned to Cooper, her eyes wide. "You got my brothers arrested?"

Xander chuckled again then walked away. "I'll meet you down there in an hour or so, but you better bring that money I mentioned, Cooper," he said over his shoulder. "I'm serious. I'm not paying their bail."

Cooper gave Everly a chagrined look. "Did I mention the part where I jumped out a ten-story window?"

Chapter 20

EVERLY SAT AT ONE OF THE WOODEN PICNIC TABLES in the SWAT compound two weeks later, soaking in the sun and nibbling on the cheeseburger Landry had brought her before heading out to play volleyball with all the other SWAT guys and some of their friends. She'd never been a huge fan of playing volleyball herself, but she definitely didn't mind watching muscular guys run around in the sand without their shirts.

Of course, she wasn't eyeing all the guys in quite the same way, especially her brother. As she watched, Tristan dove for a ball coming over the net low and fast, batting it into the air just before it hit the dirt. Landry leapt over her youngest brother, setting the ball a little higher and closer to the net so Tristan could spike the ball over for a point. Tristan and Landry high-fived, both shaking dirt out of their pants and laughing like kids.

Everly smiled. Her father and other brothers still weren't thrilled with her decision to spend her life with a werewolf, but Tristan was dealing with it much better. He'd already spent a lot of time with her and Landry, and had even hung out at the SWAT compound a couple times.

She sipped her water, focusing on Landry and how unbelievably sexy he looked with his shirt off, that beautiful wolf head tattoo flexing as he moved. It was rather funny that a werewolf had a tattoo of a wolf on his chest. Like he had a private joke no one else knew about.

But as she looked at the other muscular chests out there, she realized that all the SWAT guys had the same tattoos on their chests. *Crap*. She'd been staring at them for over an hour, and it just hit her.

Everly looked at Jayna, who was sitting with her, Mac, and Khaki, watching the guys play. Suddenly, everything fell into place, and it all made a strange kind of sense.

"Oh my God," she said. "All the guys on the SWAT team are…"

"Werewolves?" Jayna asked, as if she'd been reading Everly's mind. Was that something werewolves could do? "Yeah. The whole SWAT team is made up of werewolves—Khaki included. They're a pack like mine."

"Yours?" Everly's eyes widened. "You mean Joseph, Chris, and Moe are werewolves?"

Jayna laughed. "Yes, they're all werewolves."

"Why didn't Landry tell me? Does Mia know?"

"Cooper was waiting to tell you. He didn't want to overwhelm you with too much all at once. It's the same reason Joseph hasn't said anything to Mia yet." Jayna shrugged. "You know better than anyone. Learning something like that can be hard on some people. He'll tell her in time, if it turns out they're meant to be together. And if he thinks she can handle it."

Everly supposed she could understand why Joseph was hesitant to say anything to Mia.

"Anybody need seconds or thirds?" Alex asked, interrupting her musings as he walked by with a tray full of burgers, hot dogs, and steaks, Tuffie trailing behind him with a big doggie smile on her face.

Alex's food was so good that Everly almost said

yes, but she still had half a cheeseburger left. Jayna and Khaki obviously didn't have that problem. They each grabbed a hot dog and another burger before he moved on and started handing out food at the next table, where Gage sat with the deputy chief of police and FBI agent in charge of the Dallas field office. The SWAT commander was still trying to extend an olive branch and mend some fences with the FBI after what happened with the bombings. According to Landry, the effort was still a work in progress.

Even though Landry had technically gotten off without any official reprimand for what had happened with Jim, unofficially, the local FBI brass was still pissed at how things had gone down. While the man responsible for setting the bombs that had killed a police officer and injured dozens more was dead, and all the loose ends had been tied up, people in Dallas were giving SWAT the credit for stopping the bomber and putting North in prison. That didn't make the FBI too happy.

They weren't the only ones pissed at Landry. The detective from Internal Affairs that had made Landry see a psychologist was furious she'd signed off on his return-to-duty paperwork so quickly. The way Coletti saw it, Landry tackling a suicide bomber out a window was proof that he was unstable and unfit to remain on duty.

Then there was Gage. He hadn't been thrilled to come back from his honeymoon to find that Alex and Brooks had been arrested for getting into a physical altercation with the FBI, and that Landry had suspected who the bomber was, but hadn't said anything. Fortunately, Gage had calmed down enough to deal with IA. Even so, there was a good chance the SWAT commander was never going on vacation again.

It had also helped that the department psychologist insisted Landry's actions were completely normal and refused to consider Coletti's recommendation for a complete psychological evaluation.

Everly was just taking another bite of her cheeseburger when the volleyball game broke up. Landry ran over to her, knocking sand off his hot, glistening body, and looking good enough to eat.

As he slipped onto the bench seat beside her, the dog tags he was wearing shined in the late day sun. Dennis had gotten them from Jim's personal belongings and given them to Landry a few days after Jim's death. Everly hoped that little gesture on Dennis's part meant Landry and the FBI agent might be able to work out their issues and be friends again someday.

Everly brushed some stubborn grains of sand off Landry's back as he wiggled closer to her. That was when she noticed the scars he'd gotten from the leap out the tenth-floor window and subsequent explosion were all but gone now. There were some faint lines that crisscrossed the skin of his chest, back, shoulders, and arms. The deeper scars—the ones from Jim's death—would take much longer to heal. Landry still didn't talk about it much, but he was opening up a little more each day, and she thought that in time he would let her help him with the horrific memory in the same way that he'd helped her get past her mother's death.

Landry eyed the other half of her burger with such an adorable expression she couldn't help but slide it over to him.

He flashed her a grin as he accepted her offering. "I love you, do you know that?"

"Yes." She laughed, leaning over to kiss him and getting sand all over her clothes in the process. She didn't bother to wipe it off. She and Landry would be kissing a lot more before the barbecue was over, so she'd only get dirty again. Besides, a little sand was a small price to pay for one of his amazing kisses. "I love you, too."

He picked up the cheeseburger, but stopped with it a few inches from his mouth. She followed his gaze and realized he was looking at Gage's table.

"What's up?" she asked.

She'd gotten used to Landry being able to eavesdrop on conversations from a ridiculous distance away. She only hoped they weren't taking about him. She'd had all the drama she could stand between worrying about Landry being suspended and getting her brothers out of jail.

But Cooper shook his head and turned his attention back to his burger. "They're talking about a new drug ring that's moving cut-rate heroin through mid- and south-Texas. The feds are considering setting up a joint task force to deal with the situation and asked if Gage could put a few of us on it when needed."

Everly hoped her eyes didn't widen too much. "Drug ring? Aren't those people dangerous?"

Landry grinned. "Nah. We eat drug dealers for breakfast."

Everly shook her head, not sure she was ever going to be comfortable with the work Landry and his friends—his pack—did. But it helped knowing that since he was a werewolf, she didn't have to worry about him as much.

According to Landry—and her father—there wasn't a whole lot out there in the world that could hurt a werewolf. That made breathing a lot easier for her.

Cooper grabbed another cheeseburger when Alex passed by with more food. Everly wondered if she should get something for Mia and Joseph. They were catching some alone time at Everly's apartment, but were supposed to be here soon.

Landry had moved in with her and Mia a few days after they'd gotten back together. So far everything was working out well, but it was tight, especially when Joseph was there. Everly had talked to Mia about finding a place with Landry, and while Mia was bummed Everly was moving out, she was looking forward to having Joseph over more often. Everly was excited about the idea of her and Landry finding a place of their own, one big enough for her to have an art studio and office space, and to display Landry's paintings, as well as her artwork.

"Mia's going out with Joseph tonight," she said as she broke off a piece of Landry's cheeseburger and popped it in her mouth.

His eyes glinted gold as he watched her eat. After learning what the flash meant, Everly couldn't believe she'd ever been so foolish as to think it was sunlight reflecting off his eyes. Now she knew it meant that he was aroused. She liked a visible sign of that. It made her feel good, especially since it happened whenever she was around him.

"So we have the whole place to ourselves tonight?" He leaned over to kiss her. "You want to get naked in the studio and rub paint all over each other?"

Everly thumped him on the arm, hurting her hand more than those bulging biceps of his. "No, silly. That would be a waste of paint. But if you're willing to get naked, I could do another nude portrait."

He grinned. "That sounds good. You have a particular pose in mind?"

She nodded. "Would you consider posing for me in your wolf form? I'd like to paint you that way."

They'd been working on her werewolf issues a little at a time over the past two weeks. While she loved Landry like crazy, she still wasn't used to seeing him with fangs and claws. She was okay with the full wolf shift, but he'd only done it once since they'd gotten back together, and he hadn't let her watch the whole change, saying it might be too scary for her. When he'd come out of her studio though, she'd been mesmerized by how beautiful he was in his furry wolf form.

"This time," she added, "I want to watch you shift."

"You sure about that?" he asked softly.

She nodded. Landry was a werewolf and always would be. She needed him to know she was okay with that. "I'm sure. We have the whole night to take our time and get comfortable. Then I'm going to paint picture after picture of you in every pose you can imagine."

Landry kissed her again. "We'll take all the time you need. As long as you're in my arms as the sun comes up."

Everly smiled. "There's nowhere else I'd rather be."

Acknowledgments

I hope you had as much fun reading Cooper and Everly's story as I had writing it! If I had to pick characters most like "me," it would have to be Cooper and Everly because a lot of myself showed up in Everly, and a lot of my husband (who is my writing partner) showed up in Cooper. Like Cooper, Hubby is former Army EOD (Explosive Ordnance Disposal—twenty years), and has a lot of the same personality quirks as Cooper. He can be a bit snarky, seems to have a somewhat laissez-faire attitude toward explosives, is steady when things get stressful, and is usually a calm sounding board for people who want to talk about their problems. So I guess it makes sense that when I started thinking about Cooper's love interest, I patterned Everly after me. She's certainly in line with the kick-butt heroines I've portrayed in my other books, and when those she loves are in danger, she can be fierce in her own way. But Everly also has a soft side. Like me, she draws and paints. She also seems to have a thing for doing nude figure studies. That was my favorite class in art school too, by the way. Everly has a very boho style, she's emotional, and is quick to give her heart, which means she can fall for a guy really fast (like I did with Hubby!). In addition to all that, she's somewhat of a free spirit, just like me. For readers who know my hubby and me well, I hope you saw a bit of us in Cooper and Everly. And for readers who don't know us, I hope I gave you a glimpse.

This whole series wouldn't be possible without some very incredible people. In addition to another big thank-you to my hubby for all his help with the action scenes and military and tactical jargon, thanks to my agent, Bob Mecoy, for believing in us and encouraging us and being there when we needed to talk; my editor and go-to-person at Sourcebooks, Cat Clyne (who loves this series as much as I do and is always a phone call, text, or email away whenever I need something); and all the other amazing people at Sourcebooks, including my fantastic publicist Amelia Narigon, and their crazy-talented art department. The covers they make for me are seriously drool-worthy!

Because I could never leave out my readers, a huge thank-you to everyone who has read my books and Snoopy danced right along with me with every new release. That includes the fantastic people on my amazing Street Team, as well as my assistant, Janet. You rock!

I also want to give a big thank-you to the men, women, and working dogs who protect and serve in police departments everywhere, as well as their families.

And a very special shout-out to our favorite restaurant, P.F. Chang's, where my hubby and I bat story lines back and forth and come up with all of our best ideas, as well as a thank-you to our fantastic waiter, Andrew, who gets our order into the kitchen the moment we walk in the door!

Hope you enjoy the fifth book in the SWAT series, coming December 2016 from Sourcebooks, and look forward to reading the rest of the series as much as I look forward to sharing it with you.

If you love a man in uniform as much as I do, make sure you check out X-Ops, my other action-packed paranormal/romantic-suspense series from Sourcebooks.

Happy Reading!

About the Author

Paige Tyler is a national bestselling author of sexy romantic suspense and paranormal romance. She and her very own military hero (also known as her husband) live on the beautiful Florida coast with their adorable fur baby (also known as their dog). Paige graduated with a degree in education, but decided to pursue her passion and write books about hunky alpha males and the kick-butt heroines who fall in love with them. Visit www.paigetylertheauthor.com

She's also on Facebook, Twitter, Tumblr, Instagram, tsu, Wattpad, Google+, and Pinterest.

Hungry Like the Wolf

SWAT: Special Wolf Alpha Team

by Paige Tyler

New York Times and *USA Today* bestselling author

She's convinced they're hiding something

The team of sharpshooters is elite and ultra-secretive—they are also the darlings of Dallas. This doesn't sit well with investigative journalist Mackenzie Stone. They must be hiding something…and she's determined to find out what.

He's as alpha as a man can get

Gage Dixon, the SWAT team commander, is six-plus feet of pure muscle and keeps his team tight and on target. When he is tasked to let the persistent—and gorgeous—journalist shadow the team for a story, he has one mission: protect the pack's secrets.

He'll do everything he can to protect his secret

But keeping Mac at a distance proves difficult. She's smart, sexy, and just smells so damn good. As she digs, she's getting closer to the truth—and closer to his heart. Will Gage guard their secret at the expense of his own happiness? Or will he choose love and make her his own…

For more Paige Tyler, visit:

www.sourcebooks.com

Wolf Trouble

SWAT: Special Wolf Alpha Team

by Paige Tyler

New York Times and *USA Today* bestselling author

He's in trouble with a capital T

There's never been a female on the Dallas SWAT team and Senior Corporal Xander Riggs prefers it that way. The elite pack of alpha-male wolf-shifters is no place for a woman. But Khaki Blake is no ordinary woman.

When Khaki walks through the door, attractive as hell and smelling like heaven, Xander doesn't know what the heck to do. Worse, she's put under his command and Xander's protective instincts go on high alert. When things start heating up both on and off the clock, it's almost impossible to keep their heads in the game and their hands off each other…

Praise for Paige Tyler:

"A wild, hot, and sexy ride from beginning to end! I loved it!" —Terry Spear, *USA Today* bestselling author of *A SEAL in Wolf's Clothing*

"Hot, action-packed, and sexy as hell!" —Sara Humphreys, award-winning author of *Vampire Trouble*

For more Paige Tyler, visit:

www.sourcebooks.com

In the Company of Wolves

SWAT: Special Wolf Alpha Team
by Paige Tyler

New York Times and *USA Today* bestselling author

—◦◦◦—

The new gang of thugs in town is ruthless to the extreme—and a pack of wolf-shifters. Special Wolf Alpha Team discovers this in the middle of a shoot-out. When Eric Becker comes face-to-face with a female werewolf, shooting her isn't an option, but neither is arresting her. She's the most beautiful woman he's ever seen—or smelled. Becker hides her and leaves the crime scene with the rest of his team.

Jayna Winston has no idea why that SWAT guy hid her, but she's sure glad he did. Now what's a street-savvy thief going to do with a hot alpha-wolf SWAT officer?

—◦◦◦—

Praise for Paige Tyler's SWAT series:

"Bring on the growling, possessive alpha male… A fast-paced and super-exciting read that grabbed my attention. I loved it." —*Night Owl Reviews*, Top Pick, 5 Stars

For more Paige Tyler, visit:

www.sourcebooks.com

Her Perfect Mate

X-Ops

by Paige Tyler

New York Times and *USA Today* bestselling author

He's a high-octane Special Ops pro

When Special Forces Captain Landon Donovan is pulled from an op in Afghanistan, he is surprised to discover he's been hand-picked for a special assignment with the Department of Covert Operations (DCO), a secret division he's never heard of. Terrorists are kidnapping biologists and he and his partner have to stop them. But his new partner is a beautiful, sexy woman who looks like she couldn't hurt a fly—never mind take down a terrorist.

She's not your average Covert Operative

Ivy Halliwell is no kitten. She's a feline-shifter, and more dangerous than she looks. She's worked with a string of hotheaded military guys who've underestimated her special skills in the past. But when she's partnered with special agent Donovan, a man sexy enough to make any girl purr, things begin to heat up…

"A wild, hot, and sexy ride from beginning to end!"
—Terry Spear, *USA Today* bestselling author

For more Paige Tyler, visit:

www.sourcebooks.com

Her Lone Wolf

X-Ops

by Paige Tyler

New York Times and *USA Today* bestselling author

Leaving him was impossible…

It took everything she had for FBI Special Agent Danica Beckett to walk away from the man she loved. But if she wants to save his life, she has to keep her distance. Now, with a killer on the loose and the stakes higher than ever, the Department of Covert Ops is forcing these former lovers into an uneasy alliance…whether they like it or not.

Seeing her again is even worse

The last thing Clayne Buchanan wants is to be shackled to the woman who broke his heart. She gets under his skin in a way no one ever has and makes him want things he has no right to anymore. All he has to do is suffer through this case and he can be free of her for good. But when Clayne finds out why Danica left in the first place, everything he's tried to bury comes roaring back—and there's no way this wolf-shifter is going to let her get away this time.

"Dangerously sexy and satisfying." —Virna DePaul, *New York Times* bestselling author of the Belladonna Agency series

For more Paige Tyler, visit:

www.sourcebooks.com

Her Rogue Alpha

X-Ops

by Paige Tyler

New York Times and *USA Today* bestselling author

—···—

He'll do anything…

Former Special Forces Lieutenant Jayson Harmon is still coming to terms with the injuries he sustained in Afghanistan. His disabilities don't matter to feline-shifter Layla Halliwell, but Jayson can't understand why she'd want to saddle herself with a broken man. Determined to become the one she deserves, he agrees to try a new hybrid serum.

…to be the man for her

When the serum doesn't do what it's supposed to, Jayson finds himself on a mission to the Ukraine with a partner who's ready to kill him if things go bad. Layla knows she can't live without Jayson and goes after him. She's determined to keep him safe—even from himself.

—···—

Praise for Paige Tyler's X-Ops series:

"Does it get any better than this? Tyler…is an absolute master of the genre!" —*Fresh Fiction*

"Nonstop action and thrilling romance."
—Cynthia Eden, *New York Times* bestselling author

For more Paige Tyler, visit:

www.sourcebooks.com